THE FACES OF GOD

Mallock

THE FACES OF GOD

*Translated from the French
by Tina Kover*

Europa
editions

Europa Editions
214 West 29th Street
New York, N.Y. 10001
www.europaeditions.com
info@europaeditions.com

Copyright © 1999 by Jean-Denis Bruet-Ferreol
Published by arrangement with Agence littéraire Pierre Astier & Associés
ALL RIGHTS RESERVED
First Publication 2015 by Europa Editions

Translation by Tina Kover
Original title: *Les visages de Dieu*
Translation copyright © 2014 by Europa Editions

Library of Congress Cataloging in Publication Data is available
ISBN 978-1-60945-250-6

Mallock
The Faces of God

Book design by Emanuele Ragnisco
www.mekkanografici.com

Prepress by Grafica Punto Print – Rome

Printed in the USA

I was one of those beings divinely formed for unhappiness, who seem to have spent nine hundred years in their mother's womb before emerging woefully to spend a desolate childhood in the worthless society of men . . .

I felt as if I had fallen from some empyrean into an endless wasteland, and human beings seemed to me like so much vermin. That was my perception of human society at the age of fourteen—and it remains the same today.

One day, however, I revolted; the malice of my fellow students had finally crossed some unremembered line. Unsheathing a knife, I leapt with bombastic bravado on a group of forty young jokers. I was frothing at the mouth, crushed with blows, superb . . .

LÉON BLOY—*Le désespéré*

CONTENTS

PROLOGUE - 13

BOOK ONE - 27

BOOK TWO - 133

BOOK THREE - 229

EPILOGUE - 343

ABOUT THE AUTHOR - 349

THE FACES OF GOD

PROLOGUE
Tuesday, December 28th
3:20 A.M.

Outside, Paris was sleeping off its capital-city excesses. Parisians always gorged themselves between Christmas night and New Year's Eve dinner. Oysters, foie gras, smoked salmon . . .

The telephone rang in the darkness.

"Who is it?" Mallock barked.

"It's me, Grimaud. The Makeup Artist has just struck again. You need to come—they said—"

"Where?" Mallock got up to flick on the ceiling light.

"The entrance to Saint-Mandé. Rue du Parc, in the 12th. Do you know it?"

"I'll find it." He hung up and sat on the edge of the bed, grimacing. Throbbing migraine; aching back. He closed his eyes, stretched his neck right, then left. Forward, then backward. Another meeting in hell for the superintendent. He knew the way by heart. Forcing his protesting body to move from the bedroom to the bathroom, he splashed cold water on his face at the sink.

The battered face in the mirror stared back at him quizzically.

You think you can go on like this much longer?

He sighed. Twisted the cap delicately off the toothpaste. Turned on his electric toothbrush. Grimaced stupidly in the mirror as blood dripped into the white sink. Amédée brushed his teeth like he did everything else—with fierce determination.

Two days earlier, Raymond Grimaud had brought him the monster's file and left again without speaking. No one likes to be taken off a case right in the middle of it, but he had seemed relieved. Why? Rinsing his mouth, Amédée Mallock tried to imagine which side the first blows might come from. Everything Grimaud had told him, made worse by everything he hadn't, and by the shakiness of his voice, had been quite enough to awaken Mallock's fears. The investigation he had just been handed would be both punishing and complex. A shit-covered stick, as his colleague Bob would prosaically sum it up when they discussed it the next day.

Mallock turned away from his own gaze in the mirror and sighed. It had become a tic, a way of expelling sadness. First a deep breath drawn in—as if it were scouring the pit of his stomach for all the painful thoughts, every scrap of anguish— and then the exhalation, to push them as far away as possible. To . . . where?

He went back into the bedroom and dressed warmly. Suit, button-down shirt, black T-shirt. In the middle of the night and the dead of winter, murder scenes could be cold. Very cold.

Five feet eleven inches of muscle and bone, the superintendent had the silhouette of a wrestler and hands like a strangler's. He was fifty-five years old, and handsome despite a prominent nose with a funny little cleft in it that made it look a bit like an ass. His smile held a hint of sadness that was echoed in his green eyes, which gleamed in the imposing mass of his face. Amédée was a mixture of slight fatalism and clinging melancholy. He had an obsession with anxious types and shaggy blond hair like Depardieu.

Outside it was dark and deserted, and he shivered in his worn-out, faded trench coat. The streets were dead and the air smelled of winter. A few garlands fluttered here and there, their leaves flickers of color in the night. The parking lot was three blocks away, and it took Mallock longer than usual to pull his car out of the garage. The Jaguar, like him, wasn't fully awake. Neither of them were spring chickens anymore, and neither relished being yanked out of bed in the middle of the night.

After a few minutes on the road he turned on the heater and lit up a Havana cigar with a label that read *King of the World*, then grabbed a CD and put it in the player without looking at it: *Lacrimosa dies illa, qua resurget ex favilla Judicandus homo reus. Hulc ergo parce, Deus, Pie Jesu Domine Dona eis requiem . . .*

Mozart's requiem suited Amédée's mood. He had looked at the crime-scene photos, and one word was all it took to characterize them: horror. This was more than a puzzle to solve; it was a nightmare, lying in wait for him. The scumbag he was out to find wasn't just unbelievably perverted, he was also extremely intelligent. He'd been fingered for seven murders initially—two children, one man, and four women—but then there had been six more deaths, if Mallock had understood Grimaud correctly.

"You need to know everything," Grimaud had said, even before the waiter brought them the lunch menu. And, without giving a thought to the time or where they were, he had summarized all that horror for him. A mixture of blood, perversion, and all the foul humors that humans normally keep locked away inside. A cocktail mixed by the Devil personified.

Arriving at the Porte de Vincennes, Mallock rolled down his window to clear the car of cigar smoke and get a better view of the street signs. The air outside seemed charged with microscopic particles of fear, suicidal stars throwing themselves beneath the old Jaguar's wheels.

At the bottom of Saint-Mandé he was greeted by the lights of police cars, a forest of flashing beams. At any other time the bright shifting colors would have soothed him. Orange light reflecting off the black and white cars: His colleagues were there. They would exchange handshakes, hot coffee, and a bit of small talk.

Here, however, that wasn't the case.

On this night, only one thing awaited him: silence. The silence of the dead, and the living. In slow motion, four arms opened the rear doors of an ambulance. An old cop rubbed his forehead. Then mouths began to emit streams of words and vapor, lit by the screens of mobile telephones. Uniforms passed each other. Gazes avoided one another. And rage waited its turn. Two small dogs trembled, unsettled by the chattering lights that had invaded their night. A man vomited out his last illusions about the world behind a tree, as if ashamed. The snowflakes fell in solemn vertical columns.

Grief was here, too.

The two-story detached house had gypsy-blue shutters and was covered in new pink-and-white stucco. It looked like an English pastry shop and would have been appealing in other circumstances, a peaceful haven tucked away from the gazes of passersby. Tonight, however, it oozed death and fear.

Mallock swallowed a great gulp of death, an abject mixture of physical putrefaction and rancid terror. Here, with no way out, the horrifying stench lodged remorselessly in your nostrils: the odor of rotten eggs generated by sulphydric acid, the ammoniacal emanations of postmortem bodily evacuations, the stink of gases escaping the corpse.

Ken, who served as both captain and funnyman in the service of "Fort Mallock," their tiny state within the big government of Number 36 Quai des Orfèvres, the Paris office of the Criminal Investigation Division of the national police, had arrived before Mallock. "It's over there, Chief," he said. Unusually for him, he didn't smile or crack a joke.

Inside, gloves were snapping and plastic-covered hands rummaging as drawers told their stories. Camera flashes periodically froze positions and feelings in livid indecency. Old photos on the wall showed anachronistic scenes of happiness.

Mallock carefully wiped his shoes on the metal scraper to the right of the door, detaching both traces of mud and fragments of apprehension. He remembered his dream; him and his big clodhoppers leaving smears of dirt all over the murder scene. That wouldn't happen here. He sat down on a chair placed there for that purpose and took off his shoes, placing them on a small kitchen trolley, then stood up in his socks. Ken watched him, astonished. Yawning, Mallock took a pair of latex gloves out of his jacket pocket and then offered another pair to Ken, along with a bit of Vicks for the smell.

Ken took them, and led him upstairs.

Mallock grimaced as he entered the room. His face tensed and his body leaned forward slightly, as if someone had punched him in the stomach. The person known to insiders as the Makeup Artist was no ordinary murderer. He was a king among bastards. Emperor of the Maniacs. Amédée forced himself to look at the victim, barely managing to repress the thing that twisted his gut and rose into his throat—something between nausea, fury, and a sob.

The room was freezing. *God have mercy*, he thought.

Mallock the nonbeliever, calling upon God. He hadn't done that in forever. Even after Thomas's death he hadn't prayed. Why now, tonight?

Maybe because here, very nearby, he felt the presence of the Devil—and the need to have God by his side.

Whether he existed or not.

The body had the look and color of wax, with blotches here and there of a hue somewhere between purple and black licorice. *Zinzolin*, thought Mallock, dredging the word up from the furthest depths of his memory. A deep reddish-violet dye made from sesame seeds. *Zinzolin*, he repeated in his mind. Dark circles surrounded each puncture mark. Mallock counted a dozen of them, all located over the passage of an artery. The young woman was nude, stretched out very straight on her bed, her eyes wide open. Her eyelids had been cut away, probably with a scalpel. Blood had coagulated darkly around each eye, as if they were lined with kohl.

"Zinzolin," Amédée muttered to himself.

Her lipsticked mouth was wide open too, but it was full. A number of things would eventually be inventoried: ammonia, flour, grains of barley, formalin. Plus the dead woman's eyelids, her ripped-off fingernails, and her nipples. *Zinzolin*. The word echoed in Mallock's head. *Zinzolin*, like a mantra. Something to cling to.

The victim's thighs were spread—or rather, torn asunder, like those of a frog pinned down before dissection—and the lips of her vulva were coated with the same lipstick as on her mouth. Later, the autopsy would reveal that in both legs the rounded top of the femur, covered with articular cartilage, had been wrenched out of the cotyloid cavity in the pelvis. He had wanted the dead woman's knees to be far apart enough to touch the floor on either side of the corpse. The enarthrosis—the ball joint in the pelvis—had been crushed by the Makeup Artist, whose strength was as shocking as his rage.

The killer had finished staging the scene by tying the victim's feet so that the soles pressed together, and then binding her hands in the same way with the same bloody beige rope. The same macabre minutiae. This double positioning of the torn and obscene body as if in prayer gave the whole spectacle a particularly morbid quality, like some torture chamber out of the Inquisition.

"Zinzolin," murmured Mallock one last time.

He knew the dead. Marked with suffering, sprawling, ridiculous, and bloody, covered in piss and stinking. He knew them. Like most cops, Amédée had seen his share of cadavers, of horrors of every kind and then some. Superintendents like Mallock built up a hard shell that kept out the sadness—along with a large part of the capacity for compassion, yes, but it would have been unbearable otherwise. You had to . . . if not like it, at least develop a tolerance for the bloodiness of it. Make it into a habit. Amédée, like all his colleagues, had learned to devour a croissant and sip a hot cup of coffee while appraising a crime scene. There was no point in judging it or pretending not to notice it. That was just how it was. End of story.

Thinking about it, it was only the survivors—the relatives and close friends—who still made an impression on him. Amédée never knew what to do with their terrifying grief, undoubtedly because he knew the weight of tragedy all too well. The infinite uselessness of mumbled words of regret.

Tonight, though, was different.

It was plain even without thinking about it that the victim had suffered unimaginably. The position and condition of this body were the result of sadistic mental torture inflicted out of the psychotic desire to inflict a specific kind of physical pain. There was a ruthless quality about it all. Mallock was reminded of some perverted child tearing off an insect's legs while carefully keeping the creature alive for as long as possible. For fun.

Chest constricted, jaw clenched, teeth gritted, deeply upset, the superintendent spent more than a quarter of an hour combing the scene with his eyes, his hands clasped behind his back.

"Cover her, but don't disturb anything," he said eventually. "And close that goddamned window; it's fucking freezing in here." His voice sounded strange in his own ears; monotone, overly loud, and hoarse, as if he were getting over a lingering cold. He felt the touch of a hand on his shoulder from behind. Mordome, his friend and a brilliant specialist in anatomical pathology, had arrived.

"Hello, Superintendent," he said calmly. "I'm glad they put you on this one. Not a moment too soon."

"I'm glad you're here."

"Good, well, I suppose we'll have to tolerate one another's company again."

Mallock's face and mouth relaxed a bit. He almost smiled. "I'm going to need your insight, Barnabé. You're one step ahead of me."

Bernard Barnabé Mordome spoke quietly. "Six before this one. And a lot more really; twice as many, at least. But we'll talk about it when we get a quiet moment. Looks like he's back from his holiday."

There was a long silence, during which they tried both to absorb the reality of the situation and to distance themselves from it. Only Mordome, absorbed in his work, seemed able to escape this double impasse.

"Poor woman. Our . . . *client* . . . seems to be losing it, really. It just gets worse and worse. This lunatic comes up with new variations every time, but he's truly outdone himself to welcome you. This is . . . " Unable to find the right words, he was silent. Even Mordome was affected by this, and God knew he'd seen his share of horrors and then some—an entire catalogue of atrocities, and yet there was still something new every day.

"She died a few days ago," he said in response to Mallock's unspoken query. "I'd say within 72 hours, sometime between the 24th and 25th of December. Santa Claus can be a real bastard."

More accustomed than the others to these kinds of nightmarish scenes, the doctor had already moved into the second stage of reaction, which always followed sadness and repulsion: anger.

"That's only an estimate. The window was open," he continued, "and the cold undoubtedly slowed down the decomposition process. Fuck me, but this is terrible. Find that piece of shit for me, Amédée."

"I'm planning on it. Anyway, I'll leave you to work. You'll call me?"

"Don't worry; if I see anything useful before they take the body away I'll tell Ken, and he'll let you know. But I wouldn't count on it. See you in the fridge."

Mallock clasped Mordome's shoulder amiably. Everyone needed a bit of human warmth in moments like this. Turning to go back down to the first floor, he saw Raymond Grimaud.

Though not a huge man, RG was what might be called impressive in stature. He had the face of a former boxer, with dark olive skin that brought out everything white about him: the goatee that he always kept immaculately trimmed, his crew-cut silvery hair, and the gleaming whites of his dark eyes. He met Amédée's gaze with the hint of a smile quirking the corner of his mouth. Theoretically it was infuriating to be taken off a case like this one, but on the other hand, to be replaced by a big name like Mallock, while not exactly an honor, was at least not humiliating. They'd just gone a notch higher, and no one would say anything about it. RG was keeping his mouth shut. The Abbot Cop, as he was nicknamed, knew how to pick his battles. Tonight, though he wouldn't quite admit it to himself, he was feeling relieved. Truth be told, he couldn't take any more. Not just of not being able to solve the case, but of the case itself. All these atrocities were weighing down his policeman's soul like so many anvils. Yes, there was no doubt about it: Passing on this horrific buck would be a relief.

"Have you been here long?" Mallock asked.

"About ten minutes. You?"

"I got here almost half an hour ago. I live right nearby, so . . . "

"You were right. It's ugly in there." RG looked at him sadly. "So is the other one. Maybe even worse, don't you think?"

"What other one?"

Mallock's voice had risen nearly to a shout. The Abbot, always benevolent when it came to others, hurried to make excuses for his colleagues. "Everyone's a bit shaken up. They must have thought you already knew. Follow me; it's on the other side."

They went downstairs together and crossed the living room. Seven steps led to a study, a corridor, and, at the end of that, a bedroom. In the middle of the room was a bed, and on it lay another corpse in the same condition and in a similar position, thighs spread. But here, the eyelids and mouth had been sewn shut. As part of the by now highly systematic evidence collection procedure, a member of the crime-scene team was in the process of carefully enclosing the second victim's hands in brown paper bags. Any fibers, torn-off shreds of skin, and traces of blood or semen that might be present had to be preserved. They didn't use plastic anymore, since it tended to speed up the putrefaction of mucus and other biological matter.

One detail was especially jarring, however: the bags were much too large for the hands inside them. Amédée's throat ached and he was conscious of a rushing in his ears.

The tortured body in front of them belonged to a five- or six-year-old girl.

Back in the entryway, the superintendent sat down heavily

and pulled his shoes back on. The left shoelace snapped. He didn't swear; merely set the useless lace aside and stood up.

Ken joined him. "What are we doing?"

"I'm going back. You're staying." Mallock touched him on the shoulder to soften the curtness of the words and added, with a slight, sad smile: "You'll give me a report."

Walking down the front steps, Amédée saw a man in beige loden trying to get past the police cordon. "Oh God, it's the little girl's father," sobbed a neighbor. The man rummaged in his back pocket and pulled out his wallet. He didn't know it yet, but only a dozen yards stood between him and devastation.

Mallock had no choice. No matter what he said or did, the man in loden was going to be inconsolable forevermore. For all that, the one giving him the horrific news was inconsolable, too.

Mallock knew the language. He'd had to become familiar with all the subtleties, and all the resources, when Tom died.

The man, still being kept back by police officers, called out to Amédée. "Where's my daughter? Has something happened to my wife? Is that it? My God! I haven't been able to reach her for two days. I'm the one who called the police. What's happened?"

The poor man knew, by some strange intuition, that this tall man with the sad eyes was the one he should address.

Mallock bit his lip and fought back the urge to vomit. Looking at bodies, measuring blood spatter or the diameter of a fragment of grey matter—none of that affected him anymore. But giving painful news to family members and watching them fall to their knees—he had never gotten used to that.

The killer would always be able to find someone who would seek leniency on his behalf, but for the man in loden there would be no release, ever.

You don't heal from the death of an angel.

Another barrier to be crossed; another strip of police tape

to be lifted, and this man—this husband, this father—would be transformed into a kind of grieving monster, a silent scream, armless and legless.

The day was just breaking, beautiful and indifferent to the pain of men. Victims or torturers, the sun would warm them the same way. Mallock heard a faint noise deep inside himself, as if a delicate clockwork mechanism had broken. One day, his heart would no longer follow him on his painful journey. He knew it and, most of the time, he didn't care.

He looked up at the sky. The stars were still there, drifting slowly. How could anyone still believe in them, in guardian angels or rabbits' feet? He thought about the little girl who must have been waiting for Santa Claus, and fought back the wave of sorrow that washed over him.

The man in loden, at the end of his stumbling journey across the front garden, grasped his arm. "Just tell me. I'm begging you."

Mallock could put it off no longer. He spoke the words clearly.

"They're dead."

BOOK ONE

1.
Flashback.
Three days earlier.
Saturday, December 25th. Christmas Day

A dreadful feeling of solitude weighed heavily in his gut and tensed the muscles of his back. Anguish emanated from his body in waves, along with sadness at being alive, and a weariness that was heavy and limp, like a tongue. To top it all off, Mallock had bought a fir tree, just for the hell of it. Then he had pushed his depravity so far as to decorate it. Garlands, balls, and little styrofoam angels. Yesterday, December 24th, Christmas had come howling outside his window. Christmas as Hell, as persistent sorrow. So many sad memories and the death of his son Thomas, still and forever unacceptable.

The tree's blinking lights were almost more than he could handle. What had possessed him to buy the ridiculous thing? Mallock was stranded in that curious no-man's-land that stretches from December 20th to January 2nd—the holiday break, a sugary-sweet expanse he was loath to cross. He heaved a loud sigh that did nothing to hide his profound distress. It was in moments like this, more than at any other time, that he was at the mercy of his memories, his cruelest obsessions. Like all people who have abandoned their roots, he nursed a certain unhappiness in the deepest recesses of his heart—and on this festive day he clung to that feeling as if caressing a pebble brought back from some twilit city.

At four o'clock in the afternoon, the ringing of the telephone jerked him out of the depths.

"Hello?"

"Hello, Mallock, it's Dublin. How are you?" His boss's

voice sounded slightly embarrassed. "Sorry to disturb you on a holiday. Merry Christmas."

"You too . . . Dominique." After ten years of "Sir" and then "Boss," he still struggled with this familiarity, calling his superior by his first name, even though the head of Number 36 had encouraged it.

"Have you had a nice Christmas?"

"Can we talk about something else?"

"I have a present for you. For the new year."

"Go on."

"What would you think about taking over the investigation?" Dublin didn't even mention the Makeup Artist. He didn't have to. Cases like that came along maybe once every ten years; plus, it was the only important case that hadn't already been assigned to his subordinate. After a short, surprised silence, Mallock asked:

"Grimaud hasn't gotten anywhere with it?"

"Let's just say he's done his best with it. But obviously that wasn't good enough. So?"

"We'll see."

"Come on. I really need your touch on this one."

"I think everyone's been pretty happy without me so far, haven't they?" Mallock asked. He found himself taking out his anger on this first person he'd spoken to since the insane conversation he'd just had with that fucking Christmas tree and its goddamned blinking lights.

"People higher up have grievances with you; I don't know exactly what. There have been mutterings of *who does he think he is* and *no one is indispensable* more than once when your name comes up. You know it, or at least you suspect it. You're the kind who attracts jealousy and resentment. It has to be said. With your character—"

"My character," Mallock returned, "strongly suggests that I let those assholes stew in their own juices for a while."

*

Dublin didn't respond. He knew his superintendent by heart. As the commissioner of Number 36 his most important job was to convince Mallock. So, he would appeal—in order of importance—to his big heart, his sense of duty, and then, finally, his pride. It was better when dealing with Amédée to avoid threats or assertions of authority at all costs. Dublin had to make sure that his favorite superintendent *wanted* to take the lead of his famous combat battalion and march out to attack the piece of shit that was the Makeup Artist. The rest was just semantics.

The case was getting bogged down. They counted half a dozen crimes now; six assassinations in ceremonial robes, six Baroque tableaus, all attributed to the same bastard(s). And that didn't include the seven other murders that had been unofficially added to the tally in retrospect. By some miracle, the story had so far escaped the voraciousness of the media, thanks to a lucky set of circumstances.

Since the first homicide, Superintendent Raymond Grimaud had given free rein to his old paranoia from Central Intelligence. The victim being none other than the wife of a finance secretary, he had ensured painstaking compliance with procedure while bringing in the big guns, before hushing up the whole business. The entire case file, including photos, had been put "under embargo." And "they" had made up an official version: The secretary's wife had been stabbed and robbed of her possessions, probably by a prowler. Period, full stop. Nothing to see here; everyone go about your business.

Raymond had also been the first one to put forward the theory of a serial killer. The various murders had only had one element in common, but it was a doozy: the lavish application of makeup. More analyses had been done; they were the same products, applied in the same way. But "they" had decided not to do anything—other than convince the family to play the game and keep silent for the good of the investigation. Expressions like "the killer can't know we're on his trail" and "to achieve our ends" had been combined with "we want to get him as badly as you do" and "trust us."

To reveal the existence of a serial killer now, without having caught him, while also admitting major cover-up tactics, would make everyone look bad. Once this habitual murderer was behind bars, "they" would be able to justify their actions more easily—and even congratulate themselves on having opted for the hush-up strategy.

This was why palming the case off on Mallock now was very nearly an ideal plan. If he failed, "they" had told themselves, the great superintendent would, without the shadow of a doubt, be the perfect scapegoat. "They" had gotten the best, so "they" would have nothing to reproach themselves for.

Mallock the Wizard. Dédé the Wizard. Mallock the Tower of Strength. The superintendent owed most of his nicknames not only to his professional abilities, but also to his dazzling intuition. While he didn't deny the sobriquets, he preferred not to talk about them too much. Even though he knew it was just the ability to concentrate in a particular way, a kind of deductive reasoning, his visions might just as well be explained by a not-yet-understood genetic trait or, worse, something abnormal. Since his arrival in Paris he had conditioned himself never to think about his parents again. Blocked out all the images of his childhood, of doctors' waiting rooms and mental-institution corridors. Because madness, or anything close to it, even his famous and wonderful flashes of intuition . . . well, Mallock didn't like that at all.

Dublin, hoping the storm on Mount Mallock had passed, resumed his plea. "You know, Amédée, in their defense, no one could have imagined at the time that the investigation would go on so long. Four months and six bodies later, they're truly sorry—for covering up the whole thing, and for putting *Mallockus habilitus* out to pasture."

Dublin had thought a little stab at humor might soothe the savage beast, but the attempt was doomed to fail. Mallock was sulking. "This case has turned into a ticking time bomb," he continued. "Besides the new victims, we've got a truckload of suits with short fuses, and the whole thing could blow up at any time. See how it is?"

Mallock's silence was deafening.

"There was a meeting with poor Grimaud, who they're now blaming for everything. A clear decision has been made. The same people who chose to pass you over—against my wishes, by the way—have decided to seek you out, with their heads bowed and their dicks at half-mast. If you take over the case and succeed, which I don't doubt will be the case, they'll owe you one. And—"

"And nothing! They didn't give enough of a damn to come to me in person. I don't care about their recognition or their gratitude, and actually I'd just as soon wipe my ass with their white flag."

Mallock, for whom coarse language was a way of letting off steam, didn't see his superiors' capitulation as a victory. Instead of taking the bull by the horns and putting the best possible team on the case, "they" had insisted on playing their little power games.

"And RG? I hope he's been warned, at least?"

"Not yet. I'll call him after I get off with you. I hope he won't kick up a stink, too."

"Don't worry," said Mallock dryly. "He's not some asshole politician; he's a good cop. He has a sense of duty. He'll understand, and he'll probably be relieved. Not everyone likes marching to the front only to be booted in the ass, like your servant."

"So you're saying yes?"

"I'm thinking." Amédée looked at the Christmas tree winking at him from the corner of the room. He wanted this case as much as he feared it.

"We don't have a lot of time," Dublin persisted. "You have to decide quickly." Then, suddenly, like a summer hailstorm, he burst out:

"You're a real pain in the ass, Mallock. I've handled you with kid gloves; I've stayed calm, but shit! I know you don't give a crap, but I'm your superior. And believe me, there's a lot you don't know."

Dublin's voice was shaking. Mallock couldn't quite interpret it. Fear or anger? Both, most likely. The big boss was terrified by this case. But what else did he know about it? What was he still hiding?

"Look, don't hold it against me," Dublin tried to explain, "but there are still a few things I absolutely can't tell you. This hideous thing goes a lot further than you—well, than you—it's—the effects could be devastating. We've got to—"

"You'll give me *carte blanche*?" Mallock interrupted him.

"Naturally."

It sounded like an agreement. Dublin was relieved, but he let another moment go by without speaking.

"Why so quiet, Dominique? Do you have something else to say?"

There was a sigh on the other end of the line. "Okay . . . it's coming from upstairs. They have one condition. You have to understand—"

Amédée blew out a frustrated breath. "Spit it out!"

"Fine! Okay. We have to maintain discretion on this."

"Lovely paraphrase. Keep my trap shut; is that what you're trying to say?"

"Yes, if you like. But just for now. Ideally, until the case is resolved. Investigate without letting anything slip to the media."

Mallock's response surprised his superior. Knowing his intransigence, he fully expected to be told to go to hell.

"I'll do everything I can," was the brief and obliging answer of *Mallockus Habilis*.

Dublin, relieved to have gotten off so easily, didn't push his luck.

"I'll send you my personal case file tonight—it's a yellow binder. This is highly confidential, Mallock; I'm not even keeping a copy, if that tells you anything. You'll give it back to me next time. It's not the whole file, of course, but it's got everything that caught my attention the most, plus some photos. Anyway, you'll see. And don't go lugging it around with you—"

"Okay; send it," Mallock interrupted. "I won't move. But as a reward for my indulgence, how about you tell me who 'they' are? The ones you've been talking about for this entire enthralling conversation?"

"'They?'"

"Don't play dumb. Please."

Mallock didn't need to see Dublin's face to know he was grimacing on the other end of the line. But the boss hesitated only briefly. "There are three of them, and they're influential enough to have taken your name out of the running for this case."

"Who?"

"The chief of police, for one. And the former director of Number 36. He's working now as a consultant to the Department of the Interior. The one who—"

"Okay, enough. I know who he is. The kind of guy who doesn't have enough balls to make a pair. And the third?"

"Judge Judioni. 'Big Jack,' as the media calls him."

"That asshole? Well, that's quite a lineup of lame ducks. I had my suspicions about the first two. The chief is as dull as a shareholders' meeting. Dreary and completely spineless. That's quite a scoop about the judge, but it's not that shocking. He'd do anything to get on TV. He hasn't figured it out yet, but the Indians were right: when you let yourself be photographed with the white man's black box, your soul ends up in the camera."

Dublin, ever a pragmatist, steered the conversation back on topic. "The handover is set for Tuesday. That's three days from now. Can I confirm that's okay with you?"

Silence. A sniff. More silence. Deep breath.

"He's quite a piece of work, this Makeup Artist. Even without all this hush-hush crap. It's going to make this very complicated, and if I screw up, I'll be the one with shit all over my face."

Dublin chose not to reply. Any denial would only annoy Mallock. He would say yes or no in the end, at any rate; it was just a question of patience.

"Nothing to say?"

"I'm letting you think about it, Amédée."

"Goddamn it, Dublin, you know me too well."

"Between you and me, is there really a choice?"

Mallock chuckled. "No. You're right. Let's do it."

2.
Saturday, December 25th. Twilight

The scent of oysters and capons filled the building's courtyard. Amédée decided to go out and pay a visit to his neighbor Léon at his bookshop, for a little chat about the Makeup Artist.

The sky was darkening to violet, and the temperature hovered around freezing. The aromas of roasted chestnuts and mulled wine wafted from the cafés opening onto the square. Mallock passed his old Jaguar, immobilized by the cold. Poor little thing; just two more days to go, and then on Sunday she would have a warm place to sleep, protected from half-wits and the elements. After two years of hemming and hawing, Amédée had finally rented a space in a private garage just a few steps from his flat, on the other side of the Rue de Rivoli.

"You'll see—you'll wonder how you ever did without it," the seller had promised him.

Mallock had no doubt of it. In the meantime, he was obligated to go on foot to his old friend's bookshop on the Rue des Mauvais-Garçons. Tiny flakes of snow had begun fluttering out of the ink-purple sky. At the top of the Rue du Bourg-Tibourg the neighborhood's shopkeepers had erected an imposing flocked Christmas tree; the mixture of textile fibers and water-based glue adhering to the branches cemented the victory of artifice over nature. As a final outrage, the whole tree had been painted blue. Dazzled children circled the tree, shrieking, their backs glowing orange in the cafés' lights and their faces turned blue by the illuminated tree.

In front of his friend Léon's secondhand bookshop, Mallock stopped for a moment to contemplate the window display.

Dusted with artificial snow and adorned with two garlands and three balls, it was the same jumble of books and manuscripts as always; a treasure laid out in an order understood only by Léon Galène, "like radio sets," he told his customers. As he did every year, the elderly bookseller had put out a figure of Santa Claus in ice skates, spinning endlessly. The poor toy was so old that it had become rather horrifying, like the pieces of dusty styrofoam and the ancient yellow star dangling from a brass curtain rod.

It was Christmas Day, but the shop was open. *A book is always a treat*, Léon had written in his elegant cursive on a battered piece of cardboard. Mallock entered, causing the wind chimes that hung from the ceiling to jingle.

"Hello, Superintendent. How are things going?"

The stirring scent of old paper.

"They're going. How's business, Léon? I swear I'm coming next year on December first to throw all these decorations in the bin. Especially Father Christmas and that star."

"Why? You know the yellow star is an unforgettable memory for me." Léon gave a loud bark of harsh laughter.

"You're a lunatic, my friend."

Léonhard Scheinberg had led something of a tumultuous life. Mostly tragic. His entire family had been exterminated by Hitler's goons and he himself had spent three years in the camps. Between the ages of nine and eleven he had experienced the unspeakable, the very worst. He almost never talked about it, and Amédée, more than anyone, respected that silence.

"Must never forget . . . never forget . . . what a load of bullshit! I lived through it, and it's my right to forget," he had confided to Mallock once in a moment of temper. "It's my suffering. It belongs to me, myself, and I, and no one else. It's not just mine—it *is* me. If I want to kill it and bury it in the back garden, that's my right, isn't it?"

During the first years of his repatriation in Paris Léon had tried to regain a taste for life; first by simply learning to walk again, and then burning the candle at both ends:

"You know, Amédée, when you've been through something like that—you can't move afterward. It's like you're frozen. Stunned. Many people let themselves die afterward. Others . . . well, they gulped life down too fast and it killed them. I—after a period of recovery, I tried to pick up my life story where I'd left off, to get back into it. To go back. Good God—to go back! But they'd sent me to a country that was so far away. Even now I'm not even sure it's really a place on Earth. I went through so many train stations, over so many hills of bone, so many destroyed arches. I got good and far away . . . there was always so much death behind me. It seemed like death had won without my realizing it, like it was clinging to me with invisible hooks. Strapped to me like a god-damn pair of suspenders. That's why it just kept dropping by. Over and over . . . "

Then Léon, a master of the one-hundred-and-eighty-degree turn, had laughed at his own joke—and quickly become serious again.

"When you come back from that kind of place, you bring death with you. We brought it back on the bottoms of our shoes, in our eyes, in every pore of our skin. And God knows I washed until my skin nearly came off, but it's still there. Always. Every day. In us, and behind us. Understand?"

That was how Léon had explained things one day to his friend Amédée. One day. Only once. Mallock had said he understood, knowing perfectly well that he did not. The old man was running, running away from death that chased him even now.

For Amédée, though, like for most humans, death lay ahead.

After a long convalescence, Léon had climbed back aboard his life. He was famished, and though his heart and bones had been weakened he hadn't let a single orgy pass him by. His Zazou clothes, a few misdemeanors, his beautiful blue eyes, two or three underhanded maneuvers in casinos and betting shops, and his immoderate taste for the masculine sex had all combined to earn Léon a few stints in the capital's jails. But finally, with time, he had calmed down.

"Unless I doubled down," he had said, "I was out of the race." But first he had fallen helplessly in love and shacked up with a gorgeous young stud to whom he taught everything he knew about being an antiquary. He had given the amorous Léon everything he wanted—and then, one day, had taken off with the store's cash register. Undiscouraged, Léon had "gotten back in touch" with another beautiful young thing, and the farce had begun all over again.

In the mid-1980s, he had finally found the lid for his pot: a forty-year-old cellist, *grand, goy, et gai*, as kind as he was brilliant. Four years later, AIDS took his partner from him, and Léon had tried to join him in death. He failed. The force of his grief had brought him closer to his friend Mallock, his comrade in tragedy.

And one day, the old bookseller had found his smile again.

For Mallock, that ray of light—that movement of lips and eyes—was the victory of the heart over grief, of life over brutality, and of affection over everything else.

At sixty-something years old, when so many others his age were retiring, Léon had opened a bookshop in the heart of Le Marais. In ten years he had built a solid reputation as an expert.

"For once I'm going to spare you my recitation on the death

throes of the book," Léon announced. "Let's talk about you. What can I do for you?"

"Can you bring me those press clippings on recent unsolved murders?"

"You didn't even ask me if I have them ready. You know me well, eh?"

"Too well, and for too long," Amédée joked, holding a first edition of Harry Dickson's adventures delicately in his hands. This one was nothing less than *The Hermit of the Devil Swamp*, the first investigation of the American Sherlock Holmes, a series that had been recreated more than translated by Jean Ray, and an adolescent passion of the young Amédée's. Whenever a new episode was published, a kindhearted librarian in Caen had alerted him and Mallock had leapt on his old moped to go after it. Once back in his bedroom he would stretch out on his bed with a heap of sweets: butter toffees, jelly beans, licorice sticks. And there he would fly up out of his village, and then out of Normandy and over the Channel, higher and higher, past the white cliffs of Dover, and finally touch down a century in the past, in the notorious streets of London.

"Am I to understand that Monsieur le Superintendent has finally been let in on the action?"

Mallock started. "What action?"

Léon, putting away a pile of books, didn't bother glancing up at Mallock. "What do you take me for, some idiot journalist?"

"My dear Léon, what strange idea has taken root in that paranoid little Jewish head of yours now?"

Léon looked up, his blue gaze piercing Mallock's. "I've got all the articles here, from *Libé* and *Voici* and *Le Figaro* and *Detective*, and they're all telling me the same thing. My paranoid Jewish mind sorts information like lentils, as you cops say— except I keep the pebbles and throw out the beans, the predigested crap the police and the other bureaucrats serve up to the pencil pushers. It's fine when they don't give out complete files at press conferences today, just abstracts, the same thing they publish for public consumption. Gather the information for people so they don't tire themselves out; suggest angles so they don't have to spend time deciding which ones are the most relevant, and voilà, there's your shitty copy. Fortunately, despite everything, there's still truth in life. Little bits of it fall through the holes in the sieve. Those are my pebbles."

Mallock had listened to Léon with a smile on his face. "So what's your conclusion?"

"A whole lot of crap," Léon laughed. "There are a good half dozen murders whose descriptions don't stick. It's bullshit, if you ask me. How can I put it—it sounds hollow, like a theatre set. There's no meat to it, not even bones, just a barely-drawn outline and a lot of clichés. You're keen on linguistics; you know that what makes good information is having a balance between too much repetition, too many references, and the unpublished data. Too many original elements—too many bits of exclusive information coming one right after another—and it becomes too hard to follow. Too many repetitions and boring references, and you've got a totally empty speech. Here there's only déjà-vu and emptiness; not the slightest amount of . . . well, *news.*"

Mallock could think of no response to this, and contented himself with congratulations. "Bravo to you, but this time there's a lot more to it. It's no use trying to be cagey with you."

"I should hope not! No keeping secrets from your Léon!"

"No. But I need you to promise me something. Spit on the floor and repeat after me: '*I swear on the head of my next lover that I will not tell anyone about this.*'"

To his astonishment, Léon complied, hawking a shiny glob of phlegm onto the polished floor of his shop. It wasn't the parquet Léon loved; it was his books: ancient newspapers, illustrated magazines, paperbacks, and leather-bound histories of the Empire and tales of Puss in Boots, Gulliver, and the Musketeers. He adored the outdated sagas, still smelling of faded ink, of tigers, elephants, and maharajas; the Indian misadventures of pampered "Darjeeling darlings" in the twilight years of the British Empire. He swooned over the coarse seafaring novels with their fragrances of salt-foam and seaweed and pickled herring, their siren-haunted islands and peg-legged wizards.

Mallock told Léon everything he knew about the Makeup Artist—including the embargo.

"What a mess this is!" Léon exclaimed. "And believe me, that's exactly why they brought you in. Have you started your investigations yet?"

"Not yet—officially, at least. But let's say it won't be long . . . which is why I asked for the stories. I want to reread everything the press has said about these murders."

Though Mallock tended to limit his reading of journalists' prose to small doses, he liked looking through Léon's scrapbooks. They allowed him to trace an idea through a forest of contradictory theories, and sometimes they even triggered one of his famous hunches. The collective unconscious: this was what the "visionary superintendent" wanted to explore in Léon's books. Out of these cutout, already-yellowing articles a sort of truth would emerge; its tentacles deformed, half-smothered in various rotten digressions. You just had to know how to decode it. It was like a rose blooming on a shit heap of gossip and noise. And sometimes, though very rarely, it would contain information that came neither out of someone's crazy imaginings nor from the official version. Some journalists, bless them, still did real work.

Léon brought two scrapbooks out from the back of the shop. They were of thick black cardboard made to look like leather. They were both exactly the same size and thickness as the files in Number 36, a coincidence that Mallock chose to take as a good omen.

"Here you go. Have fun," said Léon, plunking the books down loudly on his desk.

"Do you mind if I take them with me?"

"Take them, take them. I don't worry with you. Plus I owe you one—I've put together my best scrapbooks from your investigations."

Mallock muttered a modest denial.

"Besides, one good turn deserves another," continued Léon. "I guess I'll read the rest in the newspapers—but make sure that doesn't keep you from coming to see me, kid."

"Oh—by the way, I'm going to buy that *Harry Dickson* from you. When's it from exactly, 1930?"

"Nope, '33. An excellent vintage—the year I was conceived! A few of them came out that year, as I'm sure you know. *The Red Widow*—you've already got that one, don't you?—and *The Sign of Death*, which I've looked for everywhere for you. It seems to get rarer all the time."

"Can I write you a check?"

Léon put his hand on Mallock's back and steered him firmly toward the door. "Don't waste your time; take it. I'll put it on your tab."

"Thanks again, Léon. Happy holidays."

Wind chimes. Cold outside air. Door closing behind him. Léon, smiling, watched through the window as his friend disappeared into a grey haze of snowflakes. His wrinkled features were reflected in the glass. He had eyes like a faded aquarium and a strong nose, in the middle of a face scattered with reddish splotches. He gazed at his reflection, and realized with a start that apprehension had slowly transformed his smile into a rictus. Forgetting his Jewish roots, he couldn't stop himself from murmuring an ecumenical and surprising:

"Jesus and the Virgin Mary protect you!"

It was 6:23 in the evening when Mallock banged his apartment door shut behind him. The intensifying cold, and the prospect of a good whiskey, had hastened his steps. His living room smelled of wax. Anita, his luscious housekeeper, had polished all the furniture last Thursday. He rubbed his hands together, feeling a flicker of returning joy in his heart. Santa Clauses and animated displays in department-store windows; jingle bells and sugary scents; all were forgotten.

Seven minutes later, a lovely poplar blaze crackled in the fireplace. He had turned off the Christmas tree. A glass of pure single-malt threw amber reflections on the palm of his left hand, while a double Corona Punch cigar began its slow burn.

He had a job to do. Innocent people to protect. A piece of garbage to catch. And a mystery to solve.

Truth be told, he loved it.

3.
Sunday, December 26th

The next day, Mallock woke up with a throbbing migraine crushing his forehead and the back of his neck. A ray of sunlight was in the process of finishing the insidious hammer job begun by a mixture of insomnia, smoke, and alcohol.

Getting up was painful.

Standing in front of his coffeemaker, he couldn't keep from grumbling. Nothing was going right this morning. The stupid contraption was taking forever to percolate; his goddamn cup was hiding somewhere; the bloody sugar bowl was empty and the milk sour.

He grabbed the earthenware saucer that belonged with the missing cup and flung it with all his strength down the hallway, hoping it would shatter against the bathroom door. Bingo! It exploded into shards. He felt slightly better, but not enough. The two other cups and saucers, which made up the whole rest of his coffee service, met the same fate, giving the same ceramic shrieks as they smashed on the lacquered wood of the door.

You couldn't condemn a person for murdering *things*.

The previous evening, instead of eating a quick dinner and going to bed, Mallock had dived straight into his investigation. With the files in his lap he had begun his journey—the personal itinerary that would lead to him to another man's murderous insanity.

The forest of articles clipped by Léon was immediately striking in its lack of photos. Most editors wanted illustrations; they'd get a police-artist composite sketch, a snapshot of the crime scene, or a photo of the victim—dressed up for first communion, or smiling and tanned on the beach last summer. Here, there was nothing; no serious imagery apart from a few pictures of the fronts of houses where a "*mysterious murder*," a "*sadistic crime*," or a "*terrible tragedy*" had taken place. The titles were as varied as their authors' imaginations. No matter; Mallock wasn't expecting them to shed any light on the case.

Of course, he knew the reason for it: the embargo imposed by the higher-ups. The lack of photos was glaring evidence of it, as was the obvious lack of details about the homicides. All the papers had cobbled together fantastical stories apparently supported by an interview with a neighbor or a tearful relative. *She didn't have an enemy in the world . . . it's the work of a madman . . . I don't understand; she was such a nice person.* The questions, like the photos, seemed as if they were meant to replace the scoops and other earth-shattering revelations that usually surrounded this kind of sensational news item.

The simple idea of serial crime didn't appear until three months in, at the very beginning of Léon's second scrapbook. It was in an article signed M.M. for Mallock's great friend Margot Murât, nicknamed Queen Margot. She had entitled the article "Too many police to be honest." In it, she described her surprise at the tone of the press conferences given by Number 36, and at their polite eagerness to give the newspapers an amount of information as impressively large as it was useless. "Why do I have the uncomfortable feeling that these gentlemen have just thrown a smokescreen over us?" she finished by wondering, in her inimitable style.

It was past midnight when Mallock picked up Dublin's file. He stared at it for a while without opening it, wondering if he should get some sleep and start again tomorrow. Hadn't he done enough for tonight?

But he was as meticulous as he was obstinate, and he jerked the folder open impatiently. Twenty minutes later he closed it, dismayed. He had just seen a glimpse of hell; the belly of the beast. A whole ocean of screams and flesh laid low. This new document was much crueler than Léon's scrapbooks.

Every page was adorned with grotesque illuminations. Besides the snapshots and horrifying forensic descriptions, there was one morbid detail of the killer's *modus operandi* that had never filtered down to the media; a distinctive feature of the ritual, at least with the most recent victims: they had been completely drained of their blood. Exsanguination. Not by a bite in the hollow of the neck in the grand vampirical tradition, but by the use of catheters in multiple strategically-chosen locations. The torturer—or torturers—had to have considerable medical knowledge to get such a perfect result. He would have to keep this information in mind as he pursued his investigation. A surgeon? A doctor or a nurse? A question streaked through his brain.

What had happened to all the blood?

He wouldn't find out the hideous answer until much later.

Of course, there wasn't the slightest trace of DNA; not the faintest fingerprint, only a burnt scrap of paper in a fireplace. Still legible was the end of a sentence which, it was believed, might have been written by the murderer: *death is life*.

Mallock sat up straight. Normally he would have waited, but this was urgent. It was too early; he knew. Dangerous, he suspected; even pointless, but he wanted to try. Starting tonight, against all logic, he would call on his most mysterious abilities—and on the substances that went with them.

To lift his inhibitions and give free rein to what he modestly called his intuitions, he prescribed himself his oldest, most innocent remedy to start with: whiskey and tobacco, as much as he wanted. Three good gulps to start the process and cleanse his mind of parasitic thoughts. Then the first cigar, smoked in little puffs, turning it to ensure slow and regular burning. Three more gulps. Then on to the most dubious part of the process: a sugar lump with three drops of one of his "remedies for melancholy."

He settled himself deep in an armchair, gazing at the cloud of smoke forming around him, as his whole body began to vibrate gently. Three more swallows of whiskey. Calmly, like other people eased themselves into too-cold water, he began to penetrate the icy universe of the Makeup Artist, taking with him all the data he had gleaned from Léon's scrapbooks and Dublin's files along with his own first still-fresh theories. Three more swallows. Cigar smoke like fog on a moor. His mind, skimming the rooftops of the city, disappeared beyond the horizon, into the sunlit sea spray and balmy winds of a waking dream, all above, all inside.

As with each time he plunged into the unknown this way, Mallock perceived strange and sudden things; a mixture of dreams and revelations. This kind of sleep generated images that were difficult to sort and interpret, but which might very well help him, tomorrow, to profile the killer.

The monster was waiting for him. It symbolized the murderer—but in a coded, dreamlike way. Nothing was ever said explicitly during these visions.

Sitting hunched over, damp and reptilian, the thing was writing a curious list of words on little scraps of paper, which it let fall to the ground when they were full—but not without first duly and violently stamping them.

A poppy, some poppies, an elephant, some elephants, a tent, some tents, a horse, some horses, a wop, some pizza-makers . . .

He turned suddenly. A stethoscope hung around his neck. He began talking, absurdly, saying things and then their opposites.

"Death is life. Life is pain. Pain is wine. Wine is blood. Blood is union. Union is death. Death is life."

Amédée tried to explain to him that he was talking nonsense.

"But Mallock, I'm not the one talking. You are. It's your dream, isn't it? So you're the one talking. It's your brain spouting this crap."

He burst out laughing.

"Death, you poor stupid superintendent, is the opposite of life. Life is the opposite of death. Blood is life. Life is God talking to us. Death is emptiness. Life is fullness. Death is emptiness of blood. Blood is death."

To Mallock, who felt strangely obligated to listen to this torrent of words while trying to assign some meaning to them, it seemed as if the monster was contradicting itself.

"I deny that! If I am contradicting myself it's because I am many. Like you, Superintendent. Like all of us, isn't that right?"

Then it screamed: "Look how we swarm!"

Behind it, in the shadows, a dozen forms were jeering.

"God has multiplied us, as he did with the bread and wine. Every day that God makes, we dance and piss on piles of cunts."

Then it turned suddenly serious again: "Perseverance is a great fighter."

And it picked up the chant once more: "Wine is blood. Blood is money. Money is fullness . . . "

Back in the apartment, on the other side of the dream, Mallock's cigar, having no one to smoke it, had mournfully gone out. The ice cubes in their tray had turned liquid again.

And, in the stone fireplace, two poplar logs continued to consume themselves, whispering stories of the forest.

In his nightmare, Mallock found himself wearing clunky, mud-covered shoes and standing on a staircase decorated with photos of children and beaches. On the upstairs landing was a doll dressed in chiffon with hair in two braids, and three stacks of white masks. A low, hoarse voice that sounded like it came from a pus-filled throat was singing in the next room: "Little holes, little holes, more little holes, little holes, little holes . . . "

Before venturing into the room, Mallock turned around to look for help. He realized that he was alone, and that he had left large pieces of dried mud all over the steps and the new carpet of the pretty house. The monster, emerging from the next room covered in blood, was mocking him:

"I always clean up after I visit pretty ladies."

When he finally woke up, Amédée thought they might be dealing with a case of multiple personality disorder in their killer: several individuals imprisoned in one bodily envelope. A dissident group of assassins was another possibility. Thinking about it, both theories seemed equally plausible.

After drinking a cup of coffee, Mallock went in search of the vacuum, to deal with the ceramic dust that still glittered on the carpet outside the bathroom. He was annoyed with himself. He usually treated his possessions with great care—he even talked to them sometimes, and they talked back. They'd always given him good advice, and been loyal companions when he was a child.

Amédée went into the living room. It was Sunday, and he didn't have anything much planned. The fire had gone out after struggling valiantly most of the night. Filled with sudden resolve, he began raking out the ashes choking the fireplace.

His little Tom was there, among the cold grey cinders. He had truly believed he would never recover from his son's death. The pain had stunned him, reduced him to a grief-stricken object. Incapable of rising up against the tragedy, he had found himself prostrate, bone-thin, with tears that never stopped flowing and an uncontrollable trembling that had shaken his body for almost a month.

The memory of Toto's cremation was worse than any nightmare—a series of horrifying images, a life crumbling to agonized bits. And the grief was always there, would always be there.

"Your death, Thomas . . . you, dead? How can I live with that monstrous thing?"

For a long time Mallock hadn't known what to do with his arms, or with all that love that he couldn't give anymore. Three years later, he hadn't recovered—only begun to get used to the idea that Toto would never be there again.

As he put his thoughts in order, Amédée had reached the bathroom. He shook a tablet and two capsules into his left hand and swallowed them with a mouthful of water straight from the tap. Leaning against the side of the sink, he rubbed his forehead with a bit of tiger balm and essential mint oil, then ran a bath.

Waiting for the tub to fill, he went back to the kitchen. He would stew himself a guinea fowl. Fuck it—it was Sunday!

Lots of leeks, some turnips, two big slices of pumpkin. An onion with three cloves stuck in it. Two little hot chili peppers. A quick stuffing made of chicken liver, port, and bread soaked in milk. A few morsels of black truffle between the skin and flesh of the bird. It reminded him of a black-and-white mask at a Venetian carnival. *Half-mourning*—that was the gastronomic term.

An unexpected idea occurred to him. Originally, and despite what people thought these days, the purpose of masks was to show another face, not to hide the face of the person wearing it. Another piece of information floated up from the depths of his memory: the Italian word *maschera*, meaning *false face*, *fancy dress*, or *disguise*. Mallock loved it when he received this kind of mysterious message, even though it sometimes took a while to figure out all the significance of it.

Was it possible that the killer—or killers—was putting a kind of mask on his victims by covering them with that bizarre makeup? And if so, was he veiling them, or assigning them another appearance? If so, which one? Was he erasing something, or presenting something to be seen?

Masks had two completely opposite functions. Hiding and showing.

Lost in his metaphysical wonderings, Mallock dropped the guinea fowl into the pot of stock, almost gently. Sometimes he surprised himself by murmuring a word of thanks, like an Indian after the hunt; an apology, a kind of prayer to the food he was preparing. Only with meat, though, not vegetables—no need to go overboard.

The murdered creature would be ready in an hour. Until then he would simmer in a bath of his own, just like a plump chicken. First, though, he swallowed a double whiskey in a single gulp. Bottoms up.

Too much alcohol to fight too much sadness. It was an equal exchange.

He chose a book from his library at random and put on Brian Eno for background music; then sank into the warm water with a murmur of bliss.

4.
Monday, December 27th

Arriving at Number 36 on Monday, Mallock felt a sense of apprehension, which he took for exhilaration. The guard on duty, a hulk in blue uniform and flat cap, greeted the two of them—the superintendent and his dread—with the kind of fearful respect that troubles more than it comforts. In the lobby the huge Christmas tree was already shedding its needles. The pine scent permeated the large stairway, replacing the permanent rubbery odor of worn linoleum. At the top of the building, overlooking the Seine, between the drug squad and the crime division, was his department—the kingdom of Dédé the Wizard. The only department furnished almost like new in the whole building, Fort Mallock occupied the very top in terms of reputation, mystery, and—already—legend.

The oldest and youngest of his colleagues, Bob and Francis, were on duty.

"Good morning, Guv." The ever-ceremonious Robert Daranne welcomed him by bringing two fingers to his forehead in a rough version of a military salute. As vain as a young man despite his almost sixty years, he claimed vague Irish roots, insisting people call him "Bob" and addressing Mallock as "Guv" rather than "Boss." To be fair, it was a bit hard on a man's pride to call someone "Boss" who was fifteen years younger than you, and who'd taken orders from you for a long time. He had acted as a kind of sensei to Amédée in his early days.

Bob was the index finger on the hand of Mallock's immediate team. A former army corporal and then captain, he had come to the police force late in life and by chance, finding himself promoted—thanks to age and merit—to the rank of chief inspector. Habitually dressed in a brown suit and too-wide pie-server tie, five feet five inches tall, redheaded, mustachioed, and short-tempered, Bob was fundamentally brave and viscerally narrow-minded. He favored no one but his superintendent. His obsessive authoritarianism made him the best person to relay the boss/guv's orders and ensure their perfect execution. He was a dedicated colleague, but also kind of a nuisance. The role of index finger fit him to a tee.

"How was your Christmas Eve dinner?" Mallock had asked the question because he knew they were waiting for him to ask it—for his permission to talk about it, really.

Bob launched into a recitation. "Oh, fine, fine, I managed to pull it off this year. Four out of six showed up. That's more than usual. Normally three is the record. You should have seen them; all dressed up with their hair brushed, like when they were younger. Say what you will, but family . . . that means something."

Amédée had a brief vision of a lineup of redheads; particularly the last one, Hélias, whose godfather he was. The one Bob persisted in calling "Alas," because he thought it was funny, and because the boy hadn't turned out exactly like his father would have preferred. He was too skinny, too intellectual, and he was late too much. This last pregnancy had been planned by Madame Daranne without the agreement of the paterfamilias, and seven years later His Majesty was still angry about the unauthorized use of the royal sperm.

Watching Bob was like looking back in time at the way men treated women in the 1950s. Bob was a chauvinist jackass, Mallock often thought, whom guard dogs annoyed almost as much. He imagined the four grown Daranne children, together for once to make the old man happy, wearing expressions of resigned impatience mixed with fear.

"A buddy of mine and I treated ourselves to dinner at Taillevent. I won't bore you with the details." Slimmer than Mallock, with crew-cut hair and a waistline beginning to thicken with age, Francis was a bit of a flake, taciturn and chatty at the same time. He tended to veer between one and the other, like sun and rain on the Normandy coast. "It was to die for," he continued in blatant contradiction of what he'd just promised. "All of it, amazing—except for the goddamn crappy wine. Ahhh-mazing. Cost us a hundred and fifty euros each. Not bad, eh? For the first course, I had . . . "

Francis Tremolha, nicknamed "Volunteer," always seemed as if he were trying to make up for lost time. He invariably dressed in black from head to toe, as if in mourning for his terrible childhood. Laughing one relaxed evening after three Irish coffees, he had stunned everyone with a precise and detailed comparison of the impacts of the slaps and punches delivered by his mother and father. The blows rained on him with a shoe by his mother seemed to have left as much of a mark on him as his father's complicit impassivity during these infamous "heel sessions," as he called them.

Amédée, without thinking, had taken Francis under his wing, just because the little dodo had crossed his path. "Talk about a stroke of luck," the younger man was fond of saying. At twenty-eight years old, recently promoted to chief inspector, he was just discovering all the small and large pleasures in life—especially the immeasurable freedom that money could buy.

"And for dessert," Francis continued, "we had crêpes Suzette with all the bells and whistles; the flaming Grand Marnier and the waiter in a tuxedo with the whisk and the pan and the forks. Unforgettable. And you, boss? If you don't mind me asking?"

"I got a hell of a gift, and not from just anyone. From Dublin himself."

"A tie?" asked Bob, stupidly.

"No, you idiot. I bet he finally gave that bizarre murder case to the Superintendent," said Francis.

"Bingo. But let's slow it down a little, lad. We're not officially on the case until Tuesday."

"Yes!" exclaimed the young chief inspector, pumping his fists like a tennis player after a winning serve.

Mallock couldn't hold back a smile.

"Be nice; go and see if Grimaud is here yet. But don't antagonize him, whatever you do. He's still in charge, and he's a bit touchy. Just tell him I'm here and available; he should understand." He turned to his longtime colleague. "Bob, go yell at IT. I need three extra terminals hooked up to everything that moves; Europe, the United States, and the East. And get some Mac Pros. I want as much power as we can get, to process images and films."

"How many?"

"Ken will give you the details. If you need a lucky charm, come back and get it here, okay?"

"Consider it done, Guv."

Turning back toward the window, Mallock rubbed his hands together, almost content. Sometimes everything became simple. A mission turned up like a gust of wind and blew everything else away. He was one of the good guys, on the trail of the bad guys. Forgetting his own pain for a while, he would be in the service of the people, worthy of what he wanted to be: a good and courageous man. There was a lot of Cyrano, of course—his hero—but also some Jean Valjean in Amédée. The same physical strength, the same pride and anger, the same sentimental weakness. Like Victor Hugo's hero he had a kind of monstrous destiny, the kind you could only fight with a shrewd mixture of resistance, resilience, and resignation.

For his happiness to be complete now, he only needed his two other captains: Julie, as sharp as she was pretty; and Jules, a straight, solid guy. The two of them were maintaining a long-distance romance. They'd been separated in the outside world, but not at Fort Mallock. The superintendent needed those two crazy kids . . . he just hoped they could stay discreet.

Outside, weak sunlight was filtering through the winter fog. He lingered for a few minutes, gazing at the view, trying not to think about anything at all. It was his way of wiping his hard drive, reformatting the data in his brain. Simply doing nothing, blocking out the slightest bit of information or faintest idea or smallest image from getting in.

After ten minutes of repairing authorizations, defragging, and throwing things in the trash, Mallock's brain was ready. He went back on the attack, and in three hours had torn through a heap of current business: all the incoming mail, a quick meeting with Dublin, and then a discussion with his team about three cases assigned to them: today, one rape, a disappearance, and an apartment burglary with violence. Tonight, like almost every other night, he would have to slog through a mountain of paperwork. He had decided one exasperated day to reread and sign all documents that left the Fort; he was responsible for them, so he wanted to know what they were. Aside from these pressures, which he'd brought on himself like a big boy, he did mostly what he wanted.

Spared the flattened cats, the traffic hearings, the evacuation reports and domestic disturbances, he no longer had to intervene in petty squabbles to score points with the higher-ups. For a long time now he had marched to the beat of his own drum. He kept for himself the skinheads; the hunting-down and arresting of gangsters; the most wanted criminals. Professionally speaking he really couldn't complain; he was generally left in perfect peace, or close to it. By creating his own team and fighting for materials and independence, he had succeeded in keeping useless fighting against the hierarchy, the administration, and all its parasites to a minimum. His group had not only been made more effective; it had managed to avoid dealing with the high-end rent boys, whores, and meth-heads that clogged the corridors of Number 36.

5.
Monday, December 27th. Lunch with RG

L ooking for Francis to avoid eating lunch alone, Mallock almost collided with Grimaud.

"Hello, Raymond! It's late—I was just going to lunch. Maybe we can—"

"I was just coming to ask you to have lunch with me, as a matter of fact. I'd like to brief you on the case over a bite to eat. I've got an initial written rundown with me, too."

"Great! Here, give it to me; I'll put it away."

It couldn't have worked out better. A good Bordeaux has a way of loosening tongues and numbing sensitivities. RG surveyed Mallock. He was relieved to see that the superintendent put the precious rundown in the safe and then double-locked his office door.

Amédée looked at him and smiled.

"Sorry. A leopard can't change its spots," Raymond said sheepishly.

Both men laughed as if they were old friends—which they weren't, but might become in the end.

Outside, the sun was blinding. The cold and the air, still saturated with humidity, were making a joint effort to freeze the city's pedestrians. The sidewalk outside the station was covered with corn kernels, and the pigeons taking advantage of the bounty skidded aside as the two men passed. They took the Boulevard du Palais and then the Pont au Change. The air was full of lighted garlands and also a kind of nervousness, as if the dust swirling around Paris's millions of streetlamps was electrified. Somewhere nearby, a murderer was choosing his next victim. Mallock quickened his steps, slapping his arms to warm up.

"You should have worn an overcoat."

"It's not that far! I'll be fine."

Once again Mallock cursed his phobia of coats and under-clothing. He never wore undershirts or sleeveless tops, and very rarely wore socks. His claustrophobia was getting worse and worse as he aged, and it even extended to clothing. The less he had around him, the better he felt.

Arriving in front of the restaurant, they exchanged polite "You first"s before deciding to walk in together, their laughter preceding them.

"Superintendents, hello!"

The owner extended a cordial hand to Mallock. Amédée grasped it in a crushing grip before directing his gaze toward his favorite table.

"It's all ready for you," the man confirmed, pulling back the chairs.

They had barely seated themselves when Grimaud began. "Might as well get it all out. I've seen Dublin. The big boss would like the official handover of power to happen tonight at midnight—so, tomorrow morning, really. But I've been giving it a lot of thought . . . and it can't wait. We're dealing with a madman, and the sooner you're in the know, the better."

When he wasn't running his fingers through the superb brush of silvery hair on his head, Raymond was playing nerv-ously with his fork, tracing a series of parallel grooves on the tablecloth. He paused for two or three seconds between each of his sentences; it was more a tic than any real slowness of mind.

"It's a horrendous case. I've never seen anything like it."

"Not many clues?"

"None at all! Not one lead; not even a strand of hair. And

to be frank with you, it's worse than that. I don't have a single idea or personal impression, other than my profound disgust at these murders. I'm not sure how to explain it to you. I'm just relieved you're taking over the case."

Grimaud's manner of addressing Mallock had veered between the informal *tu* and the formal *vous*, and even sometimes the hypothetical *on*, ever since they met. He had never really been comfortable around him, and undoubtedly he never would be. It was nobody's fault—that was just how things were. Amédée had always been a step ahead of him. Even now he was a chief superintendent, with the salary and expense allowance that came along with leadership, while Grimaud was only a detective chief inspector. Yet he was far from being incompetent.

"RG" wasn't only his set of initials, but a nickname earned by his obsession—albeit an effective one—for planting bugs and tapping telephone wires. He was also extremely fond of "bargain-hunting and lentil-sorting"—police jargon for searching methodically for information and then examining it with the patience and seriousness of a man panning for gold. Moreover, he was an accomplished midwife of sorts when it came to suspects; men questioned by Father Raymond tended to lie back and give birth to true confessions.

No, RG wasn't a bad detective—far from it, in fact. He was tough, meticulous, shrewd, and straightforward; qualities that Mallock appreciated greatly. He had put RG on his short list when putting together his team. If Grimaud would only relax a little, he might join the Fort one day—maybe to replace Bob when the latter retired.

"It doesn't make me particularly happy to have been taken off the case, but it's just as well," RG said again. "It's different with you . . . can't be offended when it's Mallock replacing you. I wouldn't have been too pleased if just anyone had taken over."

"Thank you, Raymond; that's a real compliment coming from you. Should we order now?"

Amédée had seen the magic words: "veal head with gribiche sauce." Grimaud, in keeping with his persona of ascetic simplicity, ordered a grilled steak with green beans. The service was speedy, and seven minutes later the plates were steaming on the table in front of them.

"*Bon appétit.*"

They ate in silence. Though impatient, Mallock had decided not to rush this meeting—and besides, his veal head was delicious, with the satisfying inclusion of a bit of tongue and brain. Not everything was rotten in God's kingdom, then. The hubbub of the dining room flowed gently around the bubble of reflection and culinary appreciation enclosing the two men. Grimaud finally set down his fork and took a drink from his glass, then wiped his mouth in a quick, almost violent gesture.

"The worst part of this whole horrible story is that crazy stitching. This guy is a maniac—a real fucking vampire. But I won't go into detail; the doc will explain it to you better than I can. I still don't understand how anyone can do this kind of thing. I've seen it with my own eyes, but this fucking Makeup Artist has really scared the crap out of me. My file is perfectly up-to-date . . . three binders, each a full foot thick, closed. But to be honest with you, none of it's terribly useful, aside from the routine investigations, which were all done very thoroughly, as you know I always do. But I'm afraid you're going to have to start over from scratch. Now, the fourth folder— there's explosive material in that one, and you need to keep it well protected."

Mallock's gaze dropped to Grimaud's fingers, which were stained with purple ink. "Carbon paper?" he asked. "Is it so secret that you can't even use a photocopier?"

"Well spotted. But then, nothing escapes our Dédé the Wizard!"

Mallock wasn't overly fond of that nickname, for a whole variety of reasons, but he smiled at Grimaud anyway.

"You're right," RG continued, "it is carbon. To avoid leaks, I've only made three copies of the file—I've got one at home, one in my safe, and another with the department. We haven't made any photocopies; I had to slog through it old-style. Carbon paper for the three copies, and I only made two copies of the photos for myself, and then encrypted the originals in the computer."

Grimaud seemed relieved to finally be able to tell everything to a colleague, someone who understood the torment he'd been through better than the political higher-ups did.

"I know I don't need to tell you that what I'm about to say is highly, highly confidential . . . for your ears only, as the English say . . . "

"For my *eyes* only," corrected Mallock.

"Fine, if you like. In any case, this stays in Number 36."

RG scooted his chair in with a horrible scraping noise and leaned toward Mallock until it looked like he might dislocate his neck. Professional corruption—wiretapping—he was all too familiar with them.

"I've spent the last two months of the investigation researching other cases, and I've managed—with the help of Mordome, your pathologist buddy—to uncover the exponential aspect of how his *modus operandi* has developed, as they say. What we really did was work backward, starting from the theory that, at the beginning, the killer must have been less . . . sick. That's how we rediscovered some older cases involving the murders of—listen to this—a man, and even kids. Everything seems to have started with the murders of two children. They're the oldest incidents and the most rudimentary ones. Then he killed a man, and then his first woman four years ago. It's gotten nastier and nastier with each victim."

At last Grimaud cut to the heart of the matter, with a wealth of details that were slightly incompatible with *tête de veau sauce gribiche*—luckily Mallock had finished eating.

"He's atypical—anomic, to use the scholarly term. A genuine psychotic, but he earns perfect marks when it comes to control. Never seen anything like it. Not even the faintest fingerprint found at any scene. No DNA. No noise at all, so no witnesses, no composite sketch. The only area where he fits into the statistics for psychopaths is his IQ. Serial killers are all geniuses, apparently. With him there's no doubt about it. His intelligence is diabolical, just like his imagination. Our killer's MO is shocking, both in its diversity and its perversity."

"Unless we put an 's' on the name, so it's Makeup Artists?" Mallock suggested. "At least for—"

Their waiter picked up his plate, making him jump. "Would you like to see the dessert menu?"

"No thanks," said Mallock. "Just coffee."

"Do you have chocolate *liégeois*?" asked Grimaud.

"Yes, but it's not part of the set menu."

"I don't care," RG cut him off. "I'll have one, with lots of whipped cream."

It was Mallock who tacked a "Please, thank you" onto the end of Grimaud's sentence, while the young man scribbled a hieroglyph on his pad, gave Amédée a quick smile, and disappeared with their empty plates.

"I don't doubt your abilities, but we're not ready to catch this guy. His rituals are long and complicated—they often take more than an hour, but he doesn't leave a trace. Zilch. The cocksucker is like a fucking ghost! As I said, we've checked every piece of evidence for fingerprints and we haven't found a single one. There's absolutely nothing human about this monster. He's worse than a devil; he is *the* Devil."

A former seminarist in the paratroopers, RG was one of the rare devout and practicing superintendents in Number 36.

"You're still talking about him in the singular. Do you have any real, valid reason for that?"

A cloud passed over Grimaud's face—a huge cumulonimbus, stuffed full of lightning bolts. When he spoke again, his voice had changed. It was shaking.

"You see, this killer has taken over my life. I'm just so relieved that I don't have to have anything more to do with him. This whole thing is a curse. You absolutely have to beware."

"Of him? I don't doubt it, my friend."

"No—of yourself. Of what he'll want you to become. He has shown me things—or rather, made me feel things . . . I'm not explaining it very well. You know I'm a religious man, a devout Catholic. People make fun of me by calling me Raymond the Priest and the Abbot Cop behind my back, as if it's craziness to have faith. But I've always considered it one of my strengths . . . until this assignment, and the . . . the things a case like this puts into our heads . . . "

Mallock allowed the silence to settle as heavily behind the last sentence as RG wished it to. Looking at Grimaud's face, he thought he could see some of those horrible things reflected in it. He had seen hints of them in the files.

"Or maybe it's because of my religious training. I'm undoubtedly more sensitive to some of the signs he leaves . . . more affected by certain symbols, and his sense of torture."

"I have to go back to this—you always say 'he,' singular. Why do you think he's acting alone? Even though there are various different rituals present?"

Grimaud plunged his spoon violently into his whipped cream. Without realizing it, his choice of dessert had made him even more likable in Amédée's eyes. There was still some of the child left, a desire for sweetness, in the big, athletic body of this ex-boxer, ex-paratrooper, ex-seminarist, and superintendent with Number 36.

"You're exactly right. I use the singular—the generic, really. There could very well be two or three murderers; a family, or a cult . . . the name *Makeup Artist* should be used in the plural, but I started out referring to him in the singular, as if . . . I don't know . . . to make him more real in my mind, I guess. And maybe, unconsciously, because I don't want to think there's more than one person on earth capable of doing such horrible things. One seems like plenty to me. But you are right, there's a very good chance that the Makeup Artist is several people."

Mallock didn't point out that last use of the singular. "Well, you've done good work. You've got nothing to feel bad about. As soon as I get going, I'll plow through all the stuff you've already figured out."

RG blushed like a schoolboy, but his honesty quickly won out. "A lot of the credit goes to Mordome, who's a hell of a guy, between you and me."

This was a double dose of pleasure for Mallock: a compliment for his friend, and the sight of a man of integrity seated across from him. Grimaud, a large smear of chocolate now adorning his white goatee, continued: "We're in the process of trying to identify exactly the molecules or the drug cocktail common to all of the cases. He'll explain it to you better than I can. It's what the Makeup Artist uses to immobilize his victims, before subjecting them to whatever's in his head. This fucking drug is all the information we have on him. If we could just find out more . . . "

"About *him*?" interjected Amédée, smiling.

"Er . . . or about *them*."

"If you'd already gotten to that point, if I'm not asking too much, would you be able to continue? I'd love to have a complete rundown on this famous cocktail."

"Of course—I've already started to do all the research on the products and the laboratories that manufacture them, and the places these drugs are available. I'll finish that up for you, if it'll help. I'd planned on adding it to my files anyway when I was done with it."

"I really appreciate it. Speaking of the files, if it isn't too much of a bother I'll send one of my boys over to your office this afternoon for the rest of them, okay?"

"I'll bring them to you. Go see Mordome at the Institute in the meantime, as soon as you can. After me, he's the one who knows the most about this case. When it comes to my conclusions, and his, about what we've found out already—that's in a fourth, separate file. There's only one copy of that and I keep it with me in my briefcase. You can leave with it from here, but promise me you'll be careful. It's explosive, this thing."

RG's paranoia was no myth. But in this case, this particular personality trait had definitely been a blessing. He put an ancient-looking leather portfolio on the table; it was actually bulging like a balloon. *Explosive*, Grimaud had said. Mallock had a vision of an old-fashioned spherical anarchist's bomb.

"Double-check it; I could be wrong about some of my conclusions. And as you'll see, it's far from being complete."

Mallock waited for RG to take his hand off the file before pulling it toward him. You had to handle these paranoid types with kid gloves. Then the two of them argued over who would pay the check, and Mallock was forced to capitulate. Grimaud wouldn't have wanted it to seem like he was handing over his goodwill in return for a simple gourmet lunch.

6.
Monday, December 27th. Evening

The sun had almost entirely disappeared behind the buildings—but, perfectionist that it was, it still touched the stones with a last salmon-pink tinge. Between dog and wolf, as the saying went. The superintendent adored this interlude before moonrise, this magic moment when you could sink silently into yourself amid the noise of others, the vast rumble walking along the sidewalks of the world, their torments filed away in the drawers of the earth, their ambitions put off until tomorrow. Sometime after six o'clock a man would go back home, contemplating his life and lingering on thoughts of soup, while God and the Devil crossed paths, keeping pointless hatred for themselves.

Amédée Mallock spent ten minutes searching for a parking spot before he remembered that his garage was waiting for him. He circled one more time, taking the Rue des Mauvais-Garçons and then the Rue du Roi-de-Sicile to reach the private parking structure. Had he paid too much for it? Without a doubt. But when you're in love, you don't do the math. He had been especially fed up with losing half an hour every evening scouring the neighborhood looking for a space, and finding one had been more of a miracle every day.

It was at this moment of intense satisfaction that he realized his mistake.

"Don't forget to come get the key card on Monday morning. Otherwise you won't be able to get back in," the seller had warned him.

Fortunately Amélie, his pretty physiotherapist, was coming today. There was no better way to keep the big bear from clawing. He avenged himself by parking in a spot marked "deliveries only" in front of the horrible little superette on the corner. The old Jaguar's blue, white, and red police sticker would protect it from the motorcycle cops.

Back at home, he smartened himself up a bit. For Amélie. The nurse and physiotherapist had been recommended to him by the blue-eyed pharmacist in the little square, her grey hair in a chignon, who had said:

"She's been giving my son his shots for years."

Coming from this charming woman, that seemed like the best reason in the world to trust her. If she, who was almost a doctor, had entrusted this young person with the fruit of her loins, there could be no doubt about her skill! Mallock, obligingly, had followed her recommendation.

He was still congratulating himself for it.

His first time seeing her through the peephole of his front door had been a shock. Love at first sight—with a whole quiverful of Cupid's arrows for good measure, which had lodged in his head as well as his heart. Not to mention other places.

To Mallock she was, quite simply, perfect. More than perfect. Even her flaws were adorable. She was a bit of a scatterbrain, her gaze always slightly unfocused, as if she were constantly thinking about what she might have forgotten. She was sweetly chaotic. The giant holdall she had once spilled on the living room floor had contained, besides her pharmacy kit and an assortment of makeup, half a dozen novels. Imagine—a woman who loves *One Hundred Years of Solitude*, *Red Dragon*, and *Book of My Mother*! She was everything a person could dream of in a partner—at least, for a misanthrope like Mallock. For this woman, he could break his solitude. But would she want him?

When Amélie arrived, he took off his shirt for the cortisone injection. And, as she plunged the needle into his back, Mallock, happy to receive this pain from her still-cold little hands, grinned like a fool.

Today, once again, they kept to the formalities.

"I didn't hurt you too much, did I?"

"I didn't feel a thing."

"Do you have time for a cup of tea?" he asked, buttoning his shirt.

"I'd love one, if it's not too much trouble."

Amédée babbled a polite denial and made for the kitchen. Three minutes later they sat silently across from each other at the table. As usual, they talked about the rain, the nice weather, the respective characters of people they knew—but there was a bit more, too. Amélie was incredibly kind; serious and harebrained at the same time; yet cultivated when the conversation required it. Always intelligent.

"I must admit, all my clients are adorable," she said.

"Naturally. You're adorable too," Mallock ventured, carefully setting his teacup down. The cup looked tiny; at least half the size of the one Amélie was drinking from. Odd. He knew they were identical.

"I'm sorry," she said; "I've got to go."

"Next Wednesday?"

"Next Wednesday. No injections next time; we're going to work on extension. Take a muscle relaxant the night before, and a painkiller when you wake up."

"And Friday? Shall we say morning or evening?"

For the sake of simplicity, and to keep Mallock from forgetting the time, she always came at either eight o'clock in the morning or eight o'clock at night.

"Morning, otherwise I can't come. Friday's the thirty-first—New Year's Eve. By five o'clock that evening I'll be slaving over a hot stove."

Amédée walked her out, imagining her adorable nose dusted with flour. At the door he shook her hand, holding it a few seconds longer for the sheer pleasure of it. He felt incredibly awkward and unfashionable around her. Awkward and clumsy, while she was pure femininity. Petite, dark-haired and green-eyed, with a swanlike neck and a mouth that was as sublime as her teeth, and the way she moved.

He stared out the window when Amélie had gone. How much longer was he going to wait before he asked her out to dinner? As enjoyable as it was, the game was beginning to go on a bit long. What if she got tired of it? The problem was that he no longer felt anything. Before, he had known when he had a chance. When his athletic body and clear green eyes were making sparks fly. Here, nothing. Flatline. He had been watching her expressions carefully, but could read nothing.

To get away from his thoughts, Mallock called his office one last time.

"Where are we, Francis?"

"We'll have the stuff by ten o'clock tomorrow morning. What should I do in the meantime?"

Mallock hesitated for a second. The little devil inside him thought of giving his colleague another job to do, but it was the big angel that won out:

"Go home. We've got a hell of a battle in front of us. You'll need your strength."

At around ten o'clock that night, Mallock finally made his way to the kitchen for something to eat. It was only when he was standing in front of his open refrigerator that he realized he wasn't really hungry. He finally reheated some broth from the previous day's chicken, using kitchen shears to snip some bits of white meat and leek into it and adding three diced turnips. Tabasco sauce; capful of port; salt and pepper.

Back in the living room, he put on a concerto for flute and harp. Mozart took him directly into the heart of his most intimate, most essential thoughts. Sipping the piping-hot soup, he gazed into the cold fireplace. Two embers had miraculously survived the fire of the previous evening; now they were staring at him like two eyes. Mallock was tempted to speak to them. But whose gaze was this? His son's? Amélie's? Or maybe the killer's?

As he came nearer, he realized that there were others. Smaller embers, nearly extinguished. Stupidly, as if they were the first stars of the evening, he began to count them. Two by two. One, two, three . . . ten, eleven, and twelve. Thirteen! A great shudder ran through him. The twelve apostles were looking back at him, and at their head the dark Christ, the fallen angel. He cursed his mediumistic abilities, and also what his mother had made religion into—a tool of domination, submission, and terror.

Behind his back he felt another kind of heat; creeping, moving, interspersed with sharp, freezing gusts of wind. It was the Devil in person, come to confront him in his own living room. There could be no doubt; he felt him, heard him, urinating powerfully in every corner and behind the sofa. Howling with laughter over the noise of his own pissing on the glass screen, the devil was now soaking the television set. Completely paralyzed, petrified with fear, Amédée couldn't move. Just before leaving, the apparition squatted on the low table to defecate some kind of blue worm, before coming very close to Amédée, and licking his ears. The odor was unspeakable.

Waking from his doze with a jolt, the former choirboy remained prostrate for a good fifteen minutes, aghast. In front of the fireplace, he waited for the embers to go out. Then, seeking some reassurance, he looked out the window. The first stars had appeared in the sky. He spoke to them about Amélie and Thomas, and then went to bed feeling almost calm.

It was that night, around 3 A.M., that the ringing of the telephone dragged him out of bed and sent him to Saint-Mandé, to look at the woman and her little daughter who had been massacred by the Makeup Artist.

The man in blue loden, after forcing his way past the security cordon, had come up to Mallock and grasped his arm.

"Where is my daughter? Has something happened to my wife?"

The two men were face to face. Mallock said:

"They're dead."

Two little puffs of breath. Two words. Two missiles. The man had just been killed in his turn. Of the person he had been, the man who believed in happiness, nothing remained now except a little head of sadness on a counterfeit body still gripping, by automatic reflex, a briefcase that had occupied his time. All the problems in that case, even the thorniest ones, no longer existed. François Modiano had worked for years as a chief engineer at Schlem. Now he was nothing more than an anguished planet frozen in a starry emptiness.

But how else could Mallock have said it? He asked himself the same question every time, always knowing that there was no answer. With time, the crushing superiority of questions over the horrible no-man's-land of answers becomes understandable. How do you announce a thing like this? Approach another person bearing filth, sadness, the end of the world? One might say it slowly, progressively, or all at once, like ripping off a bandage. But it wasn't bandage being torn away—it was the whole skin, and the heart with it. There was no other way— even though Mallock, obstinately, was still searching for one.

A few minutes earlier, François Modiano had been excited about finally getting home for Christmas Eve. In his head he had already been hugging both of his girls, and they were covering him with kisses.

"Hi, sweetheart. You're not too tired, are you?" his wife would have asked him, smiling.

His little girl would have simply murmured, "Papa," barely opening her eyes when he bent over her bed to kiss her goodnight.

Even if they hadn't been those words exactly, they would have been others. Lovelier ones. Things about Christmas; the roast capon and the gifts from Saint Sylvester, and lots and lots of sweets. Mallock carried, more than escorted, François Modiano to the ambulance, which stood useless and flickering, its rear doors wide open. There would be no miracles for the dead. No remedies or bandages for those who were deceased at the scene.

It was only an ambulance, but it knew. So why did men persist in hoping?

His face twisted in pain, the unfortunate Modiano sat down on the rear tailgate. His hands were shaking, but he couldn't cry. Amédée held back from questioning him. Later, maybe. As a medic pushed up his sleeve to give him an injection, the engineer slowly forced out a sentence.

"How did this happen?"

There was no way to answer that question. The man in loden should be spared for now, though of course he wouldn't escape it forever. It was one more thing inflicted on the survivors: the complete and exhaustive rundown of the abuses the victims had suffered during the murders. Denying them the right to a lie, to the simple but soothing "No, they didn't suffer." Subjecting them instead to an abominable array of information. It seemed like this allowed them to begin the work of grieving. Maybe, but some details killed more than once.

Mallock spoke, but of other matters. There were things the inconsolable could say to one another. They could even share quality silences. This is what he did, before going off to find the man a cup of very hot coffee. Then he waited with him for the drug that had been injected into his veins to take effect. Afterward, talking softly to him, he watched for the sister to appear, weeping, followed by the grandparents.

As he was leaving, he gave them his card. "If you need anything, please don't hesitate. I'm going to be heading the investigation personally, and I'll keep you informed."

Then, heavyhearted, he went to speak to Ken again: "You're on your own. Watch them closely. They absolutely cannot see the bodies; not inside and not when they bring them out. I'm counting on you."

The sun was beginning to rise. Everything was grey and depressing. Glacial. A garbage truck appeared in the street. The noise of garbage-bin lids clanged off sleeping façades. *Wake up, good people. Bye-bye, off to your jobs.* The banality of the sounds, more than anything else, brought home the demonic aspect of what had taken place in the very backyard, on the second floor of this suburban house with no history.

Mallock headed back toward Paris. His jaw, his whole body was rigid. At the Porte de Vincennes he took the ring road, his hands clenched tightly on the black Bakelite steering wheel. Staring straight ahead, he tried desperately to contain his rage and sadness.

After parking his old Jaguar in front of the flower market, Amédée sat down in a cafe to warm up and wait for eight o'clock to arrive.

"Coffee, double cream, and three croissants." His throat felt as if it were being squeezed. The image of the tortured little girl had joined the monstrous jumble he had built up in the pit of his stomach. He thought of the mother as well, and then of the child's father, and he watched his own right hand as it dunked the first croissant, trembling.

"Fuck," he murmured.

There was a message waiting for Mallock when he got to the office: *Call Judge Humbert back*. He would be in charge of the case of the Makeup Artist 2.0, for the time being. Could be better; could also be worse. Thirtyish, thick mustache, rumpled suit. In line with the unions, more fundamentalist than upstanding, he was a prototypical young judge, highly ambitious, full of himself and self-righteous. A real asshole, according to Mallock's criteria.

Curiously, for a police officer responsible for enforcing order and justice, Amédée was distrustful of rules and laws. Neither god nor master; an anarchist without a label; a kindly misanthrope; he abhorred religious posers and pasteurized cheese, conformism and repeat offenders, dominant thought and lack of comfort with equal fervor, just as he did all reductions, whether in sentence or price; fashion and celebrities; bad faith and anchovies; and the hypocritical semantics and repression of a democracy ashamed of itself but much too politically correct to be honest.

Add to all of that his exaggerated sense of justice, his enormous heart that fell in love easily, his profound compassion for his victims, and 50 percent fat, and the result was this curious creature: a depressive, anarchist upholder of the law with small ears and white stubble who could have had "death to assholes" as his motto—if he hadn't also had a sense of moderation, and of battles lost in advance.

Mallock cast a satisfied eye over his department. He had inherited, if not the nicest offices in Number 36, then at least the least ugly. Five rooms: two of them doubles for his four inspectors, a smaller office for Bob by himself, and a wonder-

ful common area, given the smallness of the premises, for brief-
ings and technical material. Finally, adjoining this, was his
Chief Superintendent's office, with a view of the ocean—or
practically, at least in Amédée's head, since the Seine flowed
toward the English Channel with the speed of a sustained current.

Taken as a whole, the department was something of an odd-
ity; comfortable and modern at the same time. At his request
everything had been painted off-white except, the sole conces-
sion imposed by National Heritage, the gold leaf on the rare
wood and plaster moldings miraculously surviving here and
there. The overall result had nothing in common with the traditional image of a police bureau—a stroke of luck of which
Mallock and his men were fully aware. They even felt a bit
guilty when they thought about their less fortunate comrades,
condemned to linoleum and plywood. The country treated its
police officers very shabbily indeed. Most of the station was a
joke, resembling nothing so much as a sad chicken coop.
Mallock had fought hard for high-quality feed and fodder for
his department, and he had gotten what they needed—plus a
good deal extra.

The replacement computers arrived with great fanfare at
around ten o'clock and Mallock signed the release form.
Francis ran over to the new toys like a small boy. "Hello there,
you beauties," he crooned at them.

A certificate in electronics engineering haphazardly
acquired in his younger days had earned Francis the designa-
tion of head of the department's IT service, under the unoffi-
cial surveillance of Ken. Though not as clever or highly trained
as him, Francis had eventually managed very well. Two years of
night classes in coding combined with a dogged determination
to learn had turned him into the king of the database, user-
friendly or not. These days he even went so far as to walk

around armed with automatic code executors, intrusion test platforms, and other security flaw exploitation tools like IP spoofing or buffer overflow, in FBI or Intelligence Service files. Administrative files just weren't quite enough for him anymore, and there were too few of them. So, while they waited for something to be decided, Ken, Francis, and Mallock had cobbled something together, with Amédée promising to cover for the others if a problem came up.

"But make sure one doesn't come up," he had emphasized. "For now, Francis, start putting together everything you find in the file. Digitize and touch up the best crime scene photos, and also the photos of each victim, in the same format. I want five copies of everything. Each one of us has to have a complete and consistent series to look at and think about."

"I'm on it, boss!"

"Five," repeated Mallock, thinking of Dublin and Grimaud. "No more than that."

Then he had a bathroom break, got himself a coffee, and spent a few minutes watching Francis struggle valiantly with USB, Ethernet, and FireWire cords. When the young chief inspector finally switched on the first screen, he turned to the superintendent: "It's too bad we don't have enough elements yet to attempt a portrait of the Makeup Artist, or I would have tried the new biometric morphing program we got from the Federal Bureau in New York."

Mallock's ideas often came to him in packs, like in billiards. His strength was to see or hear trajectories before anyone else did. For him, the whole universe was murmuring with clues, and his only talent was that he could hear them. This time, it was Francis's denial that gave him the idea for a suggestion:

"What if you started by doing a portrait of the victims?"

"A portrait? But we already have photos of them."

"Not portraits—*one* portrait. Singular."

"A composite sketch of a series of victims? That's a first."

"Maybe. Not really. I don't care. Try to see if they have something in common. Features, mouth, eye color, race . . . "

"You want them on different overlays, but the same file?"

"Yes, and synchronize the color correction, so it looks like they were all taken with the same light. And with equal proportions so we can superimpose them. It's possible that he's attracted by a certain facial symmetry, or a different structure: wide-set eyes, mouth close to the nose, a certain shape of eyes-mouth triangle. Look into that angle; look for common points, and make me a list."

Francis was writing everything down carefully. When he looked up to ask another question, his boss had already gone into the next room.

On the large conference table, other than his two large files, Mallock had half a dozen boxes brought by RG's assistant, filled mostly with the contents of the female victims' handbags.

"This is one of the thoughts I had recently," Grimaud had said. "Even though they were all killed in their homes, I asked the families for permission to borrow their purses. I hoped their address books and other personal details might help us establish a relationship between them. I haven't had the time to do it, so it's yours to follow up with. Don't forget to give all these things back to the families; I personally agreed to that."

Mallock spread everything out on the conference table. These personal things, exhibited anonymously and with detachment, made for a sad tableau. Key-rings, mobile phones, lipstick used with private dreams of seduction, shiny face powder: the last witnesses to see the victims alive. Coin purses and wallets, fine batiste handkerchiefs containing the final lip-print, a kiss sent from the beyond. To whom? Odors of perfume and rice powder mingled with ink and leather—the irreplaceable, inimitable scent of women's handbags.

Off to one side there were also the contents of the male victims' wallets—and, even more horribly, those of the children's schoolbags.

Ken had arrived at the office with dark bags under his eyes, which were puffy "as a cat's asshole," he thought it appropriate to specify. "I've come straight from Saint-Mandé. I stopped by for your viewing pleasure, and also to make a good impression, but I'm knackered. So just listen to me without rushing me, and then I'm going to go off and go beddy-bye, okay?"

"Sure, go on. I'm all ears."

Of Japanese and Italian heritage, Ken referred to himself as a peasant. He had lived in France since the age of eight. A stocky man of five foot nine with black hair and a mug like Jackie Chan's, his was a mixture of race and blood which, he gleefully admitted, he'd never completely understood. His origins and the tumult of his school years had made him a fairly odd character. Extremely clever, and of redoubtable physical strength, he was a good companion no matter the circumstances. To compensate occasionally for a slight lack of strictness in his work, he used dry wit and a good mood that nothing seemed able to alter. He and his wife, a pretty, voluptuous blonde called Anne and nicknamed Ninon, were expecting their first child. It was a girl whom they were calling Nina. Ken had chosen "Niwi" at first, but Ninon had objected, and no more had been said about the matter.

"I stayed until the end to sign the report," he began. "It was just a flash of intuition that I should—*à la* Mallock. As you know, it's standard procedure for a body to be turned over in case there's something hidden under it. And guess what was there?"

Sure of his effect, Ken let three seconds of silence go by.

"I don't know . . . a syringe?"

Robbed of his bombshell, Ken gasped. "How did you know?"

"Just intuition . . . *à la* Mallock," chuckled Amédée.

"You really are a goddamn wizard!"

"Where's your respect, Monsieur Inspector?"

"It went home to bed, and I plan to join it very soon. Anyway, they say 'captain' now. And since I was a senior detective, I'm actually a chief inspector—with all due respect, Monsieur Chief Superintendent . . . I mean General!"

"Yes, yes, I know. My captains are chief inspectors now; it's much simpler. So, the fingerprinting?"

"We tried at the scene, but nothing. Nada. Not even one partial fingerprint. Keep dreaming, boss."

"Okay. Before you go off to recharge your batteries, I have something to show you. I've got practically all the contents of the handbags here. Notice anything?"

Mallock was addressing not only Ken but also Bob, who had just joined them in the conference room.

"Out of the half-dozen handbags present here," he continued, not waiting for a response, "five contain a public transportation card and four have metro tickets. Same thing for one of the wallets and one of the schoolbags."

"Seems normal, boss. We're in Paris."

"You're going to look into it anyway. Call the families and ask them if the victim happened to have a usual route, maybe a daily one. If they all say it was on the same metro line, would that still seem normal to you?"

"Gotcha. I should have kept my trap shut, right?"

"Right. And if the metro's our common denominator, you get your ass down there and check it out, okay?"

Mallock had dictatorial tendencies: a kind of imperialism, watered down for everyday life. He observed all the formalities, of course, but he imposed a fanatical professionalism on his colleagues. The atmosphere in the Fort became very strained during investigations. Amédée, when stressed, was inflexible and severe in a way that only his constant kindness and attentiveness at all other times made acceptable.

He stood up and walked out the door, saying: "Call me when you have anything. I'll be back at three o'clock."

It was one o'clock in the afternoon on Tuesday, and the superintendent was exhausted and starving.

8.
Tuesday afternoon, December 28th

Mallock ordered three *croque-monsieurs*[1] and three beers at the bar, to be sent to the office for his team. For himself he chose a *croque-madame*[2] and sat down by himself in the back of the cafe. Three Santa Clauses were leaning on the bar, talking about salaries and pay raises and their lack of job security. They had stuffed their long white beards into their pockets so as not to spill anything on them. Mallock thought that public gatherings of Santa Clauses should be forbidden; they could do too much damage to children's imaginations. He thought about getting up and ordering them to circulate, but attacked his sandwich instead. A couple sat near him, talking and holding hands. He'd had that, once. Maybe he would again one day, with Amélie . . .

He thought of Margot again, too. Margot Murât. Where was she now? He'd always had a major weakness for the petite journalist. She was a hell of a reporter.

Following his train of thought, he picked up his phone. "Ken, when are our lovebirds supposed to be back?"

"Jules and Julie? They should be back on Monday morning, after New Year's Eve. I guess they have plane tickets booked. You want me to—"

"No, no, we'll leave them alone! It'll be just fine to have

[1] A toasted ham and cheese sandwich.
[2] A *croque-monsieur*, but topped with a fried egg.

them back in good form on Monday. Now, on a different note, we're going to need to do a complete inventory of all the hand-bags, item by item, and then make up a sort of table, with everything laid out like a puzzle, as Audiard would say."

"When you say 'we,' for some reason I feel like you really mean me. Am I imagining things?"

"Not really. You've always showed good analytical ability, which is a great thing!"

The men chuckled softly on both ends of the line.

"Now, what am I doing, exactly?" Ken asked eventually.

"I'll explain it. Draw a table and call one row 'lipstick,' for example, and next to that you write 'yes' or 'no.' If yes, specify the color and the brand. 'Mobile telephone,' yes or no, opera-tor, etc. Do the same thing with the photos, seeing if there are any of the same people in them. List every item; don't leave a single thing out. Pens, brushes, crosswords, pencil sharpeners, sex toys, Bibles—I want everything. Then move on to address books and bank cards."

Mallock paused just long enough to gulp down a large bite of his *croque-madame* and think for a couple of seconds about his next instruction and all the work it would involve.

"You're going to hate me, but we also have to put every-thing in the address books, mobile phones, and any iPhones or iPods in the computer, and analyze the bank statements from the victims' homes, and their handbags and pockets. You can't use your 'items' table for this, and you can't do it alone. We're going to need a drudge or two to do data entry. We have to be able to look at everything in a database, with as many fields as possible so we can cross-reference the data in every possible way. We have to find out if there's a friend or lover common to the victims, or if they did their shopping at the same place, had the same butcher or hairdresser, and that's the kind of job we need a computer for."

"I understand that, but it's going to take at least four days with three data-entry people working full time. And because of New Year's Eve and January first, we've got two days less."

Ken wasn't wrong. Getting civil servants to work was already hard enough, but during the holidays they moved slower than molasses in January. "Well, how about we say you hire six operators and I expect my results next Wednesday?"

"And when does poor Ken get to sleep, exactly?"

"Right now, if you want. Go in my office and stretch out on the sofa. In two hours you'll feel like a new man. This is war, my boy. You can sleep when we've thrown the trash away—or when you're dead."

Ken sighed on the other end of the line. It was pointless to argue with the boss when he was like this.

"After your nap, I want you to get to work. I want those listings on my desk by Thursday morning at the latest. We all need to jump on this case, and there's no more money in the budget. As of now you're on overtime *ad libitum*," Mallock said mercilessly. "As soon as you have the listings, fill out your own paper table. The Machin truc chouette lipstick you've just noticed—where was it bought? By whom? Fruits and vegetables: where were they purchased, and so on. In a nutshell, you're going to take all the information and chart it out by brand, race, shape, store, or religion."

"In a nutshell," repeated Ken, "I'm looking for the slightest thing all these things from everyday life have in common."

"Yep! But you've got to get to the very bottom of the concept."

"Meaning?"

"The very bottom of each handbag, for example. You'll find dust there. Have it analyzed, individually and then each sample against the others. Two fibers from the same carpet, matching pubic hairs, sand or gravel from the same place—we'd be incredibly pleased with any of that."

"Got it, boss! *Bon appétit*, see you soon," said Ken philo-sophically, already overwhelmed by the task in front of him.

At two o'clock Amédée returned to the office with Eskimo Pies for his team, partly out of kindness, but largely as a way of apologizing for his next idea. He noticed that Francis hadn't touched his *croque-monsieur*. The young inspector was finishing up his basic retouches on the various photos in the file. He was bent over the screen, lips parted, using the "stamp" tool.

"You'll have better luck with the healing brush or the patch. And also, don't make yourself too crazy. I don't need you to give me a work of art," fibbed Mallock, who couldn't abide botched work.

"I know you, and I don't want to have to start over."

Bob, for his part, had crammed the rest of his sandwich into his mouth so he could attack the ice cream before it melted. "Thanks for the snack, guv."

"One last thing. It's not how I usually do things, but RG has brought my attention to the necessity of keeping this information secret. So when we've got our five copies with conclusions and everything, have each one of us sign every page. I want a signature on every image and every table. If there's leak we'll know which packet it's from, and the culprit will have to answer to me."

Deafening silence. Mallock knew he might have gone a bit too far, and that he'd probably expressed himself poorly as well.

"Listen. I trust you all completely, but I've given this a lot of thought. This system will protect us as much as it will the investigation. Any copy that turns up in broad daylight and isn't signed by the Fort will exonerate us *de facto*. I'll sign my own personal copy too. Other people have been able to maintain the embargo and it's out of the question for one of us to fuck it up by being irresponsible."

Bob, Ken, and Francis had all begun crunching quietly on their Eskimo Pies. The sight was comical.

"So . . . you can cram your sensitivity up your own asses, okay?" Mallock tossed the words off as he stalked out of the room, not sure exactly who he was angry at—his men or Dublin, who had put him in this situation. No—it was himself he was furious with, and he didn't quite know how to handle it.

"Goddammit," grumbled Bob. His Eskimo Pie, neglected too long, had begun sliding down its stick toward his fist.

9

Wednesday, December 29th

During the night between Tuesday and Wednesday Mallock had a nightmare, his recurring one.

His father slammed the door to his room, clearing his throat and stomping down the stairs toward Amédée, hurling abuse at him:

"Where is the little bastard?"

Halfway down the stairs he missed a step and fell, swearing and crashing against the walls. But instead of simply falling he came apart, his limbs breaking off as if he were a gigantic porcelain doll. Making a horrible racket, the pieces of his body tumbled the rest of the way down the stairs and came to a stop a few centimeters away from Amédée. Covered with blood, his father stood up on his left arm—the only limb still attached to his torso—and cursed his incompetent, inadequate son. Then he broke into grimacing smiles and plaintive moans of "Help me, my boy!" More surreal images followed, as if to horrify the dreamer as much as possible.

Luckily, in the midst of these terrors there came a kind of patient clearing, an expression of perfect happiness. Up ahead a river flowed, populated by gigantic, phosphorescent Siamese fighting fish. Amédée found himself aboard a small boat, holding Thomas in his arms. Tom, pressed against him, alive, smelling like fresh bread. Together they rode down the river, with its eddies, its calm stretches, its blue icebergs and rapids; sometimes so wide there was nothing but sea on the horizon, and sometimes so narrow that they could touch the banks on either side. Then, insidiously, the sounds changed. Mallock continued to stroke his son's hair and inhale the scent of his skin, but now there was a horrible odor of burning coming from the boy. The water around the boat turned into lava. After a final, love-filled look at his son, Amédée fell with him, prow first, into a chasm of flames.

Mallock never emerged unscathed from these fearsome nights. This morning was no exception; he woke with an aching back. He called Amélie, who answered just as he was about to give up.

"Oh, it's you," she said. "I was about to turn on the answering machine and go out on my rounds. Are we on for eight o'clock?"

"I'm sorry to bother you, but this time I've thrown my back out completely."

"Would you like me to come earlier?"

"I'd really appreciate it. You or one of your colleagues, if you can't do it."

"I can manage it. I'll come right away. Be there in three minutes."

Amélie lived in the next square over, in an apartment above the little pharmacy where she worked.

"Thanks so much. I'll see you shortly."

Mallock stretched his back slowly, grimacing, but he was happy. She was coming over. A good cup of coffee with a froth of milk and his joy would have been complete—but he couldn't get up. Not wanting to waste time, he called his department. Here too, he had to wait a good ten rings before Ken answered.

"You've got some nerve. I've been very clear that the phone has to be answered before the third ring."

"It's been practically two nights since I got any sleep," protested Ken. "And let me remind you, with all due respect, that it's Wednesday, December 29th, and it's barely 7 A.M., and we've got neither a receptionist nor a chief here. Now then: hello, boss."

"Hello, Ken. Sorry. My sciatica's making me crazy. I'm stuck in bed."

"Your back's got some nerve," joked Ken.

Amédée knew he deserved that. "So—where are we?"

"I'm halfway done with the item chart. I'm waiting until nine o'clock before I go off in search of peons to do our data entry. Francis has finished up his part of the project, so he can show them what to do."

"And Bob?"

"I think he's almost done with his calls, but I'll let him tell you what he's found. He's a bit touchy this morning. Kind of like his beloved boss."

"Yeah, hi, guv," Bob came on the line now, having practically wrenched the phone out of Ken's hands. "I did as you asked and ended up getting the runaround three or four times. A lot of people aren't overly fond of middle-of-the-night phone calls."

"Go easy on me, Bob. What did you end up with?"

"A mixed bag, but—"

"But what?"

"Turns out seven of our nine victims took the Vincennes-La Défense line. But what dampens my enthusiasm is, that's by far the most frequently taken route."

"But it's still a significant number. We need to pursue this further."

"What should I do?"

"Routine investigation on Line One with photos of the victims in one hand and your notebook in the other. One of our vics might have spoken to a transit agent; they might remember."

"It's a needle in a haystack, boss. And Line One—Jesus! I've got no chance in that crowd! Don't get your hopes up."

"I didn't say it would be easy. It would take a stroke of luck.

But we have to try. Get two or three guys to help you—and stop by grand central video and . . . motivate them a little. Work it out for yourself. Now, put Francis back on, please."

The sound of a crashing chair heralded Francis's arrival back on the line.

"Did you fall?"

"It's okay; I've got a hard head. We're working on the address books and mobile phones. Nothing to report yet. Ken and Bob are helping me between calls. We should have four more operators around eight o'clock."

"And the composite sketch of the target victim?"

"It's done, but I don't think it's going to be very useful. The victims don't look like each other, and the morpho-biometric average I came up with doesn't correspond to anything; it doesn't show an archetype."

"Come on, try harder. Nothing at all?"

Francis hesitated for a moment. Then: "Just an impression . . . "

"Well?"

"A kind of . . . regularity."

"Meaning? What have you got?"

"Well, okay. At the end, since you told me to compare absolutely everything, I had the weird idea of cutting them in half vertically. The photos, I mean."

"And?"

"And, the two sides looked like one another. I don't know what it could mean."

"That's called beauty, Francis. No charm or seductiveness; just simple beauty. If you look at Greek statues, or painted portraits, that's what you see."

"Like in Picasso's *Weeping Woman*?" Francis, smiling at his own joke, waited for the explosion from the other end of the line.

"The exception that proves the rule. Well done, Chief Inspector. Now, while we wait for the listings, my dear exegete,

I want you to send me a printout of what you've done. I want one of the two copies of Grimaud's files—you'll see that there are three binders. As long as I'm stuck here I wouldn't mind some reading material to pass the time."

"That stuff's going to weigh a ton. I'll call one of the motorcycle cops; it should be over there in twenty minutes. Then I'll keep going with the data entry."

"Perfect, thanks. I'll let you get back to work. I'll be back tomorrow morning. Oh—don't forget to make sure my safe is closed again after you get the three binders out."

Mallock hung up on Francis, who was wondering if being called an "exegete" by his boss was positive or negative. First order of business: look the definition of the word up online.

Now for the chore of the day: Mallock returned Judge Humbert's call. Whew; he wasn't there. Amédée left his message—a few sentences recapping what had been done so far—and promised to contact the judge again when there was any news. Then he lay back down to wait for Amélie. Soon she would be there, just a few centimeters away from him. He imagined her. Her perfume and her smile. Amélie Maurel, and all the delightful things associated with her.

Waiting for her was a pleasure both strong and hazy; heavy and smooth.

After so much pain, grieving Tom.

This lightness after a weight heavy as lead had a name: joy.

He studied his hands. He looked at them often. They were as thick as Amélie's neck was long and fragile. For a millisecond, he thought of strangling her. Just like that. One of those terrifying, interfering ideas that impose themselves on men's minds when a bubble of hell floats up and breaks the surface. In truth, he would give his life to protect her. Only his son had ever inspired a feeling like this before.

Ten minutes later, the sound of the electric doorbell made him jump. Grimacing horribly, he dragged himself to the door. It wasn't Amélie, and Mallock felt ridiculous with the silly grin he wore in preparation for greeting her. A huge, helmeted motorcycle cop respectfully saluted the large man with the twisted body who was smiling at him so tenderly.

"Have a good day, Superintendent!"

Back in his room, Amédée opened the voluminous packet. Besides Grimaud's files, it contained the book of images assembled so carefully by Francis. His young chief inspector had done a beautiful job. The portraits of the victims had been retouched and cropped for a homogenous look. On the back of each photo was a brief biography printed in small letters. Mallock stretched out so he could think better. What element, what fact, what particular detail might link all these people, other than their terrible deaths?

He opened the leather portfolio RG had given him at their lunch as if it were a time bomb. At the end of the file there were photos pertaining to cases one through seven: two children, one man, and four women, all added to the list thanks to the work RG and Mordome had done.

Amédée sat up, wincing, and pulled out some of the photos. After a brief hesitation, he folded them in half vertically. A hint of a smile appeared on his pain-filled face. When pressed against the window of his room so that they became transparent, the faces showed almost perfect symmetry.

Francis's work hadn't been for nothing. Without even knowing it, the Makeup Artist—or Artists—was attracted by ancient ideals of beauty. For some reason yet to be determined, he—they—was sensitive to the harmony of a face. Was that the only criterion? And what had they wanted to do with that beauty, when they killed the victims?

The additional forensic report signed by Mordome had been added after the discovery of these seven previous murders and was fairly straightforward. All of the crimes seemed to have been perpetrated by a single individual. The first victims had been found quite literally bathing in their own blood, while the later ones had been left drained of it. But the result was the same—only the *fashion* had changed, whether it be called "ceremonial evolution" or "amplified perversion." These exsanguinations, for reasons that might be fetishist or cannibalistic, certainly corresponded to the morbid and murderous development of one and the same psychopathic individual.

Mallock decided to look back over the thirteen murders as a whole. He included the Saint-Mandé case, which he had had the sad privilege of observing up close. If they were no longer looking at this as the work of a satanic cult, as his first impression had suggested, what other possibilities might there be? When Mallock opened up the floodgates of his imagination, it meant letting in every single possibility—and also the impossibilities, which were his favorites. He even went so far as to envision, briefly and privately, the existence of a series of copycats, like father-to-son vampires, before going back to something more reasonable: a man of extraordinary intelligence and self-control, perhaps aided by one or two accomplices, whom he surprised himself by thinking of as female. Why? He didn't yet have the slightest idea.

He was mulling that over when the doorbell finally announced Amélie's arrival.

She was so damn pretty. So sweet in her full, pleated skirt, boots, and oversized gray sweater from some thrift shop. As she talked to him, she massaged and manipulated his back gently. An hour after her arrival, he was no longer in pain. It was 8:30, and the two of them went out to grab some breakfast.

"I've only got twenty minutes," she had warned him. And yet they spent an hour together, eating croissants and bread and butter. She talked, and he watched her. When he looked at her he felt as if he were tasting her; savoring her ears and her small breasts, caressing her forehead and her shoulders, sucking her lips and sliding his tongue over her little teeth. With his eyes, he was already making love to her.

She left at a run. Mallock, watching her recede in the distance, felt his throat tighten. *Amélie and Amédée.* To him, it already sounded like a fairy tale.

He spent the rest of Wednesday studying Grimaud's documents. He realized that he was excited; more excited than he had ever been before. The contents of the three files were spread out on every surface in the living room; Francis's images and the stuff from RG's leather portfolio were laid out in the bedroom. He went from room to room. Rearranged the piles. Went into the office to copy passages and do side-by-side comparisons. Racked his brain for every scrap of deductive reasoning skill. Chewed his fingernails and the skin on his fingertips. Quivered with irritation and blew out his breath like a seal to relieve his stress.

What was he so afraid of? It was only an investigation, nothing more. Was he in the habit of screwing up? No, but that was just it—this might be the time he got it wrong.

His worst fear: failure.

With every case, the same doubt, the same fear of being wrong, of missing something, filled him with anxiety. Mallock paid for his certainties with painful and permanent uncertainty.

This time, he felt he had a new reason justifying the profoundness of his worry. Never before had he dealt with so many unknowns in the equation of an investigation involving a serial killer. Normally, every murder came with a puzzle piece stuck loosely to the bottom of its boots. The police officer's job often consisted of being patient, waiting for the next murder with its crop of clues and the possibility of narrowing the field; waiting for the piece that would make it possible to see the whole picture—the image of the killer. Here, there was nothing—at least, nothing convincing. The lists were sparse, the timetables approximate, the fingerprints ghostly, the motives nonexistent, the victims dissimilar. And there was no alibi to verify because there were no suspects, or almost none. Grimaud's files were stuffed, and yet horribly empty.

There was nothing for Mallock to chew on, and he was starving.

The amount of time separating each murder had dwindled from a year to a week. If the killer was still shortening the intervals between his periods of madness, the next killing would happen on the first of January.

He had only three days to keep that from happening.

10

Thursday, December 30th. Morning

N ow that his back wasn't hurting so much, the stroll from Mallock's apartment to Number 36 was actually a pleasure; even now, after thirty years of living in Paris. It was a nice day, which allowed for a leisurely stroll to the office, reflecting on orders to be given and new strategies to be implemented. He always took the same route lately, and every morning he told himself that this probably wasn't very smart. He was not without enemies. What better moving target could there be for some crook out of prison on good behavior than Mallock on foot? For this reason, and so he wouldn't find himself staring defenselessly down the barrel of a gun, he was always armed with a weapon of his own.

He carried a 9 mm Glock 34 IPSC, loaded with 17 hollow-point FMJ bullets—except when he felt the atmosphere was more relaxed, and he traded those 700 grams of polymer for a 300-gram 340PD Smith and Wesson protected by a Cordura holster attached to his belt, loaded with five high-precision .38 special bullets.

During an assault or a period of great stress, he carried both weapons on him at all times. Mallock was a big, gentle bear of a man, but with claws and teeth befitting a beast.

Outside, the Paris that met Mallock's gaze was light grey and pearly, dry and cold. The inner edges of the gutters were still frozen, with white slashes and sheets of silver.

Amédée cut through the Place Baudoyer, beneath which

was the parking space he had just bought for his car. Turning left at the Pont d'Arcole, he walked along the Quai de Gesvres. Steam puffed from his mouth with each breath. He had a meeting with the Seine. When he reached it he gave it a quick, loving glance, as he did every day. He walked along the length of the iron-railed barrier, stopping to watch the barges and tourist boats as they passed. The noise of the water lapping against the piles. Seagulls crying above the river. Ordinary city noises. Pigeons cooing beneath the bridge.

In the Place Louis Lépine he was greeted by the scent of the flower market. He walked along the Quai de la Corse before taking a left on the Boulevard du Palais. Bridges stretched between the trees on the two banks, heavy with Christmas decorations and lights, blinking "joy" above the trees.

He decided to make a stop at the Deux Palais *bar-tabac* for three reasons: his aching back; a major craving for a croissant and a café crème; and—strangely—to gaze upon Justice. The famous court building had impressed him so much when he first came to Paris, burning to join the police force. Since then he had stopped so many times in this café to look at the great edifice that he had become friends with the owner, a taciturn man from Brittany.

It was the owner who brought him his breakfast. "Here," he said shortly, thumping the metal cups down on the round table.

"Thanks," returned Mallock with a smile and an equal economy of phrase.

Across from him the court of cassation, the assizes, the court of first instance, and the small claims court overlooked the Cour du Mai. As if to protect and ennoble all of these, an impressive gilded gate rose up in front of them, adorned with the royal arms.

Mallock surprised himself by imagining being seated at this same spot in a few days, watching as the Makeup Artist walked through those gates handcuffed between two policemen. Of course it wouldn't happen quite like that; the building adjoined Number 36 and convicted prisoners didn't use these gates anymore. But he needed to visualize the monster, to give him back a sense of reality that the violence of his crimes had taken away from him along with his humanity. Mallock needed something concrete, needed to imagine a flesh-and-blood man with a haggard face, mounting the grand staircase of justice, surrounded by the blue of uniforms, the black of ravens, the ermine rampant, and the usual army of scavengers rushing in for the kill.

Everything he had just read—theories and deductions, trails, horrors and hesitations—had turned the Makeup Artist into an abstraction, a hypothetical monster. This often happened when it took a long time to identify and arrest a culprit. You ended up even doubting his existence, as if trying to come up with some sort of excuse—that is, when you weren't imagining that he was dead, or on the other side of the world in the tropics, having a relaxed dinner with some retired dictator or a bunch of Nazi torturers in hiding. You could imagine him doing anything except having breakfast peacefully somewhere nearby, planning his next murder.

Mallock thought about ordering another croissant, but knew he should talk himself out of it. The more weight he gained, the more his back would hurt. And besides, there was Amélie now, he thought, before paying the check and getting up. He visualized the scene across the street one last time: a procession of police cars, and the infamous demon emerging with his ankles chained together, looking like an idiot. *A crazy, cruel, common criminal*, he thought to himself, enjoying the alliteration.

"Later, Mallock," called the owner.

Turning back to return the farewell, Mallock noticed the waiter serving a glass of tomato juice to a young woman in a fur coat. A question occurred to him. *What in the world could the Makeup Artist be doing with all that blood?*

A scarlet question that would dog him until the end.

Outside, Amédée saw Bob emerging, rumpled, from the Guimard exit of the Saint-Michel metro stop, a hundred meters away. He waited for him on the other side of the bridge.

"Fucking metro!" Amédée could hear Bob swearing once he was within earshot. To be fair, he smelled like a mixture of nicotine, rancid oil, and sickly farts, a combination that Mallock silently dubbed *Metropolitan Fragrance of Paris.*

"Hello to you too. How was the fishing; catch anything?"

"I went back down there at eleven o'clock last night, and didn't leave until just now. I'm totally bushed. This case really is a shit-covered stick."

Seeing that his boss didn't seem too sympathetic to his unhappiness, he continued: "In three hours, my guys and I questioned a good fifty transit agents on Line One routes. No luck, except one granny who saw one of the victims with . . . I'll give you three guesses."

"Spit it out. It's cold out here."

"With a priest. In a cassock."

"The media's going to love that."

"What should I do now?"

It was a question Mallock always answered the same way: "Keep at it. Oh—what about the videos?"

"The transit authority is about to connect all its cameras to a central surveillance hub in the near future, a security command post, which will be at their headquarters in the Gare de Lyon. Transit agents will be able to use fiber optics to directly access images from 8,000 cameras that'll be mounted on platforms and in corridors all over the transit network."

"I don't give a shit about the near future. I'm talking about today."

"I went to the new Multimodal Video Surveillance Center at Châtelet-les-Halles; it's brand-new. They're in the process of testing image analysis software and various intelligent cameras . . . "

"I don't *care*! Tell me about something that exists right now, dammit!"

Bob stammered: "For the mounted cameras, video is backed up for the fifteen minutes before and after an alarm is set off."

"I don't care. Third and last warning."

"Well, what do you want me to tell you? It would be great if we got something on film. Most of the cameras on the platforms and in the corridors take high-resolution images. The platforms are one hundred percent covered from two angles at all times. If we had someone specific to look for, we should be able to find him. For the corridors it varies a lot from station to station."

"Jesus, Bob. Did they keep the footage? Yes or no?"

"Er—no. It's that goddamn Information Commissioner's Office. You know we can't—"

"Fine," interrupted Mallock. "Do the best you can. But get back to me with something solid, or stay down there. The cold keeps things fresh."

Bob turned around to take the Pont Saint-Michel back toward the square—a square which, just a few months later, would witness true horror.[3]

Back at the department, the big digital clock read 9:39 in the morning. Amédée put a call in to Dublin's office. Geraldine, his new secretary, picked it up. "I'm sorry, but he won't be back until the end of the day. Can I do anything for you, Monsieur le Superintendent?"

Mallock asked her if she wouldn't mind coming to pick up

---

[3] *The Massacre of the Innocents*, by the same author.

the yellow personal binder that Dublin had left with him. He didn't want it lying around anymore.

After hanging up, he noticed that RG had left another report on his desk. On a fluorescent pink Post-it note on the top he had written:

"Hi Mallock, this is another little study that I had done confidentially by an independent profiler. I only showed him one case just to be safe, but in my opinion the craziest, most significant cases are bodies ten and eleven. Talk to you soon."

A second later, Mallock was reviewing the photos of the victims. The one he was looking for was in the file Dublin had loaned him. He opened it and was plunged once again into the same morbid stupefaction it had aroused in him last time.

The photo showed a man of a certain age, undoubtedly a vagrant. His Goya-like face was covered with a long, patchy beard, which his killer had taken the time to comb. His long hair had been subjected to the same treatment. All of his hair had been heavily sprayed so it would stay in a strange arrangement. His face was covered with cosmetics: pink powder on the apples of his cheeks; blue in the hollows of them—but no black kohl lining his eyelids as with the others. This time the Makeup Artist had lined the eyes with red lipstick, creating the dramatic effect of a bloody gaze. The man's dirty, skeletal body was completely nude, his back arched, laid out across the lap of a woman whose body was seated on a bench. Dressed in Chanel and drenched with perfume, she was adorned with a mass of gold necklaces and brooches. Her pink hands, smothered in rings, were posed atop the exsanguinated body of the poor tramp, who had been stripped of everything, except maybe his head lice.

The report specified that the jewelry had been taken from the previous murder victims, which was proof of the link Grimaud and Mordome had established between the different cases.

The Makeup Artist had covered the tramp's entire body in three shades of blue, emphasizing the victim's thinness by focusing on the hollow parts. In addition to his eyes, he had put lipstick on the man's penis, and the scarlet cock was screaming out its obscene nudity.

Mallock had already seen these photos, but he was stunned by them all over again. This was a descent from the cross as the Renaissance might have painted it; as could be seen in multiple interpretations in prayer books and religious images. But here, it was grotesque. Blasphemous.

He put the photo down and then turned it over before starting to read the report, which was a hopeless attempt at profiling:

This is most likely a man. A psychopath in the full clinical sense of the term. He may very well be an only son. He would be between thirty and forty-five years old. Highly complex, physically ugly, short, or ill-proportioned; he wants to make others suffer the way he has suffered, in reality or fantasy. He lives alone or with one of his parents, father or mother. Whether they are living or dead, they both play the central role in the disturbance to which he is subject.

Same diagnosis if it is a woman, with the addition of a conflict with her own homosexual impulses, consecutive to the preceding. Very importantly, he or she is much too ill not to be already on medication. Due to this, he cannot remain socialized.

I also believe there is a close but highly problematic relationship with the church and religion, concepts of God and the Devil. We're talking about a true theological conflict here. Suffering and his religious "good deeds" are part of and all-consuming in the obsessive expression of his libido. What we call "retribution" in the Catholic church seems to play a major role in his staging of scenes. Are his victims suffering for his own salvation, or that of all humanity? The double spectacle of the rich woman and the tramp can be read in different ways. The money is the blood of Christ; it gives life. Poverty is a state of death. But wealth is also a curse in terms of reversibility. If rich people have lived thanks to the blood of the poor, the needy man is redemption for humanity. He is Christ. In short, the person responsible for staging this scene belongs to the upper class, which he sees as damnation.

There will have been signs in his early childhood typical of this type of sociopath: cruelty toward animals, pyromania, and bed-wetting. Of course, multiple scenarios and other alternative archetypes may also be imagined. You will find them in order of probability in the next part of my analysis. But, more fundamentally, the crime scene photo you gave me to study leads me to recommend that you look for what we might call a kind of "theological revolutionary." A man who is beyond tormented, in whom the power of mysticism may also allow him to create a group of followers—even, for example, if we stick to the mystical Christianization of the individual, twelve apostles, recruited to his terrible cause.

Mallock put the document down, thinking. The report confirmed his own impressions—but it also contained useful reminders, like the ideas of necessary medication and abusive religion. And then there was the idea that the killer might be wealthy. Amédée was impressed. With nothing to go on but the snapshot of the well-to-do woman and the tramp, the expert had come up with the theory of a Makeup Artist and his twelve apostles. It was a way of illustrating his suggestions, of course, but the preciseness of the image had particularly struck him.

He was still thinking of the twelve embers in his fireplace, and the attack he had suffered. Twelve apostles; twelve accomplices! A nightmare.

He dialed RG's number. Even if his colleague hadn't been

able to get results, he had definitely had some good flashes of insight. He wanted to make sure Grimaud knew that, because he knew how bad the man felt. Mallock's keeping him updated would help him get over it. Amédée let the phone ring seven times, but Raymond wasn't there. He would call him back.

Just then Geraldine, Dublin's secretary, knocked timidly and poked her head through the door, as if to say, *Friend! Don't shoot! I mean no harm to your planet!*

"Come in, Geraldine. Would you like a coffee?"

Visibly intimidated, the secretary stammered a polite refusal, miring herself in a variety of excuses. "I—I don't . . . my stomach . . . I've already had one . . . heartburn . . . "

She tiptoed toward the desk for her boss's file. An inveterate old joker, Mallock couldn't resist standing up suddenly, slapping his desk, and bellowing: "Well, I'm going to have one!"

Geraldine jumped at least a meter backward, emitting a sort of *Aaaaarrrgh!* that made Mallock roar with laughter. He moved toward her and handed her the file. "Don't listen to the rumors," he said. "I only devour secretaries during leap years, and never the ones who work for my boss. That irritates him, and then I don't get a promotion."

This managed to coax a smile out of the young woman. "I've only just started," she said.

"And Dublin told you not to upset me, because I'm a pain in the ass," Mallock finished. The girl nodded uncomfortably. Amédée grinned at her. "That's one of his favorite jokes when he has a new secretary. It's kind of like hazing. Nothing nasty."

"But I have to say that you are just a bit frightening," she said.

Mallock escorted her to his office door, unable to think of any reply to this observation. Ten minutes later he was still thinking about it. He hated the idea that he might be frightening—especially to pretty young women.

Focus. Calm down. He treated himself to a few puffs on a lovely heather pipe, which had been a gift from MM—Queen Margot—and stood up to crack the window. The sky outside was dark and mouse-grey, a lowering ceiling made up of thousands of leaden clouds covering the city. Though he was only in a shirt, Amédée realized that he wasn't really cold. The temperature had risen a bit. As if to confirm his thought, it began to snow. He grabbed the large pair of binoculars that he always kept in the office. He had never stopped learning Paris, looking lovingly around him at all of its splendors, at different times of day and in different seasons, different lighting. He directed his gaze toward the Louvre, one of his favorite spots.

As he let his binoculars glide over the rooftops and the first flakes of snow attempting to settle on them, an idea occurred to him. He knew—even before it happened—that he was about to have one of his flashes. What had he seen that was noteworthy?

The snow was coming down heavily now, a vertical curtain of white marbles. His view was blocked; nothing to be done about that. He set down the binoculars, a smile hovering on his lips despite everything. This kind of weather made him as happy as a little boy.

He suddenly remembered the syringe Ken had found under the body at Saint-Mandé. He began to pace around his office. Why was he thinking of that again now? It must be something he had seen in the distance, near the Louvre. But what? On his thirteenth lap around the room the light clicked on.

The telescopic streetlamps on the Pont du Carrousel!

They needed to search not *around*, but inside the syringe, on the part of the shank that remained sunk in the body of the instrument. For safety reasons, after the AIDS scare, the needle and the plunger retracted inside the syringe in recent models.

He called the lab. In their urgency, they might overlook it.

They had just received it, marked number thirty-four among the items of evidence.

"We'll do what we have to and call you back."

His pipe had gone out. Mallock looked at the radiator, wondering if he should relight it.

How many Parisians knew that the Carrousel streetlamps were telescopic, composed of two parts, and that they got taller at night so the bridge would be better lit? Like four gigantic vertical syringes. One day, an eternity ago, the Beaux-Arts students had stuck up hundreds of posters and splattered paint on the upper parts of the lamp posts during the night. Mallock, a uniform cop at the time, still laughed about their expressions the next morning, when they believed all their work had disappeared, not realizing that the streetlamps were almost half again as short. The next night, when the four obelisks had extended again and revealed the students' handiwork, the cleaners had come with their ladders to clean it all up.

Amédée would never have believed that this student misadventure might help him one day to solve a serial crime.

At lunchtime, after checking with Bob, Ken, and Francis on the status of their tasks, Mallock went back toward Saint-Mandé to finish off his observations. Ken had left a copy of the caretaker's keys on his desk.

Outside, the snow had slowed traffic to a crawl, and it took Amédée a good hour to reach the crime scene. The guard on duty outside the house stopped stamping his frozen feet for warmth and saluted. The back garden was completely white; the house dark and silent. On the staircase leading down to the site of the tragedy, friends and neighbors had left flowers, sympathy notes. A little girl's doll.

Mallock crossed the square of snow carefully, so as not to slip. The flakes were falling heavily again, trying to cover up the unspeakable. Just then, his mobile phone rang. He stopped in the middle of the garden to answer it.

"Mallock."

"Yes, hello, this is Chief inspector Camille Sart, Super-intendent Grimaud's right-hand man. You tried to call him?"

"Yes; actually, I wanted to update him a bit on the case. Is he there?"

There was an embarrassed silence. "Well, no. In fact, that's why I'm calling you. We haven't heard from him."

Mallock stood frozen, letting snowflakes settle on him.

"He's vanished. He's not married; I don't know what to do, or whom to call."

The police, dickhead, thought Mallock. "Call Dublin," he said instead, "and keep me informed."

RG had disappeared. The last time Mallock had seen him, he had asked him to finish his investigation concerning the composition of the cocktail of drugs the killer had used. Was there a link? Had the facts taken him too close to the monsters? Raymond had the build to defend himself, but no one is invincible. Mallock stood openmouthed for a few seconds, thinking, before realizing that he was looking increasingly like a snowman built in the middle of the garden.

"I'm waiting for your next move, you bastard," he murmured.

After shaking himself thoroughly free of snow, he entered the house. Ken had told him that Modiano, the unfortunate head of the family, had been hospitalized. The house was empty and bleak, inhabited only by the filthiness of tragedy, the lingering smells of a double crime. It was intensely cold; the heating had been turned off, and the windows left half-open in the hope that the air might freshen the atmosphere. Mallock walked around the living room, his gaze taking in the many objects of a normal life destroyed. He lit a cigar, as much because it helped him think as to block out the stench of the place.

The idea of breathing in the odor of the dead little girl was unbearable.

He paced back and forth, unable to go up the stairs. He needed to get used to the place. Get himself together. The objects around him were silent. But they had lived with the victims, and they had seen the murderer go by. They had even watched while he committed his monstrous acts. Didn't they have anything to say? Mallock stared hard at them, as he would have done with recalcitrant witnesses. They were afraid, too, but of what?

He picked up an object, put it down, stroked another one, rested his hand for a long time on the wood of a table, tapped on the walls. He read the names of the films written on the spines of the DVDs and ancient VHS tapes. The titles of all the books on the shelves. Maybe a word would come back to him later. He also tried to work out whether anything might have been stolen. François Modiano hadn't noticed anything missing, but was he really in a state to be sure about anything at all?

To make sure, Amédée had brought a series of photographs of the inside of the house, taken last year by Madame Modiano for insurance purposes in case of burglary or fire.

An hour later, with the help of the snapshots, Mallock was looking at a photo of what might very well have passed as the principal motive for theft: a tiny Russian icon, ancient and made of gold. On the insurance policy it had been protected with a separate value, because it was worth a lot more than the index. Later, a call to the insurance company would confirm the price of the thing: almost one hundred thousand euros. What if all of these terrible murders had been committed to hide a much more mundane crime?

They would never had looked at it from that angle, as overwhelmed with horror as they were.

Mallock poured himself a large whiskey, somewhat unnerved that there was no one to ask permission from. But he needed it. The idea that had just occurred to him was Machiavellian. What if all these killings were only a . . . diversion?

Upstairs the shutters were closed, and Mallock had to go to the window to open them. He wanted to be able to see everything, down to the smallest detail. In the bedroom, he sat down on the edge of the bed. Normally he would have avoided doing that, but there was only one chair and it was heaped with clothes, and his back was just too painful. He opened his file again, the one he had prepared with the photos and the insurance descriptions, and pulled out the CSI report.

Outside there were occasional footsteps squeaking in the snow, cars creeping by. No children running, no birds squawking. Inside, Mallock carefully read his file without skipping a single line.

When he finally rose, he took a kind of tiny lens out of his pocket, a highly powerful magnifying glass. Then, despite his back, this Parisian Sherlock Holmes got down on all fours. Half an hour later, he did the same thing in the little girl's bedroom.

There were traces of scratches and perforation marks in the parquet floor. Mallock tested for the possible presence of blood. As always during the tours he made of the crime scene after the investigators had finished, he had brought his own little CSI kit. Provided and updated regularly by his friends at the INPS,[4] it included three lamps, one of them ultraviolet; a micro-vacuum, and droppers of oxygenated water. This method, which made the blue of benzidine show up like in the movies, was not very reliable. Fruit juice can also give off dioxygen gas. But combining this with observation under ultraviolet light resulted at least in a chance of not being wrong. In any case, when Mallock returned to Number 36 he would have the lab verify everything. They practiced two methods: one using acid to obtain the elongated violet prisms of hematine hydrochloride; the other searching via spectroscopy for alkaline hemochromogen. Finally, to be absolutely sure that they were indeed dealing with human blood, they would cause antigen-antibody agglutination to occur by adding antihuman serum to the blood, itself diluted in a saline solution.

[4] Institut national de police scientifique, or National Forensic Institute

Hunched down on the floor, Mallock began moving his lamp and Q-tips beneath the window, around the spot where he had noticed the strange perforations that were also present in the little girl's room. Under the magnifying glass he could see that the holes were recent and that they did not contain blood. Mallock also noticed that they were laid out in a triangle, but he decided not to draw any conclusions from that for the moment—not because he believed this detail was unimportant, but for the opposite reason.

An hour later he rose, aching but satisfied; his samples taken and his head full of new theories.

The victims had been moved not once, but twice.

There was the attack location, which the CSIs had identified by residual blood traces. Then there were the beds where the Makeup Artist had arranged the bodies. But there was also a third place; undoubtedly the transitional place, where each victim had visibly spent time after having been drained of her blood, but before the macabre final staging.

It made sense to imagine the spot with the perforations in the floor was where the killer had engaged in his sexual activities with the victims—but in that case, the CSIs would have found traces of sperm, and they hadn't found anything—anywhere—but a scant few hairs and epithelial cells.

So, what had he really done? What had he forced his victims to endure? What game had he played, here in this very spot?

Mallock couldn't linger at the crime scene. He had dinner plans at six-thirty; a sort of pseudo–New Year's Eve out in the suburbs. He left the house, feverish and exhausted. His head was spinning. Both his heart and his knees were filthy. Once again, the snow seemed to him like a blessing. Three children and their *maman* played in the street, laughing and throwing snowballs.

He looked up at the sky. He didn't pray, but that was not because he didn't believe in the wise man in the heavens. He was sure the bearded divinity had seen everything. Why did he stay silent? It might have been fatigue or imagination, but it seemed to Amédée as if the flakes were rising from the ground toward the sky, as if to cling to the edges of the clouds that would take them far away from this cursed place.

The world wasn't evil. It was simply indifferent.

12.
Friday, December 31st

The next day, to top off the end of the year combined with a ferocious migraine, Mallock had a meeting with the emperor of the autopsy, the king of the bone saw, the lord of the stiffs; his friend, the forensic pathologist Bernard Barnabé Mordome. At first glance, Mordome resembled nothing so much as the traditional image of a butcher: big and fat, with a face flushed pink by rosacea and large, strong hands. But just so the comparison wouldn't be too easy, he also had a head of silvery curls and an aquiline hooked nose topped with a pair of gold wire-rimmed glasses, which gave him a dignified look—as did the almost-palpable intelligence that radiated from his face, and the impressive spirituality of his gaze. You don't rub shoulders with death on a daily basis without your spirit undergoing some mutations.

The previous night, as he often did, Amédée had dined with his friends in Senlis, on the outskirts of Paris. Mallock, Michel, Claude, Gérald, and company gathered regularly near the small square where so many swashbuckler movies had been filmed. He'd gotten home late. The northern highway was deserted and, entering Saint-Denis, at the big curve that swerved left at a ninety-degree angle, just after the sign warning drivers to slow down, he had seen broken windows, a strange light, and obscene graffiti on the front of a factory. A break-in? He'd thought for a second about alerting his colleagues, and then forgotten. When he got home, he'd gone straight to the bottom of his whiskey bottle.

This morning he was paying the price.

The IML, or Institut Médico-Légal de Paris[5], a large red-brick building, looked as inviting as always. Mallock had to show his ID before entering the holy of holies, Mordome's department.

"Should I come with you?" asked the receptionist.

"No thanks. I know the way."

He went through the storage room, with its enormous scales and compartments refrigerated to thirty-nine degrees Fahrenheit. After the autopsy and the taking of samples for histological testing, bodies were stored in other drawers kept at four below zero. He arrived in the autopsy room without encountering another living soul.

The room was brightly lit by projection lamps attached to the ceiling and by bluish fluorescent cylindrical bulbs. The tiled walls also had a steel-blue tint. Mordome had explained to him once that this kind of light was necessary in order to see, besides the purplish areas in inclined parts or the lighter spots due to pressure, overall changes in corpses' color, which indicated various pathological states. The room's five white faience tables, each equipped with running water and suction systems, contained neither bodies nor the slightest trace of blood.

Mallock cleared his throat.

His son had been brought here and placed on one of these tables. A ballet of scalpels had danced across his skull. What had been done to his body? To chase the image away, Amédée contemplated the various neatly arranged instruments. Mordome had given him lessons back when the superintendent had begun to be passionately interested in forensic medicine—so now, to distract himself, he recited the names of the different instruments under his breath, like a prayer:

[5] Forensic Institute of Paris

"Granat callipers, anthropometric compasses, mallets, Rowe pliers, gouge, rugine, forceps, stripper, Mayo or Sims scissors . . . "

As he named them, he picked the tools up and put them back down. Their metallic clinking accompanied his litany. The image of Thomas's body came back, his torso charred and open.

His son's death had left him without a choice. Either he would die of sadness, or he would abandon emotion. He had hesitated, but nature had made the decision for him. For a long time his life had gone on without joy or pain, like a river subdued between oppressive banks. His feelings had been wiped clean, like pharaonic faces scoured away by the hot breath of tourists, or beautiful ancient tomb slabs ruined by the idiotic scuffing of their sandals.

He began again.

"Tongue retractor. Halstead. Backhaus scope."

He kept on with his silent recitation, not making a single mistake. On the final word, two tears escaped and fell on the shining steel of a syndesmotic hook.

He wiped them away carefully with his tie just as his phone rang.

"What are you doing? I'm waiting for you." It was Mordome.

"But I'm here. I'm in the big room, from last time."

"We could have waited for each other forever. I don't work there anymore; I'm in the new wing. I'll send someone for you; otherwise you'll get lost."

The famous pathologist knew his Mallock well.

Barnabé's office was like Grand Central Station.

An assistant was filling out evidence identification forms, while a young woman deftly pressed a stamp into a still-hot wax seal. Another operator in surgical scrubs, cap, booties, and rubber gloves delicately removed debris from under a child's fingernails, not by scraping the nails but by cutting them one by one. Each sample was then placed in a separate vial, numbered, and signed with the pathologist's initials.

"Your timing is perfect," said Mordome. "I've just finished the autopsy on the mother. My team is starting with the child. For the adult it's the usual rundown, with a few lovely innovations. As you'll have already seen, the mouth was used as a receptacle to contain various amputated parts. The nipples, the eyelids, et cetera. Want to see?"

"No thanks. I trust you."

"What's bizarre is that all the pieces were coated with some kind of flour before being placed in the mouth. And, unlike what I thought, they weren't all cut off with a scalpel like in a surgical excision. Some of them were bitten off. I'm sorry to have to tell you this, but the victims were still, if not conscious, at least alive during these amputations. As with the previous murders, this one was drained of its blood using syringes equipped with large-bore needles. The injections were all made in the same part of the body. Twelve injections, as usual. One last detail: at the end of the operation, without a doubt, this piece of shit penetrated the vagina several times with a bladed weapon. Probably a short, wide sword, Japanese-type. He then held the victim upright to drain out the rest of the blood, urine, and other physiological matter. Given the sexual nature of these perversions, I think we're dealing with a man."

"That's not what the psychologists think. We can't yet rule out the hypothesis of an insane woman."

"That's your problem."

"There's one thing I'd like to clarify. When exactly did he drain their blood?"

"Excellent question. It probably varies. At the very beginning he didn't even do it, which was worse, because they stayed alive until the very last second. His final act was the sword thrust between the legs. Now, even if he keeps them alive as long as possible, they die of hemorrhagic shock when their blood is drained, so the torture part, where he does his thing on a chemically immobilized body, doesn't last quite as long, according to my calculations."

"Okay, but in relation to the application of the makeup, and the rest of the . . . cutting?"

"I believe he starts draining the blood and applies the makeup at the same time. Then the massacre begins."

Mordome looked exhausted, but Mallock knew the doctor would hate having that pointed out.

"In one of the cases I worked on with Grimaud there was an obvious attempt at impalement. He tried that even before starting to drain the blood. A real butchery."

Mordome slammed a brown-smeared pair of Leriche surgical pliers into a stainless-steel basin. The noise reverberated in the white faience room.

"Can we have a cup of coffee before we start on the little girl?" asked Mallock, hoping to force his friend to decompress for a few seconds.

"Thanks, but I really don't have time. We'll move on to the girl. She was also given some special treatment. As with her mother, she was first injected with the famous chemical submission substance,[6] the chef's specialty. We've already identified Pavulon, dexchlorpheniramine, scopolamine, chloral hydrate, and dexedrine hydrochloride. For me, more than anything else, this is his signature. Just like the makeup. It's what made it possible for me and RG to reattribute certain crimes to him. As you already know, the use of this mixture makes dating more difficult—although I don't think that's why he used it; not many people would know it has that effect. The motherfucker—or motherfuckers—wasn't thinking about anything

---

[6] Chemical submission: the earliest clinical description in France of what was then discreetly called "medicinal submission" was generated at the Marseille Poison Control Center in 1982.

but immobilizing his victims while at the same time stimulating their hearts and keeping them conscious for as long as possible. Theoretically, in the neurocerebral sense they would unfortunately still have experienced various types of pain. That seems important to him, or them."

The doctor fell into a silence of contemplation, and of rage. He, like Mallock, thought the reason for the killer's methods was a simple one: sadism. They were wrong. The Makeup Artist was much crazier than that. And much more dangerous.

"Anyway, to get back to the little girl, the asshole put makeup on her. Same products, same designs. But, for reasons we don't know yet, he didn't perform the same sexual amputations on her. Maybe her age? Come on; we'll go over and have a look."

Amédée, struggling again, followed Mordome into another room. Three assistants, two men and a woman, had already begun working on the child. What he saw made his stomach flip over. The girl had been turned so that she was lying facedown. Her hair was scalped but still perfect, with its center part and its two braids, undoubtedly styled by her mother on the night of the murder. The incision of the scalp and the occipital region had just been completed, as well as that of the temporal muscle, and the whole had been tipped forward.

Mordome's assistant was preparing to begin the orofacial autopsy; he was far from finishing and moving on to a semblance of reconstruction. The child had virtually no face left.

"Where are we?" asked Mordome.

The assisting intern took a deep breath before reciting:

"Opening of the longitudinal sinus on the dura mater with scissors. I will then remove the encephalon in a single unit . . . "

There were a few seconds of silence. Mordome gave the intern a black look.

"Of course," the young man added quickly, aware that he had forgotten something, "that was after having sawed the skull along a frontal lateral line and obliquely incising the occipital region."

Amédée forced himself to look at the child. It was impossible to see something like that without being profoundly changed. The head was dismantled into pieces, and the rest of the body was a nameless horror. Why did he feel so obligated not to look away?

"That's fine; I'll take over," said Mordome. "As you can see, she has been disembowelled and sewn back up. Her mouth and eyes have also been sewn shut."

The pathologist's voice rasped slightly. He and Mallock shared the same feeling. Beyond disgust and pity, there was a gnawing anger deep within them, so fierce and so tightly controlled that it was becoming physically painful.

Mordome cleared his throat before continuing:

"Taking into account a slight increase of serotonin and a large dosage of histamines in the major wounds, I fear that she was also, if not conscious, at least still alive at the time of evisceration. I note over the whole surface of the body, in the same locations as those on the mother . . . correction, on number 306 . . . various needle punctures. Same arrangement and same number, twelve. These injections served to introduce the product, and then to drain the body of its blood. No liquid was found at the crime scene. The angle of perfusion is the same; that is, twenty degrees in relation to the skin surface."

Mallock remembered the expression Grimaud had used during their lunch: "This guy is a maniac; a real fucking vampire."

With a kind of enormous pair of shears plated in stainless steel, and without giving himself time to feel pity, Mordome began cutting the stitches holding the two sides of the abdomen together. With each move, each observation, he talked loudly to make sure everything would be correctly recorded. Because of the importance of this autopsy he had

had two video cameras installed. Their red lights meant that everything that happened in this room could be played back, reviewed, and analyzed.

"Resistance is relatively strong," he continued. "It's fishing line. Nylon, probably three hundredth, the kind used for carnivorous fish."

Mordome's precision made Mallock smile sadly. His friend was a fisherman during his rare moments of leisure.

"The whole has been sewn together forcefully, and the flesh could not always withstand it. The murderer realized this fairly quickly and made deeper, wider stitches beginning at the navel. From this we can deduce that this was an operation he was doing for the first time, unless it was the fragility of the child's skin that surprised him."

At that moment he cut the sixth stitch. The flesh tore apart and the abdomen fell open. The little girl's body split in two like an overfilled balloon, spilling its horrifying contents onto the floor and the feet of the people participating in the autopsy. Mordome murmured *fuck* under his breath, and a young assistant burst into tears. Mallock stayed immobile, frozen like a pillar of salt. On the ground was a vile mixture of pink and purple viscera and an appalling amount of grains of bran and shreds of newspaper. The odor was unbearable.

"Index and weigh all of that." Mordome had regained his composure in mere tenths of a second.

At his feet, Amédée recognised an organ that had fallen on the ground: a small heart, half-wrapped in the front page of an issue of *Point de vue et images du monde* showing a uniformed prince consort whose smile was still visible through a clot of coagulated blood. He was making some kind of gesture with his hand. The words *balcony*, *acclaimed*, and, further down, *happiness*, could still be read.

Fifteen minutes later, everything had been cleaned up. Mordome continued his inspection of the body.

"I'm taking advantage of the fact that the area is completely cleared out to take a sample. Using a scoop about three centimeters in diameter," he announced to the recording system, "after having incised the bladder and before proceeding with the removal of the pelvic organs, I am extracting a small quantity of urine. You okay?" he asked Mallock, before continuing.

"I don't know if I want to cry, puke, or tear that piece of shit to pieces."

"Do all three. Don't worry. He'll end up on this table too."

"That doesn't make me feel any better."

"I know. Oh! By the way—besides the twelve ceremonial punctures, I've found other needle marks, all grouped on the little girl's thighs. She must have had some kind of daily treatment, probably for diabetes. The urine analysis will confirm that."

"Did she give herself the shots?"

"Not at her age; it would have been the parents, or maybe a nurse."

Mordome moved back up to the head and pushed back the scalp with its bangs and two braids. Then, with a pair of long, curved, and very thin scissors, he began cutting the fishing line the Makeup Artist had used to sew the mouth and eyelids shut. The left eye hadn't been completely stitched. The pathologist gave a gasp. "Finally—some good news!"

He took a sort of pair of tweezers from the tray—Mallock couldn't remember the name of them—and, carefully, pushed them beneath the inner rim of the eye to draw out a fat little beige worm. Watching it squirm between the tweezers' points, he announced: "First-stage larva. Probably a bluebottle fly." He leaned toward Mallock, as if to tell him a secret. "I'm going to give it to Jo.[7] She's an intern, but she's studied forensic ento-

---

[7] Marie-Joséphine Maêcka Demaya, a big woman from Martinique, would play a more important role in the later investigations of Amédée Mallock, eventually joining his team.

mology. A brilliant recruit, between you and me. Between the
weather data for the three days preceding the discovery of the
bodies and the current size of this larva, she should be able to
tell when our victims died, almost to the hour. Incubation lasts
between twelve and twenty-four hours in the open air. Also,
the window was wide open. These charming little critters love
to lay their eggs in the mucus membranes of cadavers. Wounds,
tongues, eyes, nostrils; they love it all. It's synchronized like a
musical composition. Twenty-four hours later, they transform
into mobile larvae, and in seven days the babies reach six centimeters in length. And to give us even more information, when
they reach the pupal stage, these little police helpers turn from
white to black, with every shade of brown in between. Using a
color chart we can determine the exact ages of the creatures.
But you already know all of that by heart."

Mordome put the larva into a glass bottle, then plunged his
tweezers back into the little girl's eye to pull out some more
examples. "This time," he said, "we'll have a good idea of the
time the crime took place."

Now it only remained to finish the orofacial autopsy and
then cut the stitches on the girl's mouth so they could open it.
Except for Mordome, who kept on speaking loudly, everyone
was profoundly silent. Amédée and the three assistants stood
white-faced, hands clasped behind their backs, heads down.
When all of the stitches had been cut, Mordome asked for
help. He and Mallock had to force the jaws open; they came
apart suddenly, with a crack like a dead branch snapping.

None of them would ever forget what they found inside the
child's oral cavity—not just the nature of the things, but above
all the way the mouth was so horrifically overstuffed.

Outside in the sun, the cold was tolerable even for Mallock, who wore only a light jacket. He decided to go back to the office on foot. He needed to walk—and, more than that, he needed to let something inside him explode.

Tears or anger—it didn't matter which.

A sort of nursery rhyme had been running through his mind for several minutes; a song by Gainsbourg, about a wax doll, or a rag doll. He knew he'd never be able to erase the little girl with the braids from his memory. Crossing through the flower market, he was surprised when a sob escaped his lips. He quivered imperceptibly, unbearably full of sadness and rage. His throat tightened.

The first thing he did back in his office was to pour himself a large whiskey. The gold liquid slid down his throat, taking with it the muck that had built up in his heart and his gut. To keep on living as if nothing was wrong—was that even possible? Mallock couldn't understand how the world hadn't stopped turning, even just for a second, to weep for this little girl. To say goodbye to her.

There was only one remedy. Work.

He called Bob to give him the samples he had taken in the mysterious little holes from the house in Saint-Mandé. "Take these to the lab and have them test for blood, and if it's there, see if they can find out whose it is."

"What should I put on the label?"

"Saint-Mandé/floor holes/second floor."

Bob muttered an obliging "okay" and left the room.

The day dripped by like a marshmallow hung from a steel hook. Amédée didn't try to hold it back. There were calls to return, notably from Queen Margot, but he didn't make any of them. He wasn't sure if he wanted to talk—or if he even could.

His colleagues left one by one, popping their heads into his office to call out the traditional "Happy holidays, boss" that they repeated every December thirty-first.

At seven o'clock, weary of the silence, Mallock activated the security system and closed up the central part of the Fort. He only did that twice a year, for May first and the New Year. On the floor below, a team would continue working through the night on the data entry he had requested. He stopped by to say hello to them, partly to keep them motivated, but also out of kindness—though the old grump would never have admitted that.

Outside, the sidewalks carried the scent of oysters and lemon.

The cold had returned, bringing a few drops of rain with it—all the better to spoil the ambience. No matter; it was still a holiday. It was written on the calendar. Civilians were hurrying to celebrate, emitting occasional peals of laughter. Whatever happened, they would celebrate the New Year. And honestly, that obsession had always bothered Mallock a bit, though he had never tried to figure out why.

Those forced parties with mandatory kisses at a predetermined time, those stupid resolutions that never stuck, and the way people made sure to repeat them the following year to anyone who hadn't died in the meantime. It stressed him out. He thought the holiday was desperate and morbid, and as depressing as a funeral. And they weren't burying a year; he couldn't care less about that; it was like burying your childhood, the time you had lost, just shoving it under the carpet, along with the dust and all the regret and remorse. Three, two, one, midnight: now everyone's happy. They kiss, they throw themselves at each other, and then they ignore each other the next day and go back to the usual routine of hatred, or at best indifference.

Not only that, it reminded him too much of his childhood, and his New Year's Eves, which were never celebrated.

At home, several voicemails were waiting for him. A dozen "Happy New Year"s and three invitations to come and celebrate—including one from Margot Murât, and one from Amélie.

"If you're free, maybe we could . . . "

And how! A few seconds later, his heart thumping, he dialed her number.

"Hello, you've reached the home of Amélie Maurel. Unfortunately I'm not in, but don't leave me wondering who called—leave a message after the beep, please!"

"It's Mallock . . . Amédée," babbled the superintendent, and hung up.

Then, for more than an hour, he tried to stand being in his apartment. Around nine o'clock he gave up. Paris was at the table, having dinner. Mallock wasn't happy being inside or outside. Only Amélie's presence could pull him out of his funk. The clinking of forks and glasses in the courtyard reminded him that he hadn't had any lunch that day.

He still wasn't hungry. Gainsbourg's song had returned to his head and with it had come sadness, slowly but surely, like a flood. He thought for an instant about calling Margot back. She was often associated with his attacks of spleen, and she was the most effective remedy for them. But it wouldn't have been fair—not to her, and not to Amélie.

Not wanting to bother anyone, or to feel sorry for himself,

he was preparing to begin a long and exhaustive single-malt Scotch tasting back in his apartment when the telephone rang.

It was Léon. "Amédée, can you come here, quickly?"

"Where? Why?"

"I'm at Saint Paul's church, with a friend. Understand?"

"Canon Lasalle? Is there some problem?"

Léon didn't answer right away. Then: "I think he's your Makeup Artist."

"The canon?" Amédée laughed. "I'm not surprised; he's a nasty-looking piece of work."

"I'm not joking, Mallock. He just struck again."

"Who?"

"I think it's the Makeup Artist, but that doesn't change anything. There's a body here."

The air suddenly crackled with electricity.

"In the church?" Mallock's heart pounded.

"Yes. Get over here; hurry!"

Had the son of a bitch shortened his interval between killings again? Mallock thought back, occupying his mind while he prepared to go. He had previously calculated that it would be four days before the next murder. Saint-Mandé had been on December twenty-eighth, and now it was almost January first. The count was right.

Despite the icy sidewalks and freezing air that took his breath away, it only took him five minutes to reach his destination. Léon was waiting for him at the top of the church's six-columned forecourt, his face chalk-white. Without saying a word, he slid a large key into the lock and turned it three times. The canon was waiting for them in the ventail, trembling and red-eyed.

"Toward the baptismal fonts. On the right," he babbled. He indicated a large pillar composed of four columns with his finger. "Just behind there."

Like in most churches, the air was cold and damp, filled

with the odors of incense, mold, and cat urine. Behind him, Amédée heard the key turning three times again in the closed door. The canon was terrified by the thought that a member of his flock might think of coming in to pray.

As he walked toward the spot indicated, Mallock's breath came faster. The fear of what he might discover was mingled with that of coming across the monster. What if he was still there, hiding behind a column? The Devil in God's house. He verified the comforting presence of his guns in their holsters, but he thought twice about drawing one of them. This was a church, and the former choirboy in him was reluctant. He contented himself with resting his hand on his little .25 automatic.

A rendezvous with the Devil, in a church, on New Year's Eve. Only Mallock could have ended up in a situation like this.

Around the curve of the pillar, in a large white marble basin filled to the brim with blood, Mallock discovered a child made up like an angel in a fresco. His chest, a moonlike islet surrounded by purple, floated on the surface of the macabre scallop-shaped bathtub.

For the first time since Thomas's death, Mallock crossed himself, before taking off his coat and putting it on the floor beneath the font. He took out the small digital camera he always carried on him, just in case.

"Call Number 36," he instructed Léon, holding out his mobile phone. "Tell them to come and bring technicians."

Without waiting for a response, he began taking photos of the scene. He turned all the way around, snapping from every angle. He also took wide-angle and close-up shots, bending to take pictures from just a few centimeters away.

Léon was approaching him to relay the response to his phone call, when he saw his friend do something that froze him momentarily in his tracks. It seemed that Mallock couldn't bear to leave the child in this state, and in full view of everyone.

He saw Mallock bend his large body over the marble scallop shell and, dipping his arms into the blood filling the font, pick up the child's corpse.

A noise like dripping water. Sweet sadness. A strange fruity smell. Damp distress. Bloody drops falling on the ancient stone slabs.

With infinite care, Amédée set the small, defiled body down on his overcoat. Then he stood there, unmoving, the sleeves of his jacket drenched in blood.

Preserve traces of evidence and clues!—how many times had he screamed that at his chief inspectors? And now he had moved the body! Even though it wasn't critical, because he had taken every possible photo, it was still a thoughtless move.

He began mentally ticking off what they would find in the blood from the font: Fibers from his own coat. Hairs from Mimi, his housekeeper's kitten. Traces of whiskey and tobacco leaves. He looked again at the shell-shaped font.

All around it, the floor was spotted with thousands of red drops.

The whole life of an innocent child, fallen like rain.

The canon, who had withdrawn into the sacristy, passed in front of Mallock to place a silver crucifix on the improvised shroud. Still in shock, the three men moved closer to each other, as if to intone a last prayer.

It was midnight.

Laughs and shouts of joy from outside penetrated the church's walls and echoed in the nave.

"Four! Three! Two! One! HAPPY NEW YEAR!"

BOOK TWO

14.
Saturday morning, January 1st

Mallock got home at dawn, his heart heavy and his body soiled. He was hardly in the door before he pulled off his clothes and threw them into a bag. He didn't know yet whether he should throw them away or take them to be dry-cleaned. He decided to keep them without washing them. You never know. He'd done enough stupid things at the crime scene.

Had he really seen it? His bloody wrists and fingers didn't really leave any room for doubt. Some certainties were nightmarish: a child had been tortured and martyred and laid out like an offering to the Devil in a christening font in a church right in the middle of Paris.

One image obsessed him, ridiculous, dreadful, grotesque; that of a giant hard candy. That was what the murder scene had resembled. A piece of white sugar-candy tucked inside a scallop shell. A red fruit candy inside which someone had placed a plastic baby before filling the shell with strawberry or raspberry syrup, so the baby would stick to the inside. Red and white. The Makeup Artist definitely had a taste for the grotesque. He seemed to be obsessed with the Devil, with redemption through suffering; the same aesthetic preference for torture and hellish visions you might find in the paintings of Goya or Hieronymos Bosch, like in the right-hand panel of *The Garden of Earthly Delights*.

Mallock sat for a long time on the closed toilet lid in the bathroom, naked and sticky with blood, hands resting on his knees, head down, lost in thought.

It was only when he'd finally gotten into the shower that he placed the name of the strange odor he had identified at first as blood. Judging by the smells that were magnified now by the hot water diluting the liquid in the bottom of the shower, it seemed obvious now, and it also explained the image of sweets that had dominated his imagination. The red liquid in which the child's body had been soaking was a mixture of wine and syrup—strawberry or raspberry, he still wasn't sure which. Grenadine, maybe?

The telephone rang at ten minutes to eight.

"It's me, Margot. Happy New Year! So, my superintendent isn't calling me anymore?"

"Not after finding a baby's body in a baptism font."

There was a heavy silence. God knew, it was hard to shut Queen Margot up! But he'd struck home this time. He'd definitely been too harsh, and he knew it.

"I'm sorry," he said. "I'm pretty tense."

Margot had recovered her composure somewhat. "Well, you could at least have clued me in."

"About what?"

"I thought we had a gentlemen's agreement."

"What are you talking about? An agreement about what?"

"The Makeup Artist; what else?"

Now it was Mallock's turn to be closemouthed—or the opposite, really; hearing Margot say the suspect's name made his jaw hit the floor. "You know about it?" he asked finally. "What do you know exactly? Who tipped you off?"

"Yeah, I know about it. I know everything, or almost everything, about your serial killer. And no, no one tipped me off. It's been public knowledge since five o'clock this morning. I've been a little annoyed, as you might imagine."

Mallock acknowledged the point. With the murder of the child to top it all off, the new year was starting off with a flourish. A funereal one.

Hoarse trumpets and dented hearts.

Amédée tried to explain to Margot the series of events that had led him not to tell her anything. It wouldn't totally exonerate him in her eyes, but it might soften the reprisals she had undoubtedly planned.

"Okay, okay, my dear superintendent," she said at last. "I don't forgive you, but I understand. I won't bother you now; you're going to get enough abuse from my colleagues without my joining in. Now, on another note, I hope you've lost a little bit of weight. I wouldn't say no to the idea of dinner one of these nights, complete with dessert and sexy banter. And if you give me a tiny apology and a big exclusive between the pears and the cheese, well, then—and only then—will we call it even."

Mallock and Margot had spent six months together, two years after Thomas's death. She had helped him enormously, giving him back if not a taste for life, at least a reason not to do away with himself. Then she had gotten bored. The misanthropic homebody tendencies and sadness that had dominated Amédée back then hadn't agreed with Margot Murât, who was made for dancing and belly-laughing, weeks in the Seychelles and weekends in Venice. He adored her, though she could be a bit intrusive sometimes. Like many women she talked a lot, often too much, and the happiness she brought him made him uncomfortable. What right did he have to be happy when Thomas was dead? He wouldn't allow himself to feel joy without Thomas there. So, one day, with great tenderness and many promises, they had decided to break up. Just for a while, they had said. Since then they had held on to a strong friendship and, even though she was married now, Margot called him every now and then for a little spin in the bedroom. Stuffed suit that he was, it bothered him. It was against his principles. Margot, amused by his old-fashionedness, always laughed and reminded him that he had seniority over her dear husband.

Embarrassed by his own indecision, Mallock stammered: "Yeah—maybe, why not," before hanging up.

He really was hopeless sometimes.

Margot hadn't lied. He had barely stepped outside when he was blindsided by the banner headlines blaring from every newspaper displayed outside the corner shop. So much for the low-profile anonymity of the Makeup Artist.

Makeup Artist, Serial Murders, Mallock, and *13* were the terms that popped up the most often. For some reason, several papers contained the same mistake. Though there had been thirteen crime scenes identified, double murders had been perpetrated at two of those scenes and, counting the latest murder, which nobody was talking about yet, there were sixteen killings—and if that number had been there it would really have shattered any goodwill he still had toward the papers. Another inaccuracy was that only Superintendent Amédée Mallock's name appeared in the stories, as if he had been on the case from day one. There were no specifics given about the murders themselves. Someone had definitely spilled the beans, but no documents had been leaked, which was some consolation at least. If they had, there would have been a lot more facts and probably some images given. There was a lot of blather, but there were hardly any illustrations.

Only the rich get richer, police version: Mallock was suddenly headline news, with the pleasure of seeing himself ten years younger and thirty pounds lighter. After looking at all the front pages he went inside the shop, which featured a large and brand-new blinking plastic Santa Claus, lit up from within.

"Hello, Superintendent; you're the star today! It's all about you and your crazy lunatic! You're famous!"

The newspaper-seller and his wife stared at him, their eyes gleaming with curiosity, while he picked a copy of every newspaper, one by one.

"I could do very nicely without it," he said, forcing himself to smile at them.

He got into his car and quickly skimmed the main articles. Not all the information was there; far from it. Various theories, conjectures, and rumors were mixed with miscellaneous odd bits of information. Everything and anything, as usual. The further a journalist was from his source, the more deformed the message got.

Among the descriptions and hypotheses there was one concerning the serial killer's mobile phone. As the journalist proudly explained:

"The killer's name comes from the fact that he puts makeup on all his victims so that they all look like the woman he loved and who left him. He is endlessly repeating the fantasy murder of the same person."

Not bad, thought Mallock. Wrong, but not bad. There was something to remember in that. The fact that the makeup did give all the victims, including the men and children, a certain resemblance. Mallock didn't know the true reason for it yet, but it certainly wasn't the one claimed by the journalist. If it were, the Makeup Artist would have chosen women that already looked much more similar to one another, and never men or children.

As for the rest of the newspapers, two major facts stood out: a series of horrible murders had been committed, which meant an atypical serial killer; and the existence of a government plot to hide the truth from the French people. Depending on the paper, either the conspiracy was the star point, or the monster was. Or both. This kind of sensational double story was a real godsend for the press; they'd sell newspapers by the ton. If they could draw it out a little, it might last a month—more, with public sympathy. Heat up the presses; let hack journalists come crawling out of the woodwork. The gutter press still cherished fond memories of the case of little Gregory, the ultimate headline cash cow.

From there it wasn't much of a leap to wanting the murders to continue, to remain unsolved.

Someone had definitely leaked this, but who? Mallock's first impulse was to suspect that asshole Judge Humbert, whom Dublin had felt obligated to bring in on the case yesterday morning. Judges did love their publicity. He was definitely at the top of Amédée's list—but he was wrong, and he wouldn't realize it until much later.

Mallock's next mistake was failing to understand all the consequences these revelations would have on the rest of the investigation. He was certainly irritated at the time, but he was also relieved. It was bound to explode one of these days, so why not now? Considering the results they'd gotten up to this point, it seemed like the secrecy surrounding the case had really only benefited one person: the Makeup Artist. In revealing his existence, wasn't it possible that a hellish cycle had been broken, even unintentionally?

Mallock hoped, now that the deck had been shuffled, that he might get a better hand this time—and that the game would get a lot crappier for his adversary. In this, he underestimated the fury of the media. It wouldn't be long at all before they turned on the police, and the establishment too. Mallock was an ideal target.

They were already demanding explanations and apologies from the Secretary of the Interior. Some people were calling for his removal, or even the resignation of the whole government. Mallock was surprised to find himself smiling. Sometimes he preferred fighting in broad daylight, with one winner and one loser. Here, the arena was obviously packed to the rafters. In front of the screaming populace, the gladiators could do nothing but give themselves over to merciless combat. Thumbs would be turned up and then down.

The savage within Mallock was excited—but when he

arrived at Île de la Cité, he knew he was in for a bad time. A mob of angry journalists had gathered around the station. He glanced over the crowd. He knew everyone, and they all knew him. After a second of hesitation, he decided to plow straight through them, head down.

Galvanized by the appearance of the superintendent, the hive began buzzing, every wasp ready to sting, armed with questions. Shoving with his elbows and muttering inaudible responses, Amédée fought through the dense mass of journalists. It was a job in itself; dodging the rapacity of the press corps without giving the impression that he was trying to escape them. You had to give a nice little smile, throw out a "Hi, how are you" here and there, maybe a wink at . . . nothing. He even granted himself the luxury, once he was on the other side of the throng, of turning around and calling out: "I hope I've answered all your questions."

Then, the smile still on his lips, giving them the finger in his mind, he headed up to his office.

15.
Saturday, January 1st. Number 36

At the Quai des Orfèvres everyone was on edge. They knew heads were going to roll, promotions would be sidelined, changes ordered. All of it completely random, depending on nothing except who was the most unlucky. There was only one order of the day: *don't be in the wrong place when the shit hits the fan*. It was all a matter of guessing where lightning would strike, to avoid being the one trapped and frozen like a deer caught in a pair of headlights.

The atmosphere in the Fort, though, was completely different. Feeling protected by their temperamental boss, Bob, Ken, and Francis had their noses firmly to the grindstone. Amédée stopped to speak to each of them individually, checking, encouraging, and picking up copies. There wasn't much in the way of results yet, but they'd only been on the case for three short days. The data entry was chugging along practically without them, and they were absorbed now in dissecting RG's files.

"Those guys worked their asses off," Francis had declared, impressed.

"Yep. They did a good job," Bob had agreed.

"It corroborates pretty much everything we're doing," concluded Ken.

Without consulting each other, all three men had formed the same opinion. There wasn't much more for Mallock to say.

"Now that the embargo's been lifted, we've got our backs to the wall," he reminded them. "As far as the media's concerned we've been on the case for four months. Nobody cares about distinguishing between a Grimaud and a Mallock, which isn't really a big deal. What scares me a whole hell of a lot more is that the Makeup Artist is speeding up the rhythm of his—or their—murders. How can we work faster? Any ideas? I'm all ears."

"Jules and Julie will be back tomorrow morning. That alone will help a lot," volunteered Ken.

"Yes, I should have gotten them home more quickly. It's my own fault. Now, what else? Here's a question: how are you going to sum up this case to them on Monday?"

"We've got sixteen murders, all sharing the fact that makeup is put on the victims, their blood is drained, and they're tortured," ventured Ken.

"What else?"

"All the victims are beautiful," put in Francis. "It's not that they look like each other, but all of them—men, women, and children—have very symmetrical faces."

"And? What does that mean?"

"Well, he loves . . . beautiful people."

"*Love* is kind of a strange word to use when you see what he does to them."

"Uh . . . I meant that he's drawn to them, maybe sexually."

Mallock couldn't let it go. Francis's lack of subtlety irritated him sometimes. Especially when he needed to feel like he had help in his corner. Like today.

"Have you done any research on this facial symmetry? What are your conclusions? What are our leads?"

"I . . . well, I don't know . . . it's just telling us the type of victim, isn't it?"

"Hard work is great, my lad, but you need to reflect, too. Where do we find this same symmetry in faces or monuments? We have to try to get inside the killer's head."

"To find out what? I don't get it."

Francis got stuck quickly when he was asked to draw on his

imagination or his education, two areas in which he was sorely lacking.

"To find out, for example, that the Makeup Artist is maybe the son or grandson of an Egyptologist. Or someone who's very interested in that period, at least."

Francis looked stupefied and isolated.

"Let's imagine that he grew up among reproductions of Egyptian statues," persisted Mallock. "He might very well have been marked for life by that. Amazing studies have been done on this type of thing. The huge statues of Ramses at Luxor have perfectly symmetrical features, and it still seems impossible that they could create something like that with the tools of the time. But they did it, which is proof that this symmetry was of fundamental importance to them."

"But . . . " Francis began.

"And even then, you have to let your mind go further," continued Mallock, now wound up like a clock. "You always have to push further. Crazy people like this killer don't find their obsessions right at the edge of the forest. Even in the deepest part of their forest of madness they look for a cave or a well, searching deeper for tools to feed their psychoses. Go deeper, Francis. Go deeper, again and again and always. Don't stay on the surface of things; you'll never find anything out that way. Look—let's stay on the archaeological theme for now. What does this symmetry tell us? What were the reasons that drove the ancient Egyptians to create such incredible works of art? It's been argued that, for them, this famous symmetry was the ultimate sign of perfection, of the gods. Maybe our Makeup Artist is also looking for some kind of spiritual satisfaction, or absolution, or perfection. Which one? Why?"

Amédée paused for a moment, as if to let his words sink in. Then he continued: "And if this is a kind of obsessive-compulsive disorder focused on order and symmetry, but more . . . generally, let's say, then imagine his room, his house, his behavior at work, or even the way he walks. Would people notice him in the street? What kind of job might he want to have? Think about French-style geometrical gardens. Is it possible that he might be an arboriculturalist at Versailles?"

Francis was completely dumbfounded. He knew he really had only stayed at the edge of the forest.

"But it might also be the complete opposite. After all, he's slaughtered these women and children. So then, does he have a burning hatred for perfection, for the supreme organization that symmetry represents? Does it symbolize an anal-retentive mother? Or military school, maybe? These are the kinds of questions you should be asking yourself."

Mallock could seem harsh. But if Francis wasn't up to the task that had been assigned to him, then he—Amédée, his boss—was responsible for that, and equally guilty for his failure. Lives were at stake. You didn't come to the Fort as an intern. Everyone on his team was there to contribute his or her own science and intelligence and effectiveness.

"Anything else, boys?" he asked, turning to the others. "What is it that links all these crimes?"

"There's the substance used to immobilize the victims," suggested Ken, less out of conviction than to distract Mallock and force him to relinquish his prey.

"That might be a determining factor, yes. RG should be able to tell me more on the subject." *If we can find him*, he added to himself.

"There's also the fact that his victims take the metro," volunteered Bob, cautiously.

"Mmm . . . that point is tricky. We live in Paris. Who doesn't take the metro?"

"You don't, boss," ventured Ken, a little smile quirking the corner of his mouth.

Touché. Amédée never used public transportation. Though he'd never discussed it openly with his team, he suffered from claustrophobia and ochlophobia—the fears of enclosed spaces and crowds—as well as psychopathophobia, the fear of going crazy, which was understandable if you knew what had happened to his parents.

"Good point, Ken. A direct hit," Amédée smiled. "Now, what else have we got?"

The team continued to give their superintendent the early results of their work, and Mallock began, slowly but surely, to panic. They were going in circles. The same questions kept coming back; the same vague theories; the same dead-end trails, the same unimportant statistics. Amédée pulled himself together roughly and took the floor again:

"I have something else important to tell you. I went back to Saint-Mandé and found a new step in his MO. In a nutshell, he moves the bodies twice. There's the starting location of the murder, where he drains the blood, and then there's the end location, where he stages the final scene. But there's a middle location between the two."

Three locations for one killing. That had to be a first in the long history of criminology.

"We need to add another crucial question to our list; I've been asking myself over and over and I haven't been able to come up with a satisfactory answer. What does he do with all the blood? He drains it so he won't leave traces, and so he can cut up his victims in peace, right? Does he get rid of it afterward? Does he bathe in it? Anything is possible."

Then he added an even more disturbing possibility. "Does he drink it? Does he use it for . . . let's say . . . culinary purposes?"

Francis had a grotesque vision of a kitchen, and blood-and-apple sausages. He fought back the impulse to gag.

"Getting back to our middle location," continued Mallock. "I discovered some very strange marks there, like nail holes, and also some curved scratches."

"Little holes?" mused Ken. "Maybe they're stiletto heel prints. We might have a female Makeup Artist after all."

"No, they're more pointed than that. Anyway, I took samples. As soon as I know more, I'll . . . oh! One last thing. I noticed that an object was missing from the Modiano home: an antique Russian icon, extremely valuable. Our killer might also be a thief; they're certainly not mutually exclusive."

Even as he gave them the information, Amédée realized that there might be something else there, something even more important that he hadn't thought of at first. He didn't actually believe that the Makeup Artist had suddenly become greedy. Yes, he had stolen jewelry before, but he'd returned it all when he decorated the wealthy woman for her descent from the cross. This time, it was the very nature of the stolen object that had attracted him. A Russian icon; a Christ on the cross. Why? For what use? What pleasure? What if this theft was a key to figuring out the Makeup Artist's obsessions?

"Bob, have the photo of that icon shown around the usual circuit—antique dealers, auction houses, customs, et cetera. I'll leave you all to it."

He looked around at them all one more time, almost imploringly. "Is there anything else?"

"Yeah—about the torture," said Ken, a bit uncertainly. "I don't think we've looked deeply enough into it. I mean, it's horrible. Since it shook us all up so much, I think that— unconsciously—we kind of rushed over it, but we have to ask ourselves what it corresponds to. Aside from the sadism, it shows a hell of an imagination. So where do these fantasies come from? It suggests a certain level of education or culture, and maybe more beyond that. Something social, cultural, professional . . . it's a whole side of the murders that we need to decipher. And as of right now, we haven't gotten anywhere with that. Were you planning to give it to Jules or Julie?"

"No; don't worry, I'm on it. I'm sorry—I assigned myself

the task without thinking of talking to you about it. You're entitled to a complete rundown once I've come to any cohesive conclusions—which I haven't yet. But you're right; it's very promising. Just a couple more things. I've looked at an expert's report that was requested by RG for cases ten and eleven, the 'descent from the cross.' It's pretty telling, and it goes along with your line of thinking. In substance, the psychologist discusses the concept of 'theological conflict' and 'retribution.' To make a long story short, it's a case of inflicting pain on one person to obtain forgiveness from others. It's also been discovered that our hobo Christ was in fact the assistant manager of a bank, and the upper-class Virgin Mary draped in jewelry was actually homeless. This is the only staged scene that has a . . . social theme, let's say, so I don't think it's useful to apply that qualification to the rest of them. But I do think we should add the adjectives 'theological' and 'retributive' to our portrait of the murders, which gives us . . . "

"Sixteen murders with the common characteristics of makeup on the victims, their blood being drained, three separate sacrifice locations, the use of a chemical submission cocktail, and the use of theological-type torture in an intermediate place where there are strange traces of pointy holes," summarized Ken.

Mallock merely said: "Keep going in that direction. I'm going home. I'm planning to do some work from my end on Sunday."

From my end was Mallock's favorite way of euphemistically describing the famous waking dreams, or heightened-perception sessions, in which he engaged, escaping reality in order to plunge deeply into his own intuition—not without the occasional help of substances prohibited by both morality and the law.

16.
Sunday, January 2nd

For Amédée, who had been practicing his strange brand of magic forever, it was vital to occupy all dimensions—the rational one, the cerebral one, and the one in which occult forces were present, the great instinctual id. The Makeup Artist was present somewhere in that vast domain of madness that all people share, and that was inside Mallock too. He came and went anonymously inside the superintendent's big head like a tourist in a cave, leaving a bad smell and traces of his fingerprints.

Sometimes he screamed insane things to test the echo inside the policeman's skull—and to show that he didn't give a shit, like a scumbag yelling in a church.

Mallock hadn't had the strength to summon him immediately when he got home from the Fort. Too tired, too tense. It wouldn't have worked. He needed to let go and rest for a while. Soon enough the image of the killer and his evolution would appear more clearly. The sequences, as geographical and chronological as they were ritual, would become more logical, almost fluid.

After a long night of recuperation and data processing in the back of his mind, he woke up ready for action. It was eight-thirty in the morning. In the distance, the bells of Notre-Dame rang to summon the faithful; the day's first mass was about to begin. Mallock made his decision immediately. He also had an office to celebrate. He thought he had enough information to try and go over to the other side, and bring back—if not answers, at least good, relevant questions.

He would stake out the boulevard of the insane, and stalk the killer to the very end of his madness. Inside the box of his skull, Mallock would skip from sidewalk to sidewalk, melting into the shadows on each street corner. Patiently, he would lie in wait for the beast in window reflections and rearview mirrors. And he'd be damned if he didn't come out of it having learned something more from the fiend—or even trapping him in his head. He had to live somewhere, after all, and why not Number 13 Insanity Boulevard, dead-end street of the deranged?

No one was going to come and disturb him. From the back of the closet, in a hole he'd made in the wall, he took a brightly-colored iron box that had once contained tiger balm. What it held now was a lot more formidable.

Now he swallowed a microscopic capsule of dimethyltryptamine, a synthetic product of ayahuasca. Sometimes he took an ibogaine infusion. Then, he carefully took his opium pipe from the glass case in the living room. It was a cloisonné piece of ivory and jade. A longtime user, he preferred to keep the ceremonial aspect of all this brief. Three minutes later, he loaded the pipe with the paste he had softened and rolled into a pellet.

It was the cure for all his inhibitions.

It wasn't a habit, so much as a last resort. At his son's death, facing a pain that seemed to have no remedy and no limit, one of his friends had introduced him to it. *Opos papaver somniferum.* Morphine, to fight death and despair. He only turned to it rarely, still using bits from the same lump he had purchased back then, and only when the huge waves of sadness came back—or when he wanted, as he did this morning, to free his intuitions and let them run wild in a chaotic clog-dance in his head.

With the first inhalations he felt all of his body's mooring lines give way.

Very quickly, he found himself in a room, a sort of chapel

made of grease and rust, crowded with steel machines. At the very back a woman was suspended by chains above a kind of altar. Below her, a lance stuck in the floor seemed to be waiting for her to fall and be impaled. In the foreground, sitting at a workbench with his back turned, a person was writing. Slowly, holding back his steps, Mallock approached.

It was one of the Makeup Artists; he was sure of it. The fear and repulsion he felt couldn't lie to him. He kept moving forward, his gaze fixed on those shoulder blades and that filthy spine. He wanted to know, to discover the words the murderer was writing so carefully with a Sergent-Major fountain pen. The closer he got, the more unbearable the noise of the pen's nib on the crumpled paper became. The scraping sound reminded him of evil, of flesh ripping. In uneven handwriting that slanted to the left like the opposite of italics, the Makeup Artist was writing a poem:

831. Truth comes from the face of God,
832. Like power,
833. Lines of lava dancing,
834. The comet spinning out of control,
835. On the purple of popes,
836. Truth comes from the faces of God,
837. Mysterious arrangements,
838. Made by archangels on horseback,
838. With pyramidal antics.
839. And while God talks to us about the melancholy of volcanoes,
840. The infinitely small becomes infinitely large.

Occasionally the tip of the pen caught on the rough surface and then freed itself sharply, causing spurts of ink. Before each verse he wrote the number of the line.

841. Truth comes from the face of God,
842. From his pupils and his teeth,
843. From the clouds and the wind,
843. From his belly and his eyes,
845. Oh, divine watchtower,
846. From his heavy golden tongue,
847. From his eye that is soft and from that which bites,
848. From his mouth where resonates, hidden behind,
849. The orphan phoneme: Father!
848. And while God talks to us about the nostalgia of volcanoes,
849. The infinitely small joins the infinitely large!!!

After these three exclamation points were drawn, Mallock had a sudden flash of certainty that the killer was about to turn around. To reveal his face, and devour Mallock's own. Just then he woke up and found himself back in his own living room. His opium pipe had fallen and broken, and his sheets were soaked. Even though he had just returned, he was angry at himself for this moment of cowardice, and decided to go back. He knew he was capable of it, and he was still under the influence of the drug. He concentrated again on the assembly hall of what looked more like a factory to him now than a religious place.

But he wasn't himself anymore.

In fact, he wasn't inside his own head, or in the Makeup Artist's. Terrified, he realized that he had fallen into the very worst place: the suspended body of the victim, the one he had seen in the back of the chapel. His spirit was stuck there, like an insect caught in amber resin.

Amédée was now seeing through the eyes of the woman the killer had just captured, and whose terror now mingled with his own fear. In front of her, large, at the very back of the room, a name was written in capital letters: CAZ . . . AVE. The central letter dangled, unreadable.

Setting down his pen, the Makeup Artist approached the body, lowered it slightly, and began slobbering on it. His mouth dripped sticky, silvery drops, like a snail's trail. The victim didn't move, her eyes bulging. Through these same eyes, Mallock contemplated the monster below. The woman in whose body he was trapped was completely conscious, drunk with terror.

The Makeup Artist/writer picked up a set of dentures made of platinum set with precious gems, like a carnival prize. The teeth were sharp and overly large, almost burlesque. Like a joke, a trick. Rolled back and puffed out by the dentures, the woman's lips looked like two slugs copulating. Calmly, the mad poet pressed against the victim so he could begin cutting out various pieces: toes, lips, and other protuberances.

Blood spurted and he recoiled, disgusted by this body that had no control. Hidden behind a mask that stank like burnt rubber, a second killer appeared and advanced in his turn toward the victim, and toward the terrified Amédée trapped inside.

It was the face that interested this second killer. He began his own ritual by brushing a puff filled with rice powder over her skin, and then he dabbed rouge on her cheeks and blue eyeshadow on her eyes and the sides of her nose.

The photo session that followed, which was apparently the specialty of the masked Makeup Artist, was long and laborious. The Makeup Artist adjusted his camera to the millimeter; then he waited for the blood to flow a little, not too much; for the light to change, for the expression on the victim's face to be just right. The other killer came back to bite here and there, at the photographer's request.

The photographer, whose movements were more feminine, used a tripod that ended in three sharp points that stuck into the ground.

Amédée tried not to sink into madness. His mind was still supporting the damaged consciousness of the young woman, but he could feel the body they shared beginning, slowly, to slip away. Like a wounded animal secreting a few miraculous endorphins before being devoured, a merciful contentment began to creep over him. This was the final pause, before the worst. Through the screaming eyes of the woman he saw a brick wall, a giant inscription, a grotesque drawing on a window. Unless it was stained glass?

But the calm was brief. His photographs taken, the second Makeup Artist made way for another creature: the third monster in this cursed trinity, a flabby dwarf with reptile hands. He began licking the martyred body, sucking its breasts, its clotted blood. Everything that flowed, everything that had been forcibly extracted, down to the slightest humor. Very quickly, his movements accelerated along with his excitement. He turned around, slapped, scratched, bit, sometimes so fast that the eye couldn't even see him. His jaws, his tongue, his jaws, his tongue, his jaws, his tongue . . . Finally tired and replete, he decided to finish the job. Between the woman's legs, his eyes closed, he thrust a golden lance upward. When the point of it came out his victim's mouth, he screamed at the top of his lungs:

"*Toreador!*"

Waking up covered in cold sweat, Mallock repeated the word to himself with horror: *Toreador!* He had never experienced that degree of reality before, never so much perversity, during one of his sessions. Were there three Makeup Artists? What was the significance of this kind of trinity in all the horror? The father, the son, and the Holy Spirit? A family? The idea was as interesting as it was terrifying—a father-and-son serial killing team? With the mother as a regular accomplice? Was it possible?

In any case, he had at least come back from his expedition with the answer to one of his questions, the solution to the mystery of the little holes in the floor. Why hadn't he thought of it before? It made so much sense! The tripod of a camera.

He stood up and went into the kitchen.

Think about something else. Coffee. Wash these terrifying visions away. But his heart wouldn't stop pounding. His vision had been so brutal that he couldn't free himself from it. He had the impression, was almost positive, that somewhere in Paris a young woman was hanging, disemboweled or impaled, in a disused chapel. Go rescue her. Maybe she wasn't dead yet.

He bit his lip. It would be difficult to send his men out looking for a nightmare. Especially without giving them any explanation, any trail to follow.

Mallock knew he hadn't made any of it up or guessed any of it. With him, everything had an equal basis in reality. So? Where had this vision come from? What had he seen? Deduced? From what?

Two coffees. Ice-cold shower. Back to the living room in his white bathrobe. Cigar. Mozart.

He remembered what Mordome had said: "In one of the cases there was an obvious attempt at impalement. He tried that even before starting to drain the blood. A real butchery."

That explained the vision, but not everything. What else had he heard or seen, maybe in a file, or in the street, that made him so nearly certain that the Makeup Artist had decided to have another try at impalement?

Reflexively, during his dream, he had had the idea of counting and memorizing the number of windows in the ceiling and façade. On one of them, between two broken panes of glass, the figure of an impaled body had been clumsily painted. He had also read a half-erased inscription somewhere on the wall of the big chapel. Two pairs of letters. AZ and AV.

17.
Monday morning, January 3rd

When he woke up for the second time, Mallock felt the need to call his little team—not so much to make sure they were there as to get an update on Jules and Julie. Ken picked up the phone. "We're all here except Bob," he assured him. "The only one missing is our beloved boss."

"How are our lovebirds doing?"

"Tanned as movie stars."

Mallock smiled. He was excited to see them, and to be able to count on Julie's exceptional brain for assistance.

"Have them find me the name of a large chapel that's definitely been closed for a few years, or maybe abandoned."

"Is that it? Do you have a name?"

Hesitation.

"Well, I have the letters CAZ in a group, and then a space, and then AVE. But no idea about an address."

There was a dismayed silence on the other end of the line. The nice thing about being in charge was not always having to explain his moods and other whims. And Mallock certainly had his share of them.

"Just a red-brick chapel. I think it's red brick, at least."

"Bravo for today's mystery. You've outdone yourself, boss. Want to clue us in?"

"No." Mallock hung up, smiling. Truthfully, he didn't even know himself where the information was coming from. His dreams, certainly, but before that? What had he seen? Where? Why those letters? He knew he hadn't invented them.

It was time to go to the office. Rubber boots. The amount of snow falling outside left him no choice. Regretfully he pulled on a pair of snow boots. He'd be too hot inside, and they were hideous. Oh well.

His front door opened on the silence of his building's inner courtyard. There were at least two inches of snow on the ground. In one corner the branches of the little birch tree were covered.

Mallock struck out into the snow. The sounds of the city were muffled, cars moving silently, pedestrians struggling at the same pace against the slow, densely falling flakes. Under the bridge he saw a barge float by, also covered with snow. The riverbanks were white. In the distance, Notre-Dame was only an impression seen through the millions of flakes.

There was no way the Makeup Artist could strike in weather like this. God had turned his giant snow globe over in the night and set it down on his bedside table. It was obvious. Wherever the snow fell, you were protected. Mallock had some very bizarre certainties sometimes.

He went into the first open shoe store, chose a pair of boots specially designed for snow and ice, and left his old ones with the clerk.

"Are you sure you don't want them? I can put them in a box for you. It's a shame; they're still in pretty good shape."

Some things, especially the ugliest, least appreciated ones, never break, wear out, or get lost. You always lose the gold cigarette lighter your lover gave you, but never the horrible cheap commercial one you bought out of desperation, which will stay with you until you're dead and buried.

Mallock had no mercy for his snow boots. "Burn them and scatter the ashes in the sea," he ordered, before sweeping majestically out of the store in a huge swirl of snow.

Mallock was passing the Deux Palais bar when he heard

someone calling his name. He thought at first that it was the Breton owner haranguing him, but it was RG himself, sitting with a large coffee and a basket full of pastries in front of him.

"There you are! We thought you were lost!"

"Yeah . . . I know. I got an earful about it. But no," he grumbled, "it was my secretary. She's lost her marbles or got mud in her ears or something. I told her I was going to be gone. I took advantage of the fact that you've taken over the case to have a long New Year's weekend, fall off the face of the earth for a few days. Oh—Happy New Year, by the way."

"Happy New Year, Raymond. But how do you manage to make it so no one can find you? And why? I'd never be able to do it."

"I go to the seaside, alone. Doesn't matter which beach; doesn't matter which hotel. I spend my days outside, gazing at the horizon and reading. It works, believe me. As for why . . . well, I don't know, really. Maybe I'm hoping that my absence will make people notice my presence for a change."

There it was. Amédée promised himself he would be nicer to RG next time. Which didn't keep him from sticking to his accustomed role as a heartless bastard.

"Should I assume that you haven't made any more progress with the poison?"

"Actually I have. I didn't want to piss off Mallock. I'd finished almost everything before I left. I spent from last Wednesday to Friday working on your problem. The final results came in this morning. It's nothing special. I can sum it up for you in a few words."

Mallock pulled up a chair next to his colleague's. Sheltered beneath the bar's red awning, they were surrounded by a curtain of snowflakes falling just centimeters away from them. RG launched into an explanation of the ingredients in the famous "cocktail."

"Weirdly, chemical submission is better known by the public at large than it is correctly used by hospitals and doctors. It's a relatively recent phenomenon, but film and novels jumped on it, which explains its popularity. So as not to have to make any arrangements, our Makeup Artist—sorry, *Artists*—just made up their own blend, which I think was the first mistake on their part. In any case, it's the only thing that's given us any objective information about them: the assholes have real skill in chemistry. It's not just any cocktail, according to the experts who analyzed the components; it's an 'intelligent assortment,' well dosed and fairly . . . short-lived. A *short half-life*, it's called. The appearance of these psychoactive substances with high effectiveness and rapid elimination is a deviant side effect of advances in therapeutic medicine. They were developed for the good of the patients, but . . . "

"H'lo, Superintendent." Talkative as ever, the Breton bar owner had come to wait on his longtime customer in person.

"H'lo," responded Mallock in the same way.

"Well?"

"Macchiato," replied Mallock with a smile and a wink, going along again—as always—with the knowing brevity of their exchanges.

RG hadn't finished his speech. "Actually, I broke my vow of solitude and called Mordome Saturday morning. He would have been able to reassure you that I wasn't dead, as a matter of fact. I asked him to hurry up and take samples from the child you just found in the church, hoping he'd be able to identify traces of products in one of the little boy's three biological environments—blood, urine, and hair. It's incredibly complicated, as you know. Chemical submission substances affect different systems: GABAergic,[8] histaminic, dopaminergic, serotonergic . . . "

The macchiato arrived.

[8] Gamma-aminobutyric acid.

A little wink at the owner.

A Breton smile.

As RG spoke, Amédée couldn't help thinking that he would be a terrific recruit for the Fort. He was disciplined and hard-working, going so far as to take the time to study a science that was completely foreign to him, and memorizing some of the most obtuse terminology. Not only that, but the idea of helping Grimaud to overcome his solitude and sadness was not unappealing to the big sentimental lug that was Mallock.

"I don't know if you already know this," "Father Raymond" continued, "but what is now pompously called 'chemical submission' is an ancient practice. Datura powder[9] was used by a group of eighteenth-century bad guys calling themselves the 'Beguilers.' It happened here in Paris. They would politely offer tobacco that was mixed with Datura, and then they robbed their victims. Even back then, Datura had the double effect of causing unconsciousness and anterograde amnesia."[10]

Mallock looked at his watch. "I'm sorry, Raymond, I've got to run. The troops are waiting for me. Have you looked for suppliers?"

"Of course; we've done the rounds of 'purveyors' and other 'prescribers.' Who had the ability to manufacture this mixture? Are we talking about a lab technician in a pharmaceutical company? A doctor in a hospital, or even just a nurse?"

"Well?"

"Now it's a matter of time and patience. If you don't want to draw any attention to yourself, you calmly collect active molecules, and boom, it's done. Anyone working in the medical

---

[9] The first mentions of the term *dhattūra* are found in Sanskrit texts, notably in the treatise on the art of living and sexuality the *Kâma Sutra*. Known for its psychotropic properties, its alkaloids act by blocking the parasympathetic nervous system and are categorized as hallucinogenic drugs.

[10] The inability to memorize new facts, and thus to learn. Also called fixation amnesia.

industry could do it. None of the components are too strictly regulated except the ones that are categorized as kappa-opioid receptors, opiates, and parasympatholytics. But even then, a person could get his hands on them."

"None of this helps us very much."

RG scratched his superb white goatee violently. "Sorry, Mallock. I wish I had better news for you. But we can at least say that a person who isn't in the medical field, and has no knowledge of chemistry, would have a very hard time manufacturing this cocktail. That narrows it down a little bit at least, doesn't it?"

He was right. It was a small victory. Amédée put a ten-euro bill on the table, thanked his colleague warmly, and promised to keep him "up to speed" before disappearing once again into the snow.

By the time he arrived at the Fort, drank a coffee, swallowed an assortment of pills for his migraine and his back, drank another coffee, and read his emails while sucking anti-heartburn tablets, it was eleven o'clock. Ken, Jules, and Julie breezed into his office, followed immediately by Bob and Francis. Even though he hated it, Mallock was showered with wishes for "a happy and healthy New Year," as well as the traditional jokes about how ineffective the previous year's wishes had been. It didn't matter; they all loved being together. It was an odd atmosphere, somewhere between a family reunion and the briefing of commandos before an armed attack on enemy territory.

"They've found the solution to your . . . ahem, ecclesiastical puzzle," announced Ken triumphantly.

Julie, who was undoubtedly the reason the riddle had been solved, couldn't resist ribbing Mallock a bit. "See, boss, you should always send us on a mission on vacation, to an island, if possible. It revives all our dead brain cells. The grey matter, I mean." Even as she teased her superintendent, Julie's expression was affectionate.

"I see you've also proceeded with the standard trade-in of other cells," retorted Mallock. "Parisian squamous cells and keratinocytes."

Jules and Julie were both attractive and tanned, and it was a pleasure to look at them. She was a slim, petite brunette; he tall, blond, and solidly built. Beneath his inner-city wrestler's appearance the latter had the heart and soul—if not the manners—of a gentleman. Julie was a woman of rare refinement and intelligence combined with strong moral fiber. Jules was even-tempered, while Julie could be moody. Her Corsican roots and close, strict family explained the latter, while his gentle Béarnese parents accounted for the former. They both had the same deep-blue eyes and the same short-cropped hair.

Even as he harangued his team on a daily basis, Amédée lived in perpetual fear that something would happen to them. None of the five, except possibly Julie, knew how much their mercurial and visionary superintendent cared about them. Mallock the Rock, inflexible and upright, had a heart as mushy as a caramel at high noon in the Gobi desert. The big softie couldn't keep himself from smiling, despite the seriousness of the moment, because it was rare to see them all together, and because he had a major announcement for them. He chuckled in anticipation.

He knocked on his desk to get their attention. "I've got some big news for you. I think I've solved—for the most part—the case of the Makeup Artist."

Silence. Open mouths. Raised eyebrows. Nobody moved.

"Since the very beginning I've been asking myself one question. What could he possibly be doing with all that blood? Of course, like you I imagined morbid things, from Bloody Marys to sausage to sorbet."

"Like you," he says! Julie Gemoni gazed at him with a smile

at the corner of her mouth. She hadn't, in fact, imagined those things. She admired her boss, but he was a sicko. Ice in his veins. *A sausage sorbet?*

"And what if all those horrible rituals were only there to hide something more mundane?" Mallock continued. "What if we went back to the main motive for most crimes, the lure of money?"

Quicker than the others as usual, Julie leapt in: "Could they be contract killings? The work of one or more professional killers hiding their activity behind a cloud of smoke . . . or in this case, a curtain of blood. We'd need to review the whole case from a different angle—the settling of scores."

Mallock smiled at her. "Not a bad thought, but that isn't it."

"Have you really figured it out?" Ken was a bit taken aback.

"I'll give you the short version," Mallock said. "I went to the EFS[11] and called the IRCGN,[12] our friends and colleagues across the road. Here's a little math for you: €5,000 for one liter, and approximately five liters per person. That gives us around twenty-five thousand euros. What does that tell you?

Stupefied silence.

"Blood trafficking!" gasped Ken. "We hadn't thought of that, but it's so obvious! It's the only thing that was taken."

"I'm speechless," said Bob. "It's unbelievable."

Julies and Julie stood openmouthed. No one had imagined this kind of scenario for a single second, but now it seemed so clear. "And so typical of our world," murmured Julie, still in shock.

"A band of vampires," put in Francis.

"Shit. Unbelievable," repeated Bob.

"What's even more unbelievable," interrupted Amédée, "is

[11] French Blood Agency.
[12] Forensic Sciences Institute of the French Gendarmerie.

that I can still wind you up. No; it's not blood trafficking, my little chickens. But I had that theory checked, and it could have been. This is all to remind you how necessary it is to keep an open mind. You should have thought of that scenario. Like RG, who, by the way, still can't talk about the Makeup Artist in the plural. For him this was a single serial killer, period. In a case as important and complicated as this one, we can't leave any stone unturned. Imagine the mess if we overlook the one theory that could lead us to the culprit, singular or plural, who's killing hand over fist at this very moment. We're the last bastion here, kiddies. Us! Look around you; there's no one else. Shit! It's up to us to find him. It's our fucking job, and our fucking responsibility!"

Mallock felt anger rising within him. He knew it was due to his rage at not having been able to prevent the latest murder. This feeling of powerlessness shouldn't be redirected, much less taken out on his team. He swallowed his exasperation and continued, more calmly:

"Blood and organs are stolen mostly in poor countries. The director of the IRCGN told me on the phone that the last major case involved a group of rabbis in New Jersey who were buying kidneys to resell them. But here, in our case, stealing blood—and making sure the source wouldn't talk, every time—would be too dangerous, and not at all profitable."

Uneasiness. Deep silence.

"Hey now, I'm not the cynical one! It's the world we live in, my little ones."

In the face of his chief inspectors' uncomfortable expressions, Mallock decided to change tack. "Let's move on to something else. What have you found for me about those mysterious letters? Or the ecclesiastical enigma, as Ken so aptly put it? My chapel?"

"It'll be 'Cazenave' most likely; they were a big-name machine-tool manufacturer in the past. Does that mean anything to you? You'd pass the factory if you took the northern highway. It's just across from the big stadium. It fits with your AZ and AV. The factory isn't used anymore, but I contacted the real estate agency in charge of the complex. We can get the keys from them and go have a look at it. But what am I looking for, if it isn't too indiscreet to ask?"

Mallock dodged the question. "Are you sure? It's a factory?"

"Yeah; right near the La Chapelle metro station. Why?"

La Chapelle. It fit. Amédée couldn't hold back a small smile. Once again it hadn't been a vision, but an exaggerated form of deduction. He had passed the factory on his way back from dinner last Friday night. He remembered it now. He'd felt vaguely uncomfortable as he drove past it, suspecting a break-in or some kind of . . . unclean squatter. His mind had registered, drawn on the window of the large brick building, the silhouette of an impaled body and the two broken windows on either side of it, and part of a logo. Those letters and that brief glimpse had come back to him in his waking dream. The second vision he'd had when on the illicit substances had allowed him to connect the Makeup Artist's first attempt at impalement, the one Mordome had described, to the drawing on the window.

"Okay! Let's summarize. We've got sixteen murders, having in common the makeup on the victims, their specific beauty—see Francis about that; their blood being drained, the use of pancuronium bromide mixed with other curariform drugs to immobilize them, and tortures that we've classified as theological and retributive. I've verified it for two other crime scenes and I can also confirm now that there are definitely three distinct locations at each murder site. The middle location is used for part of the torture, but most importantly it's also used for a specific act, and it's where we find the traces of holes. And yes, I think I figured out the origin of those marks last night. I think they're made by a tripod. The Makeup Artist takes a series of photos, with painstaking care. Why? It's your job to find out. One more thing—the file must not leave these premises under any circumstances."

"'Retributive'?" asked Jules.

"Retribution is positive or negative. The good are rewarded, the bad are punished; put it that way," explained Julie.

Mallock nodded in approval before setting Francis's booklet in front of the pair. "This is a piece of visual interplay involving the victims. It'll show you what we've discovered as a common point."

Already headed out the door, he called to Ken: "Come on, hurry up; we're going to have a look at this Cazenave at La Chapelle."

18

Monday, January 3rd. Afternoon

Fifteen minutes later they were in Ken's old green Range Rover, headed through the Pleyel interchange toward Saint-Denis. First exit on the right off the highway, before the big curve leading to Bourget and Roissy. Then double back beneath the underpass.

The building was constructed of red brick. Three floors, with the logo painted in huge letters on the façade, and at the very top, two broken windows flanking a larger one with the profile of an impaled body outlined on it. This was what Mallock had seen as he drove past the other night, and he no longer had any doubt that the Makeup Artist had deliberately prepared these windows to attract attention.

And maybe my attention in particular? Amédée thought suddenly.

But how could he have known that Mallock would pass by here? What did the killer already know about him? One more reason to be paranoid. Why this place? Was it possible that he had chosen it for Mallock, knowing that he regularly drove this route when he went to dinner with his friends in Senlis? Or, even worse, was the superintendent being watched? Maybe the Makeup Artists had even more power than the police feared.

While Amédée tortured himself, Ken struggled with the keys, which gave him the perfect opportunity to use a few choice swear words in pseudo-Japanese—one of the comedy bits that always amused his friends. A dozen onomatopoeias later, he made a satisfied noise and stepped aside to let Mallock pass.

"After you, boss!"

The two men stepped into a lofty 1950s-style entry hall. To the left, behind a wide glass window, was a standard switchboard of the period. In front of them an enormous staircase wound up and off to each side, like a poor man's Château de Chambord. On the right, an army-green metal door was marked "Workshop." Ken immediately tried to open it. There was a fresh batch of curses, in French this time, and then the door was finally heaved open by Ken, who was laden with an enormous bunch of keys that must have weighed a good couple of pounds.

They found themselves on the factory floor, where half a century ago teams of specialized laborers had assembled machine tools invented by a mysterious HB, whose portrait could still be seen here and there. Cazenave was one of the many companies pushed to ruin and the unemployment of its workers by the arrival of the forces of progress in 1981. The smell of machine oil still mingled with that of the dust that had built up during the place's long years of abandonment. Turning to the left, Mallock found himself facing an assembly floor that was much different than the one in his dream. There was actually nothing to see. Beside him, Ken stepped forward, his forehead creased. Mallock caught his sleeve to hold him back.

"Look at the floor. It's covered with dust, everywhere, except for this one set of footprints."

"Just one set? No prints coming back out?"

Mallock sighed. "Let's each grab two pallets. We'll put them on the floor in front of us and walk on them. We'll have to look for some other ones. Everyone coming in here has to use them. We'll have a closer look at these footprints later."

They began moving awkwardly, bending to pick up the pallets behind them and set them down in front of their feet, stepping onto them, picking up the now-free pallets behind them, and so on and so on. They kept looking around at each step, trying to get a better grasp on the precise nature of the horror that seemed to be waiting for them at the far end of the huge space—maybe a duplication of the drawing of an impaled body on the front window of the building.

The trail of footprints they were following disappeared abruptly, as if the man making them had taken flight. Ken thought of a vampire's ability to turn into a bat. What new sorcery was this? The spectacle that awaited them pushed that question to the back burner. They continued creeping forward. In the very back of the workshop, in an area lighted by a hole in a wide transom, there finally appeared, bathed in pallid light, the impaled body of a woman.

Just like in Mallock's dream, or very close to it.

On the edge of a small red lake, surrounded by dust, Ken stopped, his face turned toward the Makeup Artist's latest work. Turning around, his heart in his mouth, he saw that Mallock, eyes closed, had sat down—or rather, sunk to the floor—at the sight of the sacrifice.

No maniacal dance; no lance made of gold, here in this fucking horrible reality. Machiavellian and rational use had been made, though, of mechanical hoists. The body had been moved using the network of pulleys, rails, and electric motors that covered the ceiling. When the Makeup Artist had finished with his victim, he had raised her into the air until she dangled vertically over the post set upright in the concrete floor. Once she was there he had undoubtedly taken some photos, and then let her literally plummet from the sky with a scream of terror.

Had he continued to photograph her?

Did he have specific prayers that he intoned at these times? A pact of contrition; a satanic mass; a reading of some diabolical Gospels? Mallock was sure, in any case, that the bastard had felt incredible excitement at seeing the iron rod penetrate between the legs of the poor woman, ripping her flesh. With a wet sound, the bar, after having torn through her internal organs, had risen up between her jaws, breaking her teeth. The body had suddenly stopped moving, impaled from vagina to mouth.

But in this horror, this macabre, disgusting, unbearable, revolting tableau, this scene to make a person weep with sadness and rage, vomit with hatred and repulsion, in this filthy spectacle of perverted obscenity and unspeakable viciousness, there was something beautiful, something horribly erotic.

Mallock, in a trance, opened his eyes to see Ken's worried face. "I'm fine, I'm fine," he said sharply, standing up and refusing the hand Ken held out to assist him.

The martyred woman rose scarlet and hieratic before the two horrified men. Her skin was yellow and waxy. Her partially oxidized blood covered the curves of her belly and breasts. Her body, as taut as a bow, seemed almost like it was part of the steel pike running it through. The metal thrust out of her mouth, in front of her light-blue eyes, which were open and staring at the ceiling. Her thighs, spread apart by the metal bar, were frozen in an impossible position. The bastard had wound a Christmas garland around the corpse from head to feet. Connected to an electrical outlet by a long white cord, its lights blinked weakly. A dark puddle the size of a football field spread across the floor.

For once, Mallock didn't have to wonder what the Makeup Artist had done with all the blood.

Time passed.

Men came.

They all looked, their eyes raised to heaven, for lack of a better alternative. Many gritted their teeth in anger and disgust. Repulsion. The kind of primal fear you feel when facing cannibal souls.

Before leaving, Mallock instructed that a whole sophisticated search procedure be put in place, almost like an archaeological dig. Nothing could be overlooked. "I want you to sift through the dust," he said. Then he turned his back on the busy men, on the impaled woman, on the *something* that had kept on rising in him since the beginning of this whole thing, which he refused to identify.

Behind the outrage and the anger a morbid fascination was hiding, throbbing, growing stronger and stronger with every murder, every corpse. Something else he would never be able to forgive himself for.

Stepping outside the factory, Mallock raised his head to look at the drawing and the two broken windows on either side of it. He took this route three times a month, and he always braked right before the big curve in the highway. The Makeup Artist had wanted to get his attention. It was obvious now.

Mallock took the highway toward Paris. He thought about Ken, saw again his face, his disbelief, his suffering. A car passed him and he had time to see a little boy smiling at him, nose pressed against the frosty rear window.

His mood shifted away from anguish and sadness, flitting from this unknown child to his own, vanished boy. Tom would never grow up. Never again stand in the sun; never again fall asleep at night. At that moment, watching him sleep was the only thing that could have calmed Mallock's rage and soothed his horror. But Tom wasn't here anymore.

Hadn't Tom escaped life? Escaped what men do to get revenge for being born, too much of this or not enough of that?

Eight-thirty. Amélie was waiting for him. He realized with

dismay that he'd completely forgotten their appointment. He babbled excuses, convinced that nothing could absolve him of such a mortal sin.

But Amélie didn't feel that way.

"Don't worry about it. It gave me the time to have a nice cup of tea in the square and rest a little bit between clients."

It occurred to Mallock that he didn't like it at all when Amélie referred to him as a client. And he liked it even less when he was lumped together with the client before him and the one after him.

"Do you still have time, or should we reschedule?"

"I have time. I've got the whole evening, actually. I cancelled my next appointment, which was the last one of the day."

Opening the front door for her, Amédée apologized to Amélie again. It really was not needed.

"You've never been late before, and I'm sure you must have a good reason," she said. The image of the impaled woman flashed through Mallock's mind. It was a good excuse, he thought, but there was no way he could talk about it with such a lovely and delicate girl.

"Not really," he lied eventually. "Just paperwork to sign."

He felt dreadfully dirty as they entered his apartment. The day's sweat, of course, but also the dust and grime of the factory—and, worse, the smells of the deceased, of female decomposition. The microscopic scarlet stars of her blood flying up in the factory's air to fall back down onto her hair, her eyelashes, her lips. Alone, he would have fallen apart already. But with Amélie there . . .

It was a bit uncomfortable, but he had to ask. "Would you just give me a few minutes? I absolutely have to have a shower."

Amélie acquiesced with a smile, reassuring him: "Don't worry. I'm used to it. Especially at the end of the day, and with older people."

Mallock took the last sentence as an insult, which wasn't how Amélie had intended it. Realizing her blunder, she hurried to explain. "I don't mean you! It isn't like that with you . . . "

Amédée reassured her by laughing and claiming he hadn't thought she was talking about him. He left to take a shower, but not without supplying Amélie with tea and cakes first.

The water streamed over his body, washing away the particles of filth. He watched them whirl around the drain as if trying to avoid being drowned, these drops of blood, drunk with rage at being evicted this way. He even imagined he could hear them screaming.

When he returned to the living room ten minutes later, Amélie was standing in front of the bay window. She hadn't turned on the big light and was in almost complete darkness. Two streetlamps glowed in the courtyard outside, and the perfection of her body was outlined for Mallock in silhouette.

She was gorgeous.

He came up behind her and put his big hands on her shoulders. Amélie didn't turn around. She did the one thing Amédée wanted most; she tilted her head slowly to the side until her cheek touched his right hand. He pressed gently against her and kissed her neck.

At around two o'clock in the morning, Amélie Maurel embraced him one last time. She had to get back. Amédée didn't ask why.

After she had gone, Mallock slept like a rock. In his dreams, a messenger came down to see him on the beach at Andernos-les-Bains.

The celestial angel looked like a combination of a manatee and a dolphin, but he couldn't really see its body; only its face, iridescent and disturbing. They began walking together along the shore, side by side, Mallock and the big, transparent figure.

Only the four parallel prints of their feet in the sand behind them attested to the angel's presence on earth. He told the angel about all his pain and anger. The despair that was stiffening his back and his soul. He screamed out his sadness, the feeling of injustice eating away at his heart. Thomas gone. His fears. The greed and jealousy of men. All his anger against God. He released his tears, his resentment; the ache gnawing at his heart. Then, suddenly, he realized that the large transparent being wasn't answering him anymore. Filled with apprehension, he turned. There was only one trail of footprints left behind him, his own steps. They were sunk deeper into the sand, weighed down by his pain, but they were alone.

He lifted his eyes toward the sky, begging for an explanation. Why had his companion disappeared? The angel spoke. It was still there, just a few centimeters from his ear.

"I'm always here," it said. "Can't you feel my arms around you? These deep prints in the sand were made by my feet, not yours.

"If there is only one set, it's because I am carrying you."

19

Tuesday, January 4th

Amédée woke with a start. For an agnostic, he'd had a lot to do with religion lately. He identified the source of his dream immediately: a Brazilian poem a friend had recited to him. But did it also have another meaning, a coded message related to the investigation? He put it to one side of his mind, to think about later. This morning he needed to focus on the torture, and the different theories and rituals surrounding it. After what he'd seen yesterday, he wanted to do some research on stakes, partly by consulting two books by Léon Bloy, which he'd already been thinking about for a a few days.

Looking through them, he stumbled on a rare example of a weekly magazine called—it was almost too perfect—*The Stake*. The cover of this issue, the third one edited by Bloy, showed four men impaled on a single rod. Examining their positions carefully, Amédée saw that the man closest to the ground was curled in the fetal position, staring at the ground. The man above him was beginning to look at the clouds, and the third man's gaze was turned toward the sky. The fourth man was extending his arms toward God. It was a perfect illustration of reversibility, the link between individual torture and collective salvation. The Makeup Artist was undoubtedly an insane mystic modeled on Bloy—only he had shifted from words to action.

It was almost eight o'clock. If he was going to get any further in his research he needed to see one person: Léon. Not the writer; the other one, his friend with the bookshop. He hesitated for a few moments. He really wanted to show Léon the photos taken at the different murder scenes, to get his opinion on them. But hadn't his friend lived through enough horror?

The best thing to do, he finally decided, was ask Léon.

Key. Door. Run. Cross the little square.

Léon was already outside. Having already shoveled the snow from the sidewalk in front of his shop, he was now scattering handfuls of coarse salt.

"Your timing is perfect, Superintendent! Mind giving me a hand? A lady with a walker and no teeth fell down yesterday, right where you're standing." Without waiting for a response, Léon handed him a plastic bag filled with grayish grains. Mallock was in a rush, but courtesy won out. It took them five minutes to complete the task.

"You came to see me?" asked Léon as they went into the shop.

"No, I just had an urge to scatter some salt on the Parisian asphalt."

"Okay, okay. New question: would the superintendent care for a little coffee?"

"A big one, actually, please. And a favor."

Mallock asked Léon if he felt able to look at the Makeup Artist's horrors, to discuss his tortures. The answer that came back was clear and concise and brooked no argument.

"Don't be an idiot."

So as not to influence him, Mallock displayed the various photos, including the one of the baby, without making any comment. Time slowed down. Mallock sat down in a deep armchair, suddenly patient. Léon picked up the snapshots one by one. He studied them calmly, sometimes with a magnifying glass. The proceedings took around fifteen minutes. Amédée, sipping his coffee, never took his eyes off Léon's face.

"So?" he asked, when the bookseller had set down the last picture.

"So . . . so. It's not clear." Léon rubbed the corners of his eyes.

"Is that all? You've studied this subject for a long time. It's that culture of suffering, inflicted voluntarily by one person on another, that I need your help with. I know it's not clear, as you say. If it were I wouldn't be here."

Léon clasped his hands behind his neck. Took a deep breath. Held it. Looked at the ceiling with a perplexed frown. Released the air in his lungs with a sigh. "You want me to give you a lesson *ex cathedra*, is that it?"

"I don't care. Talk to me. Tell me everything that's going through your head. Do you think there are multiple types of torture happening here? Do you think it's the same person? Do you see different reasons for going to such extremes?"

"Ah, that; yes, there are many reasons for torturing a fellow human being. And believe me, mankind has a hell of an imagination for constantly coming up with new ones. Even morality can be twisted for this purpose."

"Meaning?"

"Let's say you capture a guy who's planted a bomb on the metro. Do you talk to him nicely or do you burn his balls to make him talk before women and children are blown to bits all over the tiles? What does the good cop do in this case, eh?"

"Look, this isn't what I need from you right now. No philosophy lessons."

"I just wanted to make you understand that nothing is simple, even when you're talking about torture. There's more than one way to look at the subject. The number one reason to torture someone, if I can say it, is to get information. The army, the police, and intelligence organizations use it for that. You'll find all kinds of books about it—I've even got some here—but I don't think they'd apply to your raging madman. The second reason is to obtain confessions and religious conversions, like during the inquisitions, with all the lovely methods introduced

in the twelfth century by everyone's favorite funnyman, Pope
Innocent III. Right here in the shop I've got the *Malleus
Maleficarum, Le Marteau des sorcières*—reprinted in paper-
back, not expensive; *Le Manuel des Inquisiteurs*, and the
Histoire de l'Inquisition au Moyen Âge. I'll put them aside for
you."

"And the third reason?"

"The third? Ah yes . . . thirdly, we have the kind of pure,
unadulterated torture that is practiced for the simple pleasure
of making others suffer: sadism and bondage. I've got books
on that too, of course. A great set of volumes on basic sado-
masochism and onanism. I've got *S&M for Dummies* on
order," Léon joked, before turning serious again. "It's quite
possible that your Makeup Artist falls into this category. I can't
really see him doing what he does unless he finds it exciting."

"Me neither," murmured Mallock.

"And to these three," resumed Léon, "we can add a fourth
reason, a really crazy one. The aesthetics of torture. I have
books on the work of Soutine and Goya here. You should definitely have a look at *Saturn Devouring his Son*, which is really
something, and of course Bosch. Your Makeup Artist is
absolutely staging scenes here, which we can imagine are motivated by some kind of artistic desire. There is a certain aesthetic appeal, if not beauty, in what you've shown me."

Amédée looked at Léon, feeling something almost like
relief. He felt some emotion at seeing these horrifying perversions too, then. Now he could ask the question that had been
burning in him since he woke up. "I think there's another
intention at work here . . . something more mystical about what
he's doing. Don't you see a theological aspect to these sacrifices? The sanctifying value of pain?"

"The sacrality of the torturer, eh? His redemptive function?
Regenerative bloodshed? The splendor of 'the Massacre of the
innocents, the rain of rosy blood that kills only the tenderest of

bodies'? I know the whole thing by heart: 'They will go nearby, preparing for the killing on the next horizon, where millions of soldiers crouch, drawn by their metal affinity toward the masses of throat-slitters. It will be the Pentecost of slaughter and extermination, the cleansing of excessive and crumbling societies by fire . . . ' I've read and reread Léon Bloy a thousand times. You see, Amédée, I was even named after him. My father was one of that great insane mystic's few admirers. You're right; I should have thought of that. There is definitely some Bloy in these images of . . . piety turned upside down . . . it's the dogma of reversibility. In his madness, your Makeup Artist must really be convinced that he's participating in the salvation of the world. He undoubtedly believes in the Mystical Body. The only thing he hasn't done yet is impale one of his victims!"

Mallock stared openmouthed at his friend. "Why do you say that?"

"For Bloy, that's the ultimate torture. Perfection. You also find it with Bosch, and the precision he uses to inflict on the eye of the spectator—who might also be a penitent himself— the inexhaustible variety of sins, and of the sinners who have these punishments to look forward to if they don't repent. All these characters being boiled alive, drowned in barrels, dismembered. And for the most deserving: *'The indisputable beauty of the stake surpasses all in its symbolism. From the perspective of the aesthetic torturer, besides the incandescence of the tool, its verticality is vital. The man must be upright, and he must die from the bottom up.'* I can't guarantee that my memory is one hundred percent accurate, but at any rate that's not far off the original text. Against the tautological and spiraling circularity of a society that has become a howling pile of shit, soulless and helpless in a rising tide of mediocrity, the stake's verticality is, for Bloy, the sanctifying stopping point, the new axis around which society is called to change direction. It's the exclamation point that comes after the screamed-out word 'Stop.' But why does it surprise you that I mentioned the stake?"

"The most recent victim, who I haven't had a chance to tell you about yet, was impaled."

Now it was Léon's turn to stand openmouthed. "Impaled vertically?"

"Exactly. But I have to go now; I need to see the murder site near La Chapelle again, and finish my observations."

"Good God," murmured Léon, still in the grip of emotion.

There were two problems to solve: how had the Makeup Artist impaled the young woman, and how had he managed to erase his footprints on the floor?

For the first question, the technicians were theorizing that the impalement had been done horizontally, on the floor, and then the whole thing raised upright. This clearly suggested a group of killers. Two, or most likely three, the experts had estimated. But then there was Mallock's vision. He had seen her dropped violently from the air to be impaled on a pike that was already set in the floor. True, it had only been in his dream, but he was beginning to trust those experiences more and more.

He tried to combine the two puzzles in his mind; the mysterious method of impalement, and the miraculously disappearing footprints. It often happened like this; two "impossibles" could somehow be put together to create a "possible," like the technique where magicians force their audience to resolve one question while at the same time discouraging them by moving on rapidly to a different question.

Deductive reasoning led him to the spot on the floor where the Makeup Artist's footprints suddenly disappeared. As it turned out, he only needed to look up to find the answer. There, high overhead, was the start of the network of chains, motors, pulleys, and hoists that ran along the factory ceiling to be used for moving towers and the heaviest machine parts from one place to another. In all likelihood, it was this vertical and horizontal hydraulic lift that the Makeup Artist—Mallock was beginning to lean toward the singular—had used to mystify the police yet again. To further muddy the waters, before the machinery set him down he had programmed it to conceal itself at the farthest end of the factory. Even now, you could only see the horizontal rails above the footprints and the site of the sacrifice.

Amédée bent over the last two footprints. One right foot, one left foot. They were blurred. So his dream had pointed him in the right direction—unless it was the power of his conscious thoughts that had supplied the material for the dream. The chicken or the egg? Whatever the case, it had led him to the solution once again.

The Makeup Artist had arrived at the . . . takeoff site, for lack of a better word . . . carrying his victim. Then he had come back to the same spot and left the room walking backward. Mallock recreated the rest of the process in his mind. Vibration of the electric motor. Nathalie Grandet—that had been the victim's name—had felt her arms rising. Her body, attached to the freight hoist, had been lifted four meters above the floor and carried through the icy air of the factory. When she had finally realized what the monster had in mind, it was too late. Her brain fuddled with terror, she had heard the motor stop; she was suspended above the steel pike. Then the monster had released her and she had plunged downward with a scream of horror.

I'm so sorry, little Nathalie. Forgive me!

Disgusted and ashamed, Mallock prayed for the young woman as he dragged a box to the center of the factory and sat down on it, lit a cigar, drained the flask of whiskey he had brought, and tried to put himself in the killer's place.

What had the bastard done next?

If he really wanted to have a chance at understanding, Amédée would have to lose all sense of morals or moderation and become nothing but impulse. Walk up to his darkest thoughts and then keep going forward, again and always, to where the earth was flesh, the ocean blood, and the skies made of shit. Where chaos and ignorance played together, laughing in all directions. He would have to go to this mutual *there*, this collective junk pile, this hard-packed noxious magma, if he ever wanted to find the killer.

He got back to Paris at around seven o'clock. Amélie was waiting for him, sitting in the same place as yesterday evening, on the terrace of the same café. Amélie again. *Amélie for always?* Mallock asked himself.

Love. Tongues flicking everywhere, mindlessly, all over. Butterflies. Lips and kisses, like an army of little fish. Vibrations and shivers. The skin speaking, the mind going silent. The body taking over, moving as it liked. No mooring lines, no compass but the cock, stretching and thrusting straight ahead . . . and the waves, and the wind!

At two o'clock in the morning, like on the previous night, with Mallock not daring to ask her why, Amélie left quickly. The day had been emotionally draining, and he fell immediately back into a deep sleep. He began to dream. His son came back home. He was taller, and his hair had grown. With tears in his eyes, he ran into his father's arms.

"I'm sorry, Papa, I didn't mean to make you sad!"

Then he began telling Mallock everything he had done while he was away.

"I thought you were dead," babbled Amédée in his sleep.

"But I am dead, Papa."

To prove his point, Tom began to tear off big pieces of his own skin, ripping out chunks of the rotting flesh that covered his face with astonishing ease. His skull and the bones of his jaw were luminous white. Clean and pure. He only had a small spot of orange pus left on his right cheekbone. Mallocked wiped it away delicately using a handkerchief corner moistened with saliva.

"Thank you, Papa," said Thomas.

Then he had begun sticking pieces of a mask made of flesh back onto his skull, a mask modeled to look like his face from before. When he was finished, he asked: "Where is the bathroom? I need to wash up, freshen up a little."

He was holding Amélie's big makeup kit. A pool of fat beige worms squirmed at his feet.

Mallock woke at four o'clock in the morning, covered in cold sweat. How did Amélie's makeup kit figure into this whole thing? Did it symbolize the petite nurse, his new love? He decided to stick with that explanation. Still upset, he went into the bathroom, using the same square of toilet paper, folded in half, to wipe away his tears and blot a drop of urine that splashed on the seat.

He went back to sleep with the feeling that he would wake up smack in the middle of a battlefield, with bullets flying in every direction, and one of them would lodge right in his head with a noise like a seagull's shriek.

Which was exactly what happened.

I t was almost nine o'clock by the time Mallock got to Number 36. For once it seemed like the whole world had woken up earlier than him: the journalists hanging out in the lobby, the furious judge, the impatient big boss, all the way up to the Secretary of the Interior, who had gone so far as to call him personally. He and Mallock had known each for a long time and had a mutual respect for one another, kind of like two brother bears do until the day they come to blows.

Mallock's whole team was on deck. The mission of the day was to finish summarizing the different listings. The place was a madhouse, with printers shrieking in agony and Julie trying to orchestrate the whole thing. He decided to leave them alone and shut himself in his office.

At exactly noon, he had to hold a press conference organized by the higher-ups. In the pressroom he found himself dropped in front of a bristling forest of microphones. The trap had been set and there was no way he could extricate himself. Mallock would avenge himself by not making the reporters' job an easy one. He stood with his hands in his pockets, taking a fiendish pleasure in alternating "nothing really new" with "at this stage of the investigation I can't comment on that," "as soon as . . . " and "*I realize that and I understand, but . . .* "

It was tit for tat, with the press, for its part, alternating between "What is the government doing?" "Have you been pressured?" and the famous "The public has the right to know." As if the press gave a fuck about the public. Mallock only thought it silently, but so strongly that the whole room knew how he felt.

"How many victims are there exactly?" was the question repeated most often. The more deaths there were, the wider the audience would be. They were shooting for a record. Not just to sell copies or boost viewing numbers, but also so they could all bathe together in the cathartic water of this modern-day Ganges, the media. A crime like this would make all others pardonable, the major and minor sins committed by everyone else. They were professional hypocrites, making themselves unworthy so they could try to be worthy. Greedy for a clean conscience but empty of any true kindness.

These were the things Mallock thought about at times like this.

Fortunately, his contempt had the effect of keeping him silent as he endured this scene of human baseness. The quietest people are often the ones holding back from screaming out their rage, or hurling bombs. Mallock—even though he was a superintendent, even though he held the door for women and helped elderly people cross the street—was one of those people.

At the very end, like you might toss a rotting carcass to the sharks, Amédée gave the reporters one or two bits of information, along with a few salacious details. They scribbled notes, recorded, filmed. Their shining eyes, wet lips, and satisfied greediness were a lovely sight.

He got back to his office at around one o'clock, armed with a traditional ham-and-butter baguette and the beer that goes with it. Next to his telephone he found the chart with the contents of the victims' address books listed in rows. His team had done their job and left their offering on the altar of their holy superintendent, and now, famished, they'd gone off in search of a restorative lunch.

Mallock decided not to wait for them before familiarizing himself with the lists. He settled himself comfortably in his chair. Very quickly, his expression changed. The document's conclusions were so shocking that he had to reread them several times. Aside from the phone numbers of a few well-known administrative offices, a single name appeared in several address books.

Just one name!

And what a name!

Utterly stunned, he threw the report across his office, as if by doing so he could just forget about it and move on to something else. But reality is stubborn, and the facts were staggering. The implications of what he had just discovered struck him right in the heart.

He was still struggling with his thoughts half an hour later, when Ken, Francis, and Julie returned.

"Have you read it? It fits pretty well, eh boss?"

It was Ken who had spoken. Francis was next to him, nodding in excited agreement. Strangely, Julie was silent.

"When we saw the results we did a background check on her. She lives alone. According to her building manager she had a very conflicted relationship with her mother before she died."

"The mother died around six years ago," put in Francis. "The same time that the murders started."

"And as a health-care professional," Ken interrupted, "she'd know all about syringes. And—get this, we kept the best part for last—other than the injections, what's her favorite hobby?"

Amédée didn't really want to guess. Ken, sensing this, went on without waiting for an answer.

"Mademoiselle Amélie Maurel is a stage-makeup artist!"

"Specializing in tranvestites," finished Francis with a flourish, smiling.

Hearing these last three syllables pronounced with so much glee, covered in depravity and blood, was unbearable. That magical, adored name—her name—the very one he had held in his arms all night. But wait . . . no. Not quite all night. She'd left at two in the morning both times. Where had she gone after that? Home, he told himself weakly, not really believing it.

He remembered his conversation with Mordome: "Besides the twelve ceremonial punctures, I've found other needle marks, all grouped on the little girl's thighs. She must have had some kind of daily treatment, probably for diabetes. The urine analysis will confirm that." . . . "Did she give herself the shots?" . . . "Not at her age; it would have been the parents, or maybe a nurse."

As if she could hear Mordome speaking in her boss's head, Julie spoke up. "We've confirmed that the little Modiano girl was receiving daily treatment. Insulin shots for diabetes."

Ken and Francis both nodded in agreement. An unexpected silence followed. Except for Julie, who suspected something, they were anticipating well-deserved congratulations from their boss. Mallock, though, was stunned.

The coincidence was unbearably cruel. When he recovered his wits, it was to chew out his poor lieutenants, who were incredulous and appalled at so much ungratefulness.

"I don't want anything but facts and proof! Nothing else! This is nothing but a bunch of goddamn idiotic conjecture!"

Mallock had stood up behind his desk so he could scream at them more effectively. He gesticulated furiously for a good two minutes, like a caricature of an angry boss. Then, abruptly, conscious of his men's stupefied expressions and the ridiculousness of his own behavior, he broke off his tirade, like a shower suddenly running out of water.

At the same moment, his phone rang. Mallock made a grab

for it, incredibly happy for the distraction. He listened silently, leaning on his free hand, and suddenly remembered the telescopic lampposts at the Louvre. On the other end of the line, a guy from the INPS was confirming that his intuition had been spot-on. There was a partial fingerprint on the syringe found beneath Madame Modiano's body, on the tip of the plunger. They would know more soon.

Mallock thanked the technician and hung up.

Then, feeling slightly guilty about his suspicions, he opened his wallet and carefully pulled out a business card—the one Amélie had given him. *"So you'll have my private number too, in case you want to reach me more easily,"* she had said, unable to stop herself from blushing.

"Ken, dust for prints on this card and compare them with the one on the syringe."

A look of confusion passed over Francis's face, but for once he knew to keep quiet. Ken took the card gingerly, using his tie to avoid adding his own fingerprints to it, or smearing the ones already there.

"Sure, boss." He had the wisdom not to say anything else, though the voice inside him wondered—loudly—how in the world a card with the murderer's fingerprints on it had ended up in their favorite chief superintendent's wallet. He suddenly remembered one of Mallock's nicknames, "the Wizard," and feeling a troubling mixture of respect and fear, he turned to obey the order he had just been given.

Mallock called him back. "Wait, Ken, have you seen Bob? Nothing new with the metro?"

"He told me two of the victims have been formally identified. Thanks to the Louvre's surveillance center we've even got visual confirmation. Both of them were seen with a priest—Bob will have mentioned that to you; the old-fashioned kind, with the cassock and the whole shebang. That's all he's got, for now."

"Tell him to add the latest victims to his collection and keep going."

"I'll do the fingerprints first and then I'll tell Bob."

Mallock threw his sandwich into the trash can and went off in search of something more substantial, ending up back at the Deux Palais. He needed noise and warmth. Not the kind at the Fort, but a restaurant, with its comforting smells of grilled meat and coffee. The boss was there and pounced on him, almost talkative:

"Mallock twice in one day! To what do I owe the honor?"

"Just hungry," lied Mallock, kissing his waitress, who was an old friend, on the cheek.

He sat and stared out the window at the falling snow for a good twenty minutes, barely touching his cassoulet.

"Not good?" asked the bar owner.

"Not hungry," admitted Mallock.

The knockout blow came when he returned to the office. The fingerprint found on the syringe's plunger matched the ones on Amélie's business card. The dactyloscopic characteristics left no room for doubt. The technician talked to him about dermal papillae in arches, inner loops, and whorls. He was sure of himself. There were more than nine points of similarity in the different ridges, including a pool with a very specific pattern.

There were two or three other possible ways of interpreting this information, but Amédée didn't even try. Everything pointed to Amélie as the perpetrator of these crimes. Or at least as an accomplice to one of them. Not only was he going to have to arrest her, but he would have to make her talk. For a second he thought about having himself taken off the investigation. There was clearly a conflict of interest here. And then some. A lot more. Infinitely more.

He stood frozen for a good fifteen minutes. Feelings and

impressions rushed at him chaotically. He had loved the hands, the fingers that had sewn an eight-year-old girl's mouth shut after disemboweling her. He had adored the face, the features that so many people had stared at with horror. The smile, the teeth that had bitten and amputated. Amédée still wanted to believe in her innocence, but Superintendent Mallock could not.

He barely made it to the bathroom before vomiting up a combination of bile and beer.

21

Wednesday afternoon, January 5th

At three o'clock, even though he didn't need a warrant to proceed with the arrest, Mallock put in a call to Judge Humbert. Hoping to avoid giving a detailed summary of the investigation, he began the conversation by announcing: "We've got the Makeup Artist. It's a female."

But it was obvious that the judge wanted to know everything. Did he have a journalist to tip off? Amédée managed to sidestep the request by promising to call him back as soon as the arrest had been made.

By four-fifteen everything was prepared to go and take the suspect into custody. Everyone was ready . . . except Mallock. Even though he had no personal doubts about the organization of the arrest, his intuition was screaming at him to delay it. Though he hadn't sensed anything, he who had rubbed elbows so often and so intimately with the investigation, there had to be another explanation for the wall of proof that had built up so suddenly. Maybe she was connected in one way or another, even innocently, to these crimes. He couldn't deny that anymore; doing so was pointless and no one would understand it, not even Mallock himself. The time for action was now, and— all things considered—it was better if it were Superintendent Mallock, her Amédée, who did the dirty deed.

Accompanied by a special armored police van crammed full of officers, the beginnings of a migraine, and four lieutenants, Amédée went to Amélie's house. He parked his car on the Rue de Rivoli and heaved a huge sigh of sadness and stress.

The fucking stations of the cross.

Which one had he gotten to, exactly? The crown of thorns?

The killer nurse lived above the pharmacy in the little square.

He entered, and barked without any other greeting: "Amélie Maurel, which floor?"

"Fourth," babbled the pharmacist, surprised at this lack of courtesy from her usually polite customer.

"Which way do I go?"

"Uh—go back outside, and it's the green door on the right. On the left, I mean, when you're facing the display window."

This at least earned the woman a "thank you," which was a minimal bit of civility from Mallock, who was usually more than kind.

They climbed the stairs and he rang the doorbell, slightly out of breath. He had never been to her apartment, and never imagined he'd see it for the first time under this kind of circumstance. After several fruitless tries, it seemed clear that she wasn't at home. But he had to be sure. The locksmith they had brought with them opened the door, which was secured with a simple twenty-year-old lock; no dead bolt, no armor shielding. Kind of odd for a paranoid monster. There was no one inside.

"We'll search the place later," said Mallock. "Stay here and wait for her. Be discreet. Arrest her quietly if she comes back before I do. Keep in mind that she's only a suspect; I'm counting on you. I'm going to get my car and run home while we wait. It's right nearby and I'm taking up unnecessary parking space in the street."

Mallock fled. He gave himself five minutes to park his beloved car in the private garage, stop by his apartment for some migraine tablets, and return to the little square on foot.

At the bottom of his parking garage, the wonderful smell of mushrooms made him yearn for the seaside or a vacation in the country. He backed his Jaguar into the parking space, cursing his idiotic neighbor, who was edging systematically out of the space assigned to him. He slammed the door of his car and ran toward the exit. The steep slope meant for cars exiting the garage extracted a few grimaces of discomfort from him. The pain brought Amélie back to his mind.

A whole battalion of police officers was waiting to pounce on her.

How could she be the sadistic piece of garbage he'd been hunting with such hate? Would she have had the physical strength to commit the crimes alone? In his heart he didn't believe it, but the facts weren't budging. She was an accomplice, at the very least. An accomplice to the murders of children? Impalement? Evisceration? By what hellish miracle? And what about her tenderness? Her incredible sweetness? Mallock knew that he wouldn't be able to handle all these contradictory feelings for very long before they destroyed him. He decided to double the dose of his antianxiety medication as soon as he got home. It wasn't really a reasonable thing to do, but the strain was too much. He had to do everything he could to stay calm and able to make decisions. It was just then, as he entered Baudoyer Square, that he had a flash of illumination— but it was so much in Amélie's favor that he questioned it for a few moments before deciding that he would accept its consequences.

And those consequences were enormous.

In the house in Saint-Mandé during his second visit, he had realized the extent of the murderer's mania and perfectionism. The killer had managed to move the body three times with enough fastidious cleanliness to fool the police. How could it be conceivable that this same person could be foolish enough to leave a syringe at the murder scene—especially in that specific spot under the corpse's back, which was nowhere near the place on the body where the blood-draining punctures had been made? It was impossible. Even better, this fact alone put Amélie in the clear. Because this act of concealment bore the obvious signs of being a trap, the trapped person was, *de facto*, eliminated as a suspect.

In front of his apartment building Mallock saw himself yesterday, in the same place, holding Amélie's hand. He had to stop the arrest. He was so tense that he tried to unlock his apartment door with the keys to his office—which jammed in the lock, of course, so that he couldn't turn them or even pull them out. He lost a precious minute extracting them and trying again with the right set of keys.

When he finally burst into his den, an icy breeze made the door slam shut behind him. He must have left a window cracked at the other end of the apartment. That was what he thought, at least, until he reached the kitchen. It wasn't a window in there but instead the service door, wide open. In a fraction of a second his revolver was in his hand. Never for a moment did he consider that he might have left the door open, or even that there had been a break-in. The air was filled with a smell—and with it came a terrifying certainty. The Makeup Artist—the hate-filled madman who had been haunting his days and his nights—was there, mere feet away from him, hiding in a room, or a corner, or even the service staircase. An image came into his mind of a sweaty little man, flabby if not fat, with tiny hands and a clumsy walk, his face gleaming like an oil-soaked sponge. The vision was horrifying, and Mallock steeled himself to search the rest of the apartment. His difficulty opening the door should have alerted him. Waves of cold sweat poured down his body. His hands were welded to his weapon, his right index finger poised on the trigger. When he finally reached the bedroom, the shock was so overpowering that his heart froze and he couldn't breathe.

Amélie lay on the floor in the middle of the room. Her face was painted with the Makeup Artist's grotesque work. Like a nightmarish Ophelia she was immersed in a pool of blood so dark that her body was reflected in it, as if she were levitating in a scarlet abyss.

Mallock mobilized his whole team. They only had a few steps to walk. They stood, stunned, before the spectacle of their suspect, suddenly transformed into a victim. And in the very apartment belonging to their own superintendent!

A young doctor from the coroner's office arrived a few minutes after the ambulance. He and Mallock knew each other, but Amédée blanked completely on his name. He tried to remember it, just so he could think about something else. Forget what he had seen in his bedroom. Forget that an army of gloved officers was in there now, looking, photographing, touching.

"A word, Superintendent. The young lady seems to have been drugged. She's lost a lot of blood, but I think she has a chance of pulling through."

Mallock gaped at him, almost incapable of understanding the words. He squinted and managed to ask, "She isn't dead?"

"No. She's comatose, and I had trouble finding a pulse. It'll take a few hours to analyze the substances she's absorbed."

"Get in touch with Professor Mordome. He'll know which drugs they are; he's already studied them."

Only then did Mallock realize just how much of a wreck he was. His hands were shaking. He surprised himself by taking out his lighter to light a cigar he didn't even have. He was not in a normal state of mind. For him, time virtually froze right there. If he hadn't suddenly decided to run home, Amélie would be dead. If he hadn't made the mistake with the keys, there was a very good chance he would have been killed himself. He lowered his head and closed his eyes.

If Amélie survived, destiny would be treating him fairly for once.

The team of paramedics, accompanied by the doctor in charge, carried the stretcher out slowly. Amédée had time to catch a glimpse of the young woman, perfused, intubated, ventilated. Her face was white, smeared with red streaks, her hair soaked with blood. Extradural, subdural, or intracerebral hematoma; contusion? The doctors couldn't say yet.

It took all Mallock's courage to go back into his bedroom. He forced himself to squat down and examine the floor. The first thing he saw was miniscule. Laid out in an equilateral triangle were the now-familiar three little marks in the carpet, near where Amélie's head had lain. A camera tripod?

To get a definitive confirmation, he asked the crime-scene techs to make a cast of the marks in fine elastomer, and then to take tissue, dust, and hair samples inside and around the triangle. He issued an order that the sites of the other murders also be subjected to the same analyses. In the meantime, a squadron of white jumpsuits got to work dusting for fingerprints.

Mallock sat down on the edge of his bed, physically and morally exhausted. Where had he gone wrong? The piece of shit had attacked his Amélie, and he hadn't seen anything coming. His eyes burned with pain and anger.

As he struggled to regain a bit of composure, he heard a very faint sound like the rustling of wings. Not a pigeon or a crow; more like a butterfly, as if one were trapped somewhere in his apartment, fluttering against windows and curtains, trying to get out.

He soon figured out what the strange noise was.

An army of brushes loaded with granite powder was busily dusting the walls of his apartment in search of handprints.

22

Wednesday evening, January 5th

B ob, who had stayed at Amélie's building, was now wondering what he was supposed to look for. If Amélie Maurel wasn't guilty, that changed everything. His brain ground into action like rusty machinery. Fairly quickly for Bob, a bright idea occurred to him. He would listen to the voice messages on the phone. Proud of himself, he approached the answering machine with the half-grouchy, half-fearful air common to people who resist modern technology.

There was only one message:

"This is Superintendent Mallock. I've got a bad cold and my back is in really bad shape. I'd appreciate it if you could see me. Just come by whenever you can; I'll be waiting."

The voice was muffled. It bore a very slight resemblance to the superintendent's voice, especially if he had a cold, but it wasn't him. Bob knew Mallock's voice like the back of his hand.

"What the hell is going on here?" he said aloud in the empty apartment.

If he had known what the relationship was between his superintendent and the victim, the speaker's use of the formal *vous* rather than the informal *tu* would have confirmed his theory. He played the message again three times. No. It wasn't his boss.

"Goddammit, it's a goddamn fucking trap!" he realized, with unusual insight.

He searched the apartment for several more minutes but didn't find anything in particular, other than a complete professional makeup kit, which brought back his suspicion of Amélie for a few seconds until he remembered that she was comatose, a victim of the Makeup Artist.

"You're an idiot sometimes, Robert!" he bellowed aloud.

Bob knew that age had whittled away little by little his mental faculties. Soon he wouldn't really be in a condition to work anymore, and the idea scared the crap out of him. What if it was already the case? If Mallock was only keeping him around out of friendship? To avoid hurting him? To make sure he'd get full retirement benefits? He was a very nice person underneath his curmudgeonly surface, that Amédée. Almost too nice sometimes.

Just as he was about to leave the apartment, Bob noticed a Filofax sitting on a chair. Inside it was a remarkably well-organized client directory. All the people in it were listed according to the part of Paris they lived in, and each one included a passport photo or Polaroid next to his or her name, along with a brief medical note. Clearly Amélie didn't rely on her memory, or even on digital technology. The Modiano family's information was there too, with a photo of the little girl, her first name, and the dose of insulin to inject her with on each visit.

It still seemed beyond bizarre. Another coincidence? As a seasoned cop he knew that there was a word for a certain accumulation of . . . disturbing connections: guilt. The young nurse could perfectly well have been attacked by her own accomplice.

Bob went off to find his boss and give him a report. Another lovely blend of facts and mysteries. Well, it would be up to him to sort it all out.

He waved at the pharmacist as he passed her shop window. She tried to ask him some questions, but he brushed her off. "Sorry, *madame*, but there's nothing I can tell you right now."

He had no desire to be the bearer of bad news—and besides, he was in a hurry. His wife was making veal stew for dinner. "Try to be on time for once," she had requested, already annoyed.

Things weren't awful between the two of them anymore; they'd been all right for a while now, and he figured that everything would work itself out in the end—not that he felt obligated to make the slightest effort on his own end, or change his sexist, narrow-minded ways.

With traffic the way it was, there was no way he'd make it home before nine o'clock. He comforted himself by remembering that veal stew was just as good reheated.

After half a bottle of Scotch and the lightning-quick visit from Bob bringing him Amélie's things, Mallock had felt the need to get out of his apartment. It was too late to go back to the Fort, so he wandered aimlessly around the neighborhood before ending up at Léon's.

"I'll be all yours in five minutes," murmured the bookseller, who was helping a customer.

His Mallock had the look of a man who was having a bad time of things, and there was something else in his face, too, something more. Something that worried Léon.

Amédée scanned the shelves for a book—any book; something to lose himself in, to short-circuit his morbid thoughts for a few seconds, to stave off the image of an unconscious woman being loaded into an ambulance. In the very back of the store, in the religion section, among a horde of Old Testaments, Kabbalahs, and other gospels, he found a small, dog-eared missal bound in blue. Was it a subconscious desire to pray? He opened the book. Two dozen colored cards fell out of it. He stooped to pick them up; they were naïve-style icons adorned with lace and gilding, pious images, the kind grandmas offered at Holy Communion. Ecstatic faces, chromos of God and all the saints.

His childhood came flooding back to him, with its flavors of communion wine, incense, and dead flowers. Part of his youth, scattered in pieces, like so many wartime truces. When little Amédée, awkward in his red cassock and white surplice, was an altar boy. That child had had a few rare but sensational moments of happiness. Why had the Chief Superintendent forgotten these bits of his boyhood, the times when he, only a very little boy, had knelt, haloed by the glorious colors of the stained-glass windows in the Saint-Clotilde church? Smells came back to him: plaster and incense, ink and saltpeter, the nausea-inducing urine of the rectory cats. The taste of stale bread soaked in communion wine. Noises, too. Bells, the creaking of wooden pews, the rubbery squeaking of the priest's shoes as he climbed the stairs of the pulpit, weighed down with angels.

An icy chill ran through him, jolting him out of his unexpected nostalgic haze. At the very center of the riot of luminous auras, blue draperies, crosses, and robes were the faces of the saints, and of Jesus and Mary. Their faces were all made up in the same way. Waxy white skin, orange-red cheekbones, eyes raised heavenward, azure-blue eyelids, and mauve cheeks hollowed out with suffering. They were the exact same colors and characteristics used by the Makeup Artist; absolutely identical, with the same loving, meticulous attention to detail. And they were also similar to the matte pastel colors, surrounded by shining gold, of the small stolen icon.

Mallock was suddenly very far away from his childhood. The last few seconds had brought him a whole new and unexpected lead, an opening in the impenetrable wall of his investigation.

Carefully replacing the religious images in the little missal, he remembered the report on cases ten and eleven, the long discussion about Léon Bloy, and the exchange with Ken: *"Wait, Ken, have you seen Bob? Nothing new with the metro?"*

"He told me two of the victims have been formally identified. Thanks to the Louvre's surveillance center we've even got visual confirmation. Both of them were seen with a priest—Bob will have mentioned that to you; the old-fashioned kind, with the cassock and the whole shebang."

Mallock had brought Amélie's Filofax with him. He opened it now. He knew what he was looking for, but he never expected to find it so easily. On page 72, under the letter "B," he saw the face of a middle-aged parish priest, Father Bertrant. *Forty-one years old, scoliosis. 1xHp3 and C2P: 3xd.* Then she had written: *not married.* Was it a lapse in concentration, or a joke? Amédée stood there for a few moments, gazing at the oval face with its gaunt cheeks darkened by a closely-shaven black beard. The eyes were large and protruding. Very pale. The thin white lips made an almost perfect horizontal line under the long and aquiline nose. Was it a killer's face? Yes and no. The superintendent had stopped relying on morphopsychology a long time ago.

Léon's customer finally left without buying anything.

"Talk about a pain in the ass! She's worse than you!" Léon teased him, hoping to coax a smile out of him. "Come on, it's dinnertime. Let me close up and then it's my treat, okay?"

"Why not."

While Léon turned the handle of the crank that lowered the metal shutter in front of the shop, Mallock asked him:

"You know me. Do you think I'm capable of screwing up? Being completely wrong about something?"

"Anything's possible; you're not infallible. Your visions are beyond bizarre sometimes. But, paradoxically, I've never seen you be led astray without a very good reason."

"This time I have the distinct impression that I've been taken for a ride."

The iron curtain had just touched the ground and Léon stashed the crank behind a pile of books.

"It's almost like he's controlling my premonitions," Mallock said. "I don't think I should put any more stock in them at all. When I try to get a sense of him physically I don't get anything at all, except an impression of something dirty and terrifying. Bizarre features, as if they've been eaten away by water, and all coming from different faces."

"Is the great Mallock scared?"

"I have been living with a kind of fear since I saw what he's capable of. You'd be afraid too, if you'd seen it."

"I have seen it, you know."

"Yes—that's right, sorry. But now it's become very personal. He just attacked one of my friends."

"Oh, my dear boy. I'm so sorry. Did he . . . "

"Almost. She's in a coma. You know her; she lives on the other side of the square, above the pharmacy. Amélie Maurel."

"I remember her perfectly. Very pretty and a real sweetheart. A nurse, isn't she?"

"Exactly. He attacked her in my own apartment, and I almost captured him—or the other way around, actually. He might just as easily have killed me. This guy is formidable and I'm afraid that I'll fail, that I won't catch him. Unless the little priest is the killer."

"Little priest?"

"Oh—nothing."

"A new suspect?"

"Don't push, Léon. I can't tell you anything."

"At least tell me if you're serious. I mean, you sought me out to talk about Léon Bloy and other joys. You owe it to your Doctor Watson to tell me the latest."

"Okay, you're not wrong. Let's just say that this priest would be interesting to look into. It matches our theory about sanctification by torture. And all the types of rituals the killer has used correspond to different components found in the Catholic religion. I've done some research, and there are a lot more to come. There's contrition and compunction, repentance, penitence, and resipiscence. If we add retribution, reversibility, and redemption, that makes eight terms for a single . . . issue; eight missions that might correspond to all the atrocities that have been done to the victims' bodies. It all matches up very nicely, in fact."

"Well, let's go celebrate," said Léon. "You can tell me more about it."

Mallock wasn't really hungry. He ran a hand through his hair, pushing it back off his face. It had become a tic since he decided to keep his hair long. A bad-boy hairstyle for a big-city superintendent.

"A fantastic restaurant, not expensive and not kosher, to celebrate your next arrest; how does that sound?"

It wasn't often that Léon invited him out to dinner.

"I'm sorry, but I'm really not up for it," Amédée declined after a hesitation. "But I will use your phone, if you don't mind."

"Make yourself at home."

The superintendent gave his orders. Then he hung up the phone slowly, dreamily, as if the handset were made of crystal. Amélie was still fighting. The thought obsessed him.

"Actually, I think I would like to come to dinner."

Léon grinned and reached for the crank for the metal shutter again. "Let's get sloshed. Okay?"

It was okay with Amédée. Outside, pedestrians were hurrying home, their thoughts caught between a past that no longer existed and a future that was uncertain at best. Within the superintendent's heart there was a curious lapping noise, like a concert of clicking tongues.

23.

Thursday morning, January 6th

By six A.M. Mallock had almost finished installing a twenty-four-hour surveillance system outside Father Bertrant's house. There was no question of arresting the little priest. Not yet. The drug in the bodies didn't allow for a precise dating of the injections. It would still take some time to compare the timelines of the latest murders with the clergyman's schedule. Ken had been assigned the task of looking into the priest's habits as discreetly as possible, and at seven o'clock he would begin questioning every possible witness he could get his hands on: neighbors, the housekeeper, members of the congregation, the sexton. He would have to ensure their full cooperation while at the same time convincing them to keep quiet for a few hours. This was precisely why Mallock had chosen Ken for the job. He could be subtle when he chose to, and his ability to persuade people and make them like him was among the highest in Number 36. It was up to him and Julie to reconstruct the priest's activities. Back at the Fort, Jules and Francis would compare this data to the estimated times of the murders.

Mallock had another reason for setting up twenty-four-hour surveillance on the priest: to keep him from committing another crime while Amédée and his team put together the case against him. For now, they didn't have anything more than conjecture. They would have to collect a complete set of circumstantial evidence, whether it took them three hours or three days.

To add to this network of activity, Mallock had given Bob
the mission of showing the priest's picture to the witnesses
from the metro. To make the identification more conclusive,
they had collected a dozen ID photos of clergymen who resembled him—which had been no small job at five o'clock in the
morning. At seven o'clock the surveillance system was fully
installed and Mallock found himself left with nothing to do but
wait—which, truth be told, was ninety percent of an investigator's job.

He went down to the café. Not a flake of snow in the sky.
The ground was littered with confetti and scraggy islands of
dirty snow, the sad remnants of the holidays. The darkness of
night lingered, refusing to leave. In the warmth, protected by
the *bar-tabac*'s window from his phobia of crowds, Mallock
dunked his croissants and contemplated the morning's army of
the damned. Parisians streamed like human sacrifices into the
ravenous mouth of the metro.

Keeping off to one side, avoiding the head count, not participating, living on the fringes, and never giving in—never giving in or conforming—these things were vitally important to
him. Why? He didn't really know. He played with the question, flicking it around along with the crumbs that had accumulated on the little round table. He pushed them delicately
over the table's edge into the palm of his other hand and then
dumped them into his empty cup.

That was the only thing you could do with a lot of questions.

"How much do I owe you?"

"Coming, Monsieur le Superintendent."

At eight-thirty, after trying unsuccessfully to reach his
friend from the ambulance, Mallock called the hospital.
Amélie was in intensive care at the Pitié-Salpêtrière hospital.

She was under police protection and her medical bulletin was being updated regularly. Amédée asked to speak to the intern on duty.

"Her condition is stable. She's still in a coma. Sorry, Superintendent." Then: "There's no point in calling. We've been ordered to let you know if there's any change at all."

"Don't patronize me," Mallock snapped. "I want details about the coma, her MRI, her current condition."

"Yes . . . well, Superintendent, the doctor based his diagnosis principally on a clinical examination of the eyes. The reticular activating system is in a part of the brain close to the oculomotor pathways . . . "

Mallock listened carefully. The news wasn't good. He murmured a grudging "thank you" and hung up. The Makeup Artist had shown him just how strong his love for Amélie was, and it shocked him. With the brief exception of Margot, since Thomas's death he hadn't believed himself capable anymore of loving. Really loving.

At ten o'clock Jonas Paraclet, one of the crime scene technicians, came by to give Mallock his report on the three suspicious holes discovered in the floors of the different crime scenes. After submitting the superintendent to a full three-minute barrage of pseudo-scientific jargon, Jonas finally got to the point.

"It's safe to say that your guess was right, and the holes were made by a camera tripod. We analyzed all the samples found inside and around the triangles, as you instructed. We didn't find anything outside them, but inside there were traces of makeup, and hair and skin fragments from the victims."

The conclusion was simple.

After drugging them, the Makeup Artist made them up to look like religious images before photographing them. Mallock had known it already, but here was confirmation. The camera must be positioned right above the victims' heads, shooting straight down, like on a repro stand. Mallock thought about stakes again. This was also a kind of stake, a visual one. The theft of an image. Its revelation and its inversion. A beam coming from between the three posts of the tripod to impale the victims' faces, freezing life at the instant of sacrifice—the ecstatic grimace of the person offering up his or her suffering for the sake of the mystical body's health. The ceremony was perfectly choreographed; there was no room for the slightest repentance. And the preamble, the prelude to the devouring, was the makeup session, to make the victim more . . . appetizing.

Once his work was finished, the Makeup Artist moved them to the bed to mutilate them, to extract every bit of suffering still left in their poor bodies. He redesigned them according to his own madness, his aesthetic and theological ambitions. He shaped them, *molded* them, with knives and swords and his own teeth. The draining of their blood had to begin at the same time as the torture. Maybe a few minutes before it, but no more. He had to make sure they kept breathing. That their hearts kept beating.

"I don't know if . . . " Jonas began.

"Quiet!" ordered Mallock, deep in thought.

He went back over all the phases of the ceremony in his mind. Immobilization; makeup for the souvenir photo; then the blood draining, the violence to the bodies, the penetration of the sword into the lower abdomen, and the final morbid staging.

"He's not the first sicko to take pictures of his victims," Mallock mused aloud. "But it's definitely the first time I've heard of a maniac confident enough to take the time to use a tripod. What kind of photo requires that kind of equipment?"

Jonas Paraclet, it turned out, was an expert on the subject. "For me it would be a photo without flash. With normal indoor lighting and 400 ASA film, you can only shoot at an eighth of a second, and that's if you have a bright lens. With a really good-quality digital camera you can adjust the sensitivity to 3200 without too much interference. Now, with the thirtieth, the photo can still be made blurry by the slightest movement of the camera, especially if we're assuming that the photographer in question is nervous or excited. The only thing that can solve that kind of problem is a really rigid stand. If he's a maniac he might even use a shutter release to avoid vibrations, or a timer. He pushes the button, and in the time it takes for the chronometer to count ten seconds, any wobbling will stop.

"We should assume that our crazy bastard definitely needs absolutely clean, sharp photographic records . . . for some subsequent purpose I don't even want to think about."

"Photographs of victims are usually kept as trophies or used as masturbation aids, or both," Jonas found it necessary to point out, even as he realized that Mallock had no need of that kind of precision.

A normal killer, maybe, but not the Makeup Artist. He's obsessed with creating religious images, was what Amédée thought. But aloud he kept it to a polite "That's probable, Jonas. Thanks for your work. Just leave it here, please."

It was eleven-thirty and Mallock wanted desperately to call the hospital again. But just then Jonas doubled back to his desk. "Sorry, sir, but this was against the wall behind the door."

"Thanks." It was the forensic entomologist's report. He opened it.

"The death of the youngest female victim found at Saint-Mandé probably took place on the morning of Sunday, December twenty-sixth, between four and five in the morning."

The rest of the report specified the factors backing up this conclusion, complete with meteorological data and morphological and chromatic details concerning the fly larvae.

Within half an hour Ken had been informed of the new

developments. Julie and Jules added the data to their table. Shortly after that, Robert came back from his ramble through the metro looking happy.

"I've got formal identifications from two out of our three witnesses. The third one couldn't say either way; there was a lot of 'I'd need to see him in person' and 'I'd really like to see you there.' We'll have to call them for—"

"You're a bit behind on the news, Bob," Mallock interrupted with a sly smile. "Ken's already summoned them for a repeat performance this afternoon. You should really spend a little more time at the office, you know. What is this bizarre fascination you have with mass transit?"

24.
Thursday afternoon, January 6th

At one o'clock, Mallock and Bob went down to lunch. Twenty minutes later Ken rolled in, grinning. "How much is the Chief Superintendent willing to pay for some really good news?"

"A *croque-monsieur* and a half; not a penny more."

"What a bargain. I'm out of here—hell if I can't find a more generous superintendent somewhere around here," Ken retorted, pretending to turn around and leave.

"Talk or you're fired. Have a seat."

"Our little priest didn't lead services on Saturday or Sunday of the Christmas weekend. Not low mass, and not high mass. He just left a note on the church door: *Absent due to illness.* Does that make our Mallock happy?"

"So-so. It's only circumstantial."

"I said I had *really* good news. Same story on New Year's Eve. Same note on the door."

"Now you're talking. I'll call the judge and we'll run out and nab him."

"What about my sandwich?"

"You can have it when we get back."

An hour later, up in Fort Mallock, Ken was finally wolfing down his lunch, watching the little priest out of the corner of his eye. As was so often the case, the monster looked harmless on the surface—and yet there was something about him, something macabre, overly fragile and awkward.

Father Bertrant had moist yellow skin and was dressed in a

shiny old cassock that had glints of green and wine-red in it. *Zinzolin*, thought Mallock, remembering Madame Modiano's autopsy. A pair of gold-framed eyeglasses magnified the man's close-set gray eyes. His mouth hung open; his upper lip was so thin as to be almost nonexistent. Beneath a bald skull and a smooth forehead his face was incredibly thin; the skin of his cheeks looked like it was being sucked in on either side of his nose by the two deep vertical lines there.

Even though the killer's personality and the number of murders he had racked up were more than enough reason to take precautions, his weak, sickly outward appearance had dissuaded them. They didn't think they had anything to fear from this man who looked like he had one foot in the grave. Obviously in a hurry to get on with things, Mallock had simply told the little priest to sit down on an imitation-leather stool in the middle of Ken's office. He had even been reckless enough to take off the man's handcuffs, with the ludicrous rationale that *this is a clergyman; they don't commit suicide.*

Amédée had decided to let their suspect stew in his own juices for a while. He phoned Jules and Julie and told them to make an exhaustive search of the man's apartment. Then he left the priest to sweat it out. It was a full hour before he was finally ready to grill the alleged Makeup Artist.

Ken and Bob joined him in his office; they would back Mallock up during what they all expected to be a marathon interrogation. Amédée started out by talking to them about the strategy he planned to use to get what he wanted.

When they went back into Ken's office, the judge called.

"Where are we with this?"

"Nowhere. I haven't questioned him yet."

"Don't tell me you're going easy on him."

"He's only a suspect, and he's a man of the cloth. I haven't . . . "

"So what? To hell with the goddamn clergy!" retorted the

judge, in a fit of radical socialism that Mallock considered particularly inappropriate.

"I'll keep you posted," he said simply, holding his temper for once. Better to cut the conversation short than to get into an argument now. In any case, he'd do exactly as he liked. There was no reason to break out the brickbat just yet. Hunting priests had become a national pastime, but Mallock wasn't going to participate in that kind of execution—unless, of course, it turned out that the little priest was the Makeup Artist. Even though he was no believer in God himself, he knew that the balance between good and evil was infinitely more positive in clergymen than it was in the people who made a sport out of going after them. It wasn't the former altar boy speaking in Mallock's head now, but the seasoned cop who had seen them volunteering in the streets and the prisons. Still, Amélie was in a coma, and there had never been anything like these murders before. How would he react if the little priest confessed?

Mallock noticed a group of visitors at the door of the interrogation room. The whole station had come to have a look at this sideshow phenomenon: a serial killing priest.

"Get lost! Ken, close the Fort. I don't want to see one more asshole in here."

The interrogation began at four o'clock and finished at five forty-two, when the little priest—without a whole lot of pressure from Mallock's team—confessed to all his crimes.

Father Bertrant, his mouth dry and his forehead gleaming with sweat, had only lasted five minutes before cracking. Yes, he admitted it. It had been stronger than he was. A diabolical impulse. He had resisted it for a long time, but the Devil had beaten him. *As God is my witness.* It had all started five years earlier.

At that moment, Mallock's heart began to race. Confessions

always did that to him. But he was surprised by how fast the suspect had cracked this time. He'd been prepared for a long battle, not a KO at the first punch. Yes, he confessed everything—the young women, the stolen photos, all of it—but not rape. He hadn't touched them sexually, ever, in any way.

"I swear to you, Superintendent, I've never done violence to children, never caressed them. You can ask them."

Mallock thought it was strange to put those two words together, *violence* and *caress*.

"Oh, we'll ask them, Father," he said. "You can be sure of that."

The little priest began to make excuses for himself, babbling about having too much love, infinite tenderness, and a carnal temptation of which he had been the first victim.

"I didn't think I was doing anything wrong, just taking a few photos from far away. It was just the solitude . . . it's not easy, you know . . . celibacy."

"We aren't talking about your masturbation habits, or voyeurism. This is a question of murder. Women and children, slaughtered!"

Mallock knew the look of utter astonishment that came over the clergyman's face, his mouth open and his eyes wide. He recognized it. Second shock. Ken or Francis might believe the little priest was just putting on an act, but all Bob and Mallock had to do was look each other.

"Shit," muttered Bob into his mustache. This was called *experience*, and the old redhead had plenty of that.

Just then, Julie called from the rectory to tell Mallock what they had found: a complete photographer's setup, including equipment for developing and enlarging pictures. There was nothing pedophilic about the priest's photo collection. It was the work of a voyeur, pure and simple; a repressed admirer of the female form.

"Most of the pictures were taken from far away, with a tele-photo lens. Naked women in their bathrooms, mainly. There is a nude snapshot of one of the murdered women, but taken while she was alive. Looks like she'd gotten up in the middle of the night; the picture shows her naked in front of her refrigerator. Sorry, but that's it. Jules and I will keep poking around just to be absolutely sure, but don't get your hopes up; this isn't our guy, unless he's got another hideout somewhere."

The little priest had kept on babbling excuses while Mallock was on the phone. The accusation of murder was so ludicrous and unimaginable in his eyes that he had shrugged it aside and picked up his speech of repentance right where he'd left off.

"We give a lot, you know. We listen, we give comfort. And when you go back to the rectory it's so cold, and you're all alone. Nobody there to listen to our problems . . . "

Mallock had stopped listening to him. Another waste of time. Father Bertrant's sincerity was obvious. He was so visibly mortified and remorseful about his naughty pictures that there could really be no doubt of his innocence in the Makeup Artist case.

There was a banging of chairs.

The little priest, showing extraordinary strength, had seized his chair and thrown it at the window, which shattered. They were on the top floor, and it was immediately clear what he intended to do; too clear, for Mallock. He just managed to grab the priest's legs, while the rest of his body already dangled outside. His two lieutenants helped him drag the man back onto *terra firma*.

"I'd die and go to hell before I'd try to take another person's life! My God! It's always been my destiny to help people, but now destiny has forsaken me . . . "

"Now now, none of that, Father," interrupted Mallock. "Destiny's a convenient scapegoat. It's a perfect drawer to put our mistakes in. You're not the first to use it, and you won't be the last. When you choose a vocation like yours, you assume responsibility or you step down."

Mallock had been hesitating, but now he decided to continue the interrogation in spite of everything. When they accused him of murder a second time, the little priest curled in on himself, then straightened up and swore his innocence on the Bible, taking God as his witness. Without a shred of compassion, Ken spread the crime scene photos out in front of him.

"Look at your handiwork, Father. Confess, dammit! We aren't going to forgive you, so don't look for it. But your merciful God might still have pity on you, if you repent. Go on, look at them, you bastard!"

This was the signal Mallock was waiting for. There was no question of explaining to Ken—in front of the suspect—what he and Bob had already known for a good half an hour. Out of inertia, disappointment, and fatigue he'd let Ken run wild a bit, just to see what he would do, but now it had gone too far. He ended the interrogation as abruptly as he had started it. It was six o'clock, and Amédée was both discouraged and troubled. How had he taken this little priest for the unthinkable monster he was hunting?

Out of anxiety?

25

Friday, January 7th

T he next morning, the examining magistrate came for the priest. As a public prosecutor, the judge could extend custody to twenty-four hours. In cases of terrorism, drug trafficking, or prostitution, he could draw it out to a full four days.

"You'll see, I'm not going to hold back in making this guy talk," he blustered.

Mallock didn't have the heart to try to discourage Humbert, or save the little priest. He wasn't intimidated; he was just exhausted. Besides, it was like throwing a bone to a dog. As long as the judge had Bertrant to play with, he'd leave Mallock and his team alone.

Margot called him. She had already left him several messages. "I don't think I got them," lied Mallock regretfully. It was easier for him that way, and kinder to her.

He let the silence stretch out between them. It was her move.

"Don't you have anything for me?" she asked.

He hesitated; then, to show her that he trusted her, he told her about the latest developments in the case, making it clear that the information had to be kept under wraps until he gave her permission to publish it.

"It's going to be awfully hard to hold my tongue," she complained.

"Everything worthwhile is difficult," Mallock countered. Then they talked about other things—but not about Amélie.

He didn't know how to approach the subject, or even if he should.

After he hung up, it took several minutes for the smile Margot's voice had put on his face to fade away. He worked until around noon with his team, and then decided to go up and see his boss. He felt the need to tell his troubles to someone, and Dublin seemed like the perfect man for the job.

Leaving his office, Mallock glanced out a window in the corridor and saw the little priest getting into the back of a prison van in the courtyard. He was being transferred to the Palais des Toqués, where the judge would try his luck. Mallock felt a profound sense of pity for the figure in black; it represented solitude, and a shattered calling. The man had wanted to do good, in spite of others—and himself. He didn't deserve what was going to happen to him.

He promised himself he would call the judge and persuade him to go easy on the priest, before pushing open the legendary padded green leather door. Dublin was sitting behind his desk, seeming almost as if he'd been waiting for Mallock. The big boss was thin, with one of those sad gray faces that senior civil servants always develop, like a factory brand. To prove that their hard work has exhausted them, maybe.

Without asking Mallock anything, Dublin pressed the button on his intercom. "Two coffees, Annick, please." Then he resumed his position, settled deep in his chair. "I don't really like coffee," he said. "It's more the idea of it that pleases me, the concept. The fantasy of coffee, you might even say. What about you?"

Mallock thought for a few seconds before speaking. "No; for me it's the aromatic strength of coffee, and the flavor. It helps me get the taste of the world out of my mouth."

Dublin smiled, amused by Amédée's last remark. His favorite superintendent had a knack for coming up with statements like that. From now on he'd have a greater appreciation for his morning coffee. "So, how are you getting on?" he asked.

"I'm afraid we're not getting anywhere at all," Mallock said. "I don't know what to tell you."

"What about our priest?"

"Wrong track."

Dublin looked Mallock straight in the eyes, as if searching for confirmation of something. It was there.

"This case is a real nightmare. And let's be honest; I knew that perfectly well even before I gave you this . . . "

"Shit-covered stick," Mallock finished for him.

Dublin didn't contradict him. His hands were shaking.

"Yes. And I'm sorry."

Amédée felt profoundly discouraged. He'd come here for a morale boost, or maybe a good kick in the pants to get him going again, and here was his boss looking fainthearted—or worse, scared.

Right when the secretary brought in the two coffees, Dublin's desk clock—a gift from his wife—began striking twelve, and the phone began ringing at the same moment as well. Dublin calmly picked up his cup and took a sip before answering.

It was hard to describe his face during the conversation. In less than two minutes his face went from an anemic pink to pure white, and then turned absolutely green. "We'll be right there," he said into the receiver, and hung up.

There was a good twenty seconds of silence before he spoke. Mallock had the patience to wait. After all, he had all the time in the world to be punched in the gut by bad news—and this was most definitely going to be very bad news.

Kathleen Parks, one of the most popular stars in the United States and extremely talented to boot, had decided to spend the New Year holiday in Paris.

She had just been slaughtered by the Makeup Artist in her suite at the Hotel de Crillon.

It was lunchtime, and in the Madeleine-Opéra-Concorde area, even on a normal day, there was no escaping the frantic mob of cars and executives in search of their daily pittance. To top it all off, the news of the actress's death had spread like a mudslide. Dublin had the foresight to park his car in the underground garage at the Place Vendôme. The entire street of Boissy d'Anglas and the main entrance to the Crillon were jammed with people. It took the two men a full five minutes to fight their way through the crowd and into the hotel. Inside, an army of hysterical journalists thrust microphones and cameras at a group of officials and relatives still stunned by the news. Mallock and Dublin slipped authoritatively and discreetly toward the elevators.

"Which floor?" Amédée asked one of the police officers on duty, who recognized him.

"Third, Monsieur le Superintendent. The Vendôme suite."

Once in the third-floor corridor, the two men had to elbow their way through another crowd to reach the room. Dublin quickly ordered everyone to evacuate the premises, except for the hotel manager and the victim's agent and two bodyguards.

"Please stay at the door and stop e-ve-ry-bo-dy," he said to the guards, in accented but forceful English.

One of the two giants was particularly shocked. Despite himself, he couldn't stop the tears from streaming down his cheeks. His whole six-foot-six, two-hundred-and-ninety-pound body trembled. He had been the actress's bodyguard for more than ten years and was deeply attached to her. He had truly idolized her, and had no doubt ended up convincing himself that she was immortal—both in life and on the screen. She had only been attacked once before, in Detroit, and he'd risked his own life to put the assailant out of commission; an inch-long scar just above his heart bore witness to that. Now he felt like he had failed. Mallock had just enough time to grab the man by the shoulders before he collapsed. His partner, white as a sheet, helped Mallock lay him on a green-velvet damask sofa.

While they waited for the crime scene technicians, Dublin went into the star's bedroom. From behind, Mallock saw his boss's shoulders bow. His head lowered, and his long fingers groped for a wall to support him. The Makeup Artist had outdone himself.

At first glance, however, nothing seemed to have been disturbed in the room. Louis XV furniture, heavy curtains and deep-pile carpeting emblazoned with the hotel's arms, flowers and baskets of fruit—everything was in place and immaculate. The savaged body of the actress, artistically arranged on a silk sheet, was a shocking sight, its eyes, abdomen, and lower belly all wide open as if in a horrible burst of laughter. The Makeup Artist had cut away much of the flesh around her mouth so that the star's perfect teeth were clearly visible, framed by coral-pink gums. On the floor, at the foot of the bed, her intestines had been coiled into a perfect spiral. Looking at the totally hollowed-out body of Kathleen Parks, Mallock had an image of a shipwreck on some Caribbean beach, or the framework of a wooden boat in dry dock, with its ropes lovingly tied up out of the way by a conscientious fisherman. The finger- and toenails were missing.

"Christ," Dublin breathed.

Mallock silently agreed. The smell was making his stomach churn. It was a very strong mixture of perfumes, barely touched by the odor of meat and blood. Glancing at the dressing table, he understood. A series of bottles were lined up like overly made-up whores, displaying a rich variety of colors and shapes: Chanel, Dior, Guerlain, Gaultier, Lempicka, Givenchy,

Ricci. Gold, pink, blue, mauve. The bottles had only one thing in common—they were empty. The Makeup Artist had gone about his abominable butchery obscured by a dense, intense cloud of perfume.

The victim's agent and friend had followed them into the bedroom. They stood with arms dangling, sobbing, eyes fixed on the bed, babbling: *"Oh my God!" "Jesus!" "Oh, God!" "Fuck!" "Oh my God!" "Holy Christ!" "Oh my God!"*

Despite the presence of the crime scene techs and all the instructions he always gave his men for the sacrosanct preservation of traces and clues, Mallock approached the body and covered it with a silk robe. The agent, pulling himself together for a moment, came up to the body as well, intending to close its eyes.

Mallock had to explain to him that her eyelids were gone.

Three crime scene technicians took the temperature of the air in the room, and of different parts of the body. Only then were the windows opened, so the sickening smell could begin to dissipate.

Leaving the CSIs to do their job, Mallock and Dublin left the room together and took refuge in a small adjoining sitting room. They were quiet, each of them trying to recover his wits. Mallock was the first to break the silence.

"I need a complete recap of the victim's activities from the time she touched down on French soil until the tragedy. And as many photos of the premises as we can get, including the crowd, if possible."

Julie and Jules had just arrived, and Mallock's request was directed at them.

Just then someone knocked on the door of the room. An extremely well-dressed man and a woman in a suit entered. Mallock heard the man say "FBI," and was surprised to see Dublin salute as he went to greet them. What was the FBI doing on a French case, and in French territory? Dublin beck-oned Mallock over.

"Angelina Allen and Tom Marvin, I'd like you to meet Chief Superintendent Mallock, who's in charge of this case. If anyone can get us out of this, it's him."

Us? Dublin's use of that word made it clear not only that he knew the newcomers, but that they were in this together.

The woman broke into Mallock's thoughts by announcing, in perfect French: "We've requisitioned a room on the other side of the hall. Let's go."

Narrow-featured and tanned, with skin lined by too much sun exposure, she had the kind of brusque authority acquired with time. In spite of that and her drab suit, she was far from lacking charm. She walked down the corridor in front of them, a thick blonde braid reaching to the small of her back. Her calves, balanced on high heels, were muscular. She opened the door to a much smaller suite with no number on the door.

When all four of them were inside, she did something odd. She locked the door behind them. Mallock watched Dublin out of the corner of his eye; he looked exhausted, and very worried.

Tom, the other American, had ivory hair that was almost sil-ver, with glints of blue in it, a pure-white beard, and a thick-lipped mouth like the actor Lee Marvin's, with whom he also shared a last name and the same drooping eyelids. Not too far away from retirement, he gazed out on the world with the kind of swimming-pool-blue eyes that have seen too much. Mallock suddenly had the feeling that he recognized him, had maybe even worked with him before, possibly when he had been in the United States, on the NAP case? But maybe the feeling was just because of his resemblance to the actor.

The American folded his large frame into a deep armchair, leaving his partner to lay the cards out on the table.

"In the United States we were, and now we are again, in charge of the investigation of the person you call the Makeup Artist. Tom has been on the case from the start. He was part of the very first special task force created at the time and based in Quantico. He's even largely responsible for the creation of the ViCAP computer system—that's the Violent Criminal Apprehension Program—and for the implementation of the Behavior Sciences Service, which has now been renamed the Investigative Assistance Unit."

"What do you mean, 'at the time'?"

The American woman turned, not to Mallock, who had asked the question, but to Dublin. "You haven't briefed him?" she asked.

The deputy chief sighed. "We've had some pretty bad experiences with secrets and confidential information here lately. You called me specifically because the last embargo blew up in our faces. I'll admit that, at the time and even though I have complete trust in Superintendent Mallock, I had some reservations about disclosing information to anyone. I've been pretty traumatized, truthfully," he apologized, turning to Amédée.

"Am I allowed to know now? Or are you planning to keep treating me like the big dumb idiot?"

Mallock hated being out of the loop, especially when it had to do with one of his cases. Annoyed, he put his question directly to the FBI man, maybe just to piss the other two off.

"Well, Agent Marvin, can you fill me in?"

Tom seemed lost in thoughts that Amédée supposed—incorrectly, as it turned out—had nothing to do with the case. It was Angelina who answered him.

"Have a look at these."

Mallock took the packet of black-and-white prints she held out to him, but it was several seconds before he actually dropped his gaze to the photos. In that instant, he tried to guess from Angelina's eyes what she was trying to tell him. There was fear in them, made all the more disturbing by the fact that it was totally suppressed. When he finally looked at the snapshots, he understood it all immediately.

But the truth was much worse than anything his imagination, as fertile as it was, could ever come up with.

In each of the photos, corpses bore the makeup and torn-open legs that were the Makeup Artist's trademark, screaming out that he was striking on American soil as well. It was the work of the same person; there was no doubt about it. How could he be doing it? He must have two residences, or even two nationalities. Alternating murders would lighten the police pressure on him in each country. In fact, he had actually benefited from the respective embargoes that France and the United States had imposed without consulting each other. Unless there were two separate men, keeping in contact with one another. Two madmen at work on the same atrocities?

The wheels in Mallock's brain turned at top speed.

Angelina and Tom were quiet, giving him time to look at the pictures. Mallock thought there was a message in their silence, as if they wanted him to understand further, to go even deeper into the unimaginable. He was abruptly struck by the number of photos. He held proof of so very many murders in his hands. How was it possible? How long had this piece of garbage been in operation?

Tom Marvin looked him directly in the eyes and asked him to pay special attention to the oldest photos. Mallock was surprised first by the yellowish appearance of the snapshots; then he stopped at one of them.

A wide-angle shot showing the interior of a typically American apartment featured uniformed police officers standing around a body. The uniforms looked odd, as if they were from a different era. Amédée turned the photo over. "*Atlanta.*

Sharon Delanay. Alleged murderer: Needles. Date: December 28th, 1929."

"Oh yes," Marvin clarified. "'Needles' is the name we use over there for the killer you call the Makeup Artist."

26

Current day, but somewhere else

C rying with happiness before the beauty of the finished work. Crying and getting a hard-on, watering them with tears and cum, *lacrimae Christi*, all these beautiful iconic faces. They call me the Makeup Artist, but I am so much more. More than one; I am many. And not old, not young, but immortal!

In the secret room he keeps, away from prying eyes, the murderer undresses slowly, meditatively, like a priest withdrawing after the mass; stole, hood, amice, maniple, and cappa magna.

I am he who provides pain. Death, the great cleanser. Polluted with sin, contaminated by men, our Earth is bloodless, and I, I will wash it with great strokes of my tongue.

The killer moves slowly into the red-tiled bathroom. His secret chapel, covered with the number nine, written in white ink . . .

I am a harvester of faces. A fisher for pearls. I go down to the bottom of others to bring back, from God, eyes, mouth, cheeks, and hair. Holding my breath, I plunge into their caverns of flesh. And there I tear out serpents and sinew, vice and viscera . . .

Deep in thought, the Makeup Artist fills his bathtub with the blood taken from his latest victim. As always, it appeared redder to him, more luminous. In this magic liquid were millions of cells that still lived, carrying the genetic heritage of the last chosen one, fragments of the divine image. While he waits, he picks up his numbered poem again. His pen squeaks as it writes verses 832, 833, 834, and 835. He puts a large sheet of blue blotting paper on top; it sucks up the ink. He recites a few phrases from *Pilgrim of the Absolute*:

"I relish homicidal epithets and stunning metaphors . . . I invent catachreses that impale, understatements that burn alive, circumlocutions that emasculate, and hyperboles of molten lead."

The murderer lets several liters of hot water run into the tub in order to bring the mixture up to the 98.6 degrees required for the ceremony. Then he slides into the liquid body of the actress. His erection is painful.

God, I can feel you! High above, far beyond our Babel of bricks where, for want of a bandage, you think of us. Soon, I will gaze upon you, I know it. And I will know it.

He throws his head back, immerses himself completely. He stays like that, holding his breath under the surface of the little red lake. Thirty seconds pass. After the last lapping sounds stop, silence settles over this secret part of the apartment. Here, away from Mother, the great "not even" has disappeared into the blood.

Above all, death cannot be gentle!

Outside, the laughter of children rises into the sky. Tires squeak; a bicycle brakes in front of the little bakery that sells fruit tarts.

BOOK THREE

In the room at the Hotel de Crillon, twilight had slowly fallen without any of the police officers thinking to turn on the lights. His big body swathed in darkness, Marvin the FBI agent told the astonishing story of the Makeup Artist.

"His code name in the United States is 'Needles,' or 'Twelve,' the precise and unchanging number of injections he's made in the victims since the beginning."

He lit a cigarette. The flame illuminated the face of an exhausted man at the extreme limit of resignation.

"Everything I'm going to tell you about this individual has been classified top secret for seventy years now. Every theory has been imagined, even the most improbable ones, from communist plots to extraterrestrials to cults. All without success. Our only victory in this whole case is that we've managed, miraculously, to keep it confidential."

He licked his upper lip with the tip of his tongue.

"Aside from that, this is our most bitter failure. There have been more than two hundred victims now. The very first investigators on the case have died, and our man is still on the run."

Mallock was dumbfounded. The figure was terrifying. It wasn't just the death and suffering of so many people; it was also what it implied about the Makeup Artist's intelligence and cunning. It couldn't be only one person. It wasn't possible.

He asked Marvin: "Is this the first time he's attacked a well-known person?"

"Not really."

A cloud of hesitation passed over Marvin's eyes. He looked at Mallock for a few seconds. Apparently reassured by what he saw there, he made his decision. From an envelope in the inner pocket of his jacket he took a tattered photograph. It was a snapshot taken at a murder scene. The stretched-out woman was blonde. Mallock turned over the photo. On the back of it was written: *"Los Angeles. Norma Jeane Mortenson/Baker. Five Helena Drive. August 4th and 5th, 1962."*

"Is it her?"

"It was."

Marvin tucked the photo carefully, almost lovingly, back into the envelope.

"This is why there are multiple gray areas surrounding her autopsy and her death. Without doing too much damage for a change, he would have used simple barbiturate injections. An enormous quantity of drugs, which makes the suicide theory impossible. Even Sergeant Jack Clemmons, who was first on the scene, immediately realized that it was staged. She was on her stomach, her hand stretched toward the telephone. But the back already showed traces of cadaveric lividity. She'd been turned over after death. What did he do with her while she was on her back? At the time we thought maybe he'd taken photos for his subsequent use, certainly for autoerotic acts, but we couldn't tell for sure because she'd still been on her back long enough for lividity to be marked. So? For the poisoning, he used microscopic injections, which is where the nickname 'Needles' came from. Twelve of them, distributed all over the body to allow the product to be introduced and the blood to be extracted."

Mallock couldn't help but admire the quality of this cowboy's French.

"The medication theory was disproved by the autopsy," Marvin continued. "Marilyn Monroe had supposedly swallowed forty tablets of Nembutal and twenty of chloral hydrate.

But they found no trace of barbiturates or even refractive crystals in the stomach or intestines. At the same time, the concentration of chloral hydrate and barbiturates in the blood was three times the lethal dose. She would have been dead after receiving a third of what was in her blood at the time of autopsy."

Angelina added, with a curious sense of humor: "You'd have to imagine her dead on her back, then waking up—perfectly fresh and made-up, by the way—and getting out of bed to find a new syringe, which was as nonexistent as her glass of water, and injecting herself in different parts of her sublime body with two times more poison than she'd already taken, before going back to sleep for good—with one last 'boop boop be doop,' of course."

Mallock cracked a smile.

Marvin picked the story back up. "At the time, the FBI imposed a complete blackout on the case, but we couldn't prevent gossip. In fact, we just barely avoided catastrophe. The media wanted to know everything. The CIA and the FBI were right in the crosshairs. Fortunately, the actress's links to the Kennedys and the suspicions about the younger brother had their effect. Everyone was in agreement about burying the affair and confirming the suicide. The serial-killer theory was never mentioned. Even today, nobody knows who the real culprit was. One thing's for sure as far as I'm concerned, which is that she didn't take her own life. This was the work of Needles. For me there's no doubt about it. As for the fact that she was found outrageously made-up, that surprised no one. It was Marilyn. Even though everyone close to her knew perfectly well that she always took off her makeup before going to bed."

"And dressed in a drop of Chanel No. 5," finished Mallock, before asking: "Were you assigned to the investigation?"

"I almost could have been. Marilyn died in August '62. But there were already a ton of guys on the case: Don Wolfe, Jack

Clemmons, Anthony Summers. No, my first encounter with the person you call the Makeup Artist didn't happen until two years later, in '64, on Saturday, February eighth. The previous day at noon, the Fab Four had landed on American soil. I made lieutenant that same day. The next day, Saturday, I got married. In the late afternoon I was called to the scene of my first case as lead investigator. The man behind the whole thing was the one we ended up calling Needles, your Makeup Artist. I remember it like it was yesterday."

Angelina Allen shifted slightly in her chair to adjust her skirt. Her legs were superb. Who still had the nerve in this day and age to say that women didn't age well?

He was also liking Tom more and more. After all, he'd just discovered that the man was a fellow member of the huge international family of Beatles maniacs.

"So, that Saturday, February eighth, 1964? It was Beatles Day?" he encouraged him.

"You might say that. It was particularly warm for a February weekend, and for several days the media, especially Murray the K, hadn't stopped talking about the visit from the four lads from Liverpool. They were going to be live on Ed Sullivan that night and I had no intention of missing it. It was a sacred day for me. As I told you, I'd just been named lead investigator on a case, *and* married the love of my life. She's French, from Bordeaux, which is where my decent French comes from. Anyway, for me this was happiness and glory. The arrival of the Beatles, of whom I was one of the earliest fans, was the icing on the cake. I've never had another day like it since."

He stopped speaking for a moment; the emotion was still there. His eyes shone.

"Even more strangely, this was the murder that almost revealed the Makeup Artist's existence to the public at large. And the Beatles are indirectly responsible for the fact that it remained a secret. The newspapers had been brought up to speed about the crime for once, but they were far too busy covering the Fab Four's visit to America to pay much attention to anything else. The FBI took advantage of that to fix it, confuse the issue."

The American took obvious pleasure in using highly typical French expressions.

"But how has he been able to escape all these police for so long? Supposing that he was fifteen years old at the time of the first crime in 1929, he would be in his eighties today. Two hundred murders without being arrested—that's inconceivable."

"But at the time, nobody had yet made the connection between all of these deaths. My modesty will suffer from admitting this, but when I was put on that new investigation there was no question of Needles, Twelve, or any other Makeup Artist. It was a murder like any other. Unique. Like any young cop just starting out I was ambitious and stubborn; I desperately wanted this case to be more important than my superiors thought it was. The pride and vanity of youth. So I searched everywhere, dug out old files, pursued new leads."

"Uncovered a lot of tricky issues and kicked up some dust," Mallock finished for him.

"That's exactly it," smiled Marvin. "But I'm sorry; I'm going to have to stop there. This story is much too long, and we need to get over to the embassy right away. They're expecting our report."

"We're already late," confirmed Angelina, very prettily.

"Can we meet again when things calm down a bit?" suggested Marvin. "Sunday, for example?"

"Okay, Sunday. Come to my apartment. It's in Le Marais."

They agreed on an early-morning meeting, at eight o'clock.

"We'll bring the croissants. But before we go, I need to warn you about something." Marvin paused for full effect and lit a cigarette.

"Much later, after twelve years of investigation, on March

twentieth, 1979, I personally arrested the man I'd been chasing for fifteen years. Needles, in person. And yes, I did put the Makeup Artist under lock and key. To be continued in the next episode, at your apartment."

Tom Marvin closed his mouth, not too displeased with the effect of his words.

Outside, rumors and shouts continued to disturb the silence. The death of the actress was still causing tears to flow in her many admirers—and ink to flow in the presses. Mallock wondered how they would manage to preserve the secrecy of the ins and outs of this affair. France wasn't the United States; the Beatles had split up a long time ago; John had been murdered, and George, the quiet one, devoured by the big C. How could they make a diversion now?

Mallock pulled himself together. "No, no, the ambassador will wait! You've said too much now—or maybe not enough!"

Smiling, Marvin went on with his story. The capture of Needles!

"You know, I don't deserve all the credit, Mallock," he said. He had already begun using the familiar, friendly *tu* with the superintendent. "These things are always a team effort. In the early seventies, thanks to interstate cooperation and the arrival of computers, we were able to start collecting information on unsolved murders and disappearances. Then we put together a whole set of composite sketches of serial killers and mass murderers. Every time someone captured one of these monsters the lead investigator would fill out a form: age, demeanor, behavior, analytical description of *modus operandi*—we called them 'similarities' back then—and the origin of their criminal conduct. From these we built up a whole typology of archetypes, which we then used to profile this particular type of killer. That was the first version of the ViCAP system, which is used widely today. Using the criteria principle, you can code what we call the criminal signature and try to update similar, earlier cases using computer cross-referencing. Sorry to subject you to all these explanations; I know you're very familiar with these methods."

Mallock stared at him, surprised by the personal nature of the last remark. What did Tom know about him? The American agent clarified:

"I noticed that you couldn't put a name—or rather, a memory—to my face, but I could. We know each other. I met you when I worked with the BSU.[13] The FBI called you in to help catch Necros Allan Poe. That ruffled a hell of a lot of feathers. The Bureau, turning to some little Frenchie for help—that didn't sit well with a lot of people. Including me, at first, to be honest. But you did a superb job, with your own particular style . . . your French touch," he smiled. "So, still don't remember me? Subtract twenty years, forty pounds, and a lot of this hairiness."

Mallock finally recognized him. At the time, Marvin had been best friends with Amédée's partner on the American case, Scott Amish, nicknamed "Scottish" because he was as horny and pointy-nosed as the terrier.

Back then, Tom Marvin's hair wasn't yet white, and he was close-shaven like all FBI agents. Plus, he'd only ever spoken to Mallock in English. In the span of a few seconds he remembered the whole case and all its sordid details; his subsequent return to Paris, and the terrible news. He had always felt guilty about it. If he had stayed in France instead of playing American detective, he might have been able to save Thomas. Marvin seemed to hesitate, and then made his decision.

"I found out what happened to your son, your little Tom, while you were working on the investigation for us. We were all really shocked."

Mallock lowered his head, avoiding the eyes of the other

---

[13] Behavioral Science Unit, created in 1972 by the FBI to profile serial killers.

people in the room. Marvin understood that the wound was still raw, and quickly picked his explanation back up.

"I have all the results of the analysis concerning Twelve here with me. They're at your disposal. I think you may find it interesting, even though our databases aren't directly workable here in Europe. The criteria used in ViCAP aren't totally transposable to the Old World. You don't have the same kind of lunatics on this side of the Atlantic."

"Don't worry, Marvin, my team has set up a database that will serve as an interface. We had a little look around in your terminals—for the good of everyone," Mallock smiled.

The FBI agent gave him a knowing smile before continuing his story.

"One glorious day, I spotted my suspect. I was convinced of both his guilt and his identity, and I managed—thanks to a trace of sperm on a Polaroid—to arrest him and throw him in the slammer. Four hours later he slit his throat with his own fingernails. He'd kept them long and strong and sharp for that very purpose—and others as well, no doubt. It's not very politically correct to admit it, but the whole department was relieved. I even popped open a bottle of champagne with my main investigative team. We were so happy that the whole business was finally over and done with. No more murderer, no more murders. But the day after he was buried there was a new crime signed Twelve, and another one the day after that, five hundred miles away. Both killings had an identical MO to Needles. I was taken off the case, and it took me years to recover. In fact, I'm not sure I ever really have."

Marvin's eyes had drifted shut as if in slow motion, his neck bowed. He took a deep breath and continued:

"Ten years later my successor, Scott, the one you hunted the serial killer with, had the same experience, but this time he was the one who killed the suspect, a man called Ralph Barnes Bennet. Here again, we thought it was finished."

Angelina hadn't taken her eyes off her colleague. Amédée wondered if they were together. They would have made a handsome couple, like in the movies.

"A few months ago," resumed Marvin, "since we hadn't had any more murders of this type on American soil, we were going to close the case—but then we heard about the killings in France. In spite of my advanced age, they put me back on the investigation. I'm sorry to give you the news this way, Mallock, but Scott went down during a police raid three years ago. Our government and the head of the FBI officially contacted the French authorities, and then went directly to your big boss, Monsieur Dublin. Other than him and the Secretary of the Interior, only three people know about this—plus your President."

"Do you think we're looking at a copycat killer? Or several of them?"

"No, it goes a lot further than that. MO, similarities . . . down to the slightest details."

"Initiates? Or disciples?" persisted Mallock.

But Tom Marvin heaved his big body out of the armchair. "I hope you don't mind, but I don't want to go any further today. And we're . . . how do you say it in French again?"

"Running late?"

"That's it—running late. We'll see you on Sunday and then you'll know everything."

Several people had already knocked on the door. The FBI agents were expected elsewhere. It would have been stupid to trigger the journalists' curiosity even more, to hand them their next headline: *Mallock, the head of Number 36, and the FBI, together in a suite at the Crillon!*

None of them wanted to give the press a gift like that.

28.
Sunday, August 8th, 1888.
A storm on the deck of the Stella Maris

God created man with nimble hands, sturdy little legs, a brain capable of tenacity, and the irrepressible desire to reach the horizon. Here it was on the battered deck of an old caravel that the Marquis François-Henri de Salis-Viracalas tested the limits of his body's endurance.

The ocean thrust up each of its waves like so many obstacles to be overcome in order to reach America. A violent wind swelled even the smallest clouds. From high above, needle-sharp flashes of electricity speared the heavy cumulus billows, forcing them to dump their cargoes of freezing water.

François-Henri found the danger and the terrible weather thrilling.

In his eyes, the ocean was the darkroom for a symbolic revelation. By crossing it, he would finally be able to observe and immortalize what he believed to be the first humans created by God. Bloodthirsty and heavily made up with war paint, the Indians were more than screaming savages bristling with feathers. In their own primitive and impious way, the Redskins were closer to the Creator, to his first desires.

In his sweet delirium, the marquis was certain that in photographing them and studying their features, he would have a clearer vision of the image of God, of his designs and intentions. The Creator had made Man in his image, as the Holy Scriptures said; so it was enough to reverse the proposition—taking care, of course, to select the chosen ones intelligently.

Marquis François-Henri de Salis-Viracalas did not have the slightest idea then of the horde of murders his little idea would generate.

An even higher wave broke over the parapet, drenching him from head to foot. Even with his gloves soaked through and his boots full of seawater, the marquis was exultant. He readjusted his wig smoothly and settled his bicorn hat more firmly over his forehead. Above him, hanging in the rigging, drunk sailors struggled to reef the sails.

Though weighed down by its sixty thirty-pounder long guns, the first-class frigate Stella Maris, twin sister of La Boudeuse, fought valiantly. The marquis of Salis-Viracalas was only afraid of one thing: seeing his precious cameras damaged during the crossing.

For the plates, he used a pioneering technique that had yet to be officially invented at the time.[14] Potato starch fixed by resin gave particularly accurate results, which was essential if all the faces were to be harvested. There was only one pitfall, one weakness in their invention: the gaps between the grains of starch being filled with soot. This natural filter had the effect of limiting the effective sensitivity of the plates, which increased the length of posing time required when the photo was taken, and which often resulted in movement effects. Then there was also the tendency of reds to saturate.

The solution, a very simple one as it turned out, was found by the Marquis Viracalas, and he resolved to keep it a secret. All you had to do was knock out the model you wanted to photograph, drain him of his blood, put makeup on him, and wait for the final instant of death to press the shutter release. To

---

[14] The principle of autochrome would be patented by the Lumière brothers fifteen years later, in 1903.

perfect his clever system, François-Henri also used a sturdy tripod and a remote shutter release mechanism.

Before leaving for the Americas, just to be sure, he had tested his system on a couple of village peasants and a distant cousin visiting for Christmas. The results obtained with the emulsion and the whole shooting sequence had exceeded all his hopes. The victims' features were astonishingly clear.

But he had said that this voyage would be one of great revelations, as if God above had decided to come personally to his aid.

On this 8-8-1888, as François-Henri prepared to leave the deck of the Stella Maris and take refuge in his cabin, the prow of the caravel was suddenly thrust into the trough of a wave. Salis-Viracalas was thrown a full thirty feet, and two sailors fell from the rigging, shrieking like seagulls. One of them ended up in the sea, while the other was impaled on a metal rod used to coil fishing net.

He began to scream, trying to tear himself away from the trap. The rod had entered through his lower back and come out just under his neck, ripping through his lungs and intestines as it went. Pink foam bubbled out of his mouth and was blown away by the ferocious wind. His howls of pain coupled with the noise of the storm and the roaring of the waves were, for the marquis, a revelation.

Nature, God, the Devil, and the cry of men were all one and the same entity, a single mystical body. In the midst of this fury of nature, François-Henri de Salis-Viracalas gained a full understanding of the redemptive virtue of suffering.

It only made his quest more meaningful.

On a plate was a huge slice of *galette* and, on top of it, a gold cardboard crown. The day before yesterday, with the arrest of the little priest, he had missed Epiphany. Yesterday, same story; he had spent the day at the Crillon with Tom and Angelina. That made two days now that he hadn't held to tradition. On Friday night, before the weekend, the whole Fort had gathered without him to share the traditional cake and drink the champagne that ritually waters these occasions. His team knew he wasn't overly fond of these get-togethers, which he generally referred to as "bloody stupid," But Julie Gemoni also knew her Amédée and his special affection for frangipane. The added detail of the crown on top—well, that was Ken all over.

The telephone rang. His mouth full, it took Mallock a moment to answer it. It was the Secretary of the Interior.

"The two federal agents you met yesterday just left my office. I've been aware of the situation for several days now, but I was just given the details. Let's not beat around the bush; our backs are to the wall."

"I'm well aware of that," said Mallock carefully, just as he bit down on a tiny figure of a hedgehog dressed like Santa Claus.

"I don't need to tell you that I have every confidence in you, but we're in really bad shape. With the regional elections coming up it's going to become an issue, and . . . "

"I know, I know. Rest assured, I have no intention of failing."

Mallock didn't want to hear any political talk. It, and bath-room-related stories, made him very uncomfortable when he was trying to eat.

"That's exactly what I wanted to hear. What can I do to help you from my end? Don't scrimp on men. Every single lead has to be investigated, without fail, for each murder. Do you remember the Yorkshire Ripper in England? They focused on his accent, and—"

"Don't worry, I know my job. But if you can keep the media's attack dogs away from me it would be beyond help-ful."

"Journalists aren't my specialty. I'm one of their favorite tar-gets myself. I can only assure you of all my sympathy and moral support. A fat lot of good that does you, I know."

The secretary had a sense of humor, which was something, at least. Mallock smiled silently, waiting for him to continue.

"Seriously, and this is no empty promise, if you need any-thing, or if anyone bothers you, call me and I'll try to clear the way for you. If anyone can get us out of this mess, it's you. I'll talk to you soon, and good luck."

A bit dazed, Mallock continued nibbling carefully on his slice of cake—which was the right thing to do, because shortly, with a slight crunch, he extracted a second charm from his mouth, this one a tiny dinosaur wearing a Scottish kilt! He dropped it on the edge of his plate next to the hedgehog. Then he set to work writing up an assessment of the situation, an ini-tial summary. But he didn't get very far with it before he was interrupted.

Ken's head popped around the door. "Should I come back tomorrow?"

"No, relax. We won't be back on the hunt until Monday any-way, and you're going to need all your strength. You haven't stopped going for ten days now."

Without needing to be asked twice, Ken was executing a perfect military about-face when Mallock stopped him.

"Hey! It's still Saturday, and it's only eleven A.M. You weren't planning on leaving this early, were you?"

"Well, actually, yes, given my thousand and one overtime hours in hell. But since I don't want to seem like I'm disobeying my superintendent, I'll go sit in my little office, have a nice little cup of coffee, and accept your orders."

"No, get out of here. You're of no use to anyone anyway," Mallock teased him.

"How true," Ken agreed, smiling. "Thanks, Chief. You should try to relax a bit yourself."

Just before leaving, he turned around again. "Hey, what's this? You haven't put on your beautiful crown, Your Majesty!"

Mallock threw the crumpled crown at him, which hit the door as Ken yanked it quickly shut behind him. Still smiling, he stood to pick it up. He would have to decide on Monday: bring his team into the loop, or keep the secret. He tried to weigh the pros and cons. Fifteen minutes later, he was forced to acknowledge that there was no ideal solution. This was exactly where the real art of decision-making came into play, of knowing how to accept a choice and deal with its negative aspects. For once, he decided to put his final decision off until later. He wanted to wait and hear what Marvin would tell him tomorrow.

Amélie's condition tormented him and occupied a huge part of his mind. At two o'clock he made up his mind, got into his car, and drove straight through the crowd of journalists without stopping. His old Jaguar, which had previously belonged to a Chechen *mafioso*, was equipped with an ultra-powerful engine, puncture-proof tires, and an armored chassis. It had to weigh at least five tons. He surprised himself by hoping he had run over a foot or two in his escape.

He was out of the media's reach in a very short time.

The smile that the thought of flattened toes had brought to his face faded away quickly. The closer he got to Pitié-Salpêtrière Hospital, the more his heart tightened in his chest. When he parked, he noticed that his hands, which were always dry and warm, were now damp and icy-cold. Shaking. In the elevator he found it hard to breathe. He felt as if he were suffocating. When he got to intensive care it took all his courage to ask for news of Amélie.

The extern looked at him like he was an idiot. "Maurel? You're sure? No, we don't have anyone with that name here," he affirmed.

Mallock was speechless for ten seconds, then persisted. "She might have been moved to another department."

"Maybe," said White-coat, in a tone meant to be reassuring.

"Maybe you could have a look?" Mallock asked.

"Maybe," the man repeated, smirking.

Mallock exploded, and the extern feared briefly for his life. Five minutes later, almost completely calm, Amédée knocked on the door of an old room, one that Professor Ménard had turned into an office so he could be closer to his patients.

He ushered Amédée in and reassured him:

"I believe she's out of the most critical phase," he said to Mallock, who almost cried with gratitude. "I attempted to assess her level of consciousness as soon as I could. But we have to be careful, and wait to be completely sure that the various sedatives have had time to be metabolized."

"Your intern told me about your initial results. Frankly, it wasn't very encouraging."

"You know, Superintendent, nothing is simple or definite in medicine, apart from the patient's will to get better, and the doctor's desire to help that happen. And even then, it's not always clear-cut. They say sometimes that medicine consists of helping a sick person be patient while nature does its healing work, and that's not entirely untrue. The physiopathology of coma is one of the most complex things in our field. The lack of alertness may, in this case, result from both visible traumatic causes and the psychological effects of mental trauma, which are closely intertwined. There's only one thing that will help us get a clearer idea of what's going on here, and it's not easy. We just have to wait."

Mallock thanked him for his directness, and for a humility that high-level clinicians rarely possessed. Then he asked if he could see Amélie. The extern, still in shock from the telling off he had received, escorted him to her room and obsequiously opened the door for him.

Inside, an affecting scene greeted him. Still unconscious but breathing without the help of a ventilator, Amélie was lying in bed. A teenage boy bent carefully over her prone body appeared to be praying. When Mallock coughed discreetly to announce his presence, the young man turned to him with tears streaming down his face. Amédée was struck by the boy's beauty. It was her neighbor, the pharmacist's son, and one of Amélie's very first clients. She had taken care of him since he was very small. Between sobs the boy confided in Mallock, as if the older man had the power to console him.

"She moved into our building right after she passed her exams. She was twenty years old, and I was three or four. She was so nice, and she smelled so good. I really think I fell a little bit in love with her . . . or maybe a lot." The last confession made the boy smile.

"Isn't your mother here with you?"

"She was supposed to come instead and see if there was any news, but she had a problem at the pharmacy at the last minute, so she gave me the flowers—and here I am."

"Want a ride home?"

The pharmacist's son nodded silently. When you were his age, the first significant loss of someone in your life was hard to bear. But Amélie seemed to be through the worst now, and there was hope. Mallock shared this news with the boy. As they drove back, the young apprentice pharmacist talked about nothing but Amélie. She had babysat him often when he was younger. She had always been so attentive to him. She wore such pretty dresses. She . . .

Mallock was only half-listening. He savored the feeling of euphoria coursing through him. Even if not tomorrow, Amélie was going to live, and they could go back to seeing each other, to their lunches and their budding love affair. Amélie was alive, and so life would resume again. When he dropped the boy off in front of the pharmacy, the latter asked:

"Would you keep us updated, please?"

Mallock promised that he would. "What's your phone number?"

The boy fought back fresh tears. "The same as Mademoiselle Maurel's, with an eleven instead of a ten at the end. We used to get her phone calls all the time, and she'd get ours."

Mallock was preparing to head straight back to the office when Julie popped up in front of him.

"Peekaboo, Superintendent!"

"What brings you here? Nothing serious, I hope."

"Nope! We have something for you."

Jules came up behind her. "It's really hard to find a parking place in your neighborhood, boss."

Remembering the presence of the building manager's son, Amédée turned around to introduce him—and abruptly realized that he didn't remember the boy's first name. It was one of his special talents, which he called patronymic amnesia.

Julie, quick on the uptake as always, introduced herself first, which would force the young man to give his name. "I'm Julie Gemoni, chief lieutenant, and a friend of the superintendent."

"Didier Dôthem," offered the boy, making it possible for Mallock to jump in.

"Didier is my pharmacist's son," he said.

"Then he must know you very well indeed," teased Julie gently.

All four of them laughed heartily. Didier seemed transfixed by Julie; he gaped at her as if she were a holy apparition. She was used to making conquests, though, and pretended not to notice.

"Can we sit out here on the terrace for a minute, boss?"

"Of course. See you soon, Didier. I'll keep you posted about Amél—Mademoiselle Maurel."

Didier said good-bye to them and went into the pharmacy.

"Three beers!" called Jules.

Women don't like beer, as a rule—but Julie did.

"What can I do for you, my little ones?"

"Oh, it isn't what you can do for us; it's what we can do for you." Julie took an object wrapped in tissue paper out of her purse. It was a large dark-green gorilla, made out of some delicately woven material. It was a superb piece of work, and Amédée adored it immediately.

"When Jules and I saw it, we knew you absolutely had to have it."

"It looks like me, is that it?" asked Mallock, smiling.

"Let's just say it made us think of you," said Jules. "Do you like it?"

"I love it. Really. But you must have broken the bank. It's incredibly sweet of you, but why give it to me here?"

"Er . . . well, we weren't quite flush enough to buy something for everyone. So since we didn't want to make anyone jealous, we picked you. Thought we might as well suck up a little."

"I knew it!"

Mallock was touched by their kindness. Jules and Julie sensed his emotion, and hurried to lighten the mood.

"Come on, let's get out of here. If we're late to the office our grouch of a superintendent will yell at us again."

"You're not wrong. I know him, and he's completely pitiless. Hurry up; I'm sure he'll be there soon."

They all laughed again, and headed to their own cars to return to Number 36

The rest of the day was devoted to everything Mallock had shoved aside since the beginning of the case. He worked with another group, which he called his nursery, and he was pleased to find them motivated and conscientious—or maybe it was just his good mood making him see the world through rose-colored glasses.

When he got home at around eleven o'clock that night, the sky was a light chestnut color and the air had a sharp, peppery quality. In the square next to his apartment building, lit and warmed by tall outdoor lamps, people were dining outside. Mallock realized he was hungry—and that he couldn't be bothered to cook anything.

He went home and put the Beatles' third anthology on the CD player. Yesterday he would have liked to ask Marvin for more details about the Fab Four's first visit to the United States, but it wasn't the right time. He tore a large hunk off a baguette and took one of his homemade goose-liver terrines out of the fridge. No diet tonight, he told himself firmly.

The Beatles had been a big part of his life in the past, and they always would be in the future.

Amédée's passion for the Beatles had really begun in 1965. He'd been a teenager living deep in the countryside, an hour outside of Caen. His father, Ferdinand, had rented land owned by his brother Aristide. Born in Béarn in 1930, Amédée's father lived his life as if it were an ordeal, an obstacle course that he already knew he would fail. He wasn't a cowardly man, but every day he woke up defeated, and every night he went to bed aching. Well—that wasn't entirely true. Ferdinand did have his triumphant mornings. Sometimes they even lasted a whole week. At these times he was full of projects and optimism. Too much, even, because he tended to spend "willy-nilly," as his brother warned him. A new tractor, the latest combine harvester, or new show chickens: Mille Fleur and Pekin Bantams, Dark Indian Games, Sebrights, Dwarf Marans . . .

Later the sickness that ate away at Ferdinand would be given a name: manic depression. People with his symptoms would be diagnosed as bipolar, but it came too late. After failing to make a profit from his own land, located between the two big "B"s, Bayonne and Biarritz, Ferdinand had decided to join his brother Aristide Mallock, nicknamed Aristote, who had established himself successfully in Normandy.

Amédée was ten years old when he discovered Calvados. Everything was gray and muddy in Normandy, even the sun. Just a huge, confusing stretch of plain, full of wheat that surrounded everything. Sometimes there were glorious sunsets, so beautiful they were nauseating. They lacked the weighty power of the southwestern skies, in which you could still see God's Nabist brushstrokes.

In 1966, Mallock received two hits from a revolver. The first shot was fired by his mother, right after she tried to hang herself. Amédée had found her in time and held her legs up for more than an hour before his father came to the rescue. Marie, born with the maiden name of Ferré on February 29th, 1932, in a small port town in Brittany, promised she would never do it again. Two weeks later, on her birthday, she'd blown her brains out with her grandfather's old ordnance revolver. In fact it hadn't exactly been her birthday. Since that year wasn't a leap year, she didn't even have one.

It was in the morbid and tragic aftermath of this that the second revolver shot came.

For his thirteenth birthday on June fourteenth, Aristote had come over for lunch. He had brought two things with him: a Grundig pickup radio for his younger brother, whose birthday was June twenty-first, and a record of modern music for his nephew Amédée. The cover was a curious mixture of photos and drawings. The group was called the Beatles, and the album was . . . *Revolver*. Mallock would learn later, of course, that the title had nothing to do with the weapon. Paul had wanted to play on the word's double meaning in English, a mystical meaning connected to the motion of the earth, to karma, and everything that was just starting to emerge then and would later become the New Age movement—and a second, much more concrete meaning: the spinning of the record itself.

What could you say about this music? That it tore down the dark and dusty curtains smothering his childhood? That it opened the doors to rooms full of mirrors and rain? The best way to put it might be that it woke Amédée up, bogged down as he was in the Norman moors of his adolescence. Like a wild buffalo deciding to live, he dragged himself out by pulling on the music as if it were so many life-saving ropes. The essence of the sounds, the sense of vibration—all of it, from the shocking flatness of the bass drum to the blaring sharpness of the brass—all of this said *life*.

Amédée needed it. Desperately.

Three months after Marie Mallock's death, Amédée's father was institutionalized. Aristote, that kindly misanthrope, knew his duty. He took the boy into his home. Saint-Aubin was a small village by the sea. Though devastated and lost, Amédée put on a brave face. Pride, and the desire not to be a burden on someone else, made him keep his troubles to himself. It was a kind of reserve and unwavering dignity that would stay with him always.

In the face of so much sadness and loss, "What's the point?"s and "Why me?"s could easily have won out over his good nature. It's hard to stay standing, to stay upright, when the ground falls out from under your feet.

Luckily there was the sea. She and Amédée had an immediate connection. They shared the same gentleness, the same quick temper. They were both mercurial but generous; quiet but full of stories.

Every evening after he came home from school on the bus from Caen, the young Mallock headed directly for the seawall, often stopping at his best friend's house on the Rue Aumont. On the beach he would take off his socks and clunky shoes to bury his toes in the sand, and gaze out at the soothing horizontal line of the horizon. Contact was made.

Then Amédée would tell the waves about his day.

The days and nights passed in this way. Convalescing by the sea, Amédée healed gradually from the wound of his mother's death. With his father it was more complicated, and more painful. Every visit to Ferdinand ripped off the scabs, and the boy's heart would start bleeding all over again. He wished for many things, including, one day, his father's death.

He was still wishing for it.

Aristide Mallock was what you might call a man of few words, but he had a good heart, and though he never told his nephew as much, he had a great deal of compassion for Amédée. It was a feeling that turned bit by bit into friendship and then affection, encouraged by the young man's proud and responsible attitude—in which the uncle, never having had children of his own, saw something of himself. It even made him smile sometimes: watching his nephew be confronted by the indifference and nastiness of wealthy classmates or muscle-bound bullies, poor people who were scornful because they were less poor, and poor people who were violent because they were more poor. Right before Aristide's eyes it turned Amédée into a younger version of him—a kindly misanthrope.

At the end of June 1967, to reward Amédée for finishing the school year with teacher commendations and a spot on the honor roll, Aristote brought back from London a kind of blazing sun, a colorful and dazzling thing: *Sergeant Pepper's Lonely Hearts Club Band.*

This new Beatles album was like the crashing of a giant gong all over the world, exhorting the earth to wake up and sing, to look at the beauty and brilliance of things, to rediscover color after decades of gray. Paul, at the peak of his creativity, had converted George and then John and Ringo, and the whole world after them.

Mallock would always be grateful to them, because he had been one of those millions of people whose lives had been changed forever.

For dessert, Amédée put together an *omelette au rhum*. He blended whipped egg whites with three yolks he had beaten together with powdered sugar until pale. After tasting his *foie gras*, he ignited the omelette. Despite his fatigue, the eternal gourmet in him had won out again.

Just before going to bed he swallowed a sugar cube onto which he had squeezed a few drops of one of his magic potions. Lying down, he calmly allowed thoughts of the Makeup Artist to overcome him, closed his eyes, and went off to his meeting.

Seven times he woke up, body drenched in sweat and head throbbing with migraine. Seven times he went back into enemy territory. The insanity of others, as terrible as it is, lives somewhere deep inside all of us, in one of those secret rooms that we never open except in the presence of evil, or an ill wind. That night, once again, Mallock accepted the risk that his madness would awaken and take him where both his parents had gone.

This oppressive legacy only made the courage he showed at times like this more admirable.

But, ill-prepared and driven more by impatience than strategy, he didn't bring back much from this particular voyage. A few sensations of terror, smells and visions of thick walls, much too high, covered in brambles and bright scarlet vomit. A bunch of large red puddles at the bottom of a valley, held down by big carpet nails. In his dream, Mallock managed to rip out one of the nails. Imprisoned in one of these pools was the ethereal body of the little girl with blonde braids, which then rose up into the sky, while the Makeup Artist howled with rage as he watched one of the pieces in his collection get away from him.

It was a sad victory.

30.
Sunday, January 9th

A private exhibition of the Makeup Artist's latest work.
No caviar, no champagne.
No laughter.

In front of Mallock there rose up an enormous apothecary cabinet with buttons, the kind that hardly existed anymore except in those big pharmacies out in the countryside that also served as herbalists' and homeopathists' shops. This particular cabinet was definitely the largest one Amédée had ever seen. A wooden ladder slid vertically along a rail so that all the drawers could be reached.

Mallock counted around eighty drawers made of oak. The smallest ones were about three inches square; the largest a foot high by two feet wide, with the depth ranging from just over two feet for the lower drawers to about eight inches for the upper ones. Even before he opened a single drawer, Amédée knew what they would contain. A veritable anatomy lesson, a terrifying jigsaw puzzle: all the bones, muscles, and organs of Mitsuko Mitzutani, aged twelve.

Tibia, clavicles, triceps, a complete set of ribs, the deltoid muscle . . . the monster seemed to be familiar with everything. *A doctor, or a surgeon?* Mallock thought suddenly. But he might just as easily have added *poet* to the list.

On the two drawers containing the feet, the killer had written *Walk or dream*. In the two tiny compartments containing her eyes he had written *Last look*. On the drawer with her severed lips inside: *Stolen kiss*. On the one with her head inside he had written a Shakespearean *Not to be!* And on the drawer holding her still-bleeding heart, he had scrawled *Assembly required.*

Mallock felt himself falling. It felt as if his left leg were freezing, turning to ice, and soon it wouldn't be able to hold him anymore. He looked around for help, but he was alone. On the floor, a snake was lunging at a piece of wood shaped like a cross.

As he sank down to join it, Amédée woke up in his own bed. He'd been trapped by his dream visions again. While he was dreaming of this bizarre murder his bedroom window had come open, and snow had blown into the room, covering the left side of his bed and almost his entire leg.

Not having the heart to clean everything up and remake his bed, he settled for taking a very hot shower and going back to sleep on one of the huge living-room sofas.

Tomorrow is another day, as Tom Marvin would have said.

Outside, the courtyard was covered with a pretty white carpet. Mallock was woken up again, for good this time, by a curse:

"Shit, fuck!"

The FBI special agent had slipped—not on a dog turd, which was rare in Le Marais these days, but on the icy sidewalk. In the time it took him to stand up while Angelina laughed at him and brush the snow off his elegant coat, Mallock managed to pull on a shirt and trousers. He opened the door, trying to look like someone who'd been awake for hours and was expecting them.

"I've been waiting for you," he bluffed, letting them in.

"Coffee?"

"Coffee!"

But Amédée hated lying, even about small, unimportant things. "Actually . . . it was your wounded-beast impression that got me out of bed," he admitted to Marvin.

"Our meeting was for eight o'clock this morning, wasn't it?" said Angelina, looking worried.

"Oh yes. I'd just forgotten to set my alarm clock. When I don't tell it all my plans the night before and grope its hands passionately, it takes revenge. Luckily the foul mouth of a certain F . . . B . . . I . . . agent, to quote Hannibal, stepped in for its ringing."

All three of them laughed. Like yesterday with Jules and Julie, he needed it. Needed the comfort and strength of camaraderie.

"I don't need to tell you again that all of this has to stay absolutely confidential. If anything gets out we'll deny everything, but it'll really fuck things up."

Mallock agreed but, for honesty's sake, he clarified: "I do intend to give my principal colleagues an expurgated version of all of this. I can't keep them in the dark."

Marvin's mouth pursed with doubt—drawing attention to an impressive set of lips. "Expurgated how?"

"Keeping only what I think is necessary for a better overall understanding of the case."

"That's vague, but I trust you."

"You can," Mallock assured him.

"Fine, okay. I'll start over from the beginning."

Tom Marvin was finally going to tell the story of the Makeup Artist.

He moistened his full lips with a sip of coffee before beginning.

"When I was named lead investigator in '64, there was no Makeup Artist. It was just an isolated murder case. Out of ambition, pride, enthusiasm, and youthful arrogance, I . . . uncovered some tricky issues and kicked up some dust, as you said the other day. Whether by luck or sheer coincidence, I had really hit the mother lode. It took my boss a long time to believe me. I had to bring him everything on a silver platter. In his defense, though, at first I couldn't believe what was happening either. I thought I was going crazy. The more I searched, the more I found. It was like a bottomless well."

Marvin drained the last drops of his coffee with a little slurping sound and put down the cup.

"I'd started out with almost nothing to go on: the makeup, traces of multiple injections, and the double cadaveric lividity. At the time there were no computers, no databases. It would be twenty more years before Steve Jobs created Apple—he got the name from our beloved Beatles, by the way. Hey, you're a big Beatles fan. Do you know where that idea came from?"

Mallock would rather hear more about the Makeup Artist, but he decided to humor Marvin. A story for a story; it was only fair.

"London. A garden on Cavendish Avenue. Paul is directing a film crew in his private park. He goes into his living room and finds out that his old friend, the art dealer Robert Fraser, has been there without telling him and left a little painting by Paul's favorite artist, Magritte, propped against a vase. He didn't charge Paul anything and even left the door open behind him. He knows Paul wants the painting. It's a picture of a Granny Smith apple with the words *au revoir* on it. That will become the model for the famous logo."

Apple, apple turnover, *pain au chocolat*, croissant . . .

"The croissants!" The exclamation came from Amédée, who was starving.

Angelina rummaged in her bag with an apology. They hadn't forgotten. Mallock refilled the coffees and soon they were following his example and dipping their pastries in the hot liquid, *à la française*.

"Mmmmf . . . s'good," mumbled Angelina, her mouth full.

"Come on, Tom, back to the Makeup Artist. I'm dying to hear what's next."

"Okay. So, again, no computers back then, no DNA, no mobile phones or any of those things that make our lives easier today. The only communication tool I had was the telex network, which at least allowed me to send copies of reports all over the place without having to travel. I traveled back in time, like Hop-o'-My-Thumb. And every time I thought I'd found the case *princeps*, I'd discover an even older one. All the way back to the famous Sharon Delanay, killed in Atlanta in December 1929. A hundred victims in all, sixty-two of which are definite. All identical. The exact same makeup, the same MO; very simple. He photographed them paralyzed but alive, killed them, and drained their blood, not necessarily in that order. At the time I wasn't sure. Nothing else, and there was nothing spectacular about it. The needle marks were invisible, and the makeup, because he'd put it on women, didn't attract any particular attention. That's why it took the arrival of an upstart new detective like me to make the connection and set off a panic."

Tom trailed off and stared into space. But Mallock wanted more.

"But what about the capture?"

"Oh . . . nothing special. I spotted him one day, that's all. Like I told you, I was absolutely sure of his guilt because of a trace of sperm on a Polaroid. For the record, that was the very first identification through DNA in the world. A huge point of pride on top of the capture. If I hadn't been so happy and so cocky, I wouldn't have slipped up. His fingernails were as long and sharp as razors."

"You couldn't have noticed everything," Amédée tried to reassure him.

"The worst thing is that I did notice them. I thought he used them on his victims, and I wasn't too far off the mark. Ten years later, the same thing happened to Scott Amish. He was too sure of himself; he got himself into an untenable position, and he ended up having to take his suspect down without questioning him. A certain Ralph Barnes Bennet."

Amédée was impressed. It was an incredible story, the kind most police officers dreamed of. You wanted to be a hero when you became a cop, not hand out fines and knock people around with a billy club. Capturing big game like that was the top; Legion of Honor stuff.

"But how has he been able to stay one step ahead of so many police for so long?"

Mallock wanted to get into the marrow of the subject, the meat of the matter, its substance. What could they take away from this that was concrete and would help him, today?

"Assuming that he was a teenager when he started killing, he'd be a very old man now. Two hundred murders, over such a long time span and without getting caught. It's unbelievable."

"Especially because he would have to have had superhuman speed. When I cross-checked everything I found two cases in which people were killed at the same time but several hundred miles apart. It would have taken hours to drive from one location to the other. It's unlikely but not impossible by plane."

"Or we could go back to the copycat theory."

"That's not really worth considering, unfortunately. The ritualistic procedures are very precise, as you know, and they were painstakingly adhered to every time, down to the composition of the pigments used for the makeup. Also, the Makeup Artist's methods have never been revealed to the press—nor has his very existence, come to that, let alone the details."

"Look, let's be logical about this," Mallock mused. "If I'm hearing you right, given what you've just said there can only be one solution."

The two Americans stared at the Frenchman. What was he getting at?

"A cop. And moreover, a cop who's part of the investigation. Only he, knowing the ritual, would be able to duplicate it. To be so precise it would have to be him or someone close to your Needles, a relative or friend. It's a sure thing. And either way this gives us a trail to focus on for France: look for someone originally from the United States. Track the accent."

"It's far from being as clear-cut as that, Mallock. The ritual changes and gets worse as it crosses the Atlantic. In the American cases we have . . . *exsanguation*, is that the word in French?"

"We say *exsanguination*, actually."

"*Exsanguination*," repeated Tom, before continuing. "On each victim there was this practice of draining the blood through twelve puncture sites, and then the application of makeup, undoubtedly for masturbatory purposes or the souvenir photograph. But that's it. What I've seen in your photos isn't comparable to it. The guy's gone completely insane!"

"What if it's just age?" Angelina suggested. "Senile dementia combined with his obsessions?"

"That makes sense," Mallock agreed. "If we accept the idea of a hundred-year-old murderer!"

Marvin hesitated before his next words, but the idea was already on all their minds. "Someone who is somehow . . . regenerated by drinking the blood of his victims."

Mallock didn't dismiss the hypothesis. He had seen too many things. "We'd have to ask the science experts to find out if that kind of 'diet' would be possible or beneficial—if not for prolonging life, at least for good health."

"We've already asked, and the answer is no, unless the person is able to prepare and add other ingredients to this beverage. In principle, and in any other situation, I'd reject the idea. But here, after everything we've seen . . . Senile dementia could explain the horror of it, couldn't it?"

"It does fit with the age and your date of 1929. And once

you've eliminated all rational explanations," said Mallock, doing his best Sherlock imitation, "the only thing that remains is the unthinkable. It's better than nothing, no?"

"Yes," agreed the Americans, sighing.

The three of them looked at each other, almost embarrassed at having admitted their mutual disillusionment.

Silence. Fade to black.

Two or three minutes went by before anyone spoke. Snow fell softly outside. Mallock's eyes went to his whiskey cabinet. When he felt stress and discouragement overtaking him, he often indulged in a little restorative single-malt. It had the effect of a hand wiping across a fogged-up window; it was that quick and effective. And just as tenuous, too. He clearly wasn't the only one who knew this trick.

"I'd love one," said Tom, following Mallock's gaze.

"Two?"

"Three," said Angelina.

A moment later they were sipping their medicine dreamily, watching the snow fall in the courtyard. Bit by bit, it was erasing the traces left by Marvin's fall. A goddamn hundred-year-old vampire in their midst. It would make even the most hardened cop's blood run cold—or at least give him something to think about. It was Mallock who interrupted their contemplation of the courtyard.

"To sum up, we've got a first murder identified in 1929, a first guilty party who killed himself almost right before your eyes twenty years ago, and a second one a decade ago who was gunned down. Then our phoenix reappears in France. And it appears highly unlikely that we're dealing with copycats, because the information has never been released."

"That's about right."

"That leaves the cop assigned to the investigation, or . . . here's another idea: a family. Imagine a case of insanity passed down from father to son. It would only take three generations from grandfather to grandson. And that would also explain the double murders in different places—a father and son, for example."

Marvin was silent for a few seconds. He was in agreement. His French colleague's idea was, like the man himself, strange but appealing, imaginative and rational at the same time.

But instead of voicing his approval, he glanced at his watch and asked, in a worried tone:

"Is there a church nearby?"

"What for?" was Amédée's inappropriate response.

"To go to mass. It's eleven o'clock. I'll miss it."

Mallock should have directed him to Saint-Paul, but he thought better of it. The image of the child in the font was still very fresh in his mind. The church should have reopened its doors by now, but better to avoid it.

He suggested Saint-Gervais, right nearby.

No, no thanks, he wouldn't go with them. It had been a very long time since he'd taken part in that kind of rejoicing.

31.
Monday, January 10th

The snow on the ground was in its death throes. It lay in brown slabs, flakes clinging together as if trying to freeze again, die a little later. Mallock hadn't felt so awful in a long time. He was exhausted by his attempts to make contact with the killer's mind, and he couldn't seem to plant his feet firmly back in reality. He was floating somewhere a few centimeters off the ground, and only his migraine still gave him the sense that he existed. His taking of prohibited substances and his dream-devoured nights hadn't helped things either. Arriving at his office, he was pleasantly surprised to find his whole team assembled, with the exception of Robert.

Ken jumped in first. "I think I've discovered something."

"Your timing is perfect. I could really use some good news. Where?"

"The homes of the latest victims—we found similar bags. Made out of brown craft paper, pretty large and very strong, all with staple marks in the upper part. Two of the victims had reused them as garbage bags. A lot of people do that. They must have electric staplers, and—"

"Can you get to the point any faster?"

"So last night, my dear little wife went out and ran errands for the first time in her life."

"Conclusion?"

"It's the kind of bag that big stores like Monoprix use for transporting perishable foodstuffs, when they don't have their own bags with their logo on them. I noticed that they go way overboard when they seal them, with a ton of staples, and the victims' bags happened to have the same type of perforations."

There was only one Polish-Japanese man—or Nippo-Polish, as Francis called him—in the world who would use an expression like "perishable foodstuffs." Mallock decided to be a good sport and let the remark pass without comment.

"Bravo; that's a lead. How are you going to follow up on it?"

"I've asked Jules to help me find out which stores use this kind of bag, and then we'll get the names of all their delivery people, and you should have a new list to play with. And I know how much my superintendent loves lists!"

"It's nice of you to think of me, but if you do it that way it's going to take weeks. I'll be an old man by then."

"We don't have any other solutions, boss," said Jules.

Julie, who had sensed the trap, was quick to intervene. "Unless our boss has one of those simple yet brilliant ideas of his that make all our little meetings such a joy, and fill us with admiration."

"He does have one, as a matter of fact. Take a look at the victims' bank statements and you'll have the names and addresses of the stores you want. You can use the date of payment to get the delivery date, and that should make it easy to find the delivery person, or people, to bring in for questioning."

For once, Ken couldn't think of a witty comeback. He was slightly vexed that he hadn't thought of this solution himself. There was more than just humor in his little ninja's head; there was a lot of pride as well.

The silence stretched until Julie, like the good colleague that she was, stepped in with a diversion. Out of solidarity, and also because she didn't like it when Mallock, deliberately or not, made one of them look foolish.

"Jules and I have been working on another lead," she said. "A pretty good one, too."

"Tell me."

"We started with the cast you had taken of the imprint of the tripod. And we got lucky, for once. The cast was tiny to start out with; they had a lot of trouble getting anything readable out of it, even using the most state-of-the-art elastomers. But the lab techs did an amazing job. Thanks to the precision of their cast, we were able to see that the points of the tripod had been deliberately fashioned, and in a very particular way. Listen to this: there's only one brand that makes the tips of its tripods that way. Gascht!"

Flung out that way, the final word sounded like an expletive, or maybe a sneeze.

"It's German. There are only eleven vendors in France, seven of which are in Paris or the Paris metropolitan area. We'll take an inventory of everyone who's bought this model in the last ten or fifteen years. Then we can compare it with Amélie Maurel's datebook and the other lists, and voilà! *Alea iacta est!*"

Julie and Jules gave Mallock a sideways glance. Had they forgotten anything?

"Perfect. Nothing to say. Happy hunting, but hurry up. I've got a little theory of my own."

Mallock felt guilty about hiding a crucial element of the case from his own colleagues. He promised himself he would spill the beans at the first opportunity. He had gotten Tom's tacit agreement, after all.

"Don't forget the syringe! The Makeup Artist must have stolen it from Amélie Maurel, because it had her fingerprints on it. So we can reasonably assume that this individual knew her or saw her often, personally or professionally. That's why I keep going back to her appointment book. For me there's a ninety percent chance that the Makeup Artist's name is in there. We should keep it as our reference directory, our go-to list. Francis has put it in the system; he's waiting for your lists to start with the cross-checking. We'll put Bob on the bags. Let him know. Jules and Julie, you stay on the tripod. You know my favorite technique: list-comparing. In the meantime, Ken and I will take an overall look at the people in the appointment book. Anyone that might correspond to one of the possible profiles. That area is still wide open for now, unfortunately."

"You're taking me off the bags?" asked Ken, sulkily. "It was my idea!"

"I need you. Got a problem with that?"

"No, but usually . . . "

"Don't form habits, old man. I need your brain right now, not your feet."

As his colleagues filed silently out of the room, Mallock added:

"Don't ask me why, but don't hesitate to check out everyone, of *any* age whatsoever, and I mean that."

"From 7 to 77, like with Tintin?" asked Jules, smiling.

"And even older than that!"

When Francis, Jules, and Julie had gone, Ken asked: "We're starting with the letter A in the appointment book, I assume?"

"No, I want to pick out a few personally first. If I can narrow it down a bit we'll save some time."

"Other than your whim about the elderly, what criteria are we using?"

"Just let me do it."

Ken knew when to ease off. Mallock the Wizard was going to put his bizarre talents to work again. *Pretend not to notice.*

"Come back and see me at two o'clock. We'll put together the attack strategy for our interviews. I want the same method of approach to be used every time, the same questions, to get homogeneous results for all the people in the appointment book. That reminds me, where has Bob gone? He needs to be briefed about your bag story, pronto."

"It's none of my business, but I walked in when he was on the phone. He didn't want to say anything, but . . . "

"But what?"

"I think his wife might have taken off. I'm not positive, but you should have seen his face."

"I'll call him."

"Don't do that—you're not supposed to know. And plus, you know how proud he is. Also this isn't the first time she's run off."

"Really? I thought things were going better."

"No way. Bob's a good guy deep down, but frankly, he's not exactly a prize when it comes to women."

With that harsh but fair statement, Ken went off to get himself a coffee. Mallock found himself alone. This time the premonition needed no drugs, no smoky helping hand. Amédée felt himself overwhelmed by sudden and tremendous understanding.

He stood up, swearing:

"Shit!"

Fifteen minutes later he was driving up the Rue de Cronstadt toward the Georges-Brassens park, sick with worry. He parked not far away from the Deux Taureaux, remnants of an old covered meat-market. This was where Robert Daranne lived. Almost all his children had told him off and left, one by one, with haste that was highly understandable when you knew their father's character. He still lived in the family home, alone except for his exhausted wife and their youngest son, the famous "Alas."

Amédée dashed up to the second floor of Bob's building and rang the doorbell. He waited for a few seconds and rang again, then knocked with his fist. He knew Bob was there, but there was no answer, not the slightest noise. He went down to the landlord's apartment; maybe he had a set of keys.

"I'm sorry, but Monsieur Daranne isn't the trusting type," the man felt the need to explain.

Mallock didn't reply. He had made his decision. He went back upstairs, took out his Glock 34, and fired three shots into the lock. The semi-armored hollow-point bullets worked like a charm. He added to the violence by elbowing the door open. Bob was inside, sitting at the living-room coffee table, having a conversation with his revolver. He had emptied three-quarters of a bottle of Scotch.

"She's gone," he slurred.

Mallock knew from the tone of his voice that he only needed to be convinced. He had plenty of experience with this type of situation. So he talked to Bob, and let him talk. An hour later Amédée left with Bob's weapon, a snub-nosed .38. In the stairwell he changed his mind and took it back to him.

"I'll leave this right here, in case you're stupid enough to . . . "

He even went so far as pretending to make sure the gun was loaded, while Bob watched.

"I'll send over a locksmith from the office and expect to see you, cleaned up and smiling, tomorrow morning at eight o'clock sharp. Otherwise, you're fired. And I'm not kidding, believe me."

Bob nodded. Mallock, without adding anything further, turned around and walked out. When he tried to pull the door shut behind him it fell down with a giant crash. He went down the stairs, grumbling. Outside, still worried but determined not to go back up to Bob's, he drove back to the office.

By the time he'd gotten back to Number 36, an ugly migraine had reared its head. He managed to yell anyway. He desperately needed to offload the anguish that he had just transferred from Bob's heart into his own. Ken and company looked at each other discreetly. They knew what to expect. At times like this it was better to leave him alone.

"You all know your jobs; I don't need to tell you again."

But, of course, he did tell them again. This was one of his manias. He repeated himself, convinced that they hadn't fully understood him the first time, or that they had forgotten what he asked them to do.

"Ken and I are on the hunt," he said. "Every individual listed in Amélie Maurel's notebook will have to be either brought in or visited. Jules and Julie, you'll finalize the list of buyers of those tripods . . . Gouache."

"Gascht, boss!" Julie corrected him.

"Gouache or Gascht, the list needs to be finished. Robert will be here tomorrow morning. He's a little out of sorts, so be nice to him. He needs some human warmth. Francis or Ken, put him on the list of users of brown-paper bags and delivery people. I'm counting on you to be exhaustive on this, too. I'd rather have too many names than not enough. Don't forget, it's the computer that will do the sorting. Remember, above all, we can't reel in this piece of shit if we don't have the right name. Execution!"

On Tuesday morning Robert was at his desk. He tried to thank Mallock, who waved him off.

"Don't ever do anything like that again."

"I'm sorry. Thanks for bringing my gun back. It made me feel . . . "

Mallock cut him off. "I'm warning you, if you die I will fucking kill you," which got a smile out of Bob. "Let's not talk about it anymore," he added. "Go find Francis and he'll brief you. It has to do with bags and delivery people—right up your alley. I'm going to see Mordome."

"Consider it done, boss."

"I just thought of something else, too. It's the kind of large brown-paper bag, very heavy, that people reuse as garbage bags."

"So?"

"I'm not sure. Ask Ken to explain. It was his idea anyway."

When Amédée arrived at the IML, Mordome was finishing his autopsy of the actress's skull, watched by an American medical examiner who was there in an observational capacity. The largest country in the world apparently wasn't about to trust a little developing nation like France. Mordome, without overtly taking offense, ignored both of them regally and spoke loudly for the benefit of the recording system:

"I'm incising the sellar diaphragm covering the pituitary gland in order to remove the fossa hypophyseos. After sectioning the diaphragm of the sella turcica, I will sever and then

bend back the posterior clinoid processes . . . The hypophyseos has now been withdrawn from the pituitary cavity . . . I am
lifting up the sellar diaphragm and dissecting all around it . . .
Now that I've done that, and if no one has any objections, I'm
going to take a pause to greet Superintendent Mallock, who
has just entered the room, as he deserves."

The metallic *clink* of a microphone being switched off.

"I've never seen anything like it," said Mordome, talking
only to Mallock. "That maniac literally emptied out this poor
woman's body cavity like you'd do with a chicken. He widened
the pubic area by cutting the pelvic floor and ripping out the
tissue; I've noted the presence of one ragged skin edge and one
smooth edge. Then he just sank his arms into the cavity and
tore out everything he could find. A real massacre. I don't even
think he stopped there. We found beard stubble in the lower
abdomen, also head hair, neither of which belongs to the victim. Analysis should show that it's from a white man."

"He put his head inside her body?"

"I don't see any other explanation."

"I still can't believe anyone could do something like this.
And so many murders, for so many years."

"What do you mean 'so many years'? Don't exaggerate,
now; the first murder was only in—"

"Forget I said anything. I'll fill you in as soon as I can.
Okay?"

Mallock glanced sideways at the American pathologist.
Luckily the man was half-asleep thanks to jet lag.

Amédée left Mordome perplexed. It was strange, the
impressions these murders made on normal people. First there
was disgust, then anger and fear, followed rapidly by incom-
prehension. But the most surprising thing was the final feeling,
which was in the process of completely overwhelming people
like Mallock and Mordome. Not resignation, but the sense of
an almost metaphysical helplessness, like you might feel in the

face of destiny, when your child is ripped away from you in the midair explosion of an airplane.

In the main lobby, just before leaving the red-brick building, Mallock was assailed by a vision. It was fairly common for him to receive messages unprovoked, but it had already happened three times on this case. He considered it a sort of rebound effect of the drugs, especially the one he used to expand his field of vision, lysergic acid diethylamide, or LSD, the famous drug produced from rye ergot by Sandoz Laboratories. He sometimes combined it with a dose of opium.

His body had started trembling, and he had to lean against the wall. The setting of this new vision seemed familiar to him. It was the Hotel de Crillon, in the room where the actress had been slaughtered. Like in his last dream, he found himself behind the killer, trying to reach him.

The bastard was crouched a few feet away from him, head buried up to the neck in the actress's abdomen. It wasn't Kathleen Parks on the bed, but Marilyn. Amédée stood totally helpless in the lobby of the IML, mouth open and eyes closed. In the other place, the Makeup Artist's body had begun making jerking motions. He was biting, ripping, tearing body tissues apart.

Becoming aware of the superintendent's presence, the Makeup Artist pulled his head abruptly out of the corpse's crotch. Before Mallock's eyes was the image of a carrion-eater withdrawing his damp head from the belly of an antelope. A warm savanna wind wafted toward Amédée, bringing with it the sweet odor of putrefaction. Marilyn's hair was red. Dripping with blood and secretions, the Makeup Artist's face turned slowly in Mallock's direction. Running his tongue over his upper lip, he said:

"Yum yum, Superintendent! Would you like a taste?"

Mallock staggered. At almost the same instant, as if from far away, he heard:

"Superintendent? Sir?"

One of the Institute guards had come over to help him. He looked at Mallock, worried. "It happens to us all, even at our age," he added.

He clearly thought that the superintendent was still distressed by an autopsy, or maybe a difficult identification. Mallock had no problem with that. It was a useful explanation. He straightened and thanked the officer for his concern.

"I'm feeling much better now, thanks."

He took a few steps outside the building before realizing how bad he felt. Where could he find some comfort? Regain his strength before going back on the attack?

"If only Amélie . . . " he murmured under his breath.

He thought again of Margot Murât. Did he have the right? He was desperate. To lay his heavy head between her breasts and let her stroke his hair. Allow himself a moment of inelegant vulnerability. She would understand. Why then, why hesitate? Why not grant himself this little weakness?

Very simply because, for Amédée, no matter how he twisted and turned the problem in his mind, the price of that consolation would always be too high.

Pride, or moral delicacy?

Sometimes the two go hand in hand.

33.
At the same time, somewhere else

Vertigo. It was in that word that he evolved most often. After each wave of blood, each scarlet surge, the Makeup Artist cleaned all the instruments in his collection with mixed feelings. Pride and disgust. Peace and torment.

The sword gave him more unpleasant sensations than anything else. Not regret or remorse, no, but something that might be compared to a child's guilt—if his conscience had survived his childhood. After the intense rage had worn off he became a spectator of his own crimes. Without blaming himself or experiencing contrition, he felt a kind of nausea before these orange and garnet traces on the steel of the scalpels. Only the fresh blood, still alive, harvested from his latest victim continued to give him pleasure.

For the rest, he used his mouth to polish his instruments of torture, so they would regain the shining cleanliness necessary for the next sacrifice. Because there would be a new chosen one. Of that, at least, he never had any doubt. Didn't he have a mission to fulfill? Shouldn't he, despite everything it cost him, continue to the very end of the quest? He was, after all, its final custodian.

He swished the plunger from the syringes he used for "withdrawals" back and forth under the running water, which went from red to dirty pink before regaining its transparency bit by bit. He loved this resurrection. This return to the cleanliness of first creation, of newness.

For the rest, he did the best he could.

He had always told himself stories. It was a habit, a drug. A condition sine qua non of his survival. How else could he bear those two mirror shards embedded in the faces of everyone, everywhere? How could he endure his parents' gazes? He had been born ugly, but with a rare sort of ugliness, the kind that had an undeniable charm. Otherwise, why did people look at him like that? Only his mother and a few close friends pretended that he was handsome, or even sublimely beautiful, as they said. For him, that lie was the worst insult of all.

As he did every time, out of respect for his victims, he removed and changed the needles. Then he wrapped them in absorbent cotton before tossing them into the bottom of one of several brown-paper bags, those useful bags he got from his neighbor on the top floor, a rich old lady he sometimes ran errands for. At her request, though, he left the big store to deliver its own packages.

"You're not going to break your back for an old biddy like me," she said to him every time.

In fact, he never balked at doing things for her, because she was nice, and had never said anything to him about his ugliness or his beauty. Plus he liked big supermarkets. He could roam freely there, anonymous and content. And going about the peaceful act of shopping also gave him the opportunity to pick out his next model.

He was suddenly worried that he'd forgotten to take his medication. It was lucky that he had his little pills to keep him alive. Thanks to them, he'd been able to hold on for a long time. Then, one day, that hadn't been enough anymore. What would have happened if his American friend hadn't given him the mission? It had given him everything he was missing, everything that could finally fill the emptiness. Enabled him to reach a state of exaltation and bodily pleasure that his pills alone couldn't give him anymore. The happiness of choosing and then harvesting icons was a profound joy that put him in a state of sanctified beatitude.

When he walked for hours in Paris looking for a simple face, nothing else existed. Like a man prospecting for gold he sought out, hidden in the soft gray flesh of the crowds, the faces that would bring him closer to God.

He had also learned from his readings that the sound was there too, the articulation and the verb. Every word proclaimed, even by the most repugnant souls, came from God. All men, without exception, even him, the great "not even," echoed that voice. They were bearers of the first vibration of Creation: "Dreadful prophets, they could not open their mouths without shaking the stars!"

So, along with the faces, he had begun collecting phonemes and words, weighty paradigmatic columns and syntagmatic horizons, the divine origins of which he no longer had any doubt. Sometimes he integrated them, numbered, into his grand iconoclastic performances. Sometimes he carved them on his walls or in his flesh, with a needle and cuttlefish ink.

He could have survived like that if, one day, the happiness of fulfilling his mission, and his multiple harvests, wasn't enough for him anymore. All these hidden sorrows and lies had only worked for so long. He had needed to add other pleasures to the mix.

Vindicated by his quest, he had taken advantage of it to let his rage explode, and revel in a primitive sexuality that he no longer tried to control. Once the photo was taken, and the face imprisoned in the depths of the lens, he let himself go, abandoning himself body and soul to the slaughter. Barbarism was a consolation for him. Like a cannibalistic coin collector, he experienced his savagery as a redemption, a voyage to the land of Insania, among the bloody watermelons and the grenades. A sculptor of flesh and an exhibitor of bones, the Makeup Artist created a hellish fearscape with his arrangements and painstaking attention to detail.

Dazzling darkness.

Because there was no other way for him.

How else can I fill this frozen emptiness, this chasm of desolation? My dizzying despair? How do I slow down my inexorable swallowing-up by the quicksand of emotion? Express my sorrow, and my bitterness. Say the words that remain long after the lips. And tell, even if everything is smashed because of it, the reason for my torment. Say to you, at last, "Mama, you are lying."

No, I am not beautiful. Not even sad, not even normal, not even a child, not even me, not even really alive. I am the great "not even," whom no one loves, and who has given way to it. Not even taken away, not even afraid, not even fear and not even crying. I am all these "not even"s, a big "not even" who doesn't love himself. Not even compassion and not even heart. My father—what did he look like? A humpbacked zebu with a rabbit's head? A hyena or a wild boar? I don't have a single image of that lunatic; not even any words, either. No last name. No first name. Nothing. Stillborn. Fucking murderer. Something Mama said, once:

"Papa? What papa? You were born without a father, my poor baby."

That is why I'm like this. The great "not even" who doesn't love himself. Born without balls, without a dick. An orphaned wild boar with my stripes taken away. A brave killer. Because "not even" was born without a face, without hands and arms, almost without a papa. An X-ray son. I don't look like anything. Not even a white Venetian or Greek tragedy mask; nothing. Or maybe a shapeless mixture of all those things. A swollen sponge, a transparent empty space with little evil eyes.

B arely awake, Amédée headed for the kitchen. He had decided to chop two rabbits into pieces. Force of habit and a well-sharpened knife would come to his rescue. He put the pieces into a bowl and rubbed them with a mixture of cognac and fresh mustard. Salt, pepper, herbs, and Bob's your uncle. He went into the bathroom for a nice hot shower. He'd finish up the recipe tonight.

Stepping into his department, he was impressed by the deployment of forces he'd ordered himself. The big central room had proven to be too small, so they had requisitioned the whole upper floor, a kind of dusty loft above the ceiling. Now this place that time and men seemed to have forgotten was sparkling clean and boasted twelve computers connected to the network and to the seven brand-new units on the lower floor.

Since the beginning of the week, three cadets directed by Ken and supervised by Francis had been entering data as soon as it arrived into one of the five lists they had created.

The first list held the names of people who had bought a Gascht tripod in the last fifteen years, including the ones who had purchased them secondhand or borrowed them.

The second list contained the full names of all the delivery people employed by the major supermarkets identified on Mallock's advice, as well as the names of the clients who received deliveries. The Makeup Artist might very well have chosen his victims while he filled his delivery orders alongside them.

Amélie's notebook constituted the third list, which Mallock considered the most important one. It was their reference. Every person in the notebook had been or would be questioned.

The fourth was a list of every individual in the police files, not just in France but in the bordering countries as well. The offenses ranged from a simple arrest for flashing to rape to sexual murder, and the list was more or less a rundown of all the wackos in Europe whose attorneys were trying desperately to get them released back into nature.

For a long time, Mallock had still believed that everyone should have the right to a second chance, to forgiveness and clemency. But he'd seen too many victims and devastated loved ones now to have any objectivity or even compassion left toward criminals. All his compassion went to the martyrs, not the psychopaths. His job was to find them and arrest them. He wouldn't have traded places with a judge for all the tea in China.

The final list was a compilation of all the individuals who had ever been suspected, directly or indirectly, of the various crimes committed by the Makeup Artist.

The lists weren't complete yet, but Mallock was convinced that, as laborious and painstaking as it was to put them together, only this methodical approach, which allowed them to cross-reference or combine pieces of information, would give them a chance of arresting the Makeup Artist. He felt sure that the name of the killer, or one of his close friends or associates, was contained somewhere in Amélie's notebook. If they found the same name in one of the other lists, they might have a chance.

This computer-based investigation was the backbone of his research system. The technological, rational part of him.

Mallock had realized that it was all the more necessary for him because the rest of his methodology often belonged, if not in the realm of magic, at least to a highly extravagant kind of intuition. He needed the weight of the computers and lists to keep him tethered to the ground, while the weather balloon of his intuition floated above the clouds. One was a heavy trawler dragging the sea bottom, while the other, assured of having something to eat tonight, indulged in a much more unpredictable kind of line-fishing.

They made a perfect pair, the bear and the RAM, synapses and circuits, the head and the hard disk.

It had been three weeks since he inherited the case of the Makeup Artist. Never in his life had he been so afraid of overlooking something, of getting bogged down in false theories while that piece of crap kept on killing women and children. With so many open leads and the lists getting closer and closer to being complete, Mallock felt like they had cast a net finely woven enough to keep their prey from escaping it.

He still needed to tell his team the whole truth about the Makeup Artist and his earlier career. Everything Marvin had told him.

That would happen tonight. The rabbit with herbs marinating peacefully at home was for them. Four times a year he gave himself over to the little ritual of cooking dinner for his group. It bonded them even more closely, and it was relaxing for all of them.

He left Number 36 at around six o'clock to finish getting things ready. Dinner was set for nine o'clock; he had plenty of time. Lots of fresh herbs, chicken liver . . . he stopped twice on his way home to pick things up.

What if the lists yielded nothing? Amédée was petrified with nerves. There was one consolation; it had started snowing again, just the way he liked it, heavy and slow. He stopped in his Breton café to wet his dry throat with a double whiskey. A quick "Thanks, boss" and he was out the door. Now he could really enjoy the snow.

At home he jumped straight on the rabbits, wiping the surplus mustard off the pieces before browning them and then pouring generous amounts of white wine and chicken stock into the pot.

Ken, Jules, and Julie arrived like a small army at nine o'clock sharp. Bob and Francis showed up ten minutes later.

"Goddamn, that smells good," was the heartfelt greeting from both of them.

Mallock settled his little team in the living room and encouraged them to help themselves to various kinds of alcohol, then disappeared into the kitchen to mix goose liver and rabbit liver, cream, pepper, salt, and cognac. At the last minute he stirred the still-raw concoction into the dish.

Silence descended on the living room as they ate. The sounds of cutlery and the inelegant chewing of Francis, Jules, and Bob were the only sounds intruding on the culinary stillness. They liked it! Mallock decided to make his confession right in the midst of these agreeable circumstances.

"I haven't told you everything about the Makeup Artist."

He rattled off the rest without stopping to breathe.

All of it.

Everything.

From the first case to the last, just before the appearance of Needles on French soil. The only thing he left out was the Marilyn story. That wasn't necessary, and the secret had to be kept safe.

There was another silence.

Half-astonished, half-appalled, they considered this incredible story, now conjugated to the past tense, and the consequences it meant they would be the first ones to deal with in the near future. Without planning it they all began to talk at the same time, which resulted in an unintelligible jumble of noise: *How can this be possible? . . . Maybe there's more than one . . . What a fucking nightmare! . . . People are sick, aren't they . . . Would anyone like coffee? . . . I disagree . . .*

"Take turns, kiddies, please. We've got plenty of time."
Julie went first, going directly on the attack.
"But what are your thoughts about it, boss?"

As they talked, wondering about the bestial Twelve/Needles, somewhere else—not very far away—the one who called himself the great "not even" was calmly locking the three locks on the door of his secret room in his mother's house.

At the same moment as Mallock tried to comfort his troops by suggesting leads and theories, the Makeup Artist was developing his latest roll of film. While Julie tried to rationalize thoughts that hearing the facts had turned very dark, the Makeup Artist was scanning one of his best photos so he could add another face to his collection. Just as Francis and Jules divided the last morsels on the plate, the Makeup Artist was repeating to himself, "*God made man in His own image,*" the phrase that had started everything such a little while ago, and an eternity ago. And while Julie unselfconsciously wiped up the leftover sauce on the plate with big hunks of bread, the Makeup Artist was mixing his pigments for the creation of a new icon, a new *Christ Pantocrator.*

This was his passion, the sole purpose of all his torments and the ones he inflicted on others: collecting faces. Faces like the Face of God. Just one more model and his personal art gallery would be complete. She, his final specimen, had already been selected; she, a paragon of virtue, a young woman he had only just seen, would be his chosen one.

For a long time now he'd been able to spot an angel from a hundred yards away. This one would be his masterpiece, the final image to shock the unconverted, while giving him the keys to Heaven at last!

Her name was Julie, and he would have to be very careful, because she was a member of the police force.

35.

United States of America, ten years earlier

To celebrate his fifteenth birthday, or for some other reason he'd never tried to figure out, his mother had sent him to New York. Just like that. All alone, with a reservation at a YMCA and some classes to take in a school not far from Central Park. Just as remarkably, she had added an envelope containing more than enough pocket money on top of that. He was supposed to spend three weeks in America, but he ended up staying three months, for the whole summer vacation. His mother called him regularly. Sometimes from Paris, but mostly from somewhere more exotic: Marrakesh, Istanbul, Kyoto. He could only be sure about one thing: she was never alone in her room.

At first, the teenager didn't make any friends and spent his time walking the streets of the Big Apple. It was wonderful, a revelation! The feeling of freedom, and much more than that. Something intoxicating. Being able to let his feet take him anywhere they wanted, with no desire except to feel the asphalt under his feet and the exhilarating sense of the skyscrapers towering over his head. Discovering, losing himself, finding himself. No schedule. No mother. Existing without her and feeling himself spreading his wings. It was one of the happiest times of his life.

One morning he woke up feeling weightless and worn out. He had changed. A sweetish odor filled the little room, exacerbated by the warmth of the July morning. His pajamas and belly were covered with a sticky, dried substance.

He spent his first day as a man at the French-American school in a state of euphoria. At noon, forsaking the services of an overly noisy cafeteria, he opted for a stroll in Central Park instead. Classes wouldn't start again until three o'clock. A hot dog stuffed with onions and ketchup in hand, he settled himself on a bench. The grass was an odd survivor in this world of glass and steel.

It was very hot, and for the first time in his life he bought alcohol—two cans of beer. It was thanks to that bubbly fermented hops and to the sperm flowing in his genitals that, seeing a young adolescent boy with fine features and long hair coming toward him, he had the great revelation of his life. God had truly created man in his own image!

He was fascinated, and the attraction scared him. The specter of homosexuality. But then he realized that this face only appealed to him because of its resemblance to the religious images he'd been collecting since he was six years old. Nothing sexual about it—quite the opposite, in fact, he had concluded.

God created man in his own image. They were all his children, of course, but some of them had inherited his features, his magic, while others—like him—were only failures. Bad sketches he should have torn up.

The most incredible thing was that he didn't feel any resentment or despair, but rather relief. As imperfect as he was, he was part of God's destiny. Aren't abnormal children even more loved than the others?

He was surprised to find that he was smiling. Lost in Central Park, he had just found himself.

A gray squirrel approached him, looking him straight in the eyes. Its two front paws clutched a tiny human skull. He reassured himself that it must really belong to a rodent or a bird. A baby monkey, maybe. There was a zoo right nearby.

He skipped his afternoon English class and went back to

his room to sleep. The night was dreamless, colorless. He woke up at five in the morning.

Dawn was beginning to wash away the colors of the night and replace them with pastel tints. It was in that moment, standing at that window, that he surprised himself for the first time by imagining his destiny. Without knowing what shape it would take, or even worrying about it. Just feeling the delirious joy of that incredible certainty. A unique path had been laid out on this Earth just for him. All he had to do was find it. Everything could finally begin now. Quiet please, we're filming. The scene is set, the actors made up, and the camera rolling at sixty frames a second, like life. Lights! Too late to turn back. Wind machine! Bring in the extras!

Action!

Act I
In which the name of Ralph Barnes Bennet appears for the first time.

On his third day in New York he found a mimeographed note from the YMCA management under his door. Every new arrival was supposed to go and introduce himself to the director of the establishment, but in his absence you could meet with the building manager and have your presence duly noted for administrative purposes.

At 2:30, before classes started again, the young man went down and knocked on the small door behind the billiard room.

"Come in!"

Surrounded by four chrome fans, the manager, Bill Baxter, an enormous mass of fat, was waiting for him. He was impressive. Five hundred pounds of damp pink folds. In front of him there was a pile of yellow washcloths, and behind him a heap of the same cloths, soaked with water. The manager spent his time absorbing the sweat that accumulated beneath his fat folds. In the middle of that mass of flesh his face was strangely beautiful, his eyes magnificent.

"They call me BB," he said in precise French. "I'm the manager of this kid factory. And you are?"

The young Frenchman introduced himself with much more self-assurance than was typical at his age. BB noticed it, and realized that the two of them shared a kind of monstrosity and, therefore, a suffering. The incredible obesity of one, and the skinniness and startling face of the other.

"If you get lonely or have any problems, come see me. I don't get too many visitors, and I'd like the company."

That was the beginning of a bizarre friendship. An odd and atypical bond, but an essential link in the chain that would transform the teenager, little by little, into the Makeup Artist. A few days later, he surprised himself by confiding in BB about his fascination with religious icons. He even told him about his theory about the faces of God, like a confession, a violent need to finally share his secret. The other man had listened, sponging out his armpits, a funny smile on his lips. Whether by coincidence or the implacable will of destiny, his brother-in-law, who owned a trendy art gallery, had just been telling him about a painter who apparently shared a very similar kind of madness:

"He makes old-style icons," he told the boy.

They absolutely had to meet; he would call his brother-in-law to organize a get-together.

"It might be interesting for you," he added, tossing an umpteenth sweat-soaked cloth over his shoulder. "I'll figure something out and let you know when it's set up."

On the following Fourth of July the country celebrated its independence, and New York throbbed with the noise of millions of fans and air-conditioning units blowing the air around. In the street, women's high heels sank into the burning asphalt with a slight sucking noise. The city had just set a new record high temperature. In this furnace, a pale and empty child would soon change into something else, a creature with outrageous dreams, macabre and bloody.

The art-seller with whom BB had set up the meeting was a person of little interest. He tried to survive by exploiting the talent of artists whose egos he fed with hope, superlatives, and cut cocaine. Still, he and his brother-in-law were filling the roles that fate had written for them, like film extras who are superfluous but without whom the principal intrigue can't develop. He introduced the young Frenchman to Ralph Bennet, the icon-loving painter.

Bennet was a big, burly man with tiny bright-blue eyes. He seemed, despite his size, like a part of the sky. His silvery gray hair was like a mass of cumulus clouds; his gaze a retreating horizon you tried and tried to reach until you came to continents full of monsters. That was how the young Makeup Artist saw him for the first time. He instantly felt fear and respect for him, and real fascination.

They quickly started spending more time together than was reasonable. Ralph began teach him the basics necessary for making icons. He was passionate about everything, from practical work to presentations of theological theories related to it. He was particularly sensitive to the magical relationship that existed between the two domains, the spiritual "why" of the composition of the adhesive, or the alchemical symbolism of the number of days it took to dry.

It was satisfying, but the most delicious things were yet to come.

After some time had passed, Ralph confided to the boy that, in addition to the traditional dash of vodka, he added a small amount of seminal fluid to the glue for the icons. As a supreme honor and a mandatory rite of initiation, he would take some of the teenager's sperm that night for the first time.

After the preparation of a dozen icons, interrupted by touching that had nothing to do with ritual anymore, Ralph decided to initiate him into the supreme art of the hunt.

It happened in the street, in full reality. The first thing was to learn to see the auras surrounding the faces of the chosen ones, a halo of light that framed the upper part of the body.

The first time he managed it, he felt like the whole world had finally started making sense. Only a minuscule number of humans had the power to perceive what he had seen. He owed this incredible joy, this brilliance, to Ralph and his teachings. His natural tendencies had helped him, yes, but on his own he would just have kept collecting religious images for years and years without being able to go beyond, without ever being able to go through the mirror. It was thanks to Ralph that he understood that these seemingly innocent icons weren't the imaginary and symbolic representations people thought they were, but true photographs, faithful representations of a reality that had been hidden since time immemorial.

Since he owed everything to Ralph and shared his aspirations, he made no objection when the man told him the ultimate purpose of the hunt, and its corollary: the killing of the chosen ones. For the painter things were simple, even though they remained mystical. He practiced "angel hunting" the way other people collected butterflies.

Spotting the rarest species, capturing them with strings and nets, and then putting them to sleep using cotton soaked with chloroform. As with butterflies, he also practiced the art of injection. The needle had to penetrate at a very precise angle. Finally, the specimen was photographed. This took both patience and quickness. And then remembering the Marquis de Viracalas's instructions! It was incredibly important that the halo not shine at its full brightness until the exact moment of the death agony, and that it disappear just as suddenly when the subject was dead. The entire art of it therefore consisted of taking the photo using a relatively long exposure, and at the very last moment. Captured too late or with a poorly-prepared subject, the divine features would go blurry, the aura turn dull. Too soon and the halo wouldn't have yielded its full potential yet.

The limbus was as fragile as the colored dust on a butterfly's wings.

Act II
In which the Makeup Artist commits his first murder.

Ralph Bennet had asked his young disciple to pick out the next victim himself. For reasons he didn't try to go into in depth, he chose the only friend he had made in New York, Bill Baxter. He took a photo of him, zooming in close up, and showed it to Ralph. The decision was unanimous:

"His face is superb and his eyes are divine."

The operation was simple to finalize, both because he knew the sedentary habits of the huge manager by heart, and because of their friendship. He organized with BB, who never suspected a thing, the time and circumstances of his own death.

They were supposed to see each other late that night to watch the rerun of a boxing match together. At midnight the teenager went to Bill's apartment, making sure to leave the door open behind him. Five minutes later, Ralph walked in. After an instant's hesitation at the enormity of the mass of flesh in front of him, the painter moved noiselessly forward and knocked him out cleanly.

It was Scott Amish, Tom Marvin's colleague and friend, who discovered the body.

The lieutenant, a high-ranking member of the Behavioral Science Service, had been on the trail of this psycho killer for some time. It wasn't the first serial murder case of his career;

he had arrested several of them in the past few years, including the notorious Boston Strangler. When he saw the body, or rather what was left of it after the slaughter and ten days of heat, it took him several minutes of standing on the threshold before he could bring himself to take a step into the room. The victim's decapitated head had been placed on top of the television, which was running the "Star Spangled Banner" over a shot of a patriotic statue. His brain and the internal flesh of his face, liquefied by natural decomposition speeded up by the heat, had leaked out of his eyes, ears, and nose. A necklace of maggots squirmed around the severed neck.

The rest of the body was even worse. Bill Baxter had been burned alive. The floor of the room was covered with vile slices of flesh and human fat, yellowish adipose masses sliced into sections and seeming to float like so many icebergs on a sea of blood. In the middle of it all a body, made thin again by cutting, showed every muscle and a few pale bones.

Scottish had a fleeting image of a whale being carved up on the deck of a fish-packing boat before he turned and stepped back out into the hallway to throw up.

Act III
In which the Makeup Artist receives his inheritance.

One evening Ralph was late. His eyes were even more distant than usual. The Makeup Artist wondered if maybe he'd failed at his task, disappointed his mentor. That would screw up everything. The two of them were preparing to capture their third angel, a superb Face of God that the teenager had spotted two days earlier. Ralph had promised to reverse the roles for the first time. He would assist his student without intervening directly.

"In fact, you really should go alone, but wait a few days yet," Ralph had said.

And then he revealed that the boy would be the seventh in a line of hunters who had been practicing their art since the turn of the century. He gave him a small leather-covered wooden trunk containing all the Faces of God, the auras harvested and photographed, all the way back to the ones made by the first hunter, the inventor of the faces, a French nobleman who had come to America aboard the *Stella Maris*: the Marquis François-Henri de Salis-Viracalas.

The oldest shots had faded almost completely away. The eyes, mouth, and hair were still there but the rest had disappeared. At the bottom of the trunk there were three real Indian faces, scalped. Their papery skin was still stretched over a wooden mold.

In Ralph's eyes, since Viracalas had begun the line in the nineteenth century, it was only right for another Frenchman to finish the quest, by finally discovering the true Face of God. The boy had the sudden certainty, the marvelous intuition that he was, in fact, the chosen one. He would be the last of the Makeup Artists, and the first to look upon the face of the one who had made the world, the Earth and all its chaos, the whole universe with its galaxies, its planets, and him. He watched Ralph Bennet walk away, his heart too full of this overwhelmingly large dream even to say goodbye. Two hours later, Scott Amish killed Bennet while trying to arrest him.

It was August 31st, the last day of the month. The evening was scorchingly hot. Outside, everything that hides in the night was being regularly illuminated by huge bursts of light. New York was experiencing one of those dry storms that sometimes come to flash-photograph big cities. The wind rose, swirling among the buildings, erasing footprints, destroying traces, like ripples on water.

Cut!

36

Paris, present day

A decade had gone by, and now the Makeup Artist was on the point of achieving his greatest dream. It was Thursday, January 13th, and everything was cold and dull. What a path he had traveled in such a short time! He'd gone further, been stronger than all his predecessors. For him there was no question of hunting butterflies or collecting. No; it was to the ultimate dream, the supreme art, and it alone, that he had dedicated his life.

Thou shalt not make unto thee any graven image, God had ordained, and no one had listened to him. So what was he afraid of, this holy man with his white beard, his seven-pointed halo, and his benedictory hands? This numb old man on his cotton clouds? What could his son have to fear, sitting on rainbows, illuminated by his dazzling mandorla, his cross-bearing glory? Now he, the mortal, the "so ugly"; he knew. By reproducing His image he would finally have a face, and he would be the first one to unmask Him, to be able to ask him all the questions his human yearning desired.

At around two A.M., alongside his work on the Christ Pantocrator, he started smoothing down the photo of the little Modiano girl, with her braids and her sublime forehead, onto a panel of wood.

The Makeup Artist utilized his murders in two major ways. One used the computer, the most modern of technologies; the other, the ancient art of the icon as Ralph Bennet had taught it to him. Though all the victims' portraits were digitized, only the most interesting photos earned the right to the second activity.

An icon wasn't painted, but written. It wasn't the fruit of imagination but rather a work of copying, respecting models and schemas. In the beginning it was this soothing, almost scholarly aspect of it that he had loved.

Everything began with the choice of wood. He had a special affection for ash and purple beech, but since those varieties were too hard to work with he often ended up using maple, larch, or even linden or poplar, which were even softer. This time, his choice had fallen on a plank of willow.

He had prepared the mount yesterday, spending the whole day smoothing it with sandpaper and a polishing cube, always with the grain of the fibers. He had patiently polished away all the rough places, using liquid wood before impregnating the mount with a dispersion adhesive mixed with vodka and seminal fluid, according to Bennet's recipe. It was dark by the time he had laid down three intertwining coats of thin primer and gesso powder. He had a little secret to speed up the drying process, so he hardly had to wait at all between coats. If he started at five in the morning he could be done preparing the mount before midnight the next day. He was very proud of this quickness; only a couple of years ago it would have taken him two weeks to finish the job. The last step in the preparation process was damp-polishing with a half-water, half-alcohol mixture and a polishing cube wrapped in abrasive paper. After that, his technique broke with tradition a bit. He didn't draw his model, but applied it directly to the mount, a photograph he had taken and developed on special matte paper that was almost as thin as cigarette paper.

This time, without really realizing it, he had worked all night. The sun was rising and yet he didn't feel the slightest bit tired. He stopped for just half an hour to drink some Chinese tea and wolf down a baguette. Then, glancing absently out the window at the activity in the street, he took his place again, smiling widely, in front of the wooden plank he used as both workbench and drawing board.

At the very beginning of his iconostasis project, he had only depicted Blachernitissa or Kazanskaya, the mother of God. But lately he'd changed his theme. Now Christ Pantocrator was his preferred subject.

To recreate the features, he used pigments and egg tempera paint to add the beard required by the iconic representation directly to the photos. He especially favored burnt-Sienna earth and black from charred animal bones; brightness effects were created with light ochre. He dressed the bodies in traditional costumes: red madder dalmatics and crimson himations; chromium oxide green mantles. To finish, he redrew the eyebrows and refined the nose, which was never elongated or fine enough in mortals.

That same day, he made up a woman's face to create an almost perfect representation of the son of God. *Thou shalt not make unto thee any graven image.* Like a broken record of a canticle, a mantra, this phrase echoed endlessly in his head while he painted. Today, as always, it resonated within him, and he did absolutely nothing to make it stop.

The square was filled with the sound of children, like the flapping of wings. It was 4:20 in the afternoon, a cursed time of day for Mallock.

At the same moment as the Makeup Artist left his lair to prepare his gilding compound of marl, rabbit-skin glue, and pore sealer, to be spread on before the gold leaf was applied, Mallock stood up from his desk, ready to pick Thomas up from school. He had never managed to break himself of this ingrained habit, which never failed to sharpen his grief. Of course, he had never really tried very hard to break it, either. The pain was the only tangible connection he still had to his son.

He sat back down heavily, while out there, standing in a little apartment with blue balconies, a psychopath snipped pieces of gold leaf with a pair of silver scissors.

After applying the primer, he spread on the yellow adhesive and then the red gilding base made of Armenian bole, an ochreous clay with a high iron oxide content, in three successive layers. Then he went down to relieve his mother in the store. He didn't mind playing shopkeeper too much.

When she came back from running errands he went quickly upstairs again, the traditional "Thank you, sweetheart" floating after him.

It was six o'clock and the mount was perfect. Not too dry—because then the leaf wouldn't stick—and not too damp, otherwise the gold would sink. He moved on to the final procedure, which consisted of running a boar's-hair paintbrush, bizarrely called a "dog," over the surface.

Once these time-consuming preparations were finally finished it was time for the magic moment, the one he loved above anything else. With his left hand, he picked up the gilding cushion on which he had placed the cut-off sheets of gold leaf. Lighter than butterfly wings, they seemed like they had a life of their own, like they could fly. He laid the first one on the cushion, turned it over, and blew on it to flatten it. Then he cut it with his gilding knife. Before applying it, he rubbed his palette over his cheek to charge it with static electricity and placed it carefully on the still-damp part of the object. Using a special gilding brush called an *appuyeux*,[15] he delicately tamped

[15] A very soft brush, round with a flat top, made of Siberian squirrel's hair and mounted on a feather.

the gold leaf down to get rid of any residual moisture, and then started the process over again with another leaf.

Next it was time for the hook-shaped burnishing agates. He applied himself to the task, startled as always by the velvety, sensual touch of the agate against the still-wrinkled gold leaves.

The gold began to gleam.

Before his eyes, thanks to his dedicated perseverance, the halo appeared at last, glowing in the already shadow-filled room. It was at these moments that he would have liked to call the world in to see. Show it that, if this mandorla around the lord shone miraculously in the darkness of this winter evening, it was because of him. Maybe then people would understand that he was right to do what he did. Maybe then he would even be loved and admired like he deserved to be.

But this weakness never lasted more than a fraction of a second. He preferred to remain misunderstood. It was what he enjoyed. Feeling different from everyone else, monstrously unique, with the solitude and the horror draped around him like a cloak.

37.
Friday, January 14th

Mallock had been up since four o'clock in the morning, unable to get back to sleep. He suffered from insomnia sometimes, when the day's results hadn't lived up to his expectations. Sometimes he slept like a baby, with the reassuring feeling of having conducted his day in ways that were helpful for himself and others. Work as remedy for depression and guilt.

At six o'clock he turned on the radio, to keep the silence from whispering hateful things that he didn't want to hear.

The news hit like an exploding bomb. France was at the mercy of the most fearsome murderer of all time. A super-killer, a bloody monster, a butchering psychopath . . . there was no lack of titles and superlatives. Worse, the number of two hundred victims was mentioned for the first time. Someone hadn't been able to hold their tongue, and the journalists had pounced on the case with their customary voracity.

Carnage like this was a godsend! A victim tally like that, how lucky! What joy, for the press.

At seven A.M. Amédée went out to buy the newspapers. It was even worse than he ever could have imagined. After seventy years of blackout, everything was now revealed in the light of day, with various versions that were more or less precise but all relatively complete. Some of them wallowed in the horror, in more or less realistic descriptions of the different murders; others preferred to focus on the mystery, the fantastical aspect of this unprecedented series of killings.

And the ultimate question: how old could the murderer be?

They had published old photos of the chief superintendent, taken on various cases. Some of the captions allowed readers to believe that the shots had been taken yesterday, while others wrote: *Chief Superintendent Mallock, seen here trying to dodge our cameras, has refused to comment on this incredible case.*

He should have become immune to their mudslinging a long time ago, but this really infuriated him. You might get wiser over the years, better at turning the other cheek, but you don't get used to everything.

At eight o'clock, like a gladiator marching back into the arena, Mallock headed for the Fort. Snow had started falling again on the mob of journalists bunched at the main door of the police station. After a brief hesitation, he began making his way through this crowd of people he had liked at one time, but couldn't feel any affection for now that they had replaced ethics with grandstanding, sources with the gutter, objectivity with ideology, and information with spectacle. Every journalist now followed his paper's editorial line the way an addict followed a line of coke; there was no question of anything anymore except staying in the good graces of the editor-in-chief. To be honest, if you added to all of that the lobbies and networks, the cronyism and mutual back-scratching, the commercial and financial pressures—both those on the media and those on journalists at the end of the month—how could you still believe for a single second that the information being diffused could still have the slightest bit of value?[16]

Mallock was very careful not to make any statements. These guys were only going to write down what they wanted to hear. He made sure to say nothing at all. They loved nothing more

[16] Author's note: I am fully conscious of having done absolutely nothing at all to make the job of my press agent at Fleuve Editions any easier.

than zooming in on one little sentence or even a single word, if it was on the blacklist of terms forbidden by the semantics police.

This time they managed to crucify him even when he didn't say a word.

They drew their own conclusions from his silence, especially because he made the mistake of accompanying it with a fixed, rather idiotic smile. That same rictus would be splashed across the front page of every newspaper that very afternoon. The journalists, poor darlings, professed themselves to be completely scandalized by the irresponsible attitude of this superintendent who smiled so mockingly when so many unfortunate victims had been tortured and all of France trembled with fear. Some of them called unhesitatingly for the resignation of this monster of cynicism—or reactionary, or anarchist, depending on the political leanings of the publication. Comparing three newspapers' versions of the same photo, Francis noticed that one of them had retouched the smile so that the scum-sucking cop looked even more repugnant. It was Photoshop's smoothness slider, Amédée realized, not sure whether to laugh or cry.

The morning passed without Mallock's being able to get much done. Phone calls and visits came thick and fast; it was like everything was made so the pressure would reach unprecedented levels. From the DA to the president of the bar association by way of Humbert and a host of other examining magistrates, from the lowest asshole of an umbrella-holder to various goddamn cabinet members, everyone piled on him, directly or through some middleman. All of them were careful to cover their asses as quickly as possible in case of a possible failure and the victims to come.

For Mallock, it was already a failure.

Only the Secretary of the Interior, and God knew this wasn't typical of either his position or his character, acted halfway civilized. Which didn't stop him from warning Mallock, in his low, gravelly voice:

"I've only got one piece of advice for you: hurry. The wolves have been released. I can't do anything for you unless I get some tangible results as soon as possible, some bone to throw to the dogs. They'd be all too happy to pin the blame on me, so let's not beat around the bush. I'll support you for as long as I can, and not a minute longer. I'm well aware that you're a good detective, which makes you my best chance—and the country's. Give me another demonstration of your talents as fast as you possibly can, if you don't want to end up as the fall guy."

He hung up without giving Mallock time to respond. The phone immediately rang again. It was Queen Margot, who was none too pleased either.

"You asshole! Everyone's put out an article and I've got zilch! I'm furious! I kept everything to myself, and now I look like an idiot in front of my editors-in-chief. I promised them reliable, exclusive info. Wasn't that our deal?"

"You're right. But the info you're talking about didn't come from me. There was a leak. I give you my word; I didn't see any of this coming, and frankly I feel terrible for you."

An embarrassed silence fell between them. She wasn't wrong, but neither was he. It had just worked out badly. Murphy's Law. He explained it to her calmly, and Margot, magnanimously, took it on the chin.

"I'm not angry at you," she said at last. "Your investigation comes before I do, and that's normal. But seeing all these articles everywhere when you swore me to silence . . . it made me livid. Especially because they completely destroyed you."

"I understand. I wasn't particularly happy about it either."

"The only information they have is your wonky smile. Incredible. Sometimes I'm ashamed to be a journalist."

"Those people aren't journalists anymore. You still are, and there are a few others, thank goodness. The ones outside, they're . . . "

"Cocksuckers?"

Mallock laughed. "You said it, not me."

"Okay, I'll let you get back to work, my big bear. Try to think of me next time."

Mallock made a quick decision. "Wait, don't hang up. Get out your tape recorder; you're going to have the only official and exclusive interview given by Chief Superintendent Amédée Mallock, my girl. That's better than the scuttlebutt, don't you think?"

After the improvised interview with Margot Murât, Amédée organized a series of meetings in his office. Then he spent his lunch hour listening, eyes closed, to the reports of the various lieutenants and inspectors who had been conducting house-to-house inquiries. Maybe some detail would tell him something, awaken that particular brand of inspiration he'd abused so many times. He met with all of them, one by one, without a break, from eleven A.M. to half past four.

At exactly 4:20, as like he had yesterday, he started and stood up abruptly at his desk, thinking of Toto and classes getting out. He sat down again once he remembered that Tom didn't go to school anymore, now that he was dead. At the same moment a call from the hospital came, telling him that Amélie Maurel's condition had taken a new turn for the worse. They'd had to put her back on the ventilator.

"You seem to know her quite well," ventured Dr. Ménard on the telephone.

Ménard was an old-school gentleman, and a man of courage and duty. Mallock had liked him right away.

"Not for too long, but we . . . get along very well."

"Her father is dead," said the doctor, "and her mother lives out in the country with the rest of her family. Would you be so kind as to bring us her things? Identity papers, social security, insurance—anything you can find within the next couple of days. I'm very much afraid she won't be with us a great deal longer."

"I'll try."

"Thank you very much."

Half an hour later Amédée was standing despondently at Amélie's door. He didn't have very much trouble locating the various documents. Her home was neat as a pin, arranged very much like her notebook, with fanatical precision. In her wallet, which was in the pocket of a raincoat, he found her ID—and a photo of himself. She'd taken it when she visited him for the third time.

"It's for my notebook," she had explained. "It helps me remember each client."

But she had never put this photo in her planner. It seemed almost worn out, as if she'd often taken it out of her wallet and held it between her beautiful fingers so she could look at it more closely. That meant . . . he hadn't known . . . Amélie had always kept Amédée's face within reach.

He put the picture back in her wallet.

Her condition once again made any hope illusory that she would be able to give evidence or describe the face of her attacker. She was the only one of the Makeup Artist's victims who was still alive. Had she seen him? Would she recognize him again? Could she give them any physical description to go on?

His back had been hurting him again since noon. He decided to replenish his stock of painkillers in the little pharmacy on the ground floor of the same building. His young friend, Amélie's patient, was behind the counter.

"How are you, Superintendent?"

The youth seemed happy to see Mallock again. They loved

the same woman, and instead of pitting them against each other, the feeling had brought them together—undoubtedly because neither of them could hold her in his arms now.

"I could be better, if my back didn't hurt so much."

The handsome young man bent his athletic six-foot-three-inch frame toward the tile floor. His eyes were glistening. "We miss her too," he murmured. He hesitated for a few seconds, then asked: "Is there any news?"

He still seemed deeply upset. Mercifully, Mallock lied to him, as he would have liked to be lied to himself: "She's doing better. Don't worry. I think I may even be able to question her soon."

The apprentice pharmacist's emotions kept him speechless for a brief instant. Mallock thought he might start crying again.

"Thank God," the boy said eventually. "Do you still have your prescription?"

Mallock handed it over, and he went off in search of the life-saving pills. From the back of the pharmacy he called out:

"Do you want a care sheet?"

"If you don't mind."

He filled the form out once, made a mistake, tossed it into a garbage can behind him, started over. As he was leaving, the young man walked him out and held the door for him.

"Thank you . . . Didier," said Amédée, proud of himself for remembering this time.

38.
Saturday, January 15th. In the crypt

The Makeup Artist didn't understand it. Some days he was so cold that nothing could warm him up. It wasn't the temperature, but solitude that chilled his bones. As far back as he could remember he had been alone, shut away with his mother, who was always calm and never got angry and never kissed him. Alone, with the ugliness he and everyone else pretended not to see. All alone, with the hands he had so much trouble keeping busy. So alone that the cold froze his heart and put a coating of frost on his guts and his forehead. And his cock.

Why wasn't he dead? Why did he have to do what he did? Why didn't he have any love in him, or around him? Why could his life only happen through the death of others? His only company was these thousands of *why*s and the silence that answered them.

Why live alone, and why cry?

Why did the great "not even" have a father who never appeared? Who didn't love him, who had hidden himself away out of guilt after ejaculating in his mother's womb?

The dirty, lying whore.

One day all these whys would come flooding out of him like rain on the earth, rivers in the sea. The question marks would float for a few seconds and then sink, screaming in terror.

Everyone had their turn to be afraid.

The great "not even" normally used water for gilding, but

today he had decided to try it with oil. What he had come up with this time was very different from his usual creations, and he thought he'd have better results this way.

This time the circumstances, which he had organized himself, would give him all the time he needed. With the movie star at the Crillon he'd had to hurry, and he hated that. Rushing your work was a crime. Here, safe in the crypt of the church, he could take his time.

He had prepared the surfaces for this new staging. The blood had been drawn, and he had even injected a condensed formalin-based solution, which would extend the subject's life. A bolt of rage sizzled through him. He knew that when the bodies were found, after the autopsy, the families would surely opt for cremation. The idiots! But those iconoclasts weren't worth making himself sick over. He waited for his hands to stop shaking. To relax himself, he pulled a picture of his next face from his pocket.

The young woman had been photographed with a tele-photo lens. A huge guy was walking next to her with heavy strides. It was the man he called his hunter, Superintendent Amédée Mallock. The Makeup Artist had no interest in him. It was his colleague, Julie. She was an angel. Her face would be perfect for completing the quest, and he had a very special treatment in store for her. He had planned everything needed to trap her. It was foolproof. He was the only person in the world who knew that she was going to die, and that gave him immense satisfaction, almost like a penetration, but without the unclean things that went along with that. Possessing the power of death over her . . . *that* was possessing her.

The Makeup Artist tenderly kissed the photo before tucking it back in his pocket.

For the woman he had prepared yesterday, he'd brought white and sky-blue veils today. As if dressing a doll, he transformed her smoothly into the Virgin Mary in a matter of seconds. He'd always been talented with fabric.

"It's too bad; you could have been a great designer," his mother had reproached him more than once.

Not a designer, not a dancer, not a hairdresser. The Makeup Artist, forgetting his American activities, never missed an opportunity to express his hatred of queers.

His Virgin Mary was already made up; the only thing left now was to put her in place. Using metal rods, he managed without too much effort to get her in the perfect position. It was harder with her face. She had to be looking up at the sky, with her mouth and eyes open. In the end he had to remove her eyeballs and replace them with glass marbles.

Yes—that made it look so much more lifelike!

Somewhat irritated, he reapplied her makeup, making it a bit more over-the-top to hide the unfortunate condition of her eyelids. Two coats of foundation on her hands. Powder and clear polish on her nails. Done. He backed away to look at his handiwork.

She was splendid. He smiled.

There was another body waiting for him. A baby's. He was excited.

He was going to try a new technique for the first time: gilding with oil. The whole body, from head to toe, would be completely covered with twenty-four-carat gold leaf. No one had ever done anything like it. Not on wood, but on a real baby, and he had thought for a long time about the best technique to use. Because the skin was so soft, he had decided on oil.

The crypt was perfectly silent. All around him hundreds of candles were burning, opening their fiery little mouths to exclaim:

"Oh! How incredible! Marvelous! So beautiful!" they seemed to be singing in concert, their little amber lips quivering with admiration.

The yellow adhesive, made of glue and pigments heated together, was the first coat he applied to the baby. Next came a coat of blended Armenian bole and rabbit-skin glue, painted on using a "dog." Determined to perfect his masterpiece, he applied a coat of flatting lacquer to make sure he would be able to achieve *simili brunis*, in which the shiniest parts imitated what was naturally obtained with water gilding. It held, especially on the forehead, eyelids, and belly. It was incredibly sensual, the meeting of his materials with the baby's skin. The pores were so fine that he only needed one coat of primer.

Patiently, he waited for the mixture to be "in love"—that is, dry and sticky enough for the three-inch square sheets of gold leaf to stay in place. Abandoning his usual technique of using a cushion to place them, he employed the booklet technique, applying whole sheets without cutting them up beforehand. He had large surfaces to cover—stomach, back, thighs, and calves—and they were wide and smooth. Perfect for this new technique.

It took him almost three hours to transform the baby into a golden angel.

Sleep, golden child. Mama will be back soon, sang the great "not even" to his creation.

Then, exhausted, he left the crypt, locking its three heavy padlocks behind him.

39.
Sunday, January 16th

Amédée had meant to spend his Sunday at the office, but his friends decided otherwise. Six of them descended on his apartment. They had all read the papers, and they were absolutely furious. None of them had a single doubt about their Amédée's morals, and they had plotted together to come and cheer him up.

"We're sick of not having any news, and of not seeing Your Majesty much anymore, so we decided to come harass you a bit."

"I'm thrilled to see you, but . . . "

"No discussion, no debate; I don't care if you're Chief Superintendent. Put on your swimming trunks and some casual clothes and follow us."

Mallock didn't try to argue. He knew this outing with his friends would do him a lot of good. This wasn't the first time the clan of seven had come beating on the hermit-superintendent's door. Their friendship had often been the best remedy for the miseries he suffered. For a long time he had taken care of himself, preferring to believe that you can and must pull yourself up by your own bootstraps. When Thomas died, he had given up the fight. You needed other people. And his friends had risen to the challenge with tenderness and discretion. They had done everything anyone could do in that type of situation. Made sure he knew they were there, and that they loved him. The simple fact that Mallock was still alive today was proof of their delicate effectiveness.

With what had happened to Amélie, he really needed them now.

He went into his bedroom to change, thinking that sometimes it was nice to obey without discussion, to let himself be carried along by the will of others. All he asked was for them to stop by his office so he could give instructions to his team. At ten o'clock, leaving his colleagues to work and not without feeling guilty, he got back into one of his friends' two cars. Without asking him anything, either about his preference of restaurant or the case that was on the front page of every newspaper, they headed for the Bois de Boulogne.

They had a long ramble and then a wonderful meal with wine at Pétrus, followed by a film. At five o'clock they decided to go swim a few laps before heading back. When they split up, Amédée decided to stay in the water a little longer.

The pool was practically deserted and, through a wall of floor-to-ceiling windows, he could see snow drifting lazily onto the street. What would his friends think if they knew the exact nature of his dreams? For days now, he had been giving the hardest part of the investigation over to the night. Before falling asleep, in the little coma that preceded drowsiness, he went over all the horrors he had seen since the start of the investigation. Once asleep he visited a terrible world, populated with evil and terrifying fantasies. In the morning he wasn't sure anymore what came from the killer and what was just the expression of his own impulses. But he had learned a few small things which, put together, were beginning to yield results.

This cocksucker wasn't just highly intelligent; he hadn't committed all of these crimes alone. He had also sensed around the Makeup Artist an idea of cleanliness, a great ugliness, the color green, and the haunting presence of a cross. There were also the bags, and the piece of furniture with the buttons. A snake.

He couldn't tolerate the visions this investigation was forcing on him anymore. For them, and for all the innocent people who had been sacrificed, he bore the Makeup Artist a burning hatred. Outside, the night and the snow had covered up the warmth of the automobiles. After one last lap, Mallock pulled himself easily out of the water. His towel was rough. He dried himself off slowly, sloshing through the water pooled on the tiles.

He would never have moved so calmly if he'd known about Julie.

40.
Monday, January 17th. Dawn

I t was the first day of a week he would never forget, and yet he didn't notice anything special. He woke up at four in the morning, convinced that the phone was about to ring. He got up and took the handset with him into the kitchen. Even before he'd lit the gas burner, the ring shattered the silence.

"Hi, chief. Sorry to wake you."

"Don't worry; I was expecting your call. Has he struck again?"

"A young woman and a baby this time," answered Ken, no longer surprised by his boss's strange abilities. "Should I come by and get you?"

"I'm ready."

Mallock hung up. His weekend had ended in the best way possible; it almost seemed normal for the week to begin with news of the worst. Tossing a couple of children's toys into the backseat, he got into his colleague's little Renault, grim-faced. Ken didn't even try to lighten the mood. He was none too happy himself; he was just as tired of counting bodies. His wife was just about to give birth again, and he would rather have devoted himself to thinking about life.

Without exchanging a word, they drove to the crime scene. Parking in front of the police station on the Rue Bonaparte, which overlooked the square, Ken said simply:

"First indications point to the murder's happening two days ago."

He led them toward the church of Saint-Sulpice, crossing the vast esplanade with its two fountains.

"Don't tell me he's managed to hide in there! It's always jammed with people," said Mallock.

"The bastard staged his scene in the crypt. It was closed for renovations and no one thought to go down and check on it."

Mallock felt like he'd been slapped in the face. He knew the Saint-Sulpice crypt. At his wife's insistence, Thomas had been baptized there.

As Ken spoke, he pulled out a jar of Vicks. "Want some, boss?"

Mallock took a dab of the camphor-eucalyptus jelly on the tip of his index finger and smeared it under his nose. He'd cut his upper lip shaving that morning. The Vicks made it sting cruelly.

There was something nightmarish about the atmosphere that reigned in the crypt. Besides the light given off by hundreds of flickering candles, one element gave the scene a particularly theatrical air: a sort of white calm, compact and oily. They were in a church crypt, which was a reason to whisper his orders as well as his curses. The noise of shoes scraping on the stone, and the voices distorted by individual radios linked to the central command post, only gave more weight and significance to this pallid silence.

In front of Mallock were the sacrificed bodies of a mother and her baby. He had actually been expecting something like this for several days now. The mother and child, the Madonna and Christ, an emblematic and recurring theme in religious imagery. It also reminded him, for the first time, of Russian icons.

Contrary to what some people thought at the time, the strand of iron around the child's arms wasn't a remnant of torture; just a simple brace to hold the subject, arms raised, in the position of the benedictory infant. But the most astonishing aspect was the gold covering the baby's entire body. Mallock was certain now that the Makeup Artist must be creating images, duplicating existing ones. It was incredible that he was able to make them up more and more while they were alive, or almost.

"As soon as we get back to the Fort," he murmured to Ken, "put one of the guys on the purchase of decorative gold leaf. There's a ton of it here; we've got a chance. Then have him put the list of major buyers in the database, as usual."

Then he turned his attention back to the victims.

The woman's arms were raised heavenward. She was draped in floor-length blue and white veils. But her stomach was bare. Worse, it had been hollowed out like a cave. The Makeup Artist had eviscerated and disemboweled her. In the empty space, where only the spinal column and a few ribs remained, he had placed two candles. Their flickering light danced on the bloody walls around them and on the group of small, traditional Christmas figurines that also filled the cavity: a cow, a donkey, Joseph, the three Kings, and, on a bed of straw, a little pink baby Jesus.

Mallock turned his head to look at the baby. He wanted to say goodbye to the little martyred body, whisper a few snatches of prayer over it. He moved closer to it. No one had dared to do that yet. A smell of sweat and feces rose from it. He thought at first of the putrefaction of death, but one detail stunned him. The golden stomach was moving. It was almost imperceptible, but he had to be sure. He put his ear up to the baby's mouth. Nothing. But he felt compelled to hold the lenses of his glasses right up against the child's lips.

"For the love of Christ!"

The curse echoed in the crypt, immediately followed by orders.

"Call the paramedics, quickly. He's still breathing! Pulse very weak, respiration almost nil, but there's something alive in there. Move your asses!"

To the astonishment of the two priests and everyone else present, he began ripping the gold leaf off the child's body. Ken joined him and removed the iron brace. Like damned souls hovering over the poor golden angel, they looked like two birds of prey tearing apart their victim. Flakes of gold floated in the air of the crypt, gleaming in the light of the candles, like so many miniature suns.

While Ken continued to pull off all the gold leaf he could, Amédée began artificial resuscitation. His big body breathed air into the child's lungs, like a giant blowing up a balloon. One deep breath and then three chest compressions, gently, using two fingers. He tried to get a look at the baby's eyes, verify the presence of movement, but the butcher had glued his eyelids shut.

Fifteen minutes later, exhausted, Amédée left the crypt. There had been nothing he could do. Near the door he stepped on a little rubber giraffe, undoubtedly left there during a previous christening. The toy let out a ridiculous squeak, punctuated by the superintendent's low *"Shit."* More than the repulsive spectacle or the smell coming from the corpses, it was this noise, the cry of Sophia the giraffe, that made him want to throw up.

Ken stayed on to coordinate operations, but Mallock went straight back to the office. He could have used a short break to get a grip on his emotions, but there wasn't time. If he wanted to capture the monster he would have to start moving even faster.

The Makeup Artist seemed to be sailing through.

And yet, the police weren't exactly doing nothing. Fort Mallock was like a beehive. Dozens of inspectors and computer techs in shirtsleeves were coming and going in every direction. Faxes, printers, telephones, and other technological aids were each contributing their own particular brand of

racket to the unusual hubbub in the superintendent's department. "Work in silence" was one of his favorite instructions,
but this morning he didn't have the strength or even the desire
to quiet down the cacophony. He gave Bob his request concerning the gold leaf.

"Ken will speak to you about it again, but go ahead and
make a start. Call the main suppliers of gilding necessities and
have them give you a list of their clients, with each one marked:
'new customer,' 'larger order than usual,' and so on."

Then he went to see Francis. The young lieutenant looked
absolutely terrible. Had he slept at all in the last forty-eight
hours?

"Will you be ready soon?" was all Mallock said by way of
encouragement.

"Just about, boss. I just started the overall comparison of
the five lists. The answers will be on your desk in twenty minutes."

"You've done a good job."

Even so, Francis thought.

Bob, who had joined them, couldn't resist asking:

"Are we going to catch him, boss?"

"What do you think?" Mallock barked. "Go work on the
gold."

In the corridor that led to his office, he realized that his
anger hadn't cooled at all. It was even keeping him from walking upright. He was broken, head bowed, teeth gritted, aching.
His feet dragged slightly on the floor, betrayed by his knees.

A baby covered in gold. My God.

He had pinned all his hopes on his list idea. If the comparison results didn't turn up anything he'd be right back where
he started, but with the weight of the whole world on his
shoulders and—he had no doubt—a lot of explaining to do to
the mob of spectators. And to himself.

Worse yet, the Makeup Artist would have a wide-open path ahead of him.

In his office he poured himself a generous glass of single-malt, hoping the liquor might untie the inextricable knots in his stomach. Francis had said twenty minutes, and Mallock started counting them down. He didn't even try to think anymore. It was too late.

The roulette wheel was already spinning.

The die was cast. No more bets, please. He couldn't change anything now; there would be no changing of bets, no altering the track, no adding chips to a number that was suddenly obvious. Nothing.

Nothing but the clicking sound of that fucking roulette wheel.

All he could do was count down the minutes. Still ten to go. He'd never been in this situation before, at the mercy of a goddamn printout of a list. It was a bizarre feeling. Then, a flash of inspiration: light a cigar. That would take up a good three minutes.

When Francis came in with the computer printout in his arms, Amédée didn't try to read the results of the database-matching in his eyes. He listened, pulling slowly on his Havana cigar. Francis was stunned by his superintendent's calm. If only he'd known!

"Here it is. I assigned a sort of coefficient to each of the lists, according to their importance. I gave four points to the names present in the Maurel notebook; four as well for people who own the famous tripod; two points to people listed in the supermarket file, two for the list generated by the door-to-door questioning, and finally two for all the suspects in the police files. That gives us a grade out of fourteen."

Francis turned the page. His hands were shaking.

"I didn't get any fourteens. No twelves, no tens—"

"It's fucking worthless," Mallock burst out.

He had rarely felt a failure so cruelly. He could have cried.

"But I did get three sixes. One of them is on both the tripod list and in our files. The two others are in Amélie's notebook and their names came up during the door-to-door investigation."

"It's not enough."

"Wait! I saved the best for last! We also have an eight. This guy is on the supermarket list, the tripod list, and both police lists. Interesting, right?"

Nose buried in his papers, Francis didn't dare look up at his boss. "He isn't on Amélie's list though, unfortunately," he admitted.

"It's not your fault; it's mine," sighed Mallock. "You did a fine job, but I don't think there's much to your eight. It's crucial for the name to be in Amélie's book. Shit, shit, shit! Call Ken and the others; have them verify the eight and the three sixes anyway. See if you can get with Bob too, for the gold leaf list."

Francis was relieved for a few seconds, before realizing that he would almost have preferred a dressing-down. He started for the door, but Mallock called him back.

"Don't tell the others I know about this, okay? We need to keep morale up."

Francis agreed, wondering how much good the morale of the Fort's inspectors would be without their boss's own.

Half an hour later, Bob and Julie were standing in front of Mallock. Jules was too busy checking and sorting the hundreds of complaints that had flooded into the Fort over the past three days; apparently everyone in France had spent their weekend adding to the stream of invective. When Ken joined them in the office he had come straight from the crypt, and the others were surprised to see him covered in flakes of gold.

Mallock gave them a quick rundown without letting them

in on his disappointment. They weren't fooled, but they all pretended to be.

"I'll have to call home," said Ken. "We might be here all night."

He picked up the phone and stood, his gaze unfocused, without dialing. "Shit. What's my home number again?"

"You forgot your own phone number?"

"Oh, like it's never happened to you. We changed it three months ago, and it's not like I call myself very often."

"Look in your address book, dummy," Julie advised.

A minute later Ken snapped the notebook shut, swearing. "This is so goddamn stupid. It's not in there. I never put it in. Usually I can remember it."

"You know what we're going to do? We're going to buy you a pretty little bracelet with your name and address engraved on it, and a little note underneath that saying: 'Reward to anyone who brings little Ken back to the police station.'"

Mallock put an end to the teasing by shooing them out of his office. "Get a move on; I want be absolutely sure. If none of these suspects is our bastard, we're back to square one."

When his colleagues had gone he realized that he was hungry and exhausted. Waking up at dawn, the sight of the corpses, the lack of breakfast, and the panicked fear of failure were taking their toll. But his troubles weren't over yet. At twelve-thirty came the call to battle stations. There was a big meeting at one o'clock sharp with the biggest boss of all, the honorable Secretary of the Interior.

A motorcycle cop in an impeccable uniform came to give him the secretary's invitation, and Mallock knew he was about to find out the true limits of this unusual politician's friendship. The telephone rang a few seconds later. It was Dublin.

"Shall we go over together? I've already called my car."

His voice was shaking. He was sitting on an ejection seat, and those weren't made to hold civil servants—even when they were members of the police force. Mallock let the ghost of a smile cross his lips. He would have to hold his hand in front of the big boss. He imagined it moist and trembling. In Dublin's defense, he, like the other directors of the 36, had always refused promotion to stay in his job. Mallock had certainly made the most of that.

"I'll meet you downstairs in three minutes," were the only words of comfort he could offer.

It was six o'clock in the evening.

When he thought about it, it hadn't really gone all that badly, Mallock told himself as he headed home. Dublin had been a bit of a chickenshit, naturally, but not too much. The secretary had raised his voice, naturally, but only moderately. Everyone had tried to avoid being blamed, naturally, and naturally, the final responsibility had fallen right on him. He hadn't been fazed. After more than an hour of buck-passing, when the secretary and the whole audience had turned on their freshly and unanimously nominated scapegoat, he had faced them head-on.

"It is my fault," he had said, to general astonishment. "I have no excuses to make. If it'll make you feel better, I'm happy to accept all your complaints. Frankly, I don't give a damn. On the other hand, I'm still convinced that searching for the killer should be the principal and only concern of this venerable assembly, rather than pointing fingers and coming after me with torches and pitchforks. Think less about your salaries and more about this butcher, and things might go much better."

Dublin's face had gone from milk-white to a lovely pastel green, while the yes-men were bright red. The Secretary of the Interior, undoubtedly because he was an old hand, gave Mallock his support.

"You've run a good investigation. Criticism is easy, gentlemen, but apprehending an individual as formidable as this . . . Makeup Artist . . . is a whole different ball game."

After that, the meeting had gone in a much more constructive direction. They tried to answer one question together: what could be done to improve the system while satisfying the press at the same time?

A series of measures were taken, and Mallock couldn't escape what looked very much like a competitive pitch. Particularly the involvement on the ground, and even in the investigation, of outside authorities answerable directly to the secretary.

Though some of these decisions were intended to boost the effectiveness of the search, most of them, as always, were as demagogic as they were useless, and were made only to give the newspapers and the politicians something to chew on. They created SCAG, the Specific Coordinated Action Group, for some reason no one would ever figure out, and also a group for the Ethical Computer Information Research Collective, or ECIRC. The call for Mallock's resignation put forward by a television program was rejected at the last minute, as was some overzealous attaché's heat-of-the-moment suggestion of a referendum to declare a countrywide state of emergency. At the time no one could have suspected that, one day, a measure like that would in fact be taken for a simple police investigation—least of all Mallock, who would be the one to initiate it.[17]

During the entire meeting and on his drive home, Amédée couldn't shake the niggling worry that he'd forgotten something. Something someone had said or done that afternoon; something extremely important. A number, maybe. He was virtually certain that it was crucial. He'd been given the solution to the mystery, and he'd shoved it aside.

Home at last, he decided, cigar and whiskey in hand, to set-

[17] *The Massacre of the Innocents.*

tle into a comfortable armchair and try to locate the stowaway passenger hiding somewhere in the back of his mind.

He fell asleep on the sofa without finding it.

The helpless, powerless Mallock, the unconscious one, was finally going to pay the price for his inadequacies. The latest of them, falling asleep like that in his apartment without locking the door, had made it possible for the Makeup Artist to capture him, as if he were a complete novice.

Amédée was trussed up hand and foot now, a spectator of the Makeup Artist's latest relaxation exercise. In front of him, clamped to the wall by means of a neoprene adhesive, was a woman bound in the shape of a cross, her eyes bulging with terror, begging mutely, desperately for his help. Mallock tried to move, but with no success at all.

Without even a glance at his old enemy, the Makeup Artist approached the cross-shaped body and, empty-eyed, began with jerky movements to beat the woman to a pulp. First he explained, in a metallic-sounding voice, that the first thing was to tenderize the flesh so it would be easier to remove the skin. Then, without waiting, without hearing the sacrificed woman's screams, he began beating her with all his strength using an iron bar. *That voice!* Mallock screamed. He recognized it. My God, it was Julie!

He tried again to free himself, but nothing made any difference. He could only watch. Robotically, with somewhat clumsy regularity, the Makeup Artist pounded his weapon against what no longer bore any resemblance to skin. The petite Julie's flesh and muscles, fat, bones, and bodily fluids were now just one indistinguishable, nauseating mass.

After long minutes punctuated by rhythmic cracking sounds, Mallock suddenly realized that he must be dreaming. But how could he hear the cracks so distinctly, as if they were coming from inside the room? He opened his eyes.

*

A snowstorm had broken over Paris, and one of the living-room shutters had come loose. He had been hearing its regular banging noises, even in his dream. Relieved, he got up to pull the shutters closed.

It was then, standing naked in front of his window, letting his gaze wander among the millions of crystalline snowflakes, that he realized the solution to his mystery. It was simple and complicated, cold and ephemeral like the snowflakes whirling before his eyes. He murmured a *thank you*; then, before the revelation could melt away, he closed the window again.

On a piece of paper, he wrote the Makeup Artist's name.

It was only five in the morning but he got dressed, downed a cup of boiling coffee, and ran for his garage. Paris was completely white, with a violent wind whistling through the narrow streets. He turned up the collar of his coat. For once, he had deigned to bundle up. Bluish vapor puffed from his mouth. He thought of Tom, and the six Christmases they had spent together. He loved the wind, for a bunch of reasons he'd never tried to analyze. Now, he thought, there was a new reason.

Little Tom was here, in this wind.

Like all the life energy in the world, all the lives of the pure and the just. It was their breath.

41.

Tuesday, January 18th

At Number 36, Quai des Orfèvres, the lists were still asleep on his desk. He looked at the tripod list. The name he had written down on a scrap of paper just after he woke up was typed on it.

This suspect was the eight out of fourteen he had been hoping for. And to be honest, he was deeply indebted to Ken's forgetfulness. When the captain hadn't been able to find his own number in his address book, something had clicked in Amédée's brain.

There were only two phone numbers Amélie hadn't found it necessary to write down in her notebook. Hers, because like everyone she knew it by heart, and the one belonging to her patient and neighbor, the pharmacist's son. A number so similar to her own that she couldn't help but remember it. Suddenly everything was so clear, so obvious. Irritating in its simplicity.

All the details came back to him. The paper garbage bag he had unwittingly glimpsed in the pharmacy. The moment when the first, incorrectly filled-out insurance slip had been thrown away by the apprentice pharmacist. The young man's handwriting on that document, a calligraphy that was astonishingly similar to the writing he'd deciphered in his nightmares—and that he had seen once before, on the famous fragment of burnt paper found in a crime scene fireplace: *Death is life.*

Of course he'd had no problem stealing a syringe from his nurse. He was certainly in the best position to do it, and

Mallock was angry with himself for not assigning the neighborhood investigations more importance—and for not relying enough on his own intuition. The repeated visions he'd had of the color green connected with a cross sign—together they made a pharmacy cross, a precious clue that should have led him to the Makeup Artist much sooner. Like the snake and the cross, or the big wooden chest with buttons, a miniature version of which was part of the decorations in the pharmacy window.

His visions were none other than a higher level of reflection and lucidity; why was he still so afraid to trust them? When he had seen Didier Dôthem at Amélie's bedside, he . . .

Terror shot through him, paralyzing his hand as he reached toward the coffee machine.

What had he said to Didier Dôthem, the Makeup Artist, to reassure him about Amélie's condition?

She was the only person who could identify him formally, and he had been stupid enough to pretend she was better—and even worse, that she was almost ready to talk.

Mallock lunged for his coat. Luckily, at six o'clock in the morning you could still drive in Paris at ninety miles an hour. Once outside, his heart sank. In this kind of storm, the snow would be blocking everything, and it would take him at least half an hour to reach the hospital—assuming that his old Jaguar could manage the treacherous roads at all. Without really thinking, he started to run in the direction of the Pitié-Salpêtrière, on foot, like an idiot, in the middle of the night. Blessing the rubber soles of the snow boots he'd bought at the start of the case, he managed to attain a reasonable, sustained speed.

Snowplows were already at work on the Quai Saint-Barnard, pushing the snow onto the sidewalks and scattering generous amounts of salt. He was glad he hadn't taken his car.

But dear God, why had he told Didier that Amélie was better, that she would be able to describe her attacker? Why, of all people, had he said that to *Didier*? What a fool!

His heart pounded and his breathing made him regret the hours spent sitting and smoking Coronas. Fifteen minutes later the hospital was in view. He slowed down. He needed to prepare himself for battle, regain his strength, his breath, his clear-headedness.

Mallock was just about to enter the building when two police cars caught up with him and smashed into one another, the first one crashing into the steps of the main entrance.

"Superintendent Mallock! Who contacted you? We just got a call. The Makeup Artist has been seen . . . "

The young inspector's face was red with cold.

"Let's go. Just follow us!"

Mallock ran for the elevator in the third building. Amélie's room was on the second floor, in Doctor Ménard's unit. Inside, on the ventilator, the young woman looked like she was sleeping, protected from the outside world by the depth of her dreams. On her chest the Makeup Artist had left a red carnation and a letter. Had he come all this way, taken such a huge risk, just to leave a flower and a note?

Mallock moved forward and opened the envelope.

Neither alive nor dead. That suits me fine. Sleep.
Stay between the sky and the earth, Heaven and Hell, heat and ice
In this fleeting eternity.
Where your lips breathe, your marble sweats,
And I feared the worst.
You live; good.
I, the great "not even," the pearl diver,
I would have accomplished the essential and the substantial.

Brought back, from God, the eyes, the mouth, and the broken nose.

Holding my breath, I have penetrated caverns of flesh.

An esoteric cannibal, I have tasted the ineffable bitterness of spiritual meats.

Here below, I will miss only you, and the wind in the streets.

The face of God? I have seen it, and it is suffocating.

It is the face of a child.

Mallock didn't waste time analyzing the killer's prose. Twenty minutes later he pulled up in one of the police cars at the little square in Le Marais. The pharmacy wasn't open yet. He had called Francis and Ken, who were waiting for him outside. They were both covered with snow.

"That was fast! What's going on, boss?"

"We're here to arrest the Makeup Artist. I thought that might interest you."

"But how did you—"

"There isn't time. I'll explain later. Let's go."

Like most of the buildings in Le Marais, the one Amélie and the Makeup Artist lived in didn't have an elevator. They pounded up the stairs, Mallock in the lead. Much, much later, Ken and Francis would tell their grandchildren for the thousandth time about how cold and snowy it had been on the famous day they arrested one of the greatest criminals of all time.

When they hit the third floor, the smell of leek soup—which must have been from the previous evening—suddenly made the adventure seem a bit more commonplace. They cursed the anonymous housewife who had decided to stink up the stairwell on that particular day. Reaching the top floor, Mallock missed a step and let out an oath.

"Get ready."

"Should we knock?"

"Nope. We're breaking the door down."

Accompanying his words with action just like in the movies, Mallock smashed the lock off the door with a violent kick. Behind it was a second door, this one armored. An alphanumeric keypad on the wall next to it waited for the correct code. Mallock examined it while Ken called the station for an emergency locksmith. Mallock punched in three names before hitting on the right one. It was an image from his last dream, one that made his throat tighten and whisper the word: *Julie.*

The admiring, lovestruck look that had come across the Makeup Artist's face when he saw her standing next to Amédée.

"Are you going to tell us how you figured that out?"

"No, I can't. But we can be on our guard. There's a monster hiding behind this door. Get out your Pythons and shoot on sight. Do I make myself clear?"

"Crystal."

Their superintendent's face and the deadly seriousness in his voice left no room for doubt. Ken and Francis both checked the content of their cylinders, more out of nervous habit than because they really needed to. Every police officer knows perfectly well how many bullets he has in his gun. If he doesn't, he should find a new job.

"Go on three. Me first, Ken second, and Francis covering. One, two, three."

There was nothing special about the apartment. It was clean and tidy. Ordinary. A large room that served as both living and dining area; a small tiled kitchen, and a tiny bathroom. The Makeup Artist wasn't there. His absence frightened Mallock. His gaze swept the room. A bulky table, two rustic chairs, and a superb chest of drawers that had apparently lost its marble top—maybe broken during a move, he thought to himself. At the far end of the room, to the right, opposite the window, was a door. Behind it they found a large office filled with computers, printers, enlargers, and screens.

Francis sat down in front of the main unit.

"Should I, chief?"

"No, wait. The suspect isn't here. We need two witnesses."

Three minutes later Francis came back with two neighbors, who were openmouthed and visibly stunned by the young assistant pharmacist's activities.

"I would be shocked if he'd done anything. He's a very nice boy; very ordinary, Superintendent."

Mallock turned to Francis, who was waiting. "Go ahead. We'll need all the information we can get to find him."

Francis pulled a chair on wheels up to the computer. "Look, there are only two files, but they're super heavy."

"Can you open them?"

"I'll try."

They spent the next few minutes trying various codes. It was Francis who finally hit on the right one: 000. The Makeup Artist hadn't exactly given it a lot of thought. Unless he didn't really think the two documents in the file were worth protecting. The first one was a long poem. The other file was much heavier.

"Almost a terabyte," announced Francis. "999 gigabytes exactly. This guy's a fucking maniac."

"Open it."

The second file was called "Faces of God."

Inside, the first set contained all of the victim photos taken using the famous tripod, still in their untreated format, not touched up at all. Two things made these portraits special. The makeup, of course, but also the light that illuminated the faces themselves. A kind of aura, a halo, that no flash or light bulb could simulate. Mallock didn't try to figure it out.

"Is that all he has?"

Francis opened the file marked "Final." This one was more complicated; reading it required a whole series of programs. Luckily, the young lieutenant knew what he was doing. Two minutes later the incredible quest of the Makeup Artist began scrolling past the eyes of the three men.

Every face of every victim of the whole line of Makeup Artists was there, but they were arranged in a specific order and had been retouched. A morphing program had been used to soften the transition from one face to the next, and the result was fascinating. Played back in a loop, the faces seemed to melt into one another. Francis, who was very familiar with this kind of programming, had a connoisseur's appreciation of it.

"Fantastic work," he murmured.

God made us in His image, and the Makeup Artists had believed that it was possible to follow the opposite route to find the face of God. To do that, they had chosen their victims—mostly women—for their resemblance to what they considered the divine.

Suddenly, Mallock and his lieutenants realized where the animation between the different visuals was leading. And the miracle happened.

They were no longer looking at a stream of similar faces, but a single face formed from the sum of all the others. And what a face! Francis tried to speak, but he couldn't get the words out. A benevolent spirituality and a terrifying kind of power radiated from what they were seeing.

Nothing else existed anymore except that look and those features.

Outside, the wind and the snow had joined forces to shake the buildings. Windows clattered open. The vibrations coming from the computer seemed to be trying to push the face out of the screen, to help it escape and fill the room, and Paris, and the whole universe. Covered in cold sweat, they shivered, powerless, motionless, their hearts pounding wildly.

"Is that God's face?" asked Ken, with something like a sob.

No one dared, or wanted, to stop the machine. They stood frozen, openmouthed, their eyes full of tears.

"My God," whispered Mallock.

He was the first one to look away.

42.
The final reversal

During the seventy-two hours that followed, every police officer, legal expert, and journalist in Paris moved heaven and earth to get into the Makeup Artist's lair for even a second. Mallock's investigation was described in the minutest detail in the papers, turning him into a national hero. The accolades, coming from the same people who had tried to destroy him, were greeted by Amédée with utter contempt.

He had only one thing on his mind: two days after the guilty party had been identified he was still at large, and only when he had been captured would Mallock relax. Until he locked him up or gunned him down, he could neither rest nor think about anything else.

They had found the photo of Julie, and Mallock, his fears confirmed, had taken drastic steps.

"I don't give a shit what you or the big bosses think. You're getting out of here and that's final. Take Jules as a bodyguard. One condition: don't tell anyone where you're hiding."

"But it's disgraceful. I—"

"It's nothing of the kind. This guy is too dangerous. We don't even know where he is, and you're his next victim. I don't want to have to worry about you."

"So you care about little old Julie after all, Superintendent?"

"What do you think, you little idiot?" Mallock barked.

He knew that sometimes you couldn't hold back with the people you loved, especially during the good times.

He went to Didier Dôthem's apartment very early the next morning after a sleepless night, accompanied by a dozen men, to carry away everything that might possibly yield clues or proof: all the computer equipment and backup systems, plus the contents of every closet, drawer, and garbage can. The rest was left *in situ* to await the specialists.

And then another nightmare began.

Even though every police force in Europe had set out the widest net ever conceived to trap a criminal, blocking train stations and airports. Even though the surveillance system in France had been maintained and expanded. Even though multiple photographs of Dôthem were on the front pages of every newspaper in the country. Even though they had mobilized every yokel in every corner of every shithole town. Twelve days after discovering the killer's hiding place and his identity, Mallock and his team were still in the same place. There was no trace of the Makeup Artist, not a single tangible sign. The monster had well and truly vanished off the face of the Earth.

"Well, shit! There's never been this kind of manhunt for anyone before. He can't get away," grumbled Ken, whose rage had been building slowly but surely.

"A few more days and the press will eat us alive," said Bob, who for his part had become much more cheerful. He seemed to be getting real pleasure out of the search operations. Even though they'd been unsuccessful so far, like a good hunter he appreciated the scenery and the outdoor exercise.

Mallock had only one worry. "I don't give a shit about the press. But if he starts up again . . . "

"What does your . . . intuition say?" ventured Francis—who had, just yesterday, decided to go by the name "Frank," with a *k*.

"There's no particular reason!" he had barked. "Robert goes by Bob! And 'Francis' sounds stupid! I'm just tired of it, okay?"

Childish, Mallock had said to himself. As if this were any time to get all fussy over a name.

For a month now, the setting up of the dragnet and the fantastical reports coming in from all over France had taken up all his attention. The monster had taken the ferry to Corsica. He'd been officially seen in Marseille two days ago. He was in German Switzerland; at the top of the Eiffel Tower; in the Black Forest; on a billionaire's yacht off Saint Martin.

Every time a sighting was reported Mallock had to check into it, to the detriment of more creative thought. Unconsciously he had disconnected himself from the hell that reigned inside the Makeup Artist's head, happy to be finished with all the drugs and the nightmares. But he must have done it too soon.

Now, realizing this, he decided to go home early.

He poured himself a glass of his favorite whiskey and lit up a double Corona. Then he watched the sunset, his gaze lost somewhere deep inside himself, in that place where the universe according to Mallock was made and unmade. A fragile heap of feelings and traces, of plastic objects. Of illusions, impulses, and fears. In the deepest part of himself, where the always-dark sky was forever lapped by icy waves. Within his very core, in search of vestiges of the essential, scraps of truth clinging to rotted masts, a shred of reality on the rafts of fortune. Even deeper, in a sort of intoxicating free dive, he traveled immense spaces enclosed by gigantic walls. At the center he saw a pool of translucent water, and at the bottom of it, a marble tomb. The specific shape of the sepulcher reminded him that he was far from being all-knowing.

The next morning he set out for the little square. It was January 30th, and temperatures had gotten milder. His experience of the night before had made him sleep until nine o'clock.

As he approached the pharmacy, his back gave a twinge. He looked for a bench to sit down. You can never argue with your own vertebrae.

It was the last day of the month, and city employees were taking down the big blue spruce. They were using long rakes to tear off the tree's flocking, which was made of several layers of vinyl adhesive mixed with shredded cotton/rayon fabric. It was sad to see such a beautiful tree being skinned alive. The little Styrofoam angels decorating the tree were falling to the ground, one after another.

There were still pretty shades of green under the spruce's flocking. They could have replanted it. But two gardeners approached the tree in cherry-picker baskets and began cutting off its branches. Mankind has a strange way of thanking the plants and animals that make life more beautiful.

Amédée turned back toward the pharmacy building and looked up at the apartment's three windows.

The small one on the left corresponded to the bathroom, right next to the front door. The two other, larger ones were the living room and office windows, respectively. Nothing to report. Mallock took out his cigar case and selected an *Especial no. 1*. He lit it without taking his eyes off the windows. What was he hoping to learn from these old dormers?

Time passed. It could have been a minute or an hour; Mallock couldn't tell. And then suddenly, everything was clear. Slightly stiff from sitting for so long, he stood up and went into the building. He broke the police tape sealing off the Makeup Artist's door.

As required by procedure, the main pieces of evidence had been removed from the apartment and stored in a safe place. He'd taken charge of that himself, with his team and the crime-scene techs. Otherwise, after having taken all the necessary photos and samples, dusted for every possible fingerprint, and confiscated objects and documents, the Criminal Investigation Division normally used a specialized Parisian municipal cleaning service to scrub everything, erase the smallest trace of blood and violence, and make the physical memory of the murders perpetrated on these premises disappear forever. Next, more often than not, the place would be resold or rented out and, in time, forgotten.

Here, even though it was practically empty, after the various visits from the superintendent and his men the apartment had been left as it was. The request had come from the great Mallock himself, who, in his wisdom, had given the famous and pithy explanation: "You never know."

Amédée walked quickly into the other room, the office. Looking at the window, he breathed a sigh of relief. It wasn't the only other room, after all. There was one more. And then he knew he had finally won. There would be no more killings.

He started playing a bizarre game. Like an Indian on the warpath he crouched on the floor to observe any traces there, then began tapping on the walls.

A few minutes later he gave a triumphant shout. The opening mechanism was perfectly hidden, and there would have been almost no chance of finding the concealed room without really searching for it.

Three facts had put Mallock on the trail of this secret room, the Makeup Artist's studio. One was the permanent presence of his mother. How had he been able to conduct all his rituals without having a hidey-hole? Another fact was the absence of icons and the originals of the photos Dôthem had digitized on the computer. There was no way he would have been separated from them when they meant to much to him. And finally, there was the location of the office window.

Seen from the outside, there were at least ten feet unaccounted for between the office window and the façade of the next building to the left. But inside the office itself, the wall was only a foot to the right of that same window.

It took him another hour to figure out how to slide open the wall. Once he was finally in the studio, he groped around for a light switch. Light flooded a small space. To the left there was an enormous armoire; to the right a bathroom done in red ceramic tile. A large closet, obviously homemade, took up almost all of the six-and-a-half-foot space noticeable from the outside. Opening the closet switched on another light. The interior held no clothing; it was completely filled with icons.

All of the Makeup Artist's work was there, as well as the exhibition of his principal victims. It was a terrible sight, an admirable and macabre spectacle: a five-row iconostasis, his masterpiece, including icons of the Virgin of the Sign, an Annunciation, a Moses, a David, several representations of the Madonna and Child, and, in the center, a Christ Pantocrator and an astonishing Deisis, which included the recognizable faces of the two men Dôthem had murdered at the start of his quest and, as Mary, the little Modiano girl, whose gilded braids, pinned high on her head, formed the base of a halo.

Nervously, Mallock drew on his cigar, but it had gone out. The whole display might well have been repugnant, but it exuded an intoxicating blend of spirituality and sensuality. A dazzling cocktail. He recognized certain scenes: a disembow-eled saint holding his own head in his hands. A "Saint Mandé" with thighs spread wide and eyes covered in gold leaf. The baby in its sugared shell. The actress, like an empty-hulled boat on the shore of a black lake. A female Jesus, impaled atop a Golgotha made of seashells.

He ran his tongue across his upper lip. There was a perverse pleasure in looking at these icons. He shut the closet door, thinking that you could have terrible suspicions about yourself.

To the right, an odor wafted from the bathroom that was unpleasant, but not quite as bad as he had expected. Like the rest of the space, it was completely red. From the tiles down to the contents of the bathtub, which was filled to the brim with blood. Mallock knew he'd reached the end of his investigation. Here, finally, was the answer to the question of what the Makeup Artist had done with all the blood he took from his victims. He bathed in it.

Mallock thanked his lucky stars and closed his eyes for a few seconds before putting on a pair of elbow-length rubber gloves, leaning over the tub, and pulling its plug. The liquid, which had still been red a month ago, had taken on the brown color and appearance of mud. As the fluid level began slowly to go down, his eyes riveted to the surface of the syrupy substance, Amédée relit his cigar—maybe in part to relax, but mainly to hide the stink coming off this sludge of water, formalin, and decomposing blood. When the tub had drained halfway a long, flat object began to be revealed. A smile of satisfaction and relief, slightly twisted with disgust, appeared on Mallock's lips. He hadn't been wrong.

As always, he had doubted his own visions. He shouldn't have. Feverishly, he heaved the heavy marble slab upward.

It wasn't as heavy as he had worried it would be, and beneath it he found what he had come looking for.

The Makeup Artist hadn't left it up to anyone else to seal the door to his tomb. Pulling the marble top of the chest of drawers from the living room over himself, he hadn't given his body any chance of escaping the sacrifice. So that the smell of his decomposing body wouldn't give away the location of his lair, he had added several liters of formalin to the blood, then zipped himself into one of the waterproof bags used to transport bodies during wars or major catastrophes. It was a terrible death, but a fitting suicide for the man, drowning in the blood of his last Faces.

Above all, death cannot be gentle, the corpse seemed to whisper to Mallock.

Maybe they would have found this hidden room eventually, and discovered the body, but it would have taken a very long time, and in the meantime his legend, and the uncertainty about his death, would have terrified the whole world. Mallock, fighting his repulsion, decided to open the plastic bag. Dôthem was inside, but he had to be sure. The zipper opened with a soggy ripping noise. It was him, and despite the dreadful death he had inflicted upon himself, despite what he had always thought of himself, he was still beautiful.

So beautiful. Monstrously beautiful.

Contrary to what he had believed all his life, on this point at least, his mother had never lied to him.

Mallock switched on his mobile phone and made a few calls. The body had to be formally identified—not the slightest doubt could be allowed to remain—and autopsied, then cremated. He also called François Modiano, as he had promised to do. The man in loden thanked him. "Courage," Amédée said, and hung up.

Then he decided to wait for the team downstairs in the square, outside in the fresh air.

His heart full, he closed the front door of the building behind him and went to sit down on the same bench he had occupied that morning. The pharmacy was closed. It would never open again.

Amédée just sat. Breathed. Let his heart slow down. Felt himself grow calmer.

The case was over. He had won. He could let it all go. Lie down and stretch out and sleep deeply at last.

Empty.

But he knew it didn't work like that. The Mallock machine had a lot of momentum built up in it. The train would keep chugging and chugging, for days and hours, probably even years, carried along by the insane race he had just run. And so would his emotions and his terrors, which would smolder for months.

Little blonde braids . . . a baby's chest like an island of white sand. Amédée felt tears rising to the surface. The release of pressure after combat has its own dangers.

To distract his mind and force it to dwell on happy things, he thought about Margot. Her loyalty had never faltered, and—it had to be said—she hadn't exactly been well-rewarded for it. She'd been left empty-handed all throughout this case. He took out his phone and called her. She had earned exclusive rights to the story's epilogue.

Just as he hung up, a man sat down next to him. Raymond Grimaud had heard the call on his CB.

"Fuck, it's hard to find a parking space in this neighborhood! Anyway, bravo, Amédée. The knight has slain the dragon."

Mallock smiled at him. "I don't know about a knight, but it was a fucking nightmare of a dragon."

He relit his cigar; RG lit a cigarette. There was a long silence.

"You're sure he's dead?"

"He is. Don't worry."

A flock of angels went by. This time they were Styrofoam, floating along in the gutter.

"And you're sure it's him?"

"Positive."

Raymond lit another cigarette with the stub of the first. He shifted around on the bench, and finally asked:

"Mind if I just have a look?"

Realizing that Mallock still wasn't understanding him—the bear could be dense sometimes—he went on:

"Mallock, this guy has been haunting me for so long. He ended up convincing me that he was immortal."

"But we got him, your piece of shit immortal! You and me, and our teams! He's up there in his bathtub, underneath a black marble tombstone!"

"So it would bother you if I . . . "

"No, no! Go ahead!"

RG stood up and went to the little green door on the left of the pharmacy. He felt slightly ridiculous, but he needed to see the body.

Just as he was about to open the door, Mallock called out to him:

"You do have your gun, right? Now that I think about it, he might still have been moving a little!"

Raymond was laughing as he entered the Makeup Artist's lair.

It was almost noon. A new squadron of city employees had arrived to clean up the last remnants of the Christmas tree. A big black man in an orange parka whistled *Marlborough s'en va-t-en guerre, mironton, mironton, mirontaine,*" as he swept up little blue angels, the corpses of red balls, and green needles. The clock of the Saint-Gervais church chimed twelve times. Servers in the cafes lining the square began lighting tall torches and setting out tables for the lunch crowd. The clinking of glasses and steel cutlery, punctuated by the regular passage of cars on the Rue de Rivoli, were like a sort of modern symphony.

In Mallock's head, a phrase repeated itself over and over: *Thou shalt not make unto thee any graven image.*

EPILOGUE
Tuesday, April 1st

Two months passed without Mallock, almost despite him. Mallock, who couldn't go forward anymore, couldn't walk toward an emptiness of things and feelings anymore. This always happened to him after a good collar, as the police jargon went. First there was a happiness that was almost painful; then a calmer sense of relief. But the mind kept seeking and worrying, running on empty, like a bicycle on a hamster wheel. And then, three or four days later, came the rebound effect, the decompensation. At those times, the only thing to do was to get away, go off to some island with a lover, or the kids. Mallock no longer had either of those. Thomas was gone, and Amélie, it seemed, didn't want to wake up.

So he turned into the ghost of Mallock; a sharp, terse man, a stone, who didn't give a damn about anyone, or the rain and the wind, or the path he was traveling.

But for Easter, he made the heroic effort of going away to his cottage in Normandy. His friends had decided to join him for ten days or so, "to watch the idiot tourists and eat until we make ourselves sick." He had agreed, but only because he was in no condition to argue.

Besides, he had a strong suspicion that they were really doing it for him. And that it might do him some good.

As he drove toward the highway, he made a detour to see Amélie one more time. Her condition had improved slightly; she was more reactive. But could she hear him, from the depths of her coma? Did she feel even the slightest sensation when Mallock slipped his mother's ring onto the third finger of her left hand, a diamond as insignificant and solitary as its owner?

Confession. He spoke to her softly, told her about his overwhelming sadness; his son, lost forever, and her, gone as well. He whispered in her ear:

"You're the only one I love."

After navigating the tollbooths on the Normandy highway, Mallock opened the shutters of his cottage, turned on the heating, and went out to the beach.

It was seven o'clock in the evening. On the seawall, the sunset had broken out its choicest palette. The Channel was milky, beige and blue-green by turns, a vast and liquid sea of hope. The air smelled of iodine. The last tide had formed an army of black dunes made of heaped mussel shells. He walked between them to the water's edge, where the tongues of salty water murmured to those who knew how to hear their tales of scuppered vessels and dastardly pirates.

Mallock, who was an expert at listening to the waves, settled down on the damp sand and, despite the cold, exhausted by too much Paris, too many drugs, and too much savagery, fell asleep.

In his dream, he was walking hand in hand with Thomas along this same beach, on this very night. He told his son about the pain that can lead to horror, about the hideously beautiful apprentice pharmacist, and about his dysmorphophobia, the sickness that had driven him to do such terrible things. And then he talked about forgiveness and compassion, even for a murderer like that.

The Mallock of his waking hours would never have thought or said this; he wasn't even truly opposed to the death penalty for cold-blooded killers and repeat murderers. But the sleeping papa teaching his son about clemency and mercy for young pharmacists believed it with all his heart.

Night had fallen and the moon was full. His cottage was waiting for him, warm and cozy. Amédée stood up with difficulty, noting that God still hadn't done anything about his back. Well, He wasn't perfect either.

Observing the ground behind him, next to his big footprints he saw traces of a small child with bare feet, the prints exactly parallel. Were they from his dream; were they his Tom's?

He looked up toward the stars, toward God, and he laughed.

That crafty little boy of his would get him to love God one of these days, even though He didn't exist.

Amédée made his way back up the beach, careful not to step on the miraculous prints of his son. Tomorrow his friends would be there for lunch. He had a sudden urge to stew two nice chickens, the old-fashioned way, like he'd done last month. He'd need to buy cognac and some chicken livers for the stuffing. But this time, since it was for his friends, he would also use the wonderful truffles he had in a jar, the *tuber melanosporum*, which Jules had bought directly from some people he knew who hunted them. He would cut them into wide, thin rounds with a mandoline and slide them between the skin and the flesh. His friends would love it. The idea brought the beginnings of a smile back to the superintendent's face.

As for the little bare footprints next to his on the beach, Mallock had come to a conclusion of his own:

You don't need shoes in Heaven.

About the Author

Jean-Denis Bruet-Ferreol, who writes under the pseudonym Mallock, was born in Neuilly-sur-Seine in 1951. He is an author, painter, photographer, designer, inventor, artistic director, and composer. Since 2000, he has dedicated himself to digital painting and crime novels.